THE PLAYS OF GILBERT AND SULLIVAN

THE PLAYS OF

Gilbert and Sullivan

ILLUSTRATED BY W. S. GILBERT

THE BOOK LEAGUE OF AMERICA

New York

CL
Manufactured in the United States of America

CONTENTS

CHRONOLOGICAL TABLES

Sir W. S. Gilbert

Born in London November 18th, 1836
Became contributor to *Fun* 1861
Became Barrister-at-Law 1866. Practised to 1870
First play (*Dulcamara*) produced December 29th, 1866
Bab Ballads first published 1869
First meeting with Arthur Sullivan autumn of 1870
Palace of Truth produced November 19th, 1870
First Gilbert and Sullivan collaboration (*Thespis*) produced December 23rd, 1871
Trial by Jury (with Sullivan) produced March 25th, 1875
The Sorcerer (first D'Oyly Carte production, music by Sullivan) November 17th, 1877
H.M.S. Pinafore (with Sullivan) produced May 25th, 1878
The Pirates of Penzance (with Sullivan) produced April 3rd, 1880
Patience (with Sullivan) produced April 23rd, 1881
Iolanthe (with Sullivan) produced November 25th, 1882
Arthur Sullivan knighted, May 27th, 1883
Princess Ida (with Sullivan) produced January 5th, 1884
The Mikado (with Sullivan) produced March 14th, 1885
Ruddigore (with Sullivan) produced January 22nd, 1887
The Yeomen of the Guard (music by Sullivan) produced October 3rd, 1888
The Gondoliers (with Sullivan) December 7th, 1889
Breach between Gilbert and Sullivan 1889–1893
The Mountebanks (music by Alfred Cellier) produced January 4th, 1892
His Excellency (music by Osmond Carr) produced October 27th, 1894
Utopia, Limited (music by Sullivan) produced October 7th, 1893
The Grand Duke (music by Sullivan) produced March 7th, 1896

Death of Sir Arthur Sullivan November 22nd, 1900
Wm. S. Gilbert knighted, June 30th, 1907
Drowned May 29th, 1911

Sir Arthur Sullivan

Born in London May 13th, 1842
Won Mendelssohn Scholarship at the Royal Academy of Music, 1856
Student in Leipzig 1858
Composed incidental music for *The Tempest*, performed at the Crystal Palace, London, 1862
Kenilworth Cantata produced 1864
L'Ile Enchantée produced at Covent Garden 1864
Irish Symphony produced at Crystal Palace 1866
Cox and Box (in collaboration with F. C. Burnand) a musical extravaganza 1866
In Memoriam Overture 1866
Contrabandista (in collaboration with F. C. Burnand) 1867
Marmion Overture 1867
Discovered many lost Schubert manuscripts 1867
The Window (in collaboration with Tennyson) 1871
Di Ballo 1870
The Prodigal Son an oratorio 1871
Met W. S. Gilbert 1871
Thespis (their first collaboration) 1871
Onward, Christian Soldiers! 1872
Te Deum 1872
The Light of the World 1873
Trial by Jury (with Gilbert) produced March 25th, 1875
The Sorcerer (first D'Oyly Carte production, libretto by Gilbert), November 17th, 1877
Henry VIII 1877
The Lost Chord 1877
H.M.S. Pinafore (with Gilbert) produced May 25th, 1878
The Pirates of Penzance (with Gilbert) produced April 3rd, 1880
The Martyr of Antioch 1880
Patience (with Gilbert) produced April 23rd, 1881
Iolanthe (with Gilbert) produced November 25th, 1882
Arthur Sullivan knighted, May 27th, 1883
Princess Ida (with Gilbert) produced January 5th, 1884
The Mikado (with Gilbert) produced March 14th, 1885
The Golden Legend 1886

Ruddigore (with Gilbert) produced January 22nd, 1887
The Yeomen of the Guard (with Gilbert) produced October 3rd, 1888
The Gondoliers (with Gilbert) December 7th, 1889
Breach between Gilbert and Sullivan 1889–1893
Ivanhoe (libretto by Julian Sturgis) 1891
Haddon Hall (libretto by Sydney Grundy) 1892
Utopia, Limited (libretto by Gilbert) 1893
The Chieftain 1894
The Grand Duke (libretto by Gilbert) 1896
Victoria and Merrie England (Ballet) 1897
The Beauty Stone (libretto by A. W. Pinero and J. C. Carr) 1898
The Rose of Persia (libretto by Captain Basil Hood) 1900
Died of heart failure November 22nd, 1900
The Emerald Isle (posthumous) (libretto by Captain Basil Hood) produced in 1901

THESPIS

OR

THE GODS GROWN OLD

DRAMATIS PERSONÆ

GODS

Jupiter Apollo Mars Diana	*Aged Deities*

Mercury

THESPIANS

Thespis	Stupidas
Sillimon	Sparkeion
Timidon	Nicemis
Tipseion	Pretteia
Preposteros	Daphne

Cymon

ACT I

RUINED TEMPLE ON THE SUMMIT OF OLYMPUS

ACT II

THE SAME SCENE, WITH THE RUINS RESTORED

Produced at the Gaiety Theatre, under the management of J. Hollingshead, Tuesday, December 23rd, 1871.

THESPIS

OR

THE GODS GROWN OLD

ACT I

SCENE.—*The ruins of The Temple of the Gods on summit of Mount Olympus. Picturesque shattered columns, overgrown with ivy, etc.,* R. *and* L., *with entrances to temple [ruined]* R. *Fallen columns on the stage. Three broken pillars* 2 R. E. *At the back of stage is the approach from the summit of the mountain. This should be "practicable" to enable large numbers of people to ascend and descend. In the distance are the summits of adjacent mountains. At first all this is concealed by a thick fog, which clears presently. Enter [through fog] Chorus of Stars coming off duty, as fatigued with their night's work.*

Chorus of Stars

Throughout the night
  The constellations
Have given light
  From various stations.
When midnight gloom
  Falls on all nations,
We will resume
  Our occupations.

SOLO

Our light, it's true,
  Is not worth mention;
What can we do
  To gain attention,
When, night and noon,
  With vulgar glaring,
A great big Moon
  Is *always* flaring?

CHORUS

Throughout the night, &c.

During Chorus Enter DIANA, *an elderly Goddess. She is carefully wrapped up in Cloaks, Shawls, etc. A Hood is over her head, a Respirator in her mouth, and Goloshes on her feet. During the chorus she takes these things off, and discovers herself dressed in the usual costume of the Lunar Diana, the Goddess of the Moon.*

DIA. [*shuddering*] Ugh! How cold the nights are! I don't know how it is, but I seem to feel the night air a great deal more than I used to. But it is time for the sun to be rising. [*Calls*] Apollo.

AP. [*within*] Hollo!

DIA. I've come off duty—it's time for you to be getting up.

Enter APOLLO. *He is an elderly "buck" with an air of assumed juvenility, and is dressed in dressing gown and smoking cap.*

AP. [*yawning*] I shan't go out to-day. I was out yesterday and the day before and I want a little rest. I don't know how it is, but I seem to feel my work a great deal more than I used to.

DIA. I'm sure these short days can't hurt you. Why, you don't rise till six and you're in bed again by five: you should have a turn at *my* work and see how you like that—out all night!

AP. My dear sister, I don't envy you—though I remember when I did—but that was when I was a younger sun. I don't think I'm quite well. Perhaps a little change of air will do me good. I've a great mind to show myself in London this winter, they'll be very glad to see me. No! I shan't go out to-day. I shall send them this fine, thick wholesome fog and they won't miss me. It's the best substitute for a blazing sun—and like most substitutes, nothing at all like the real thing. [*To fog*] Be off with you.

[*Fog clears away and discovers the scene described.*

Hurried Music. MERCURY *shoots up from behind precipice at back of stage. He carries several parcels afterwards described. He sits down, very much fatigued.*

MER. Home at last. A nice time I've had of it.

DIA. You young scamp you've been down all night again. This is the third time you've been out this week.

MER. Well *you're* a nice one to blow me up for that.

DIA. *I* can't help being out all night.

MER. And I can't help being down all night. The nature of Mercury requires that he should go down when the sun sets, and rise again, when the sun rises.

DIA. And what have you been doing?

MER. Stealing on commission. There's a set of false teeth and a box of Life Pills—that's for Jupiter—An invisible peruke and a bottle of hair dye—that's for Apollo—A respirator and a pair of goloshes—that's for Cupid—A full bottomed chignon, some auricomous fluid, a box of pearl-powder, a pot of rouge, and a hare's foot—that's for Venus.

DIA. Stealing! you ought to be ashamed of yourself!

MER. Oh, as the god of thieves I must do something to justify my position.

DIA. and AP. [*contemptuously*] Your position!

MER. Oh I know it's nothing to boast of, even on earth. Up here, it's simply contemptible. Now that you gods are too old for your work, you've made me the miserable drudge of Olympus—groom, valet, postman, butler, commissionaire, maid of all work, parish beadle, and original dustman.

AP. Your Christmas boxes ought to be something considerable.

MER. They ought to be but they're not. I'm treated abominably. I make everybody and I'm nobody—I go everywhere and I'm nowhere—I do everything and I'm nothing. I've made thunder for Jupiter, odes for Apollo, battles for Mars, and love for Venus. I've married couples for Hymen, and six weeks afterwards, I've divorced them for Cupid—and in return I get all the kicks while they pocket the halfpence. And in compensation for robbing me of the halfpence in question, what have they done for me?

AP. Why they've—ha! ha! they've made you the god of thieves!

MER. Very self-denying of them—there isn't one of them who hasn't a better claim to the distinction than I have.

Song—MERCURY

Oh, I'm the celestial drudge,
From morning to night I must stop at it,
On errands all day I must trudge,
And I stick to my work till I drop at it!
In summer I get up at one
(As a good-natured donkey I'm ranked for it),
Then I go and I light up the Sun,
And Phœbus Apollo gets thanked for it!
Well, well, it's the way of the world,
And will be through all its futurity;
Though noodles are baroned and earled,
There's nothing for clever obscurity!

I'm the slave of the Gods, neck and heels,
And I'm bound to obey, though I rate at 'em;
And I not only order their meals,
But I cook 'em, and serve 'em, and wait at 'em.
Then I make all their nectar—I do—
(Which a terrible liquor to rack us is)
And whenever I mix them a brew,
Why all the thanksgivings are Bacchus's!
Well, well, it's the way of the world, &c.

Then reading and writing I teach,
And spelling-books many I've edited!
And for bringing those arts within reach,
That donkey Minerva gets credited.

Then I scrape at the stars with a knife,
And plate-powder the moon (on the days for it),
And I hear all the world and his wife
Awarding Diana the praise for it!
Well, well, it's the way of the world, &c.

[*After song—very loud and majestic music is heard.*

DIA. and MER. [*looking off*] Why, who's this? Jupiter, by Jove!

Enter JUPITER, *an extremely old man, very decrepit, with very thin straggling white beard, he wears a long braided dressing-gown, handsomely trimmed, and a silk night-cap on his head.* MERCURY *falls back respectfully as he enters.*

JUP. Good day, Diana—ah Apollo—Well, well, well, what's the matter? what's the matter?

DIA. Why, that young scamp Mercury says that we do nothing, and leave all the duties of Olympus to him! Will you believe it, he actually says that our influence on earth is dropping down to *nil.*

JUP. Well, well—don't be hard on the lad—to tell you the truth, I'm not sure that he's very far wrong. Don't let it go any further, but, between ourselves, the sacrifices and votive offerings have fallen off terribly of late. Why, I can remember the time when people offered us human sacrifices—no mistake about it—human sacrifices! think of that!

DIA. Ah! those good old days!

JUP. Then it fell off to oxen, pigs, and sheep.

AP. Well, there are worse things than oxen, pigs, and sheep.

JUP. So I've found to my cost. My dear sir—between ourselves, it's dropped off from one thing to another until it has positively dwindled down to preserved Australian beef! What do you think of that?

AP. I don't like it at all.

JUP. You won't mention it—it might go further——

DIA. It couldn't fare worse.

JUP. In short, matters have come to such a crisis that there's no mistake about it—something must be done to restore our influence, the only question is, *What?*

Quartette

MER. [*coming forward in great alarm*]

Enter MARS

Oh incident unprecedented!
I hardly can believe it's true!
MARS Why, bless the boy, he's quite demented!
Why, what's the matter, sir, with you?
AP. Speak quickly, or you'll get a warming!
MER. Why, mortals up the mount are swarming,
Our temple on Olympus storming,
In hundreds—aye in thousands, too!

ALL Goodness gracious,
How audacious;
Earth is spacious,
Why come here?
Our impeding
Their proceeding
Were good breeding,
That is clear.

DIA. Jupiter, hear my plea;
Upon the mount if *they* light,
There'll be an end of me,
I won't be seen by daylight!

AP. Tartarus is the place
These scoundrels you should send to—
Should they behold my face
My influence there's an end to!

JUP. [*looking over precipice*] What fools to give themselves so much exertion!

DIA. " " A government survey I'll make assertion!

AP. " " Perhaps the Alpine club at their diversion!

MER. " " They seem to be more like a "Cook's Excursion."

ALL Goodness gracious, etc.

AP. If, mighty Jove, you value your existence,
Send them a thunderbolt with your regards!

JUP. My thunderbolts, though valid at a distance,
Are not effective at a hundred yards.

MER. Let the moon's rays, Diana, strike 'em flighty,
Make 'em all lunatics in various styles!

DIA. My Lunar rays unhappily are mighty
Only at many hundred thousand miles.

ALL Goodness gracious, etc.

[*Exeunt* JUPITER, APOLLO, DIANA, *and* MERCURY *into ruined temple.*

Enter SPARKEION *and* NICEMIS *climbing mountain at back.*

SPAR. Here we are at last on the very summit, and we've left the others ever so far behind! Why, what's this?

NICE. A ruined palace! A palace on the top of a mountain. I wonder who lives here? Some mighty king, I dare say, with wealth beyond all counting, who came to live up here—

SPAR. To avoid his creditors! It's a lovely situation for a country house, though it's very much out of repair.

NICE. Very inconvenient situation.

SPAR. Inconvenient?

NICE. Yes—how are you to get butter, milk, and eggs up here? No pigs—no poultry—no postman. Why, I should go mad.

SPAR. What a dear little practical mind it is! What a wife you will make!

NICE. Don't be too sure—we are only partly married—the marriage ceremony lasts all day.

SPAR. I've no doubt at all about it. We shall be as happy as a king and queen, though we are only a strolling actor and actress.

NICE. It's very kind of Thespis to celebrate our marriage day by giving the company a pic-nic on this lovely mountain.

SPAR. And still more kind to allow us to get so much ahead of all the others. Discreet Thespis! [*Kissing her.*

NICE. There now, get away, do! Remember the marriage ceremony is not yet completed.

SPAR. But it would be ungrateful to Thespis's discretion not to take advantage of it by improving the opportunity.

NICE. Certainly not; get away.

SPAR. On second thoughts the opportunity's so good it don't admit of improvement. There! [*Kisses her.*

NICE. How dare you kiss me before we are quite married?

SPAR. Attribute it to the intoxicating influence of the mountain air.

NICE. Then we had better do down again. It is not right to expose ourselves to influences over which we have no control.

Duet—SPARKEION and NICEMIS

SPAR. Here far away from all the world,
Dissension and derision,
With Nature's wonders all unfurled
To our delighted vision,
With no one here
(At least in sight)
To interfere
With our delight,
And two fond lovers sever,
Oh do not free,
Thine hand from mine,
I swear to thee
My love is thine,
For ever and for ever!

NICE. On mountain top the air is keen,
And most exhilarating,
And we say things we do not mean
In moments less elating.
So please to wait,

For thoughts that crop,
En tête-à-tête,
On mountain top,
May not exactly tally
With those that you
May entertain,
Returning to
The sober plain
Of yon relaxing valley.

SPAR. Very well—if you won't have anything to say to me, I know who will.

NICE. Who will?

SPAR. Daphne will.

NICE. Daphne would flirt with anybody.

SPAR. Anybody would flirt with Daphne. She is quite as pretty as you and has twice as much back-hair.

NICE. She has twice as much money, which may account for it.

SPAR. At all events, *she* has appreciation. *She* likes good looks.

NICE. We all like what we haven't got.

SPAR. *She* keeps her eyes open.

NICE. Yes—one of them.

SPAR. Which one?

NICE. The one she doesn't wink with.

SPAR. Well, I was engaged to her for six months and if she still makes eyes at me, you must attribute it to force of habit. Besides—remember—we are only half-married at present.

NICE. I suppose you mean that you are going to treat me as shamefully as you treated her. Very well, break it off if you like. *I* shall not offer any objection. Thespis used to be very attentive to me, and I'd just as soon be a manager's wife as a fifth-rate actor's!

Chorus heard, at first below, then enter DAPHNE, PRETTEIA, PREPOSTEROS, STUPIDAS, TIPSEION, CYMON, *and other members of* THESPIS' *company climbing over rocks at back. All carry small baskets.*

*Chorus—[with dance]**

Climbing over rocky mountain,
Skipping rivulet and fountain,
Passing where the willows quiver,
By the ever rolling river,
Swollen with the summer rain.
Threading long and leafy mazes,

**Afterwards transplanted to Act I of "The Pirates of Penzance."*

Dotted with unnumbered daisies,
Scaling rough and rugged passes,
Climb the hardy lads and lasses,
Till the mountain-top they gain.

FIRST VOICE
Fill the cup and tread the measure,
Make the most of fleeting leisure,
Hail it as a true ally,
Though it perish bye and bye!

SECOND VOICE
Every moment brings a treasure
Of its own especial pleasure,
Though the moments quickly die,
Greet them gaily as they fly!

THIRD VOICE
Far away from grief and care,
High up in the mountain air,
Let us live and reign alone,
In a world that's all our own.

FOURTH VOICE
Here enthroned in the sky,
Far away from mortal eye,
We'll be gods and make decrees,
Those may honour them who please.

CHORUS
Fill the cup and tread the measure,
etc.

After CHORUS *and* COUPLETS *enter* THESPIS *climbing over rocks.*

THES. Bless you, my people, bless you. Let the revels commence. After all, for thorough, unconstrained unconventional enjoyment give me a pic-nic.

PREP. [*very gloomily*] Give him a pic-nic somebody!

THES. Be quiet, Preposteros—don't interrupt.

PREP. Ha! ha! shut up again! But no matter.

STUPIDAS *endeavours, in pantomime, to reconcile him. Throughout the scene* PREP. *shows symptoms of breaking out into a furious passion, and* STUPIDAS *does all he can to pacify and restrain him.*

THES. The best of a pic-nic is that everybody contributes what he pleases, and nobody knows what anybody else has brought till the last moment. Now, unpack everybody, and let's see what there is for everybody.

NICE. I have brought you—a bottle of soda water—for the claret-cup.

DAPH. I have brought you—a lettuce for the lobster salad.

SPAR. A piece of ice—for the claret-cup.

PRETT. A bottle of vinegar—for the lobster-salad.

CYMON. A bunch of burrage for the claret-cup!

TIPS. A hard-boiled egg—for the lobster-salad!

STUP. One lump of sugar for the claret-cup!

PREP. He has brought one lump of sugar for the claret-cup? Ha! Ha! Ha! [*Laughing melodramatically.*

STUP. Well, Preposteros, and what have *you* brought?

PREP. *I* have brought *two* lumps of the very best salt for the lobster salad.

THES. Oh—is that all?

PREP. All! Ha! Ha! He asks if it is all! [STUPIDAS *consoles him.*

THES. But, I say—this is capital so far as it goes—nothing could be better, but it doesn't go far enough. The claret, for instance! I don't insist on claret—or a lobster—I don't insist on lobster, but a lobster salad without a lobster, why, it isn't lobster salad. Here, Tipseion!

TIPSEION [*a very drunken bloated fellow, dressed, however, with scrupulous accuracy and wearing a large medal round his neck*]. My Master? [*Falls on his knees to* THES. *and kisses his robe.*

THES. Get up—don't be a fool. Where's the claret? We arranged last week that you were to see to that.

TIPS. True, dear master. But then I was a drunkard!

THES. You were.

TIPS. You engaged me to play convivial parts on the strength of my personal appearance.

THES. I did.

TIPS. You then found that my habits interfered with my duties as low comedian.

THES. True——

TIPS. You said yesterday that unless I took the pledge you would dismiss me from your company.

THES. Quite so.

TIPS. Good. I have taken it. It is all I have taken since yesterday. My preserver! [*Embraces him.*

THES. Yes, but where's the wine?

TIPS. I left it behind, that I might not be tempted to violate my pledge.

PREP. Minion! [*Attempts to get at him, is restrained by* STUPIDAS.

THES. Now, Preposteros, what *is* the matter with you?

PREP. It is enough that I am down-trodden in my profession. I will not submit to imposition out of it. It is enough that as your heavy villain I get the worst of it every night in a combat of six. I will *not* submit to insult in the day time. I have come out, ha! ha! to enjoy myself!

THES. But look here, you know—virtue only triumphs at night from seven to ten—vice gets the best of it during the other twenty-three hours. Won't that satisfy you? [STUPIDAS *endeavours to pacify him.*

PREP. [*irritated to* STUP.] Ye are odious to my sight! get out of it!

STUP. [*in great terror*] What have I done?

THES. Now *what* is it, Preposteros, *what* is it?

PREP. I a—hate him and would have his life!

THES. [*to* STUP.] That's it—he hates you and would have your life. Now go and be merry.

STUP. Yes, but why does he hate me?

THES. Oh—exactly. [*To* PREP.] Why do you hate him?

PREP. Because he is a minion!

THES. He hates you because you are a minion. It explains itself. Now go and enjoy yourselves. Ha! ha! It is well for those who *can* laugh—let them do so—there is no extra charge. The light-hearted cup and the convivial jest for them—but for me—what is there for me?

SILLIMON. There is some claret-cup and lobster salad. [*Handing some.*

THES. [*taking it*] Thank you. [*Resuming*] What is there for me but anxiety—ceaseless gnawing anxiety that tears at my very vitals and rends my peace of mind asunder? There is nothing whatever for me but anxiety of the nature I have just described. The charge of these thoughtless revellers is my unhappy lot. It is not a small charge, and it is rightly termed a lot, because they are many. Oh why did the gods make me a manager?

SILL. [*as guessing a riddle*] *Why* did the gods make him a manager?

SPAR. Why did the *gods* make him a manager?

DAPH. Why did the gods make *him* a manager?

PRETT. Why did the gods make him a *manager?*

THES. No—no—what are you talking about? what do you mean?

DAPH. I've got it—don't tell us——

ALL No—no—because—because——

THES. [*annoyed*] It isn't a conundrum—it's a misanthropical question. Why cannot I join you? [*Retires up centre.*

DAPH. [*who is sitting with* SPARKEION *to the annoyance of* NICEMIS *who is crying alone*] I'm sure I don't know. We do not want you. Don't distress yourself on our account—we are getting on very comfortably—aren't we, Sparkeion?

SPAR. We are so happy that we don't miss the lobster or the claret. What are lobster and claret compared with the society of those we love? [*Embracing* DAPHNE.

DAPH. Why, Nicemis, love, you are eating nothing. Aren't you happy, dear?

NICE. [*spitefully*] *You* are *quite* welcome to *my* share of *everything. I* intend to console *myself* with the society of my manager. [*Takes* THESPIS' *arm affectionately.*

THES. Here I say—this won't do, you know—I can't allow it—at least before my company—besides, you are half-married to Sparkeion. Sparkeion, here's your half-wife impairing my influence before my company. Don't you know the story of the gentleman who undermined his influence by associating with his inferiors?

ALL Yes, yes,—we know it.

PREP. [*furiously*] *I* do not know it! It's ever thus! Doomed to disappointment from my earliest years——

[STUPIDAS *endeavours to console him.*

THES. There—that's enough. Preposteros—you *shall* hear it.

Song—THESPIS

I once knew a chap who discharged a function
On the North South East West Diddlesex junction,
He was conspicu*ous* exceeding,
For his affable ways and his easy breeding.
Although a Chairman of Directors,
He was hand in glove with the ticket inspectors,
He tipped the guards with brand-new fivers,
And sang little songs to the engine drivers.
'Twas told to me with great compunction,
By one who had discharged with unction,
A Chairman of Directors' function,
On the North South East West Diddlesex junction.
Fol diddle, lol diddle, lol lol lay.

Each Christmas Day he gave each stoker
A silver shovel and a golden poker,
He'd button-hole flowers for the ticket sorters,
And rich Bath-buns for the outside porters.
He'd mount the clerks on his first-class hunters,
And he built little villas for the road-side shunters,
And if any were fond of pigeon shooting,
He'd ask them down to his place at Tooting.
'Twas told to me, etc.

In course of time there spread a rumour
That he did all this from a sense of humour,
So instead of signalling and stoking,
They gave themselves up to a course of joking.
Whenever they knew that he was riding,
They shunted his train on lonely siding,
Or stopped all night in the middle of a tunnel,
On the plea that the boiler was a-coming through the funnel.
'Twas told to me, etc.

If he wished to go to Perth or Stirling,
His train through several counties whirling,
Would set him down in a fit of larking,
At four a.m. in the wilds of Barking.
This pleased his whim and seemed to strike it,

But the general Public did not like it,
The receipts fell, after a few repeatings,
And he got it hot at the annual meetings,
'Twas told to me, etc.

He followed out his whim with vigour,
The shares went down to a nominal figure,
These are the sad results proceeding
From his affable ways and his easy breeding!
The line. with its rails and guards and peelers,
Was sold tor a song to marine store dealers,
The shareholders are all in the work'us,
And he sells pipe-lights in the Regent Circus.
'Twas told to me with much compunction,
By one who had discharged with unction
A Chairman of Directors' function,
On the North South East West Diddlesex junction,
Fol diddle, lol diddle, lol lol lay!

[*After song.*

THES. It's very hard. As a man I am naturally of an easy disposition. As a manager, I am compelled to hold myself aloof, that my influence may not be deteriorated. As a man, I am inclined to fraternize with the pauper—as a manager I am compelled to walk about like this: Don't know yah! Don't know yah! Don't know yah!

Strides haughtily about the stage, JUPITER, MARS, *and* APOLLO, *in full Olympian costume appear on the three broken columns. Thespians scream.*

JUPITER, MARS and APOLLO [*in recit.*] Presumptuous mortal!

THES. [*same business*] Don't know yah! Don't know yah!

JUP., MARS and APOLLO [*seated on three broken pillars, still in recit.*] Presumptuous mortal!

THES. I do not know you, I do not know you.

JUP., MARS and APOLLO [*standing on ground, recit.*] Presumptuous mortal!

THES. [*recit.*] Remove this person.

[STUP. *and* PREP. *seize* AP. *and* MARS.

JUP. [*speaking*] Stop, you evidently *don't* know me. Allow me to offer you my card. [*Throws flash paper.*

THES. Ah yes, it's very pretty, but we don't want any at present. When we do our Christmas piece I'll let you know. [*Changing his manner.*] Look here, you know, this is a private party and we haven't the pleasure of your acquaintance. There are a good many other mountains about, if you must have a mountain all to yourself. Don't make me let myself down before my company. [*Resuming*] Don't know yah! Don't know yah!

Jup. I am Jupiter, the King of the Gods. This is Apollo. This is Mars. [*All kneel to them except* Thespis.

Thes. Oh! then as I'm a respectable man, and rather particular about the company I keep, I think I'll go.

Jup. No—no—stop a bit. We want to consult you on a matter of great importance. There! Now we are alone. Who are you?

Thes. I am Thespis of the Thessalian Theatres.

Jup. The very man we want. Now as a judge of what the public likes, are you impressed with my appearance as the father of the gods?

Thes. Well to be candid with you, I am not. In fact I'm disappointed.

Jup. Disappointed?

Thes. Yes, you see you're so much out of repair. No, you don't come up to my idea of the part. Bless you, I've played you often.

Jup. You have!

Thes. To be sure I have.

Jup. And how have you dressed the part?

Thes. Fine commanding party in the prime of life. Thunderbolt—full beard—dignified manner—A good deal of this sort of thing "Don't know yah! Don't know yah! don't know yah!" [*Imitating, crosses* L.

Jup. [*much affected*] I—I'm very much obliged to you. It's very good of you. I—I—I used to be like that. I can't tell you how much I feel it. And do you find I'm an impressive character to play?

Thes. Well no, I can't say you are. In fact we don't use you much out of burlesque.

Jup. Burlesque! [*Offended, walks up.*

Thes. Yes, it's a painful subject, drop it, drop it. The fact is, you are not the gods you were—you're behind your age.

Jup. Well, but what are we to do? We feel that we ought to do something, but we don't know what.

Thes. Why don't you all go down to Earth, incog., mingle with the world, hear and see what people think of you, and judge for yourselves as to the best means to take to restore your influence?

Jup. Ah, but what's to become of Olympus in the meantime?

Thes. Lor bless you, don't distress yourself about that. I've a very good company, used to take long parts on the shortest notice. Invest us with your powers and we'll fill your places till you return.

Jup. [*aside*] The offer is tempting. But suppose you fail?

Thes. Fail! Oh, we never fail in our profession. We've nothing but great successes!

Jup. Then it's a bargain?

Thes. It's a bargain. [*They shake hands on it.*

Jup. And that you may not be entirely without assistance, we will leave you Mercury, and whenever you find yourself in a difficulty you can consult him.

Enter Mercury [*trap* c.]

Quartette

JUP. So that's arranged—you take my place, my boy,
  While we make trial of a new existence.
At length I shall be able to enjoy
  The pleasures I have envied from a distance.
MER. Compelled upon Olympus here to stop,
  While other gods go down to play the hero,
Don't be surprised if on this mountain top
  You find your Mercury is down at zero!
AP. To earth away to join in mortal acts,
  And gather fresh materials to write on,
Investigate more closely several facts,
  That I for centuries have thrown some light on!
DIA. I, as the modest moon with crescent bow,
  Have always shown a light to nightly scandal,
I must say I should like to go below,
  And find out if the game is worth the candle!

Enter all the Thespians, summoned by MERCURY

MER. Here come your people!
THES. People better now!

Air—THESPIS

While mighty Jove goes down below
  With all the other deities,
I fill his place and wear his "clo,"
  The very part for me it is.
To mother earth to make a track,
  They all are spurred and booted, too,
And you will fill, till they come back,
  The parts you best are suited to.

CHORUS Here's a pretty tale for future Iliads and Odys-
  seys,
Mortals are about to personate the gods and goddesses.
Now to set the world in order, we will work in
  unity.
Jupiter's perplexity is Thespis's opportunity.

Solo—SPARKEION

Phœbus am I, with golden ray,
The god of day, the god of day,
When shadowy night has held her sway,
I make the goddess fly.
'Tis mine the task to wake the world,
In slumber curled, in slumber curled,
By me her charms are all unfurled,
The god of day am I!

CHORUS
The god of day, the god of day,
That part shall our Sparkeion play.
Ha! ha! &c.
The rarest fun and rarest fare,
That ever fell to mortal share!
Ha! ha! &c.

Solo—NICEMIS

I am the moon, the lamp of night.
I show a light—I show a light.
With radiant sheen I put to flight
The shadows of the sky.
By my fair rays, as you're aware,
Gay lovers swear—gay lovers swear,
While greybeards sleep away their care,
The lamp of night am I!

CHORUS
The lamp of night—the lamp of night,
Nicemis plays, to her delight.
Ha! ha! ha! ha!
The rarest fun and rarest fare,
That ever fell to mortal share.
Ha! ha! ha! ha!

Solo—TIMIDON

Mighty old Mars, the God of War,
I'm destined for—I'm destined for—
A terribly famous conqueror,
With sword upon his thigh.
When armies meet with eager shout,
And warlike rout, and warlike rout,
You'll find me there without a doubt.
The God of War am I!

CHORUS The God of War, the God of War.
Great Timidon is destined for!
Ha! ha! ha! ha!
The rarest fun and rarest fare,
That ever fell to mortal share.
Ha! ha! ha! ha! &c.

Solo—DAPHNE

When, as the fruit of warlike deeds,
The soldier bleeds, the soldier bleeds,
Calliope crowns heroic deeds,
With immortality.
From mere oblivion I reclaim
The soldier's name, the soldier's name,
And write it on the roll of fame,
The muse of fame am I!

CHORUS The muse of fame, the muse of fame,
Calliope is Daphne's name,
Ha! ha! ha! ha!
The rarest fun and rarest fare,
That ever fell to mortal share!
Ha! ha! ha! ha!

TUTTI. Here's a pretty tale!

Enter procession of old Gods, they come down very much astonished at all they see, then passing by, ascend the platform that leads to the descent at the back.

Gods [JUPITER, DIANA, *and* APOLLO] *in corner are together.*

We will go,
Down below,
Revels rare,
We will share.
Ha! ha! ha!

With a gay
Holiday,
All unknown,
And alone.
Ha! ha! ha!

TUTTI. Here's a pretty tale!

The Gods, including those who have lately entered in procession, group themselves on rising ground at back. The Thespians [*kneeling*] *bid them farewell.*

ACT II

SCENE.—*The same scene as in Act I with the exception that in place of the ruins that filled the foreground of the stage, the interior of a magnificent temple is seen, showing the background of the scene of Act I, through the columns of the portico at the back. High throne* L.U.E. *Low seats below it.*

All the substitute gods and goddesses [that is to say, Thespians] are discovered grouped in picturesque attitudes about the stage, eating, drinking, and smoking, and singing the following verses:—

Chorus

Of all symposia,
The best by half,
Upon Olympus, here, await us,
We eat Ambrosia,
And nectar quaff—
It cheers but don't inebriate us.

We know the fallacies
Of human food,
So please to pass Olympian rosy,
We built up palaces,
Where ruins stood,
And find them much more snug and cosy.

Solo—SILLIMON

To work and think, my dear,
Up here, would be,
The height of conscientious folly,
So eat and drink, my dear,
I like to see,
Young people gay—young people jolly.
Olympian food, my love,
I'll lay long odds,
Will please your lips—those rosy portals,
What is the good, my love
Of being gods,
If we must work like common mortals?

CHORUS Of all symposia, &c.

Exeunt all but NICEMIS, *who is dressed as* DIANA, *and* PRETTEIA, *who is dressed as* VENUS. *They take* SILLIMON'S *arm and bring him down.*

SILLIMON. Bless their little hearts, I can refuse them nothing. As the Olympian stage-manager I ought to be strict with them and make them do their duty, but I can't. Bless their little hearts, when I see the pretty little craft come sailing up to me with a wheedling smile on their pretty little figure-heads, I can't turn my back on 'em. I'm all bow, though I'm sure I try to be stern!

PRETT. You certainly are a dear old thing.

SILL. She says I'm a dear old thing! Deputy Venus says I'm a dear old thing!

NICE. It's her affectionate habit to describe everybody in those terms. *I* am more particular, but still even *I* am bound to admit that you are certainly a very dear old thing.

SILL. Deputy Venus says I'm a dear old thing, and deputy Diana, who is much more particular, endorses it! Who could be severe with such deputy divinities?

PRETT. Do you know, I'm going to ask you a favour.

SILL. Venus is going to ask me a favour!

PRETT. You see, I am Venus.

SILL. No one who saw your face would doubt it.

NICE. [*aside*] No one who knew her *character* would.

PRETT. Well Venus, you know, is married to Mars.

SILL. To Vulcan, my dear, to Vulcan. The exact connubial relation of the different gods and goddesses is a point on which we must be extremely particular.

PRETT. I beg your pardon—Venus is married to Mars.

NICE. If she isn't married to Mars, she ought to be.

SILL. Then that decides it—call it married to Mars.

PRETT. Married to Vulcan or married to Mars, what does it signify?

SILL. My dear, it's a matter on which I have no personal feeling whatever.

PRETT. So that she is married to some one!

SILL. Exactly! so that she is married to some one. Call it married to Mars.

PRETT. Now here's my difficulty. Presumptios takes the place of Mars, and Presumptios is my father!

SILL. Then why object to Vulcan?

PRETT. Because Vulcan is my grandfather!

SILL. But, my dear, what an objection! You are playing a part till the real gods return. That's all! Whether you are supposed to be married to your father—or your grandfather, what does it matter? This passion for realism is the curse of the stage!

PRETT. That's all very well, but I can't throw myself into a part that has already lasted a twelvemonth, when I have to make love to my father. It interferes with my conception of the characters. It spoils the part.

SILL. Well, well, I'll see what can be done. [*Exit* PRETTEIA L.U.E.] That's always the way with beginners, they've no imaginative power. A true artist ought to be superior to such considerations. [NICEMIS *comes down* R.] Well, Nicemis—I should say Diana—what's wrong with you? Don't you like your part?

NICE. Oh, immensely! It's great fun.

SILL. Don't you find it lonely out by yourself all night?

NICE. Oh, but I'm *not* alone all night!

SILL. But—I don't want to ask any injudicious questions—but who accompanies you?

NICE. Who? why Sparkeion, of course.

SILL. Sparkeion? Well, but Sparkeion is Phœbus Apollo. [*Enter* SPARKEION] He's the Sun, you know.

NICE. Of course he is; I should catch my death of cold, in the night air, if he didn't accompany me.

SPAR. My dear Sillimon, it would never do for a young lady to be out alone all night. It wouldn't be respectable.

SILL. There's a good deal of truth in that. But still—the Sun—at night—I don't like the idea. The original Diana always went out alone.

NICE. I hope the original Diana is no rule for *me*. After all, what *does* it matter?

SILL. To be sure—what *does* it matter?

SPAR. The sun at night, or in the daytime!

SILL. So that he shines. That's all that's necessary. [*Exit* NICEMIS R.U.E.] But poor Daphne, what will she say to this?

SPAR. Oh, Daphne can console herself; young ladies soon get over this sort of thing. Did you never hear of the young lady who was engaged to Cousin Robin?

SILL. Never.

SPAR. Then I'll sing it to you.

Song—SPARKEION

Little maid of Arcadee
Sat on Cousin Robin's knee,
Thought in form and face and limb,
Nobody could rival him.
He was brave and she was fair.
Truth, they made a pretty pair.
Happy little maiden, she—
Happy maid of Arcadee!

Moments fled as moments will
Happily enough, until,
After, say, a month or two,
Robin did as Robins do.
Weary of his lover's play,
Jilted her and went away.

Wretched little maiden, she—
Wretched maid of Arcadee!

To her little home she crept,
There she sat her down and wept,
Maiden wept as maidens will—
Grew so thin and pale—until
Cousin Richard came to woo!
Then again the roses grew!
Happy little maiden, she—
Happy maid of Arcadee!

[*Exit* SPARKEION.

SILL. Well, Mercury, my boy, you've had a year's experience of us here. How do we do it? I think we're rather an improvement on the original gods—don't you?

MER. Well, you see, there's a good deal to be said on both sides of the question; you are certainly younger than the original gods, and, therefore, more active. On the other hand, they are certainly older than you, and have, therefore, more experience. On the whole I prefer *you*, because your mistakes amuse me.

Song—MERCURY

Olympus is now in a terrible muddle,
  The deputy deities all are at fault;
They splutter and splash like a pig in a puddle,
  And dickens a one of 'em's earning his salt,
For Thespis as Jove is a terrible blunder,
  Too nervous and timid—too easy and weak—
Whenever he's called on to lighten or thunder,
  The thought of it keeps him awake for a week!

Then mighty Mars hasn't the pluck of a parrot,
  When left in the dark he will quiver and quail;
And Vulcan has arms that would snap like a carrot,
  Before he could drive in a tenpenny nail!
Then Venus's freckles are very repelling.
  And Venus should *not* have a squint in her eyes;
The learned Minerva is weak in her spelling,
  And scatters her h's all over the skies.

Then Pluto, in kindhearted tenderness erring,
  Can't make up his mind to let anyone die—
The *Times* has a paragraph ever recurring,
  "Remarkable instance of longevi*ty*."

On some it has come as a serious onus,
  To others it's quite an advantage—in short,
While ev'ry Life Office declares a big bonus,
  The poor undertakers are all in the court!

Then Cupid, the rascal, forgetting his trade is
  To make men and women impartially smart,
Will only shoot at pretty young ladies,
  And never takes aim at a bachelor's heart.
The results of this freak—or whatever you term it—
  Should cover the wicked young scamp with disgrace,
While ev'ry young man is as shy as a hermit,
  Young ladies are popping all over the place!

This wouldn't much matter—for bashful and shy men,
  When skilfully handled, are certain to fall,
But, alas! that determined young bachelor Hymen
  Refuses to wed anybody at all!
He swears that Love's flame is the vilest of arsons,
  And looks upon marriage as quite a mistake;
Now, what in the world's to become of the parsons,
  And what of the artist who sugars the cake?

In short, you will see from the facts that I'm showing,
  The state of the case is exceedingly sad;
If Thespis's people go on as they're going,
  Olympus will certainly go to the bad!
From Jupiter downwards there isn't a dab in it,
  All of 'em quibble and shuffle and shirk;
A premier in Downing Street, forming a Cabinet,
  Couldn't find people less fit for their work!

Enter THESPIS, L.U.E.

THES. Sillimon, you can retire.

SILL. Sir, I—

THES. Don't pretend you can't when I say you can. I've seen you do it—go! [*Exit* SILLIMON *bowing extravagantly*, THESPIS *imitates him*] Well, Mercury, I've been in power one year to-day.

MER. One year to-day. How do you like ruling the world?

THES. Like it! Why it's as straightforward as possible. Why there hasn't been a hitch of any kind since we came up here. Lor! The airs you gods and goddesses give yourselves are perfectly sickening. Why it's mere child's play!

MER. Very simple, isn't it?

THES. Simple? Why I could do it on my head.

MER. Ah—I daresay you will do it on your head very soon.

THES. What do you mean by *that*, Mercury?

MER. I mean that when you've turned the world *quite* topsy-turvy you won't know whether you're standing on your head or your heels.

THES. Well, but, Mercury, it's all right at present.

MER. Oh yes—as far as we know.

THES. Well, but, you know, we know as much as anybody knows; you know, I believe, that the world's still going on.

MER. Yes—as far as we can judge—much as usual.

THES. Well, then, give the Father of the Drama his due, Mercury. Don't be envious of the Father of the Drama.

MER. Well, but you see you leave so much to accident.

THES. Well, Mercury, if I do, it's my principle. I am an easy man, and I like to make things as pleasant as possible. What did I do the day we took office? Why I called the company together and I said to them: "Here we are, you know, gods and goddesses, no mistake about it, the real thing. Well, we have certain duties to discharge, let's discharge them intelligently. Don't let us be hampered by routine and red tape and precedent, let's set the original gods an example, and put a liberal interpretation on our duties. If it occurs to any one to try an experiment in his own department, let him try it, if he fails there's no harm done, if he succeeds it is a distinct gain to society. Take it easy," I said, "and at the same time, make experiments. Don't hurry your work, do it slowly, and do it well." And here we are after a twelvemonth, and not a single complaint or a single petition has reached me.

MER. No—not yet.

THES. What do you mean by "no, not yet"?

MER. Well, you see, you don't understand these things. All the petitions that are addressed by men to Jupiter pass through my hands, and it's my duty to collect them and present them once a year.

THES. Oh, only once a year?

MER. Only once a year.

THES. And the year is up—?

MER. To-day.

THES. Oh, then I suppose there are *some* complaints?

MER. Yes, there *are some*.

THES. [*disturbed*] Oh. Perhaps there are a good many?

MER. There are a good many.

THES. Oh. Perhaps there are a thundering lot?

MER. There are a thundering lot.

THES. [*very much disturbed*] Oh!

MER. You see you've been taking it so very easy—and so have most of your company.

THES. Oh, who has been taking it easy?

MER. Well, all except those who have been trying experiments.

THES. Well but I suppose the experiments are ingenious?

MER. Yes; they are ingenious, but on the whole ill-judged. But it's time to go and summon your court.

THES. What for?

MER. To hear the complaints. In five minutes they will be here. [*Exit.*

THES. [*very uneasy*] I don't know how it is, but there is something in that young man's manner that suggests that the Father of the Gods has been taking it *too* easy. Perhaps it would have been better if I hadn't given my company so much scope. I wonder what they've been doing. I think I will curtail their discretion, though none of them appear to have much of the article. It seems a pity to deprive 'em of what little they have.

Enter DAPHNE, *weeping*

THES. Now then, Daphne, what's the matter with you?

DAPH. Well, you know how disgracefully Sparkeion——

THES. [*correcting her*] Apollo——

DAPH. Apollo, then—has treated me. He promised to marry me years ago, and now he's married to Nicemis.

THES. Now look here. I can't go into that. You're in Olympus now and must behave accordingly. Drop your Daphne—assume your Calliope.

DAPH. Quite so. That's it! [*Mysteriously*

THES. Oh—that is it? [*Puzzled*

DAPH. That is it, Thespis. I am Calliope, the Muse of Fame. Very good. This morning I was in the Olympian library, and I took down the only book there. Here it is.

THES. [*taking it*] Lemprière's Classical Dictionary. The Olympian Peerage.

DAPH. Open it at Apollo.

THES. [*opens it*] It is done.

DAPH. Read.

THES. "Apollo was several times married, among others to Issa, Bolina, Coronis, Chymene, Cyrene, Chione, Acacallis, and Calliope."

DAPH. *And* Calliope.

THES. [*musing*] Ha! I didn't know he was *married* to them.

DAPH. [*severely*] Sir! This is the Family Edition.

THES. Quite so.

DAPH. You couldn't expect a lady to read any other?

THES. On no consideration. But in the original version——

DAPH. I go by the Family Edition.

THES. Then by the Family Edition, Apollo is your husband.

Enter NICEMIS *and* SPARKEION

NICE. Apollo your husband? He is my husband.

DAPH. I beg your pardon. He is *my* husband.

NICE. Apollo is Sparkeion, and he's married to me.

DAPH. Sparkeion is Apollo, and he's married to me.

NICE. He's my husband.

DAPH. He's your brother.

THES. Look here, Apollo, whose husband are you? Don't let's have any row about it; whose husband are you?

SPAR. Upon my honour I don't know. I'm in a very delicate position, but I'll fall in with any arrangement Thespis may propose.

DAPH. I've just found out that he's my husband, and yet he goes out every evening with that "thing"!

THES. Perhaps he's trying an experiment.

DAPH. I don't like my husband to make such experiments. The question is, who are we all and what is our relation to each other.

Quartette

SPAR. You're Diana, I'm Apollo—
And Calliope is she.
DAPH. He's you're brother.
NICE. You're another.
He has fairly married me.
DAPH. By the rules of this fair spot
I'm his wife, and you are not—
SPAR. and DAPH. By the rules of this fair spot,
{I'm / She's} his wife, and you are not.
NICE. By this golden wedding ring,
I'm his wife, and you're a "thing."
DAPH., NICE. and SPAR. By this golden wedding ring,
{I'm / She's} his wife, and you're a "thing."
ALL Please will some one kindly tell us,
Who are our respective kin?
All of {us / them} are very jealous,
Neither of {us / them} will give in.
NICE. He's my husband I declare,
I espoused him properlee.
SPAR. That is true, for I was there,
And I saw her marry me.
DAPH. He's you're brother—I'm his wife,
If we go by Lemprière,
SPAR. So she is, upon my life,
Really that seems very fair.
NICE. You're my husband and no other
SPAR. That is true enough I swear,
DAPH. I'm his wife, and you're his brother.
SPAR. If we go by Lemprière.

NICE. It will surely be unfair,
To decide by Lemprière.
[*Crying*]
DAPH. I will surely be quite fair,
To decide by Lemprière,
SPAR. and THES. How you settle I don't care,
Leave it all to Lemprière.
[*Spoken*] The Verdict.
As Sparkeion is Apollo
Up in this Olympian clime,
Why, Nicemis, it will follow,
He's *her* husband, for the time
—[*indicating* DAPHNE]
When Sparkeion turns to mortal,
Join once more the sons of men,
He may take *you* to his portal
[*indicating* NICEMIS]
He will be *your* husband then.
That oh that is my decision,
'Cording to my mental vision.
Put an end to all collision,
That oh that is my decision.
My decision—my decision,
ALL That oh that is his decision,
His decision—his decision! &c.

[*Exeunt* THES., NICE., SPAR., *and* DAPHNE, SPAR. *with* DAPHNE, NICEMIS *weeping with* THESPIS.

Mysterious Music. Enter JUPITER, APOLLO, *and* MARS, *from below, at the back of stage. All wear cloaks as disguise and all are masked.*

Recitative

Oh rage and fury! Oh shame and sorrow!
We'll be resuming our ranks to-morrow,
Since from Olympus we have departed,
We've been distracted and brokenhearted,
Oh wicked Thespis! Oh villain scurvy;
Through him Olympus is topsy-turvy!
Compelled to silence to grin and bear it!
He's caused our sorrow, and he shall share it.
Where is the monster! Avenge his blunders,
He has awakened Olympian thunders.

Enter MERCURY

JUP. [*recit.*] Oh Monster!
AP. [*recit.*] Oh Monster!
MARS [*recit.*] Oh Monster!

MER. [*in great terror*] Please sir, what have I done sir?

JUP. What did we leave you behind for?

MER. Please sir, that's the question I asked for when you went away.

JUP. Was it not that Thespis might consult you whenever he was in a difficulty?

MER. Well, here I've been, ready to be consulted, chockful of reliable information—running over with celestial maxims—advice gratis ten to four—after twelve ring the night bell in cases of emergency.

JUP. And hasn't he consulted you?

MER. Not he—he disagrees with me about everything.

JUP. He must have misunderstood me. I told him to consult you whenever he was in a fix.

MER. He must have thought you said *in*sult. Why whenever I opened my mouth he jumps down my throat. It isn't pleasant to have a fellow constantly jumping down your throat—especially when he always disagrees with you. It's just the sort of thing I can't digest.

JUP. [*in a rage*] Send him here, I'll talk to him.

Enter THESPIS. *He is much terrified.*

JUP. [*recit.*] Oh Monster!
AP. [*recit.*] Oh Monster!
MARS [*recit.*] Oh Monster!

THESPIS *sings in great terror, which he endeavours to conceal*

JUP. Well Sir, the year is up to-day.

AP. And a nice mess you've made of it.

MARS You've deranged the whole scheme of society.

THES. [*aside*] There's going to be a row! [*Aloud and very familiarly*] My dear boy—I do assure you——

JUP. [*in recit.*] Be respectful!
AP. [*in recit.*] Be respectful!
MARS [*in recit.*] Be respectful!

THES. I don't know what you allude to. With the exception of getting our scene-painter to "run up" this temple, because we found the ruins draughty, we haven't touched a thing.

JUP. [*in recit.*] Oh story teller!
AP. [*in recit.*] Oh story teller!
MARS [*in recit.*] Oh story teller!

Enter THESPIANS

THES. My dear fellows, you're distressing yourselves unnecessarily. The court of Olympus is about to assemble to listen to the complaints of the year, if any. But there are none, or next to none. Let the Olympians assemble!

Enter THESPIANS

THESPIS *takes chair.* JUP., AP. *and* MARS *sit below him*

THES. Ladies and gentlemen. It seems that it is usual for the gods to assemble once a year to listen to mortal petitions. It doesn't seem to me to be a good plan, as work is liable to accumulate; but as I'm particularly anxious not to interfere with Olympian precedent, but to allow everything to go on as it has always been accustomed to go—why, we'll say no more about it.[*Aside*] But how shall I account for your presence?

JUP. Say we are gentlemen of the press.

THES. That all our proceedings may be perfectly open and aboveboard I have communicated with the most influential members of the Athenian press, and I beg to introduce to your notice three of its most distinguished members. They bear marks emblematic of the anonymous character of modern journalism. [*Business of introduction.* THESPIS *very uneasy*] Now then, if you're all ready we will begin.

MER. [*brings tremendous bundles of petitions*] Here is the agenda.

THES. What's that? The petitions?

MER. Some of them. [*Opens one and reads*] Ah, I thought there'd be a row about it.

THES. Why, what's wrong now?

MER. Why, it's been a foggy Friday in November for the last six months and the Athenians are tired of it.

THES. There's no pleasing some people. This craving for perpetual change is the curse of the country. Friday's a very nice day.

MER. So it is, but a Friday six months long!—it gets monotonous.

JUP., AP. and MARS [*in recit. rising*] It's perfectly ridiculous.

THES. [*calling them*] It shall be arranged. Cymon!

CYM. [*as Time with the usual attributes*] Sir!

THES. [*introducing him to* THREE GODS] Allow me—Father Time—rather young at present but even Time must have a beginning. In course of Time, Time will grow older. Now then, Father Time, what's this about a wet Friday in November for the last six months?

CYM. Well, the fact is, I've been trying an experiment. Seven days in the week is an awkward number. It can't be halved. Two's into seven won't go.

THES. [*tries it on his fingers*] Quite so—quite so.

CYM. So I abolished Saturday.

JUP., AP. and MARS Oh but—— [*Rising.*

THES. Do be quiet. He's a very intelligent young man and knows what he is about. So you abolished Saturday. And how did you find it answer?

CYM. Admirably.

THES. You hear? He found it answer admirably.

CYM. Yes, only Sunday refused to take its place.

THES. Sunday refused to take its place?

CYM. Sunday comes after Saturday—Sunday won't go on duty after Friday, Sunday's principles are very strict. That's where my experiment sticks.

THES. Well, but why November? Come, why November?

CYM. December can't begin till November has finished. November can't finish because he's abolished Saturday. There again my experiment sticks.

THES. Well, but why wet? Come now, why wet?

CYM. Ah, that is your fault. You turned on the rain six months ago, and you forgot to turn it off again.

JUP., MARS and AP. [*rising—recitative*] Oh this is monstrous!

ALL Order, order.

THES. Gentlemen, pray be seated. [*To the others*] The liberty of the press, one can't help it. [*To the three gods*] It is easily settled. Athens has had a wet Friday in November for the last six months. Let them have a blazing Tuesday in July for the next twelve.

JUP., MARS and AP. But——

ALL Order, order.

THES. Now then, the next article.

MER. Here's a petition from the Peace Society. They complain that there are no more battles.

MARS [*springing up*] What!

THES. Quiet there! Good dog—soho; Timidon!

TIM. [*as* MARS] Here.

THES. What's this about there being no battles?

TIM. I've abolished battles; it's an experiment.

MARS [*springing up*] Oh come, I say——

THES. Quiet then! [*To* TIM] Abolished battles?

TIM. Yes, you told us on taking office to remember two things, to try experiments and to take it easy. I found I couldn't take it easy while there are any battles to attend to, so I tried the experiment and abolished battles. And then I took it easy. The Peace Society ought to be very much obliged to me.

THES. Obliged to you! Why, confound it! since battles have been abolished war is universal.

TIM. War universal?

THES. To be sure it is! Now that nations can't fight, no two of 'em are on speaking terms. The dread of fighting was the only thing that kept them civil to each other. Let battles be restored and peace reign supreme.

MER. [*reads*] Here's a petition from the associated wine merchants of Mytilene.

THES. Well, what's wrong with the associated wine merchants of Mytilene? Are there no grapes this year?

MER. Plenty of grapes; more than usual.

THES. [*to the gods*] You observe, there is no deception; there are more than usual.

MER. There are plenty of grapes, only they are full of ginger beer.

THREE GODS Oh, come I say.

[*Rising, they are put down by* THESPIS.

THES. Eh? what. [*Much alarmed*] Bacchus?

TIPS. [*as* BACCHUS] Here!

THES. There seems to be something unusual with the grapes of Mytilene; they only grow ginger beer.

TIPS. And a very good thing too.

THES. It's very nice in its way, but it is not what one looks for from grapes.

TIPS. Beloved master, a week before we came up here, you insisted on my taking the pledge. By so doing you rescued me from my otherwise inevitable misery. I cannot express my thanks. Embrace me!

[*Attempts to embrace him.*

THES. Get out, don't be a fool. Look here, you know you're the god of wine.

TIPS. I am.

THES. [*very angry*] Well, do you consider it consistent with your duty as the god of wine to make the grapes yield nothing but ginger beer?

TIPS. Do you consider it consistent with my duty as a total abstainer to grow anything stronger than ginger beer?

THES. But your duty as the god of wine——

TIPS. In every respect in which my duty as the god of wine can be discharged consistently with my duty as a total abstainer, I will discharge it. But when the functions clash, everything must give way to the pledge. My preserver! [*Attempts to embrace him.*

THES. Don't be a confounded fool! This can be arranged. We can't give over the wine this year, but at least we can improve the ginger beer. Let all the ginger beer be extracted from it immediately.

JUP., MARS, AP. [*aside*] We can't stand this,
We can't stand this,
It's much too strong,
We can't stand this.
It would be wrong,
Extremely wrong,
If we stood this,
If we stand this,
If we stand this,
We can't stand this.

DAPH., SPAR., NICE. Great Jove, this interference,
Is more than we can stand;
Of them make a clearance,
With your majestic hand.

JOVE This cool audacity, it beats us hollow
[*removing mask*] I'm Jupiter!
MARS I'm Mars!
AP. I'm Apollo!

Enter DIANA *and all the other gods and goddesses.*

ALL [*kneeling with their foreheads on the ground*].
Jupiter, Mars and Apollo,
Have quitted the dwellings of men;
The other gods quickly will follow,
And what will become of us then.
Oh, pardon us, Jove and Apollo,
Pardon us, Jupiter, Mars;
Oh, see us in misery wallow,
Cursing our terrible stars.

Enter other gods.

Chorus and Ballet

ALL THE THESPIANS Let us remain, we beg of you pleadingly!
THREE GODS Let them remain, they beg of us pleadingly!
THES. Life on Olympus suits us exceedingly.
GODS Life on Olympus suits them exceedingly.
THES. Let us remain, we pray in humility!
GODS Let 'em remain, they pray in humility.
THES. If we have shown some little ability.
GODS If they have shown some little ability.
Let us remain, etc.
JUPITER Enough, your reign is ended;
Upon this sacred hill
Let him be apprehended,
And learn our awful will.
Away to earth, contemptible comedians,
And hear our curse, before we set you free;
You shall all be eminent tragedians,
Whom no one ever goes to see!
ALL We go to earth, contemptible comedians,
We hear his curse before he sets us free,
We shall all be eminent tragedians,
Whom no one ever, ever goes to see!
SILL. Whom no one—
SPAR. Whom no one—
THES. Whom *no* one—
ALL Ever, ever goes to see.

The Thespians are driven away by the gods, who group themselves in attitudes of triumph.

THES. Now, here you see the arrant folly
Of doing your best to make things jolly.
I've ruled the world like a chap in his senses,
Observe the terrible consequences.
Great Jupiter, whom nothing pleases,
Splutters and swears, and kicks up breezes,
And sends us home in a mood avengin',
In double quick time, like a railroad engine.
And this he does without compunction,
Because I have discharged with unction
A highly complicated function,
Complying with his own injunction.
Fol, lol, lay.

CHORUS All this he does, etc.

The gods drive the Thespians away. The Thespians prepare to descend the mountain as the curtain falls.

TRIAL BY JURY

DRAMATIS PERSONÆ

The Learned Judge
The Plaintiff
The Defendant
Counsel for the Plaintiff
Usher
Foreman of the Jury
Associate
First Bridesmaid

First produced at the Royalty Theatre, March 25, 1875.

TRIAL BY JURY

SCENE.—*A Court of Justice. Barristers, Attorneys, and Jurymen discovered.*

Chorus

Hark, the hour of ten is sounding:
Hearts with anxious fears are bounding,
Hall of Justice crowds surrounding,
  Breathing hope and fear—
For to-day in this arena,
Summoned by a stern subpœna,
Edwin, sued by Angelina,
  Shortly will appear.

Enter USHER

Solo—USHER

Now, Jurymen, hear my advice—
All kinds of vulgar prejudice
  I pray you set aside:
With stern judicial frame of mind
From bias free of every kind,
    This trial must be tried.

Chorus

From bias free of every kind,
This trial must be tried.

During Chorus, USHER *sings fortissimo, "Silence in Court!"*

USHER
Oh, listen to the plaintiff's case:
Observe the features of her face—
The broken-hearted bride.
Condole with her distress of mind:
From bias free of every kind,
This trial must be tried!

CHORUS
From bias free, etc.

USHER
And when amid the plaintiff's shrieks,
The ruffianly defendant speaks—
Upon the other side;
What *he* may say you needn't mind—
From bias free of every kind,
This trial must be tried!

CHORUS
From bias free, etc.

Enter DEFENDANT

Recitative—DEFENDANT

Is this the Court of the Exchequer?
ALL It is!
DEFENDANT [*aside*] Be firm, be firm, my pecker,
Your evil star's in the ascendant!
ALL Who are you?
DEFENDANT I'm the Defendant!

Chorus of Jurymen [*shaking their fists*]

Monster, dread our damages.
We're the jury,
Dread our fury!

DEFENDANT
Hear me, hear me, if you please,
These are very strange proceedings—
For permit me to remark
On the merits of my pleadings,
You're at present in the dark.

DEFENDANT *beckons to* JURYMEN—*they leave the box and gather round him as they sing the following:*

That's a very true remark—
On the merits of his pleadings
We're at present in the dark!
Ha! ha!—ha! ha!

Song—Defendant

When first my old, old love I knew,
  My bosom welled with joy;
My riches at her feet I threw—
  I was a love-sick boy!
No terms seemed too extravagant
  Upon her to employ—
I used to mope, and sigh, and pant,
  Just like a love-sick boy!
          Tink-a-Tank—Tink-a-Tank.

But joy incessant palls the sense;
And love, unchanged, will cloy,
And she became a bore intense
  Unto her love-sick boy!
With fitful glimmer burnt my flame,
  And I grew cold and coy,
At last, one morning, I became
  Another's love-sick boy.
          Tink-a-Tank—Tink-a-Tank.

Chorus of Jurymen [*advancing stealthily*]

Oh, I was like that when a lad!
  A shocking young scamp of a rover,
I behaved like a regular cad;
  But that sort of thing is all over.
I'm now a respectable chap
  And shine with a virtue resplendent
And, therefore, I haven't a scrap
  Of sympathy with the defendant!
      He shall treat us with awe,
      If there isn't a flaw,

Singing so merrily—Trial-la-law!
Trial-la-law—Trial-la-law!
Singing so merrily—Trial-la-law!

[*They enter the Jury-box.*

Recitative—USHER [*on Bench*]

Silence in Court, and all attention lend.
Behold your Judge! In due submission bend!

Enter JUDGE *on Bench*

Chorus

All hail great Judge!
To your bright rays
We never grudge
Ecstatic praise.
All hail!

May each decree
As statute rank
And never be
Reversed in banc.
All hail!

Recitative—JUDGE

For these kind words accept my thanks, I pray.
A Breach of Promise we've to try to-day.
But firstly, if the time you'll not begrudge,
I'll tell you how I came to be a Judge.

ALL He'll tell us how he came to be a Judge!

Song—JUDGE

When I, good friends, was called to the bar,
I'd an appetite fresh and hearty,
But I was, as many young barristers are,
An impecunious party.
I'd a swallow-tail coat of a beautiful blue—
A brief which I bought of a booby—
A couple of shirts and a collar or two,
And a ring that looked like a ruby!

CHORUS A couple of shirts, etc.

JUDGE In Westminster Hall I danced a dance,
Like a semi-despondent fury;
For I thought I should never hit on a chance
Of addressing a British Jury—
But I soon got tired of third-class journeys,
And dinners of bread and water;
So I fell in love with a rich attorney's
Elderly, ugly daughter.

CHORUS So he fell in love, etc.

JUDGE The rich attorney, he jumped with joy,
And replied to my fond professions:
"You shall reap the reward of your pluck, my boy
At the Bailey and Middlesex Sessions.
You'll soon get used to her looks," said he,
"And a very nice girl you'll find her!
She may very well pass for forty-three
In the dusk, with a light behind her!"

CHORUS She may very well, etc.

JUDGE The rich attorney was good as his word;
The briefs came trooping gaily,
And every day my voice was heard
At the Sessions or Ancient Bailey.

All thieves who could my fees afford
  Relied on my orations,
And many a burglar I've restored
  To his friends and his relations.

CHORUS — And many a burglar, etc.

JUDGE — At length I became as rich as the Gurneys—
  An incubus then I thought her,
So I threw over that rich attorney's
  Elderly, ugly daughter.
The rich attorney my character high
  Tried vainly to disparage—
And now, if you please, I'm ready to try
  This Breach of Promise of Marriage!

CHORUS — And now if you please, etc.

JUDGE — For now I am a Judge!
ALL — And a good Judge too.
JUDGE — Yes, now I am a Judge!
ALL — And a good Judge too!
JUDGE — Though all my law is fudge,
Yet I'll never, never budge,
But I'll live and die a Judge!
ALL — And a good Judge too!
JUDGE — [*pianissimo*] It was managed by a job—
ALL — And a good job too!
JUDGE — It was managed by a job!
ALL — And a good job too!
JUDGE — It is patent to the mob,
That my being made a nob
Was effected by a job.
ALL — And a good job too!

Enter COUNSEL *for* PLAINTIFF. *He takes his place in front row of* **Coun-***sels' seats.*

Recitative—COUNSEL

Swear thou the Jury!

USHER — Kneel, Jurymen, oh, kneel!

All the JURY *kneel in the Jury-box, and so are hidden from audience.*

USHER — Oh, will you swear by yonder skies,
Whatever question may arise,
'Twixt rich and poor, 'twixt low and high,
That you will well and truly try?

JURY [*raising their hands, which alone are visible*]

To all of this we make reply
By the dull slate of yonder sky:
That we will well and truly try.
[*All rise with the last note.*]

Recitative—COUNSEL

Where is the Plaintiff?
Let her now be brought.

Recitative—USHER

Oh, Angelina! Come thou into Court!
Angelina! Angelina!!

Enter the Bridesmaids

Chorus of Bridesmaids

Comes the broken flower—
Comes the cheated maid—
Though the tempest lower,
Rain and cloud will fade.
Take, oh take these posies:
Though thy beauty rare
Shame the blushing roses,
They are passing fair!
Wear the flowers till they fade;
Happy be thy life, oh maid!

The* JUDGE, *having taken a great fancy to* FIRST BRIDESMAID, *sends her a note by* USHER, *which she reads, kisses rapturously, and places in her bosom.

Enter PLAINTIFF

Solo—PLAINTIFF

O'er the season vernal,
Time may cast a shade;
Sunshine, if eternal,
Makes the roses fade!
Time may do his duty;
Let the thief alone—
Winter hath a beauty,
That is all his own.
Fairest days are sun and shade:
I am no unhappy maid!

The JUDGE *having by this time transferred his admiration to* PLAINTIFF, *directs the* USHER *to take the note from* FIRST BRIDESMAID *and hand it to* PLAINTIFF, *who reads it, kisses it rapturously, and places it in her bosom.*

Chorus of Bridesmaids

Comes the broken flower, etc.

JUDGE Oh, never, never, never, since I joined the human race,
Saw I so exquisitely fair a face.

THE JURY [*shaking their forefingers at him*] Ah, sly dog! Ah, sly dog!

JUDGE [*to* JURY] How say you? Is she not designed for capture?

FOREMAN [*after consulting with the* JURY] We've but one word, my lord, and that is—Rapture.

PLAINTIFF [*curtseying*] Your kindness, gentlemen, quite overpowers!

JURY We love you fondly and would make you ours!

THE BRIDESMAIDS [*shaking their forefingers at* JURY]

Ah, sly dogs! Ah, sly dogs!

Recitative—COUNSEL for PLAINTIFF

May it please you, my lud!
Gentlemen of the jury!

Aria

With a sense of deep emotion,
I approach this painful case;
For I never had a notion
That a man could be so base,
Or deceive a girl confiding,
Vows, *etcetera*, deriding.

ALL He deceived a girl confiding,
Vows, *etcetera*, deriding.

PLAINTIFF *falls sobbing on* COUNSEL's *breast and remains there*

COUNSEL See my interesting client,
Victim of a heartless wile!
See the traitor all defiant
Wear a supercilious smile!
Sweetly smiled my client on him,
Coyly woo'd and gently won him.

ALL Sweetly smiled, etc.

COUNSEL Swiftly fled each honeyed hour
Spent with this unmanly male!

Camberwell became a bower,
  Peckham an Arcadian Vale,
Breathing concentrated otto!—
An existence *à la* Watteau.

ALL — Bless, us, concentrated otto! etc.

COUNSEL — Picture, then, my client naming,
  And insisting on the day:
Picture him excuses framing—
  Going from her far away;
Doubly criminal to do so,
For the maid had bought her *trousseau!*

ALL — Doubly criminal, etc.

COUNSEL — [*to* PLAINTIFF, *who weeps*]
Cheer up, my pretty—oh, cheer up!

JURY — Cheer up, cheer up, we love you!

COUNSEL *leads* PLAINTIFF *fondly into Witness-box; he takes a tender leave of her, and resumes his place in Court.*

[PLAINTIFF *reels as if about to faint*]

JUDGE — That she is reeling
  Is plain to see!

FOREMAN — If faint you're feeling
  Recline on me!
[*She falls sobbing on to the* FOREMAN'S *breast.*

PLAINTIFF [*feebly*]
I shall recover
  If left alone.

ALL [*shaking their fists at* DEFENDANT]
Oh, perjured lover,
  Atone! atone!

FOREMAN — Just like a father
  I wish to be. [*Kissing her.*

JUDGE [*approaching her*]
Or, if you'd rather,
  Recline on me!

She jumps on to Bench, sits down by the JUDGE, *and falls sobbing on his breast.*

COUNSEL Oh! fetch some water
From far Cologne!

ALL For this sad slaughter
Atone! atone!

JURY [*shaking fists at* DEFENDANT]
Monster, monster, dread our fury–
There's the Judge, and we're the Jury!
Come! Substantial damages,
Dam–

USHER Silence in Court!

Song–DEFENDANT

Oh, gentlemen, listen, I pray,
Though I own that my heart has been ranging,
Of nature the laws I obey,
For nature is constantly changing.
The moon in her phases is found,
The time and the wind and the weather,
The months in succession come round,
And you don't find two Mondays together.
Consider the moral, I pray,
Nor bring a young fellow to sorrow,
Who loves this young lady to-day,
And loves that young lady to-morrow.

BRIDESMAIDS [*rushing forward, and kneeling to* JURY]

Consider the moral, etc.
You cannot eat breakfast all day,

Nor is it the act of a sinner,
When breakfast is taken away,
To turn your attention to dinner;
And it's not in the range of belief,
That you could hold him as a glutton,
Who, when he is tired of beef,
Determines to tackle the mutton.
But this I am willing to say,
If it will appease her sorrow,
I'll marry this lady to-day,
And I'll marry that lady to-morrow!

BRIDESMAIDS [*rushing forward as before*]

But this he is willing to say, etc.

Recitative—JUDGE

That seems a reasonable proposition,
To which, I think, your client may agree.

COUNSEL But, I submit, my lord, with all submission,
To marry two at once is Burglaree!

[*Referring to law book.*

In the reign of James the Second,
It was generally reckoned
As a very serious crime
To marry two wives at one time.

[*Hands book up to* JUDGE, *who reads it.*

ALL — Oh, man of learning!

Quartette

JUDGE — A nice dilemma we have here,
That calls for all our wit:

COUNSEL — And at this stage, it don't appear
That we can settle it.

DEFENDANT [*in Witness-box*]
If I to wed the girl am loth
A breach 'twill surely be—

PLAINTIFF — And if he goes and marries both,
It counts as Burglaree!

ALL — A nice dilemma, etc.

Duet—PLAINTIFF and DEFENDANT

PLAINTIFF [*embracing him rapturously*]

I love him—I love him—with fervour unceasing
I worship and madly adore;
My blind adoration is always increasing,
My loss I shall ever deplore.
Oh, see what a blessing, what love and caressing
I've lost, and remember it, pray,
When you I'm addressing, are busy assessing
The damages Edwin must pay!

DEFENDANT [*repelling her furiously*]

I smoke like a furnace—I'm always in liquor,
A ruffian—a bully—a sot;
I'm sure I should thrash her, perhaps I should kick her,
I am such a very bad lot!
I'm not prepossessing, as you may be guessing,
She couldn't endure me a day;
Recall my professing, when you are assessing
The damages Edwin must pay!

She clings to him passionately; after a struggle, he throws her off into arms of COUNSEL.

JURY — We would be fairly acting,
But this is most distracting!

Recitative—JUDGE

The question, gentlemen—is one of liquor;
You ask for guidance—this is my reply:
He says, when tipsy, he would thrash and kick her,
Let's make him tipsy, gentlemen, and try!

COUNSEL With all respect
I do object!

PLAINTIFF I do object!

DEFENDANT I don't object!

ALL With all respect
We do object!

JUDGE [*tossing his books and papers about*]

All the legal furies seize you!
No proposal seems to please you,
I can't stop up here all day,
I must shortly go away.
Barristers, and you, attorneys,
Set out on your homeward journeys;
Gentle, simple-minded Usher,
Get you, if you like, to Russ*her;*
Put your briefs upon the shelf,
I will marry her myself!

He comes down from Bench to floor of Court. He embraces ANGELINA.

FINALE

PLAINTIFF Oh, joy unbounded,
With wealth surrounded,
The knell is sounded
Of grief and woe.

COUNSEL With love devoted
On you he's doated
To castle moated
Away they go.

DEFENDANT I wonder whether
They'll live together
In marriage tether
In manner true?

USHER
It seems to me, sir,
Of such as she, sir,
A judge is he, sir,
And a good judge too.

JUDGE
Yes, I am a Judge.

ALL
And a good Judge too!

JUDGE
Yes, I am a Judge.

ALL
And a good Judge too!

JUDGE
Though homeward as you trudge,
You declare my law is fudge.
Yet of beauty I'm a judge.

ALL
And a good Judge too!

CURTAIN

THE SORCERER

DRAMATIS PERSONÆ

SIR MARMADUKE POINTDEXTRE, *an Elderly Baronet*

ALEXIS, *of the Grenadier Guards—his Son*

DR. DALY, *Vicar of Ploverleigh*

NOTARY

JOHN WELLINGTON WELLS, *of J. W. Wells & Co., Family Sorcerers*

LADY SANGAZURE, *a Lady of Ancient Lineage*

ALINE, *her Daughter—betrothed to Alexis*

MRS. PARTLET, *a Pew-opener*

CONSTANCE, *her Daughter*

CHORUS OF VILLAGERS

ACT I

EXTERIOR OF SIR MARMADUKE'S MANSION. MID-DAY.

(*Twelve hours are supposed to elapse between Acts I and II*)

ACT II

EXTERIOR OF SIR MARMADUKE'S MANSION. MIDNIGHT.

First produced at the Opéra Comique on November 17, 1877

THE SORCERER

ACT I

SCENE.—*Exterior of* SIR MARMADUKE'S *Elizabethan Mansion.*

Chorus of Villagers

Ring forth, ye bells,
With clarion sound—
Forget your knells,
For joys abound.
Forget your notes
Of mournful lay,
And from your throats
Pour joy to-day.

For to-day young Alexis—young Alexis Pointdextre
Is betrothed to Aline—to Aline Sangazure,
And that pride of his sex is—of his sex is to be next her
At the feast on the green—on the green, oh, be sure!

Ring forth, ye bells, etc.

[*Exeunt the men into house.*

Enter MRS. PARTLET *with* CONSTANCE, *her daughter*

Recitative

MRS. P. Constance, my daughter, why this strange depression?
The village rings with seasonable joy,
Because the young and amiable Alexis,
Heir to the great Sir Marmaduke Pointdextre,
Is plighted to Aline, the only daughter
Of Annabella, Lady Sangazure.
You, you alone are sad and out of spirits;
What is the reason? Speak, my daughter, speak!

CON. Oh, mother, do not ask! If my complexion
From red to white should change in quick succession,
And then from white to red, oh, take no notice!
If my poor limbs should tremble with emotion,
Pay no attention, mother—it is nothing!
If long and deep-drawn sighs I chance to utter,
Oh, heed them not, their cause must ne'er be known!

MRS. PARTLET *motions to* CHORUS *to leave her with* CONSTANCE. *Exeunt ladies of* CHORUS.

Aria—CONSTANCE

When he is here,
  I sigh with pleasure—
When he is gone,
  I sigh with grief.
My hopeless fear
  No soul can measure—
His love alone
  Can give my aching heart relief!

When he is cold,
  I weep for sorrow—
When he is kind,
  I weep for joy.
My grief untold
  Knows no to-morrow—
My woe can find
  No hope, no solace, no alloy!

MRS. P. Come, tell me all about it! Do not fear—
I, too, have loved; but that was long ago!
Who is the object of your young affections?
CON. Hush, mother! He is here!

Enter DR. DALY. *He is pensive and does not see them*

MRS. P. [*amazed*] Our reverend vicar!
CON. Oh, pity me, my heart is almost broken!
MRS. P. My child, be comforted. To such an union
I shall not offer any opposition.
Take him—he's yours! May you and he be happy!
CON. But, mother dear, he is not yours to give!
MRS. P. That's true, indeed!
CON. He might object!
MRS. P. He might.
But come—take heart—I'll probe him on the subject.
Be comforted—leave this affair to me.

Recitative—DR. DALY

The air is charged with amatory numbers—
  Soft madrigals, and dreamy lovers' lays.
Peace, peace, old heart! Why waken from its slumbers
  The aching memory of the old, old days?

Ballad

Time was when Love and I were well acquainted.
Time was when we walked ever hand in hand.
A saintly youth, with worldly thought untainted,
None better-loved than I in all the land!
Time was, when maidens of the noblest station,
Forsaking even military men,
Would gaze upon me, rapt in adoration—
Ah me, I was a fair young curate then!

Had I a headache? sighed the maids assembled;
Had I a cold? welled forth the silent tear;
Did I look pale? then half a parish trembled;
And when I coughed all thought the end was near!
I had no care—no jealous doubts hung o'er me—
For I was loved beyond all other men.
Fled gilded dukes and belted earls before me—
Ah me, I was a pale young curate then!

[*At the conclusion of the ballad,* Mrs. Partlet *comes forward with* Constance.

Mrs. P. Good day, reverend sir.

Dr. D. Ah, good Mrs. Partlet, I am glad to see you. And your little daughter, Constance! Why, she is quite a little woman, I declare!

Con. [*aside*] Oh, mother, I cannot speak to him!

Mrs. P. Yes, reverend sir, she is nearly eighteen, and as good a girl as ever stepped. [*Aside to* Dr. D.] Ah, sir, I'm afraid I shall soon lose her!

DR. D. [*aside to* MRS. P.] Dear me, you pain me very much. Is she delicate?

MRS. P. Oh no, sir—I don't mean that—but young girls look to get married.

DR. D. Oh, I take you. To be sure. But there's plenty of time for that. Four or five years hence, Mrs. Partlet, four or five years hence. But when the time *does* come, I shall have much pleasure in marrying her myself—

CON. [*aside*] Oh, mother!

DR. D. To some strapping young fellow in her own rank of life.

CON. [*in tears*] He does *not* love me!

MRS. P. I have often wondered, reverend sir (if you'll excuse the liberty), that *you* have never married.

DR. D. [*aside*] Be still, my fluttering heart!

MRS. P. A clergyman's wife does so much good in a village. Besides that, you are not as young as you were, and before very long you will want somebody to nurse you, and look after your little comforts.

DR. D. Mrs. Partlet, there is much truth in what you say. I am indeed getting on in years, and a helpmate would cheer my declining days. Time was when it might have been; but I have left it too long—I am an old fogy, now, am I not, my dear? [*to* CONSTANCE]—a very old fogy, indeed. Ha! ha! No, Mrs. Partlet, my mind is quite made up. I shall live and die a solitary old bachelor.

CON. Oh, mother, mother! [*Sobs on* MRS. PARTLET'S *bosom*]

MRS. P. Come, come, dear one, don't fret. At a more fitting time we will try again—we will try again.

[*Exeunt* MRS. PARTLET *and* CONSTANCE.

DR. D. [*looking after them*] Poor little girl! I'm afraid she has something on her mind. She is rather comely. Time was when this old heart would have throbbed in double-time at the sight of such a fairy form! But tush! I am puling! Here comes the young Alexis with his proud and happy father. Let me dry this tell-tale tear!

Enter SIR MARMADUKE *and* ALEXIS

Recitative

DR. D. Sir Marmaduke—my dear young friend, Alexis—
On this most happy, most auspicious plighting—
Permit me, as a true old friend, to tender
My best, my very best congratulations!
SIR M. Sir, you are most obleeging!
ALEXIS Dr. Daly,
My dear old tutor, and my valued pastor,
I thank you from the bottom of my heart!
[*Spoken through music*]
DR. D. May fortune bless you! may the middle distance
Of your young life be pleasant as the foreground—
The joyous foreground! and, when you have reached it,
May that which now is the far-off horizon
(But which will then become the middle distance),
In fruitful promise be exceeded only
By that which will have opened, in the meantime,
Into a new and glorious horizon!
SIR M. Dear Sir, that is an excellent example
Of an old school of stately compliment
To which I have, through life, been much addicted.
Will you obleege me with a copy of it,
In clerkly manuscript, that I myself
May use it on appropriate occasions?
DR. D. Sir, you shall have a fairly-written copy
Ere Sol has sunk into his western slumbers!

[*Exit* DR. DALY.

SIR M. [*to* ALEXIS, *who is in a reverie*] Come, come, my son—your *fiancée* will be here in five minutes. Rouse yourself to receive her.

ALEXIS Oh rapture!

SIR M. Yes, you are a fortunate young fellow, and I will not disguise from you that this union with the House of Sangazure realizes my fondest wishes. Aline is rich, and she comes of a sufficiently old family, for she is the seven thousand and thirty-seventh in direct descent from Helen of Troy. True, there was a blot on the escutcheon of that lady—that affair with Paris—but where is the family, other than my own, in which there is no flaw? You are a lucky fellow, sir—a very lucky fellow!

ALEXIS Father, I am welling over with limpid joy! No sicklying taint of sorrow overlies the lucid lake of liquid love, upon which, hand in hand, Aline and I are to float into eternity!

SIR M. Alexis, I desire that of your love for this young lady you do not speak so openly. You are always singing ballads in praise of her beauty, and you expect the very menials who wait behind your chair, to chorus your ecstasies. It is not delicate.

ALEXIS Father, a man who loves as I love—

SIR. M. Pooh pooh, sir! fifty years ago I madly loved your future mother-in-law, the Lady Sangazure, and I have reason to believe that she returned my love. But were we guilty of the indelicacy of publicly rushing into each other's arms, exclaiming—

"Oh, my adored one!" "Beloved boy!"
"Ecstatic rapture!" "Unmingled joy!"

which seems to be the modern fashion of love-making? No! it was "Madam, I trust you are in the enjoyment of good health"—"Sir, you are vastly polite, I protest I am mighty well"—and so forth. Much more delicate—much more respectful. But see—Aline approaches—let us retire, that she may compose herself for the interesting ceremony in which she is to play so important a part.

[*Exeunt* SIR MARMADUKE *and* ALEXIS.

Enter ALINE, *on terrace, preceded by Chorus of Girls*

Chorus of Girls

With heart and with voice
  Let us welcome this mating:
To the youth of her choice,
  With a heart palpitating,
    Comes the lovely Aline!

May their love never cloy!
  May their bliss be unbounded!
With a halo of joy
  May their lives be surrounded!
    Heaven bless our Aline!

Recitative—ALINE

My kindly friends, I thank you for this greeting,
And as you wish me every earthly joy,
I trust your wishes may have quick fulfilment!

Aria—ALINE

Oh, happy young heart!
  Comes thy young lord a-wooing
With joy in his eyes,
  And pride in his breast—
Make much of thy prize,
  For he is the best

That ever came a-suing.
  Yet–yet we must part,
          Young heart!
  Yet–yet we must part!

Oh, merry young heart,
  Bright are the days of thy wooing!
But happier far
  The days untried–
No sorrow can mar,
  When Love has tied
The knot there's no undoing.
  Then, never to part,
          Young heart!
  Then, never to part!

Enter LADY SANGAZURE

Recitative–LADY S.

My child, I join in these congratulations:
Heed not the tear that dims this aged eye!
Old memories crowd upon me. Though I sorrow,
'Tis for myself, Aline, and not for thee!

Enter ALEXIS, *preceded by Chorus of Men*

Chorus of Men and Women

With heart and with voice
  Let us welcome this mating;
To the maid of his choice,
  With a heart palpitating,
    Comes Alexis the brave!

SIR MARMADUKE *enters.* LADY SANGAZURE *and he exhibit signs of strong emotion at the sight of each other, which they endeavour to repress.* ALEXIS *and* ALINE *rush into each other's arms.*

Recitative

ALEXIS Oh, my adored one!

ALINE Beloved boy!

ALEXIS Ecstatic rapture!

ALINE Unmingled joy!

[*They retire up.*]

Duet—Sir Marmaduke and Lady Sangazure

Sir M. [*with stately courtesy*]
Welcome joy, adieu to sadness!
As Aurora gilds the day,
So those eyes, twin orbs of gladness,
Chase the clouds of care away.
Irresistible incentive
Bids me humbly kiss your hand;
I'm your servant most attentive—
Most attentive to command!

[*Aside with frantic vehemence*]
Wild with adoration!
Mad with fascination!
To indulge my lamentation
No occasion do I miss!
Goaded to distraction
By maddening inaction,
I find some satisfaction
In apostrophe like this:
"Sangazure immortal,
"Sangazure divine,
"Welcome to my portal,
"Angel, oh be mine!"

[*Aloud with much ceremony*]
Irresistible incentive
Bids me humbly kiss your hand;
I'm your servant most attentive—
Most attentive to command!

Lady S. Sir, I thank you most politely
For your graceful courtesee;
Compliment more true and knightly
Never yet was paid to me!
Chivalry is an ingredient
Sadly lacking in our land—
Sir, I am your most obedient,
Most obedient to command!

[*Aside with great vehemence*]
Wild with adoration!
Mad with fascination!
To indulge my lamentation
No occasion do I miss!
Goaded to distraction
By maddening inaction,

I find some satisfaction
In apostrophe like this:
"Marmaduke immortal,
"Marmaduke divine,
"Take me to thy portal,
"Loved one, oh be mine!"

[*Aloud with much ceremony*]
Chivalry is an ingredient
Sadly lacking in our land;
Sir, I am your most obedient,
Most obedient to command!

[*During this the* NOTARY *has entered, with marriage contract.*

Recitative—NOTARY

All is prepared for sealing and for signing,
The contract has been drafted as agreed;
Approach the table, oh, ye lovers pining,
With hand and seal come execute the deed!

[ALEXIS *and* ALINE *advance and sign*, ALEXIS *supported by* SIR MARMADUKE, ALINE *by her Mother.*

Chorus

See they sign, without a quiver, it—
Then to seal proceed.
They deliver it—they deliver it
As their Act and Deed!

ALEXIS I deliver it—I deliver it
As my Act and Deed!

ALINE I deliver it—I deliver it
As my Act and Deed!

Chorus

With heart and with voice
Let us welcome this mating;
Leave them here to rejoice,
With true love palpitating,
Alexis the brave,
And the lovely Aline!

[*Exeunt all but* ALEXIS *and* ALINE.

ALEXIS At last we are alone! My darling, you are now irrevocably betrothed to me. Are you not very, very happy?

ALINE Oh, Alexis, can you doubt it? Do I not love you beyond all on earth, and am I not beloved in return? Is not true love, faithfully given and faithfully returned, the source of every earthly joy?

ALEXIS Of that there can be no doubt. Oh, that the world could be persuaded of the truth of that maxim! Oh, that the world would break down the artificial barriers of rank, wealth, education, age, beauty, habits, taste, and temper, and recognise the glorious principle, that in marriage alone is to be found the panacea for every ill!

ALINE Continue to preach that sweet doctrine, and you will succeed, oh, evangel of true happiness!

ALEXIS I hope so, but as yet the cause progresses but slowly. Still I have made some converts to the principle, that men and women should be coupled in matrimony without distinction of rank. I have lectured on the subject at Mechanics' Institutes, and the mechanics were unanimous in favour of my views. I have preached in workhouses, beershops and Lunatic Asylums, and I have been received with enthusiasm. I have addressed navvies on the advantages that would accrue to them if they married wealthy ladies of rank, and not a navvy dissented!

ALINE Noble fellows! And yet there are those who hold that the uneducated classes are not open to argument! And what do the countesses say?

ALEXIS Why, at present, it can't be denied, the aristocracy hold aloof.

ALINE Ah, the working man is the true Intelligence after all!

ALEXIS He is a noble creature when he is quite sober. Yes, Aline, true happiness comes of true love, and true love should be independent of external influences. It should live upon itself and by itself—in itself love should live for love alone!

Ballad—ALEXIS

Love feeds on many kinds of food, I know,
  Some love for rank, and some for duty:
Some give their hearts away for empty show,
  And others love for youth and beauty.
To love for money all the world is prone:
  Some love themselves, and live all lonely:
Give me the love that loves for love alone—
  I love that love—I love it only!

What man for any other joy can thirst,
  Whose loving wife adores him duly?
Want, misery, and care may do their worst,
  If loving woman loves you truly.
A lover's thoughts are ever with his own—
  None truly loved is ever lonely:
Give me the love that loves for love alone—
  I love that love—I love it only!

ALINE Oh, Alexis, those are noble principles!

ALEXIS Yes, Aline, and I am going to take a desperate step in support of them. Have you ever heard of the firm of J. W. Wells & Co., the old-established Family Sorcerers in St. Mary Axe?

ALINE I have seen their advertisement.

ALEXIS They have invented a philtre, which, if report may be believed, is simply infallible. I intend to distribute it through the village, and within half an hour of my doing so there will not be an adult in the place who will not have learnt the secret of pure and lasting happiness. What do you say to that?

ALINE Well, dear, of course a filter is a very useful thing in a house; but still I don't quite see that it is the sort of thing that places its possessor on the very pinnacle of earthly joy.

ALEXIS Aline, you misunderstand me. I didn't say a filter—I said a philtre.

ALINE [*alarmed*] You don't mean a love-potion?

ALEXIS On the contrary—I *do* mean a love-potion.

ALINE Oh, Alexis! I don't think it would be right. I don't indeed. And then—a real magician! Oh, it would be downright wicked.

ALEXIS Aline, is it, or is it not, a laudable object to steep the whole village up to its lips in love, and to couple them in matrimony without distinction of age, rank, or fortune?

ALINE Unquestionably, but—

ALEXIS Then unpleasant as it must be to have recourse to supernatural aid, I must nevertheless pocket my aversion, in deference to the great and good end I have in view. [*Calling*] Hercules.

Enter a PAGE *from tent*

PAGE Yes, sir.

ALEXIS Is Mr. Wells there?

PAGE He's in the tent, sir—refreshing.

ALEXIS Ask him to be so good as to step this way.

PAGE Yes, sir. [*Exit* PAGE.

ALINE Oh, but, Alexis! A real Sorcerer! Oh, I shall be frightened to death!

ALEXIS I trust my Aline will not yield to fear while the strong right arm of her Alexis is here to protect her.

ALINE It's nonsense, dear, to talk of your protecting me with your strong right arm, in face of the fact that this Family Sorcerer could change me into a guinea-pig before you could turn round.

ALEXIS He *could* change you into a guinea-pig, no doubt, but it is most unlikely that he would take such a liberty. It's a most respectable firm, and I am sure he would never be guilty of so untradesmanlike an act.

Enter MR. WELLS *from tent*

MR. W. Good day, sir. [ALINE *much terrified*]

ALEXIS Good day—I believe you are a Sorcerer.

MR. W. Yes, sir, we practise Necromancy in all its branches. We've a choice assortment of wishing-caps, divining-rods, amulets, charms, and counter-charms. We can cast you a nativity at a low figure, and we have a horoscope at three-and-six that we can guarantee. Our Abudah chests, each containing a patent Hag who comes out and prophesies disasters, with spring complete, are strongly recommended. Our Aladdin lamps are very chaste, and our Prophetic Tablets, foretelling everything—from a change of Ministry down to a rise in Unified—are much enquired for. Our penny Curse—one of the cheapest things in the trade—is considered infallible. We have some very superior Blessings, too, but they're very little asked for. We've only sold one since Christmas—to a gentleman who bought it to send to his mother-in-law—but it turned out that he was afflicted in the head, and it's been returned on our hands. But our sale of penny Curses, especially on Saturday nights, is tremendous. We can't turn 'em out fast enough.

Song—MR. WELLS

Oh! my name is John Wellington Wells,
I'm a dealer in magic and spells,
In blessings and curses
And ever-filled purses,
In prophecies, witches, and knells.

If you want a proud foe to "make tracks"—
If you'd melt a rich uncle in wax—
You've but to look in
On our resident Djinn,
Number seventy, Simmery Axe!

We've a first-class assortment of magic;
And for raising a posthumous shade
With effects that are comic or tragic,
There's no cheaper house in the trade.
Love-philtre—we've quantities of it;
And for knowledge if any one burns,
We keep an extremely small prophet, a prophet
Who brings us unbounded returns:

For he can prophesy
With a wink *of* his eye,
Peep with security
Into futurity,
Sum up your history,
Clear up a mystery,
Humour proclivity
For a nativity—for a nativity;
With mirrors so magical,
Tetrapods tragical,
Bogies spectacular,
Answers oracular,
Facts astronomical,
Solemn or comical,
And, if you want it, he
Makes a reduction on taking a quantity!
Oh!

If any one anything lacks,
He'll find it all ready in stacks,
If he'll only look in
On the resident Djinn,
Number seventy, Simmery Axe!

He can raise you hosts
Of ghosts,
And that without reflectors;
And creepy things
With wings,
And gaunt and grisly spectres.
He can fill you crowds
Of shrouds,

And horrify you vastly;
He can rack your brains
With chains,
And gibberings grim and ghastly!

Then, if you plan it, he
Changes organity,
With an urbanity,
Full of Satanity,
Vexes humanity
With an inanity
Fatal to vanity—
Driving your foes to the verge of insanity!

Barring tautology,
In demonology,
'Lectro-biology,
Mystic nosology,
Spirit philology,
High-class astrology,
Such is his knowledge, he
Isn't the man to require an apology!

Oh!
My name is John Wellington Wells,
I'm a dealer in magic and spells,
In blessings and curses
And ever-filled purses,
In prophecies, witches, and knells.

If any one anything lacks,
He'll find it all ready in stacks,
If he'll only look in
On the resident Djinn,
Number seventy, Simmery Axe!

ALEXIS I have sent for you to consult you on a very important matter. I believe you advertise a Patent Oxy-Hydrogen Love-at-first-sight Philtre?

MR. W. Sir, it is our leading article. [*Producing a phial*]

ALEXIS Now I want to know if you can confidently guarantee it as possessing all the qualities you claim for it in your advertisement?

MR. W. Sir, we are not in the habit of puffing our goods. Ours is an old-established house with a large family connection, and every assurance held out in the advertisement is fully realised. [*Hurt*]

ALINE [*aside*] Oh, Alexis, don't offend him! He'll change us into something dreadful—I know he will!

ALEXIS I am anxious from purely philanthropical motives to distribute this philtre, secretly, among the inhabitants of this village. I shall of course require a quantity. How do you sell it?

MR. W. In buying a quantity, sir, we should strongly advise you taking it in the wood, and drawing it off as you happen to want it. We have it in four-and-a-half and nine gallon casks—also in pipes and hogsheads for laying down, and we deduct 10 per cent for prompt cash.

ALEXIS I should mention that I am a Member of the Army and Navy Stores.

MR. W. In that case we deduct 25 per cent.

ALEXIS Aline, the villagers will assemble to carouse in a few minutes. Go and fetch the tea-pot.

ALINE But, Alexis—

ALEXIS My dear, you must obey me, if you please. Go and fetch the tea-pot.

ALINE [*going*] I'm sure Dr. Daly would disapprove of it.

[*Exit* ALINE.

ALEXIS And how soon does it take effect?

MR. W. In twelve hours. Whoever drinks of it loses consciousness for that period, and on waking falls in love, as a matter of course, with the first lady he meets who has also tasted it, and his affection is at once returned. One trial will prove the fact.

Enter ALINE *with large tea-pot*

ALEXIS Good: then, Mr. Wells, I shall feel obliged if you will at once pour as much philtre into this tea-pot as will suffice to affect the whole village.

ALINE But bless me, Alexis, many of the villagers are married people!

MR. W. Madam, this philtre is compounded on the strictest principles. On married people it has no effect whatever. But are you quite sure that you have nerve enough to carry you through the fearful ordeal?

ALEXIS In the good cause I fear nothing.

MR. W. Very good, then, we will proceed at once to the Incantation.

The stage grows dark

Incantation

MR. W. Sprites of earth and air—
Fiends of flame and fire—
Demon souls,
Come here in shoals,
This dreadful deed inspire!
Appear, appear, appear.

MALE VOICES Good master, we are here!

MR. W. Noisome hags of night—
Imps of deadly shade—
Pallid ghosts,
Arise in hosts,
And lend me all your aid.
Appear, appear, appear!

FEMALE VOICES Good master, we are here!

ALEXIS [*aside*] Hark, they assemble,
These fiends of the night!

ALINE [*aside*] Oh, Alexis, I tremble,
Seek safety in flight!

Aria—ALINE

Let us fly to a far-off land,
Where peace and plenty dwell—
Where the sigh of the silver strand
Is echoed in every shell
To the joy that land will give,
On the wings of Love we'll fly;
In innocence there to live—
In innocence there to die!

Chorus of Spirits

Too late—too late
It may not be!
That happy fate
Is not for thee!

ALEXIS, ALINE, and MR. WELLS

Too late—too late,
That may not be!
That happy fate
Is not for { me! / thee! }

MR. WELLS

Now shrivelled hags, with poison bags,
Discharge your loathsome loads!
Spit flame and fire, unholy choir!
Belch forth your venom, toads!
Ye demons fell, with yelp and yell,
Shed curses far afield—
Ye fiends of night, your filthy blight
In noisome plenty yield!

MR. WELLS [*pouring phial into tea-pot—flash*]
Number One!
CHORUS It is done!
MR. W. [*same business*] Number Two! [*flash*]
CHORUS One too few!
MR. W. [*same business*] Number Three! [*flash*]
CHORUS Set us free!
Set us free—our work is done
Ha! ha! ha!
Set us free—our course is run!
Ha! ha! ha!

ALINE and ALEXIS [*aside*]

Let us fly to a far-off land,
Where peace and plenty dwell—
Where the sigh of the silver strand
Is echoed in every shell.

Chorus of Fiends

Ha! ha! ha! ha! ha! ha! ha! ha! ha! ha!

[*Stage grows light.* MR. WELLS *beckons villagers. Enter villagers and all the dramatis personæ, dancing joyously.* MRS. PARTLET *and* MR. WELLS *then distribute tea-cups.*

Chorus

Now to the banquet we press;
Now for the eggs, the ham;
Now for the mustard and cress,
Now for the strawberry jam!

Now for the tea of our host,
Now for the rollicking bun,
Now for the muffin and toast,
Now for the gay Sally Lunn!

WOMEN The eggs and the ham, and the strawberry jam!

MEN The rollicking bun, and the gay Sally Lunn!
The rollicking, rollicking bun!

Recitative—SIR MARMADUKE

Be happy all—the feast is spread before ye;
Fear nothing, but enjoy yourselves, I pray!
Eat, aye, and drink—be merry, I implore ye,
For once let thoughtless Folly rule the day.

Tea-cup Brindisi

Eat, drink, and be gay,
  Banish all worry and sorrow,
Laugh gaily to-day,
  Weep, if you're sorry, to-morrow!
Come, pass the cup round–
  I will go bail for the liquor;
It's strong, I'll be bound,
  For it was brewed by the vicar!

Chorus

None so knowing as he
At brewing a jorum of tea,
    Ha! ha!
A pretty stiff jorum of tea.

Trio–MR. WELLS, ALINE, and ALEXIS [*aside*]

See–see–they drink–
  All thought unheeding,
The tea-cups clink,
  They are exceeding!
Their hearts will melt
  In half-an-hour–
Then will be felt
  The potion's power!

[*During this verse* CONSTANCE *has brought a small tea-pot, kettle, caddy, and cosy to* DR. DALY. *He makes tea scientifically.*

Brindisi, 2nd Verse–DR. DALY [*with the tea-pot*]

Pain, trouble, and care,
  Misery, heart-ache, and worry,
Quick, out of your lair!
  Get you all gone in a hurry!
Toil, sorrow, and plot,
  Fly away quicker and quicker–
Three spoons to the pot–
  That is the brew of your vicar!

Chorus

None so cunning as he
At brewing a jorum of tea,
    Ha! ha!
A pretty stiff jorum of tea!

Ensemble—ALEXIS and ALINE [*aside*]

Oh love, true love—unworldly, abiding!
  Source of all pleasure—true fountain of joy,—
Oh love, true love—divinely confiding,
  Exquisite treasure that knows no alloy,—
O love, true love, rich harvest of gladness,
  Peace-bearing tillage—great garner of bliss,—
Oh love, true love, look down on our sadness—
  Dwell in this village—oh, hear us in this!

[*It becomes evident by the strange conduct of the characters that the charm is working. All rub their eyes, and stagger about the stage as if under the influence of a narcotic.*

TUTTI (*aside*)	ALEXIS, MR. WELLS, *and* ALINE (*aside*)
Oh, marvellous illusion!	A marvellous illusion!
Oh, terrible surprise!	A terrible surprise
What is this strange confusion	Excites a strange confusion
That veils my aching eyes?	Within their aching eyes—
I must regain my senses,	They must regain their senses,
Restoring Reason's law,	Restoring Reason's law,
Or fearful inferences	Or fearful inferences
Society will draw!	Society will draw!

Those who have partaken of the philtre struggle in vain against its effects, and, at the end of the chorus, fall insensible on the stage.

END OF ACT I

ACT II

SCENE.—*Exterior of* SIR MARMADUKE'S *mansion by moonlight. All the peasantry are discovered asleep on the ground, as at the end of Act I.*

Enter MR. WELLS, *on tiptoe, followed by* ALEXIS *and* ALINE. MR. WELLS *carries a dark lantern.*

Trio—ALEXIS, ALINE, and MR. WELLS

'Tis twelve, I think,
  And at this mystic hour
The magic drink
  Should manifest its power.
Oh, slumbering forms,
  How little have ye guessed
The fire that warms
  Each apathetic breast!

ALEXIS But stay, my father is not here!
ALINE And pray where is my mother dear?

MR. WELLS I did not think it meet to see
A dame of lengthy pedigree,
A Baronet and K.C.B.
A Doctor of Divinity,
And that respectable Q.C.,
All fast asleep, al-fresco-ly,
And so I had them taken home
And put to bed respectably!
I trust my conduct meets your approbation.

ALEXIS Sir, you have acted with discrimination,
And shown more delicate appreciation
Than we expect in persons of your station.

MR. WELLS But stay—they waken, one by one—
The spell has worked—the deed is done!
I would suggest that we retire
While Love, the Housemaid, lights her kitchen fire!

[*Exeunt* MR. WELLS, ALEXIS, *and* ALINE, *on tiptoe, as the villagers stretch their arms, yawn, rub their eyes, and sit up.*

MEN Why, where be oi, and what be oi a doin',
A sleepin' out, just when the dews du rise?

GIRLS Why, that's the very way your health to ruin,
And don't seem quite respectable likewise!

MEN [*staring at girls*] Eh, that's you!
Only think o' that now!

GIRLS [*coyly*] What may you be at, now?
Tell me, du!

MEN [*admiringly*] Eh, what a nose,
And eh, what eyes, miss!
Lips like a rose,
And cheeks likewise, miss!

GIRLS [*coyly*] Oi tell you true,
Which I've never done, sir,
Oi loike you
As I never loiked none, sir!

ALL Eh, but oi du loike you!

MEN If you'll marry me, I'll dig for you and rake for you!

GIRLS If you'll marry me, I'll scrub for you and bake for you!

MEN If you'll marry me, all others I'll forsake for you!

ALL All this will I du, if you'll marry me!

GIRLS If you'll marry me, I'll cook for you and brew for you!

MEN — If you'll marry me, I've guineas not a few for you!

GIRLS — If you'll marry me, I'll take you in and du for you!

ALL — All this will I du, if you'll marry me!
En, but oi du loike you!

Country Dance

At end of dance, enter CONSTANCE *in tears, leading* NOTARY, *who carries an ear-trumpet.*

Aria—CONSTANCE

Dear friends, take pity on my lot,
My cup is not of nectar!
I long have loved—as who would not?—
Our kind and reverend rector.
Long years ago my love began
So sweetly—yet so sadly—
But when I saw this plain old man,
Away my old affection ran—
I found I loved him madly.
Oh!

[*To* NOTARY] You very, very plain old man,
I love, I love you madly!

CHORUS — You very, very plain old man,
She loves, she loves you madly!

NOTARY — I am a very deaf old man,
And hear you very badly!

CONSTANCE — I know not why I love him so;
It is enchantment, surely!
He's dry and snuffy, deaf and slow
Ill-tempered, weak, and poorly!
He's ugly, and absurdly dressed,
And sixty-seven nearly,
He's everything that I detest,
But if the truth must be confessed,
I love him very dearly!
Oh!

[*To* NOTARY] You're everything that I detest,
But still I love you dearly!

CHORUS — You're everything that girls detest,
But still she loves you dearly!

NOTARY I caught that line, but for the rest,
I did not hear it clearly!

[*During this verse* ALINE *and* ALEXIS *have entered at back unobserved.*

ALINE and ALEXIS

ALEXIS Oh joy! oh joy!
The charm works well,
And all are now united.

ALINE The blind young boy
Obeys the spell,
The troth they all have plighted!

Ensemble

ALINE and ALEXIS

Oh joy! oh joy!
The charm works well,
And all are now united!
The blind young boy
Obeys the spell,
Their troth they all have plighted.
True happiness
Reigns everywhere,
And dwells with both the sexes,
And all will bless
The thoughtful care
Of their beloved Alexis.

CONSTANCE

Oh, bitter joy!
No words can tell
How my poor heart is blighted!
They'll soon employ
A marriage bell,
To say that we're united.
I do confess
A sorrow rare
My humbled spirit vexes,
And none will bless
Example rare
Of their beloved Alexis!

NOTARY

Oh joy! oh joy!
No words can tell
My state of mind delighted.
They'll soon employ
A marriage bell,
To say that we're united.
True happiness
Reigns everywhere
And dwells with both the sexes,
And all will bless
Example rare
Of their beloved Alexis!

[*All, except* ALEXIS *and* ALINE, *exeunt lovingly.*

ALINE How joyful they all seem in their new-found happiness! The whole village has paired off in the happiest manner. And yet not a match has been made that the hollow world would not consider ill-advised!

ALEXIS But we are wiser—far wiser—than the world. Observe the good that will become of these ill-assorted unions. The miserly wife will check the reckless expenditure of her too frivolous consort, the wealthy husband will shower innumerable bonnets on his penniless bride, and the young and lively spouse will cheer the declining days of her aged partner with comic songs unceasing!

ALINE What a delightful prospect for him!

ALEXIS But one thing remains to be done, that my happiness may be complete. We must drink the philtre ourselves, that I may be assured of your love for ever and ever.

ALINE Oh, Alexis, do you doubt me? Is it necessary that such love as ours should be secured by artificial means? Oh, no, no, no!

ALEXIS My dear Aline, time works terrible changes, and I want to place our love beyond the chance of change.

ALINE Alexis, it is already far beyond that chance. Have faith in me, for my love can never, never change!

ALEXIS Then you absolutely refuse?

ALINE I do. If you cannot trust me, you have no right to love me—no right to be loved *by* me.

ALEXIS Enough, Aline, I shall know how to interpret this refusal.

Ballad—ALEXIS

Thou hast the power thy vaunted love
To sanctify, all doubt above,
Despite the gathering shade:
To make that love of thine so sure
That, come what may, it must endure
Till time itself shall fade.
Thy love is but a flower
That fades within the hour!
If such thy love, oh, shame!
Call it by other name—
It is not love!

Thine is the power and thine alone,
To place me on so proud a throne
That kings might envy me!
A priceless throne of love untold,
More rare than orient pearl and gold.
But no! Thou wouldst be free!
Such love is like the ray
That dies within the day:
If such thy love, oh, shame!
Call it by other name—
It is not love!

Enter DR. DALY

DR. D. [*musing*] It is singular—it is very singular. It has overthrown all my calculations. It is distinctly opposed to the doctrine of averages. I cannot understand it.

ALINE Dear Dr. Daly, what has puzzled you?

DR. D. My dear, this village has not hitherto been addicted to marrying and giving in marriage. Hitherto the youths of this village have not been enterprising, and the maidens have been distinctly coy. Judge then of my surprise when I tell you that the whole village came to me in a body just now, and implored me to join them in matrimony with as little delay as possible. Even your excellent father has hinted to me that before very long it is not unlikely that he also may change his condition.

ALINE Oh, Alexis—do you hear that? Are you not delighted?

ALEXIS Yes. I confess that a union between your mother and my father would be a happy circumstance indeed. [*Crossing to* DR. DALY] My dear sir—the news that you bring us is very gratifying.

DR. D. Yes—still, in my eyes, it has its melancholy side. This universal marrying recalls the happy days—now, alas, gone for ever—when I myself might have—but tush! I am puling. I am too old to marry—and yet, within the last half-hour, I have greatly yearned for companionship. I never remarked it before, but the young maidens of this village are very comely. So likewise are the middle-aged. Also the elderly. All are comely—and [*with a deep sigh*] all are engaged!

ALINE Here comes your father.

Enter SIR MARMADUKE *with* MRS. PARTLET, *arm-in-arm*

ALINE and ALEXIS [*aside*] Mrs. Partlet!

SIR M. Dr. Daly, give me joy. Alexis, my dear boy, you will, I am sure, be pleased to hear that my declining days are not unlikely to be solaced by the companionship of this good, virtuous, and amiable woman.

ALEXIS [*rather taken aback*] My dear father, this is not altogether what I expected. I am certainly taken somewhat by surprise. Still it can hardly be necessary to assure you that any wife of yours is a mother of mine. [*Aside to* ALINE] It is not quite what I could have wished.

MRS. P. [*crossing to* ALEXIS] Oh, sir, I entreat your forgiveness. I am aware that socially I am noth everythink that could be desired, nor am I blessed with an abundance of worldly goods, but I can at least confer on your estimable father the great and priceless dowry of a true, tender, and lovin' 'art!

ALEXIS [*coldly*] I do not question it. After all, a faithful love is the true source of every earthly joy.

SIR M. I knew that my boy would not blame his poor father for acting on the impulse of a heart that has never yet misled him. Zorah is not perhaps what the world calls beautiful—

DR. D. Still she is comely—distinctly comely. [*Sighs*]

ALINE Zorah is very good, and very clean, and honest, and quite, quite sober in her habits: and that is worth far more than beauty, dear Sir Marmaduke.

DR. D. Yes; beauty will fade and perish, but personal cleanliness is practically undying, for it can be renewed whenever it discovers symptoms of decay. My dear Sir Marmaduke, I heartily congratulate you. [*Sighs*]

Quintette

ALEXIS, ALINE, SIR MARMADUKE, ZORAH, and DR. DALY

ALEXIS I rejoice that it's decided,
Happy now will be his life,
For my father is provided
With a true and tender wife.

Ensemble

She will tend him, nurse him, mend him,
  Air his linen, dry his tears;
Bless the thoughtful fates that send him
  Such a wife to soothe his years!

ALINE No young giddy thoughtless maiden,
  Full of graces, airs, and jeers—
But a sober widow, laden
  With the weight of fifty years!

SIR M. No high-born exacting beauty,
  Blazing like a jewelled sun—
But a wife who'll do her duty,
  As that duty should be done!

MRS. P. I'm no saucy minx and giddy—
  Hussies such as them abound—
But a clean and tidy widdy
  Well be-known for miles around!

DR. D. All the village now have mated,
  All are happy as can be—
I to live alone am fated:
  No one's left to marry me!

ENSEMBLE She will tend him etc.

[*Exeunt* SIR MARMADUKE, MRS. PARTLET, *and* ALINE, *with* ALEXIS. DR. DALY *looks after them sentimentally, then exits with a sigh.*

Enter MR. WELLS

Recitative—MR. WELLS

Oh, I have wrought much evil with my spells!
  And ill I can't undo!
This is too bad of you, J. W. Wells—
  What wrong have they done you?
And see—another love-lorn lady comes—
  Alas, poor stricken dame!
A gentle pensiveness her life benumbs—
  And mine, alone, the blame!

LADY SANGAZURE *enters. She is very melancholy*

LADY S. Alas, ah me! and well-a-day!
I sigh for love, and well I may,
For I am very old and grey.
    But stay!

[*Sees* MR. WELLS, *and becomes fascinated by him*]

Recitative

LADY S. What is this fairy form I see before me?
MR. W. Oh, horrible!—she's going to adore me!
This last catastrophe is overpowering!
LADY S. Why do you glare at one with visage lowering?
For pity's sake recoil not thus from me!
MR. W. My lady, leave me—this may never be!

Duet—LADY SANGAZURE and MR. WELLS

MR. W. Hate me! I drop my H's—have through life!
LADY S. Love me! I'll drop them too!
MR. W. Hate me! I always eat peas with a knife!
LADY S. Love me! I'll eat like you!
MR. W. Hate me! I spend the day at Rosherville!
LADY S. Love me! that joy I'll share!
MR. W. Hate me! I often roll down One Tree Hill!
LADY S. Love me! I'll join you there!

LADY S. Love me! my prejudices I will drop!
MR. W. Hate me! that's not enough!
LADY S. Love me! I'll come and help you in the shop!
MR. W. Hate me! the life is rough!
LADY S. Love me! my grammar I will all forswear!
MR. W. Hate me! abjure my lot!
LADY S. Love me! I'll stick sunflowers in my hair!
MR. W. Hate me! they'll suit you not!

Recitative—MR. WELLS

At what I am going to say be not enraged—
I may not love you—for I am engaged!
LADY S. [*horrified*] Engaged!
MR. W. Engaged!
To a maiden fair,
With bright brown hair,
And a sweet and simple smile,
Who waits for me
By the sounding sea,
On a South Pacific isle.
MR. W. [*aside*] A lie! No maiden waits me there!
LADY S. [*mournfully*] She has bright brown hair;
MR. W. [*aside*] A lie! No maiden smiles on me!
LADY S. [*mournfully*] By the sounding sea!

Ensemble

LADY SANGAZURE

Oh, agony, rage, despair!
The maiden has bright brown hair,
  And mine is as white as snow!
False man, it will be your fault,
If I go to my family vault,
  And bury my life-long woe!

MR. WELLS

Oh, agony, rage, despair!
Oh, where will this end—oh, where?
  I should like very much to know!
It will certainly be my fault,
If she goes to her family vault,
  To bury her life-long woe!

BOTH

The family vault—the family vault.
It will certainly be {your / my} fault.
If {I go / she goes} to {my / her} family vault,
  To bury {my / her} life-long woe!

[*Exit* LADY SANGAZURE, *in great anguish, accompanied by* MR. WELLS.

Enter ALINE, *Recitative*

Alexis! Doubt me not, my loved one! See,
Thine uttered will is sovereign law to me!
All fear—all thought of ill I cast away!
It is my darling's will, and I obey!

[*She drinks the philtre.*

The fearful deed is done,
  My love is near!
I go to meet my own
  In trembling fear!
If o'er us aught of ill
  Should cast a shade,
It was my darling's will,
  And I obeyed!

[*As* ALINE *is going off, she meets* DR. DALY, *entering pensively. He is playing on a flageolet. Under the influence of the spell she at once becomes strangely fascinated by him, and exhibits every symptom of being hopelessly in love with him.*

Song—DR. DALY

Oh, my voice is sad and low
And with timid step I go—
For with load of love o'erladen
I enquire of every maiden,
"Will you wed me, little lady?
Will you share my cottage shady?"

Little lady answers "No!
Thank you for your kindly proffer—
Good your heart, and full your coffer;
Yet I must decline your offer—
I'm engaged to So-and-so!"
So-and-so!
So-and-so! [*flageolet solo*]
She's engaged to So-and-so!
What a rogue young hearts to pillage;
What a worker on Love's tillage!
Every maiden in the village
Is engaged to So-and-so!
So-and-so!
So-and-so! [*flageolet solo*]
All engaged to So-and-so!

[*At the end of the song* DR. DALY *sees* ALINE, *and, under the influence of the potion, falls in love with her.*

Ensemble—ALINE and DR. DALY

Oh, joyous boom! oh, mad delight;
Oh, sun and moon! oh, day and night!
Rejoice, rejoice with me!
Proclaim our joy, ye birds above—
Yet brooklets, murmur forth our love,
In choral ecstasy:

ALINE Oh, joyous boon!
DR. D. Oh, mad delight!
ALINE Oh, sun and moon!
DR. D. Oh, day and night!
BOTH Ye birds, and brooks, and fruitful trees,
With choral joy delight the breeze—
Rejoice, rejoice with me!

Enter ALEXIS

ALEXIS [*with rapture*] Aline my only love, my happiness! The philtre—you have tasted it?
ALINE [*with confusion*] Yes! Yes!
ALEXIS Oh, joy, mine, mine for ever, and for aye!

[*Embraces her.*

ALINE Alexis, don't do that—you must not!

[DR. DALY *interposes between them*]

ALEXIS [*amazed*] Why?

Duet—ALINE and DR. DALY

ALINE — Alas! that lovers thus should meet:
Oh, pity, pity me!
Oh, charge me not with cold deceit;
Oh, pity, pity me!
You bade me drink—with trembling awe
I drank, and, by the potion's law,
I loved the very first I saw!
Oh, pity, pity me!

DR. D. — My dear young friend, consolèd be—
We pity, pity you.
In this I'm not an agent free—
We pity, pity you.
Some most extraordinary spell
O'er us has cast its magic fell—
The consequence I need not tell.
We pity, pity you.

Ensemble

Some most extraordinary spell
O'er {us / them} has cast its magic fell—
The consequence {we / they} need not tell.
{We / They} pity, pity {thee! / me.}

ALEXIS [*furiously*] — False one, begone—I spurn thee,
To thy new lover turn thee!
Thy perfidy all men shall know,

ALINE [*wildly*] — I could not help it!

ALEXIS [*calling off*] — Come one, come all!

DR. D. — We could not help it!

ALEXIS [*calling off*] — Obey my call!

ALINE [*wildly*] — I could not help it!

ALEXIS [*calling off*] — Come hither, run!

DR. D. — We could not help it!

ALEXIS [*calling off*] — Come, every one!

Enter all the characters except LADY SANGAZURE *and* MR. WELLS

Chorus

Oh, what is the matter, and what is the clatter?
He's glowering at her, and threatens a blow!
Oh, why does he batter the girl he did flatter?
And why does the latter recoil from him so?

Recitative—ALEXIS

Prepare for sad surprises—
My love Aline despises!
No thought of sorrow shames her—
Another lover claims her!
Be his, false girl, for better or for worse—
But, ere you leave me, may a lover's curse—

DR. D. [*coming forward*] Hold! Be just. This poor child drank the philtre at your instance. She hurried off to meet you—but, most unhappily, she met me instead. As you had administered the potion to both of us, the result was inevitable. But fear nothing from me—I will be no man's rival. I shall quit the country at once—and bury my sorrow in the congenial gloom of a Colonial Bishopric.

ALEXIS My excellent old friend! [*Taking his hand—then turning to* MR. WELLS, *who has entered with* LADY SANGAZURE] Oh, Mr. Wells, what, what is to be done?

MR. W. I do not know—and yet—there is one means by which this spell may be removed.

ALEXIS Name it—oh, name it!

MR. W. Or you or I must yield up his life to Ahrimanes. I would rather it were you. I should have no hesitation in sacrificing my own life to spare yours, but we take stock next week, and it would not be fair on the Co.

ALEXIS True. Well, I am ready!

ALINE No, no—Alexis—it must not be! Mr. Wells, if he must die that all may be restored to their old loves, what is to become of me? I should be left out in the cold, with no love to be restored to!

MR. W. True—I did not think of that. [*To the others*] My friends, I appeal to you, and I will leave the decision in your hands.

Finale

MR. W. Or I or he
Must die!
Which shall it be?
Reply!
SIR M. Die thou!
Thou art the cause of all offending!
DR. D. Die thou!
Yield thou to this decree unbending!
ALL Die thou!
MR. W. So be it! I submit! My fate is sealed.
To public execration thus I yield!

[*Falls on trap*]

Be happy all—leave me to my despair—
I go—it matters not with whom—or where!

[*Gong*]

[*All quit their present partners, and rejoin their old lovers.* SIR MARMADUKE *leaves* MRS. PARTLET, *and goes to* LADY SANGAZURE. ALINE *leaves* DR. DALY, *and goes to* ALEXIS. DR. DALY *leaves* ALINE, *and goes to* CONSTANCE. NOTARY *leaves* CONSTANCE, *and goes to* MRS. PARTLET. *All the* CHORUS *make a corresponding change.*

ALL

GENTLEMEN Oh, my adored one!
LADIES Unmingled joy!
GENTLEMEN Ecstatic rapture!
LADIES Beloved boy!

[*They embrace*]

SIR M. Come to my mansion, all of you! At least
We'll crown our rapture with another feast!

Ensemble

SIR MARMADUKE, LADY SANGAZURE, ALEXIS, and ALINE

Now to the banquet we press—
Now for the eggs and the ham—
Now for the mustard and cress—
Now for the strawberry jam!

CHORUS Now to the banquet, etc.

DR. DALY, CONSTANCE, NOTARY, and MRS. PARTLET

Now for the tea of our host—
Now for the rollicking bun—
Now for the muffin and toast—
Now for the gay Sally Lunn!

CHORUS Now for the tea, etc.

[*General Dance*]

[*During the symphony* MR. WELLS *sinks through trap, amid red fire.*

CURTAIN

H.M.S. PINAFORE

OR

THE LASS THAT LOVED A SAILOR

DRAMATIS PERSONÆ

THE RT. HON. SIR JOSEPH PORTER, K.C.B. [*First Lord of the Admiralty*]
CAPTAIN CORCORAN [*Commanding H.M.S. Pinafore*]
TOM TUCKER [*Midshipmite*]
RALPH RACKSTRAW [*Able Seaman*]
DICK DEADEYE [*Able Seaman*]
BILL BOBSTAY [*Boatswain's Mate*]
BOB BECKET [*Carpenter's Mate*]
JOSEPHINE [*the Captain's Daughter*]
HEBE (*Sir Joseph's First Cousin*)
MRS. CRIPPS (LITTLE BUTTERCUP) [*a Portsmouth Bumboat Woman*]
First Lord's Sisters, his Cousins, his Aunts, Sailors, Marines, etc.

Scene: QUARTER-DECK OF H.M.S. *Pinafore*, OFF PORTSMOUTH

ACT I—*Noon.* ACT II—*Night.*

First produced at the Opéra Comique on May 25, 1878

H.M.S. PINAFORE

OR

THE LASS THAT LOVED A SAILOR

ACT I

SCENE.—*Quarter-deck of H.M.S. Pinafore. Sailors, led by* BOATSWAIN, *discovered cleaning brasswork, splicing rope, etc.*

Chorus

We sail the ocean blue,
And our saucy ship's a beauty;
We're sober men and true,
And attentive to our duty.
When the balls whistle free
O'er the bright blue sea,
We stand to our guns all day;
When at anchor we ride
On the Portsmouth tide,
We have plenty of time to play.

Enter LITTLE BUTTERCUP, *with large basket on her arm*

Recitative

Hail, men-o'-war's men—safeguards of your nation,
Here is an end, at last, of all privation;
You've got your pay—spare all you can afford
To welcome Little Buttercup on board.

Aria

For I'm called Little Buttercup—dear Little Buttercup,
Though I could never tell why,
But still I'm called Buttercup—poor little Buttercup,
Sweet Little Buttercup I!

I've snuff and tobaccy, and excellent jacky,
I've scissors, and watches, and knives;
I've ribbons and laces to set off the faces
Of pretty young sweethearts and wives.

I've treacle and toffee, I've tea and I've coffee,
Soft tommy and succulent chops;
I've chickens and conies, and pretty polonies,
And excellent peppermint drops.

Then buy of your Buttercup—dear Little Buttercup;
  Sailors should never be shy;
So, buy of your Buttercup—poor Little Buttercup;
  Come, of your Buttercup buy!

BOAT. Aye, Little Buttercup—and well called—for you're the rosiest, the roundest, and the reddest beauty in all Spithead.

BUT. Red, am I? and round—and rosy! Maybe, for I have dissembled well! But hark ye, my merry friend—hast ever thought that beneath a gay and frivolous exterior there may lurk a canker-worm which is slowly but surely eating its way into one's very heart?

BOAT. No, my lass, I can't say I've ever thought that.

Enter DICK DEADEYE. *He pushes through sailors, and comes down*

DICK *I* have thought it often. [*All recoil from him*]

BUT. Yes, you look like it! What's the matter with the man? Isn't he well?

BOAT. Don't take no heed of *him;* that's only poor Dick Deadeye.

DICK I say—it's a beast of a name, ain't it—Dick Deadeye?

BUT. It's not a nice name.

DICK I'm ugly too, ain't I?

BUT. You are certainly plain.

DICK And I'm three-cornered too, ain't I?

BUT. You are rather triangular.

DICK Ha! ha! That's it. I'm ugly, and they hate me for it; for you all hate me, don't you?

ALL We do!

DICK There!

BOAT. Well, Dick, we wouldn't go for to hurt any fellow-creature's feelings, but you can't expect a chap with such a name as Dick Deadeye to be a popular character—now can you?

DICK No.

BOAT. It's asking too much, ain't it?

DICK It is. From such a face and form as mine the noblest sentiments sound like the black utterances of a depraved imagination. It is human nature—I am resigned.

Recitative

BUT. [*looking down hatchway*]
    But, tell me—who's the youth whose faltering feet
      With difficulty bear him on his course?
BOAT. That is the smartest lad in all the fleet—
          Ralph Rackstraw!
BUT. Ha! That name! Remorse! remorse!

Enter RALPH *from hatchway*

Madrigal—RALPH

The Nightingale
Sighed for the moon's bright ray,
And told his tale
In his own melodious way!
He sang "Ah, well-a-day!"

ALL He sang "Ah, well-a-day!"
The lowly vale
For the mountain vainly sighed,
To his humble wail
The echoing hills replied.
They sang "Ah, well-a-day!"

ALL They sang "Ah, well-a-day!"

Recitative

I know the value of a kindly chorus,
But choruses yield little consolation
When we have pain and sorrow too before us!
I love—and love, alas, above my station!

BUT. [*aside*] He loves—and loves a lass above his station!
ALL [*aside*] Yes, yes, the lass is much above his station!
[*Exit* LITTLE BUTTERCUP.

Ballad—RALPH

A maiden fair to see,
The pearl of minstrelsy,
A bud of blushing beauty;
For whom proud nobles sigh,
And with each other vie
To do her menial's duty.
ALL To do her menial's duty.

A suitor, lowly born,
With hopeless passion torn,
And poor beyond denying,
Has dared for her to pine
At whose exalted shrine
A world of wealth is sighing.
ALL A world of wealth is sighing.

Unlearned he in aught
Save that which love has taught
(For love had been his tutor);
Oh, pity, pity me—
Our captain's daughter she,
And I that lowly suitor!
ALL And he that lowly suitor!

BOAT. Ah, my poor lad, you've climbed too high: our worthy captain's child won't have nothin' to say to a poor chap like you. Will she, lads?

ALL No, no.

DICK No, no, captains' daughters don't marry foremast hands.

ALL [*recoiling from him*] Shame! shame!

BOAT. Dick Deadeye, them sentiments o' yourn are a disgrace to our common natur'.

RALPH But it's a strange anomaly, that the daughter of a man who hails from the quarter-deck may not love another who lays out on the fore-yard arm. For a man is but a man, whether he hoists his flag at the main-truck or his slacks on the main-deck.

DICK Ah, it's a queer world!

RALPH Dick Deadeye, I have no desire to press hardly on you, but such a revolutionary sentiment is enough to make an honest sailor shudder.

BOAT. My lads, our gallant captain has come on deck; let us greet him as so brave an officer and so gallant a seaman deserves.

Enter CAPTAIN CORCORAN

Recitative

CAPT. My gallant crew, good morning.
ALL [*saluting*] Sir, good morning!
CAPT. I hope you're all quite well.
ALL [*as before*] Quite well; and you, sir?
CAPT. I am in reasonable health, and happy
To meet you all once more.
ALL [*as before*] You do us proud, sir!

Song—CAPTAIN

CAPT. I am the Captain of the *Pinafore;*
ALL And a right good captain, too!
CAPT. You're very, very good,
And be it understood,
I command a right good crew,
ALL We're very, very good,
And be it understood,
He commands a right good crew.

CAPT. Though related to a peer,
I can hand, reef, and steer,
And ship a selvagee;
I am never known to quail
At the fury of a gale,
And I'm never, never sick at sea!

ALL What, never?
CAPT. No, never!
ALL What, *never?*
CAPT. Hardly ever!
ALL He's hardly ever sick at sea!
Then give three cheers, and one cheer more,
For the hardy Captain of the *Pinafore!*

CAPT. I do my best to satisfy you all—
ALL And with you we're quite content.
CAPT. You're exceedingly polite,
And I think it only right
To return the compliment.
ALL We're exceedingly polite,
And he thinks it's only right
To return the compliment.
CAPT. Bad language or abuse,
I never, never use,
Whatever the emergency;
Though "Bother it" I may
Occasionally say,
I never use a big, big D—
ALL What, never?
CAPT. No, never!
ALL What, *never?*
CAPT. Hardly ever!
ALL Hardly ever swears a big, big D—
Then give three cheers, and one cheer more,
For the well-bred Captain of the *Pinafore!*

[*After song exeunt all but* CAPTAIN.

Enter LITTLE BUTTERCUP

Recitative

BUT. Sir, you are sad! The silent eloquence
Of yonder tear that trembles on your eyelash
Proclaims a sorrow far more deep than common;
Confide in me—fear not—I am a mother!

CAPT. Yes, Little Buttercup, I'm sad and sorry—
My daughter, Josephine, the fairest flower
That ever blossomed on ancestral timber,
Is sought in marriage by Sir Joseph Porter,
Our Admiralty's First Lord, but for some reason
She does not seem to tackle kindly to it.

BUT. [*with emotion*] Ah, poor Sir Joseph! Ah, I know too well
The anguish of a heart that loves but vainly!
But see, here comes your most attractive daughter.
I go—Farewell! [*Exit.*

CAPT. [*looking after her*] A plump and pleasing person! [*Exit.*

Enter JOSEPHINE, *twining some flowers which she carries in a small basket.*

Ballad—JOSEPHINE

Sorry her lot who loves too well,
Heavy the heart that hopes but vainly,
Sad are the sighs that own the spell,
Uttered by eyes that speak too plainly;
Heavy the sorrow that bows the head
When love is alive and hope is dead!

Sad is the hour when sets the sun—
Dark is the night to earth's poor daughters,
When to the ark the wearied one
Flies from the empty waste of waters!
Heavy the sorrow that bows the head
When love is alive and hope is dead!

Enter CAPTAIN

CAPT. My child, I grieve to see that you are a prey to melancholy. You should look your best to-day, for Sir Joseph Porter, K.C.B., will be here this afternoon to claim your promised hand.

JOS. Ah, father, your words cut me to the quick. I can esteem—reverence—venerate Sir Joseph, for he is a great and good man; but oh, I cannot love him! My heart is already given.

CAPT. [*aside*] It is then as I feared. [*Aloud*] Given? And to whom? Not to some gilded lordling?

JOS. No, father—the object of my love is no lordling. Oh, pity me, for he is but a humble sailor on board your own ship!

CAPT. Impossible!

JOS. Yes, it is true—too true.

CAPT. A common sailor? Oh fie!

JOS. I blush for the weakness that allows me to cherish such a passion. I hate myself when I think of the depth to which I have stooped in permitting myself to think tenderly of one so ignobly born, but I love him! I love him! I love him! [*Weeps*]

CAPT. Come, my child, let us talk this over. In a matter of the heart I would not coerce my daughter—I attach but little value to rank or wealth, but the line must be drawn somewhere. A man in that station may be brave and worthy, but at every step he would commit solecisms that society would never pardon.

JOS. Oh, I have thought of this night and day. But fear not, father, I have a heart, and therefore I love; but I am your daughter, and therefore I am proud. Though I carry my love with me to the tomb, he shall never, never know it.

CAPT. You *are* my daughter after all. But see, Sir Joseph's barge approaches, manned by twelve trusty oarsmen and accompanied by the admiring crowd of sisters, cousins, and aunts that attend him wherever he goes. Retire, my daughter, to your cabin—take this, his photograph, with you—it may help to bring you to a more reasonable frame of mind.

JOS. My own thoughtful father!

[*Exit* JOSEPHINE. CAPTAIN *remains and ascends the poop-deck.*

Barcarolle [*invisible*]

Over the bright blue sea
Comes Sir Joseph Porter, K.C.B.,
Wherever he may go
Bang-bang the loud nine-pounders go!
Shout o'er the bright blue sea
For Sir Joseph Porter, K.C.B.

[*During this the Crew have entered on tiptoe, listening attentively to the song.*

Chorus of Sailors

Sir Joseph's barge is seen,
And its crowd of blushing beauties,
We hope he'll find us clean,
And attentive to our duties.
We sail, we sail the ocean blue,
And our saucy ship's a beauty.
We're sober, sober men and true
And attentive to our duty.

We're smart and sober men,
And quite devoid of fe-ar,
In all the Royal N.
None are so smart as we are.

Enter SIR JOSEPH'S FEMALE RELATIVES

[*They dance round stage*]

RELATIVES Gaily tripping,
Lighting skipping,
Flock the maidens to the shipping.
SAILORS Flags and guns and pennants dipping!
All the ladies love the shipping.
RELATIVES Sailors sprightly
Always rightly
Welcome ladies so politely.
SAILORS Ladies who can smile so brightly,
Sailors welcome most politely.
CAPT. [*from poop*] Now give three cheers, I'll lead the way
ALL Hurrah! hurrah! hurrah! hurray!

Enter SIR JOSEPH with COUSIN HEBE

Song—SIR JOSEPH

I am the monarch of the sea,
The ruler of the Queen's Navee,
Whose praise Great Britain loudly chants.
COUSIN HEBE And we are his sisters, and his cousins and his aunts!
RELATIVES And we are his sisters, and his cousins, and his aunts!
SIR JOSEPH When at anchor here I ride,
My bosom swells with pride,
And I snap my fingers at a foeman's taunts;
COUSIN HEBE And so do his sisters, and his cousins, and his aunts!
ALL And so do his sisters, and his cousins, and his aunts!
SIR JOSEPH But when the breezes blow,
I generally go below,
And seek the seclusion that a cabin grants;
COUSIN HEBE And so do his sisters, and his cousins, and his aunts!

ALL And so do his sisters, and his cousins, and
his aunts!
His sisters and his cousins,
Whom he reckons up by dozens,
And his aunts!

Song—SIR JOSEPH

When I was a lad I served a term
As office boy to an Attorney's firm.
I cleaned the windows and I swept the floor,
And I polished up the handle of the big front door.
I polished up that handle so carefullee
That now I am the Ruler of the Queen's Navee!

CHORUS—He polished, etc.

As office boy I made such a mark
That they gave me the post of a junior clerk.
I served the writs with a smile so bland,
And I copied all the letters in a big round hand—
I copied all the letters in a hand so free,
That now I am the Ruler of the Queen's Navee!

CHORUS—He copied, etc.

In serving writs I made such a name
That an articled clerk I soon became;
I wore clean collars and a brand-new suit

For the pass examination at the Institute,
    And that pass examination did so well for me,
    That now I am the Ruler of the Queen's Navee!

CHORUS—And that pass examination, etc.

Of legal knowledge I acquired such a grip
That they took me into the partnership.
And that junior partnership, I ween,
Was the only ship that I ever had seen.
    But that kind of ship so suited me,
    That now I am the Ruler of the Queen's Navee!

CHORUS—But that kind, etc.

I grew so rich that I was sent
By a pocket borough into Parliament.
I always voted at my party's call,
And I never thought of thinking for myself at all.
    I thought so little, they rewarded me
    By making me the Ruler of the Queen's Navee!

CHORUS—He thought so little, etc.

Now landsmen all, whoever you may be,
If you want to rise to the top of the tree,
If your soul isn't fettered to an office stool,
Be careful to be guided by this golden rule—
    Stick close to your desks and never go to sea,
    And you all may be Rulers of the Queen's Navee!

CHORUS—Stick close, etc.

SIR JOSEPH You've a remarkably fine crew, Captain Corcoran.

CAPT. It *is* a fine crew, Sir Joseph.

SIR JOSEPH [*examining a very small midshipman*] A British sailor is a splendid fellow, Captain Corcoran.

CAPT. A splendid fellow indeed, Sir Joseph.

SIR JOSEPH I hope you treat your crew kindly, Captain Corcoran.

CAPT. Indeed I hope so, Sir Joseph.

SIR JOSEPH Never forget that they are the bulwarks of England's greatness, Captain Corcoran.

CAPT. So I have always considered them, Sir Joseph.

SIR JOSEPH No bullying, I trust—no strong language of any kind, eh?

CAPT. Oh, never, Sir Joseph.

SIR JOSEPH What, *never?*

CAPT. Hardly ever, Sir Joseph. They are an excellent crew, and do their work thoroughly without it.

SIR JOSEPH Don't patronise them, sir—pray, don't patronise them.

CAPT. Certainly not, Sir Joseph.

SIR JOSEPH That you are their captain is an accident of birth. I cannot permit these noble fellows to be patronised because an accident of birth has placed you above them and them below you.

CAPT. I am the last person to insult a British sailor, Sir Joseph.

SIR JOSEPH You are the last person who did, Captain Corcoran. Desire that splendid seaman to step forward.

[DICK *comes forward*]

SIR JOSEPH No, no, the other splendid seaman.

CAPT. Ralph Rackstraw, three paces to the front—march!

SIR JOSEPH [*sternly*] If what?

CAPT. I beg your pardon—I don't think I understand you.

SIR JOSEPH If you *please.*

CAPT. Oh, yes, of course. If you please. [RALPH *steps forward*]

SIR JOSEPH You're a remarkably fine fellow.

RALPH Yes, your honour.

SIR JOSEPH And a first-rate seaman, I'll be bound.

RALPH There's not a smarter topman in the Navy, your honour, though I say it who shouldn't.

SIR JOSEPH Not at all. Proper self-respect, nothing more. Can you dance a hornpipe?

RALPH No, your honour.

SIR JOSEPH That's a pity: all sailors should dance hornpipes. I will teach you one this evening, after dinner. Now tell me—don't be afraid—how does your captain treat you, eh?

RALPH A better captain don't walk the deck, your honour

ALL Aye; Aye!

SIR JOSEPH Good. I like to hear you speak well of your commanding officer; I daresay he don't deserve it, but still it does you credit. Can you sing?

RALPH I can hum a little, your honour.

SIR JOSEPH Then hum this at your leisure. [*Giving him MS. music*] It is a song that I have composed for the use of the Royal Navy. It is designed to encourage independence of thought and action in the lower branches of the service, and to teach the principle that a British sailor is any man's equal, excepting mine. Now, Captain Corcoran, a word with you in your cabin, on a tender and sentimental subject.

CAPT. Aye, aye, Sir Joseph. [*Crossing*] Boatswain, in commemoration of this joyous occasion, see that extra grog is served out to the ship's company at seven bells.

BOAT. Beg pardon. If what, your honour?

CAPT. If what? I don't think I understand you.

BOAT. If you *please,* your honour.

CAPT. What!

SIR JOSEPH The gentleman is quite right. If you *please.*

CAPT. [*stamping his foot impatiently*] If you *please!*

[*Exit.*

SIR JOSEPH For I hold that on the seas
The expression, "if you please",
A particularly gentlemanly tone implants.

COUSIN HEBE And so do his sisters, and his cousins, and his aunts!

ALL And so do his sisters, and his cousins, and his aunts!

[*Exeunt* SIR JOSEPH *and* RELATIVES.

BOAT. Ah! Sir Joseph's true gentleman; courteous and considerate to the very humblest.

RALPH True, Boatswain, but we are not the very humblest. Sir Joseph has explained our true position to us. As he says, a British seaman is any man's equal excepting his, and if Sir Joseph says that, is it not our duty to believe him?

ALL Well spoke! well spoke!

DICK You're on a wrong tack, and so is he. He means well, but he don't know. When people have to obey other people's orders, equality's out of the question.

ALL [*recoiling*] Horrible! horrible!

BOAT. Dick Deadeye, if you go for to infuriate this here ship's company too far, I won't answer for being able to hold 'em in. I'm shocked! that's what I am–shocked!

RALPH Messmates, my mind's made up. I'll speak to the captain's daughter, and tell her, like an honest man, of the honest love I have for her.

ALL Aye, aye!

RALPH Is not my love as good as another's? Is not my heart as true as another's? Have I not hands and eyes and ears and limbs like another?

ALL Aye, aye!

RALPH True, I lack birth—

BOAT. You've a berth on board this very ship.

RALPH Well said–I had forgotten that. Messmates–what do you say? Do you approve my determination?

ALL We do.

DICK *I* don't.

BOAT. What is to be done with this here hopeless chap? Let us sing him the song that Sir Joseph has kindly composed for us. Perhaps it will bring this here miserable creetur to a proper state of mind.

Glee—RALPH, BOATSWAIN, BOATSWAIN'S MATE, and CHORUS

A British tar is a soaring soul,
  As free as a mountain bird,
His energetic fist should be ready to resist
  A dictatorial word.
His nose should pant and his lip should curl,
His cheeks should flame and his brow should furl,
His bosom should heave and his heart should glow,
And his fist be ever ready for a knock-down blow.

CHORUS—His nose should pant, etc.

His eyes should flash with an inborn fire,
  His brow with scorn be wrung;
He never should bow down to a domineering frown,
  Or the tang of a tyrant tongue.
His foot should stamp and his throat should growl,
His hair should twirl and his face should scowl;
His eyes should flash and his breast protrude,
And this should be his customary attitude—[*pose*]

CHORUS—His foot should stamp, etc.

All dance off excepting RALPH, *who remains, leaning pensively against bulwark.*

Enter JOSEPHINE *from cabin*

Jos. It is useless—Sir Joseph's attentions nauseate me. I know that he is a truly great and good man, for he told me so himself, but to me he seems tedious, fretful, and dictatorial. Yet his must be a mind of no common order, or he would not dare to teach my dear father to dance a hornpipe on the cabin table. [*Sees* RALPH] Ralph Rackstraw! [*Overcome by emotion*]

RALPH Aye, lady—no other than poor Ralph Rackstraw!

Jos. [*aside*] How my heart beats! [*Aloud*] And why poor, Ralph?

RALPH I am poor in the essence of happiness, lady—rich only in never-ending unrest. In me there meet a combination of antithetical elements which are at eternal war with one another. Driven hither by objective influences—thither by subjective emotions—wafted one moment into blazing day, by mocking hope—plunged the next into the Cimmerian darkness of tangible despair, I am but a living ganglion of irreconcilable antagonisms. I hope I make myself clear, lady?

Jos. Perfectly. [*Aside*] His simple eloquence goes to my heart. Oh, if I dared—but no, the thought is madness! [*Aloud*] Dismiss these foolish fancies, they torture you but needlessly. Come, make one effort.

RALPH [*aside*] I will—one. [*Aloud*] Josephine!

Jos. [*indignantly*] Sir!

RALPH Aye, even though Jove's armoury were launched at the head of the audacious mortal whose lips, unhallowed by relationship, dared to breathe that precious word, yet would I breathe it once, and then perchance be silent evermore. Josephine, in one brief breath I will concentrate the hopes, the doubts, the anxious fears of six weary months. Josephine, I am a British sailor, and I love you!

Jos. Sir, this audacity! [*Aside*] Oh, my heart, my beating heart! [*Aloud*] This unwarrantable presumption on the part of a common sailor! [*Aside*] Common! oh, the irony of the word! [*Crossing, aloud*] Oh, sir, you forget the disparity in our ranks.

RALPH I forget nothing, haughty lady. I love you desperately, my life is in your hand—I lay it at your feet! Give me hope, and what I lack in education and polite accomplishments, that I will endeavour to acquire. Drive me to despair, and in death alone I shall look for consolation. I am proud and cannot stoop to implore. I have spoken and I wait your word.

Jos. You shall not wait long. Your proffered love I haughtily reject. Go, sir, and learn to cast your eyes on some village maiden in your own poor rank—they should be lowered before your captain's daughter.

Duet—JOSEPHINE and RALPH

Jos. Refrain, audacious tar,
Your suit from pressing,
Remember what you are,
And whom addressing!

[*Aside*] I'd laugh my rank to scorn
In union holy,
Were he more highly born
Or I more lowly!

RALPH Proud lady, have your way,
Unfeeling beauty!
You speak and I obey,
It is my duty!
I am the lowliest tar
That sails the water,
And you, proud maiden, are
My captain's daughter!

[*Aside*] My heart with anguish torn
Bows down before her,
She laughs my love to scorn,
Yet I adore her!

[*Repeat refrain, ensemble, then exit* JOSEPHINE *into cabin.*

RALPH [*Recit.*] Can I survive this overbearing
Or live a life of mad despairing,
My proffered love despised, rejected?
No, no, it's not to be expected!
[*Calling off*]
Messmates, ahoy!
Come here! Come here!

Enter SAILORS, HEBE, *and* RELATIVES

ALL Aye, aye, my boy,
What cheer, what cheer?
Now tell us, pray,
Without delay,
What does she say—
What cheer, what cheer?

RALPH [*to* COUSIN HEBE] The maiden treats my suit with scorn,
Rejects my humble gift, my lady;
She says I am ignobly born,
And cuts my hopes adrift, my lady.

ALL Oh, cruel one.

DICK She spurns your suit? Oho! Oho!
I told you so, I told you so.

SAILORS and RELATIVES

Shall {we / they} submit? Are {we / they} but slaves?
Love comes alike to high and low—

Britannia's sailors rule the waves,
And shall they stoop to insult? No!

DICK — You must submit, you are but slaves;
A lady she! Oho! Oho!
You lowly toilers of the waves,
She spurns you all—I told you so!

RALPH — My friends, my leave of life I'm taking,
For oh, my heart, my heart is breaking.
When I am gone, oh, prithee tell
The maid that, as I died, I loved her well!

ALL [*turning away, weeping*] Of life, alas! his leave he's taking,
For ah! his faithful heart is breaking;
When he is gone we'll surely tell
The maid that, as he died, he loved her well.

[*During Chorus* BOATSWAIN *has loaded pistol, which he hands to* RALPH.

RALPH — Be warned, my messmates all
Who love in rank above you—
For Josephine I fall!

[*Puts pistol to his head. All the sailors stop their ears.*

Enter JOSEPHINE *on deck*

JOS. — Ah! stay your hand! I love you!
ALL — Ah! stay your hand—she loves you!
RALPH [*incredulously*] Loves me?
JOS. — Loves you!
ALL — Yes, yes—ah, yes,—she loves you!

Ensemble

SAILORS and RELATIVES and JOSEPHINE

Oh joy, oh rapture unforeseen,
For now the sky is all serene;
The god of day—the orb of love—
Has hung his ensign high above,
The sky is all ablaze.

With wooing words and loving song,
We'll chase the lagging hours along,
And if {I find / we find} the maiden coy,
{I'll / We'll} murmur forth decorous joy
In dreamy roundelays!

DICK DEADEYE

He thinks he's won his Josephine,
But though the sky is now serene,
A frowning thunderbolt above
May end their ill-assorted love
Which now is all ablaze.

Our captain, ere the day is gone,
Will be extremely down upon
The wicked men who art employ
To make his Josephine less coy
In many various ways. [*Exit* DICK.

JOS. This very night,
HEBE With bated breath
RALPH And muffled oar—
JOS. Without a light,
HEBE As still as death,
RALPH We'll steal ashore
JOS. A clergyman
RALPH Shall make us one
BOAT. At half-past ten,
JOS. And then we can
RALPH Return, for none
BOAT. Can part them then!
ALL This very night, etc.

[DICK *appears at hatchway*]

DICK Forbear, nor carry out the scheme you've planned;
She is a lady—you a foremast hand!
Remember, she's your gallant captain's daughter,
And you the meanest slave that crawls the water!
ALL Back, vermin, back,
Nor mock us!
Back, vermin, back,
You shock us!

[*Exit* DICK.

Let's give three cheers for the sailor's bride
Who casts all thought of rank aside—
Who gives up home and fortune too
For the honest love of a sailor true!
For a British tar is a soaring soul
As free as a mountain bird!
His energetic fist should be ready to resist
A dictatorial word!

His foot should stamp and his throat should growl,
His hair should twirl and his face should scowl,
His eyes should flash and his breast protrude,
And this should be his customary attitude—[*pose*]

General Dance

END OF ACT I

ACT II

Same Scene. Night. Awning removed. Moonlight. CAPTAIN *discovered singing on poop-deck, and accompanying himself on a mandolin.* LITTLE BUTTERCUP *seated on quarter-deck, gazing sentimentally at him.*

Song—CAPTAIN

Fair moon, to thee I sing,
Bright regent of the heavens,
Say, why is everything
Either at sixes or at sevens?
I have lived hitherto
Free from breath of slander,
Beloved by all my crew—
A really popular commander.
But now my kindly crew rebel,
My daughter to a tar is partial,
Sir Joseph storms, and, sad to tell,
He threatens a court martial!
Fair moon, to thee I sing,
Bright regent of the heavens,
Say, why is everything
Either at sixes or at sevens?

BUT. How sweetly he carols forth his melody to the unconscious moon! Of whom is he thinking? Of some high-born beauty? It may be! Who is poor Little Buttercup that she should expect his glance to fall on one so lowly! And yet if he knew—if he only knew!

CAPT. [*coming down*] Ah! Little Buttercup, still on board? That is not quite right, little one. It would have been more respectable to have gone on shore at dusk.

BUT. True, dear Captain—but the recollection of your sad pale face seemed to chain me to the ship. I would fain see you smile before I go.

CAPT. Ah! Little Buttercup, I fear it will be long before I recover my accustomed cheerfulness, for misfortunes crowd upon me, and all my old friends seem to have turned against me!

BUT. Oh no—do not say "all", dear Captain. That were unjust to one, at least.

CAPT. True, for you are staunch to me. [*Aside*] If ever I gave my heart again, methinks it would be to such a one as this! [*Aloud*] I am touched to the heart by your innocent regard for me, and were we differently situated, I think I could have returned it. But as it is, I fear I can never be more to you than a friend.

BUT. I understand! You hold aloof from me because you are rich and lofty—and I poor and lowly. But take care! The poor bumboat woman has gipsy blood in her veins, and she can read destinies.

CAPT. Destinies?

BUT. There is a change in store for you!

CAPT. A change?

BUT. Aye—be prepared!

Duet—LITTLE BUTTERCUP and CAPTAIN

BUT. Things are seldom what they seem,
Skim milk masquerades as cream;
Highlows pass as patent leathers;
Jackdaws strut in peacock's feathers.
CAPT. [*puzzled*] Very true,
So they do.
BUT. Black sheep dwell in every fold;
All that glitters is not gold;
Storks turn out to be but logs;
Bulls are but inflated frogs.
CAPT. [*puzzled*] So they be,
Frequentlee.
BUT. Drops the wind and stops the mill;
Turbot is ambitious brill;
Gild the farthing if you will,
Yet it is a farthing still.
CAPT. [*puzzled*] Yes, I know.
That is so.
Though to catch your drift I'm striving,
It is shady—it is shady;
I don't see at what you're driving,
Mystic lady—mystic lady.
[*Aside*] Stern conviction's o'er me stealing,
That the mystic lady's dealing
In oracular revealing.
BUT. [*aside*] Stern conviction's o'er him stealing,
That the mystic lady's dealing

In oracular revealing.

BOTH — Yes, I know—
That is so!

CAPT. — Though I'm anything but clever,
I could talk like that for ever:
Once a cat was killed by care;
Only brave deserve the fair.

BUT. — Very true,
So they do.

CAPT. — Wink is often good as nod;
Spoils the child who spares the rod;
Thirsty lambs run foxy dangers;
Dogs are found in many mangers.

BUT. — Frequentlee,
I agree.

CAPT. — Paw of cat the chestnut snatches;
Worn-out garments show new patches;
Only count the chick that hatches;
Men are grown-up catchy-catchies.

BUT. — Yes, I know,
That is so.

[*Aside*] — Though to catch my drift he's striving,
I'll dissemble—I'll dissemble;
When he sees at what I'm driving,
Let him tremble—let him tremble!

Ensemble

Though a mystic tone { I / you } borrow,
{ You will / I shall } learn the truth with sorrow,
Here to-day and gone to-morrow;
Yes, I know—
That is so!

[*At the end exit* LITTLE BUTTERCUP *melodramatically*.

CAPT. Incomprehensible as her utterances are, I nevertheless feel that they are dictated by a sincere regard for me. But to what new misery is she referring? Time alone can tell!

Enter SIR JOSEPH

SIR JOSEPH Captain Corcoran, I am much disappointed with your daughter. In fact, I don't think she will do.

CAPT. She won't do, Sir Joseph!

SIR JOSEPH I'm afraid not. The fact is, that although I have urged my suit with as much eloquence as is consistent with an official utterance, I have done so hitherto without success. How do you account for this?

CAPT. Really, Sir Joseph, I hardly know. Josephine is of course sensible of your condescension.

SIR JOSEPH She naturally would be.

CAPT. But perhaps your exalted rank dazzles her.

SIR JOSEPH You think it does?

CAPT. I can hardly say; but she is a modest girl, and her social position is far below your own. It may be that she feels she is not worthy of you.

SIR JOSEPH That is really a very sensible suggestion, and displays more knowledge of human nature than I had given you credit for.

CAPT. See, she comes. If your lordship would kindly reason with her and assure her officially that it is a standing rule at the Admiralty that love levels all ranks, her respect for an official utterance might induce her to look upon your offer in its proper light.

SIR JOSEPH It is not unlikely. I will adopt your suggestion. But soft, she is here. Let us withdraw, and watch our opportunity.

Enter JOSEPHINE *from cabin.* FIRST LORD *and* CAPTAIN *retire*

Scene—JOSEPHINE

The hours creep on apace,
My guilty heart is quaking!
Oh, that I might retrace
The step that I am taking!
Its folly it were easy to be showing,
What I am giving up and whither going.
On the one hand, papa's luxurious home,
Hung with ancestral armour and old brasses,
Carved oak and tapestry from distant Rome,
Rare "blue and white" Venetian finger-glasses,
Rich oriental rugs, luxurious sofa pillows,
And everything that isn't old, from Gillow's.
And on the other, a dark and dingy room,
In some back street with stuffy children crying,
Where organs yell, and clacking housewives fume,
And clothes are hanging out all day a-drying.
With one cracked looking-glass to see your face in,
And dinner served up in a pudding basin!

A simple sailor, lowly born,
Unlettered and unknown,
Who toils for bread from early morn
Till half the night has flown!
No golden rank can he impart—
No wealth of house or land—
No fortune save his trusty heart
And honest brown right hand!

And yet he is so wondrous fair
That love for one so passing rare,
So peerless in his manly beauty,
Were little else than solemn duty!
Oh, god of love, and god of reason, say,
Which of you twain shall my poor heart obey!

SIR JOSEPH *and* CAPTAIN *enter*

SIR JOSEPH Madam, it has been represented to me that you are appalled by my exalted rank. I desire to convey to you officially my assurance, that if your hesitation is attributable to that circumstance, it is uncalled for.

JOS. Oh! then your lordship is of opinion that married happiness is *not* inconsistent with discrepancy in rank?

SIR JOSEPH I am officially of that opinion.

JOS. That the high and the lowly may be truly happy together, provided that they truly love one another?

SIR JOSEPH Madam, I desire to convey to you officially my opinion that love is a platform upon which all ranks meet.

JOS. I thank you, Sir Joseph. I *did* hesitate, but I will hesitate no longer. [*Aside*] He little thinks how eloquently he has pleaded his rival's cause!

Trio

FIRST LORD, CAPTAIN, and JOSEPHINE

CAPT. Never mind the why and wherefore,
Love can level ranks, and therefore,
Though his lordship's station's mighty,
Though stupendous be his brain,
Though your tastes are mean and flighty
And your fortune poor and plain,
CAPT. and SIR JOSEPH Ring the merry bells on board-ship,
Rend the air with warbling wild,
For the union of {his / my} lordship
With a humble captain's child!
CAPT. For a humble captain's daughter—
JOS. For a gallant captain's daughter—
SIR JOSEPH And a lord who rules the water—
JOS. [*aside*] And a *tar* who ploughs the water!
ALL Let the air with joy be laden,
Rend with songs the air above,
For the union of a maiden
With the man who owns her love!
SIR JOSEPH Never mind the why and wherefore,
Love can level ranks, and therefore,

Though your nautical relation [*alluding to* CAPT.]
In my set could scarcely pass—
Though you occupy a station
In the lower middle class—
CAPT. and SIR JOSEPH Ring the merry bells on board-ship,
Rend the air with warbling wild,
For the union of {my / his} lordship
With a humble captain's child!
CAPT. For a humble captain's daughter—
JOS. For a gallant captain's daughter—
SIR JOSEPH And a lord who rules the water—
JOS. [*aside*] And a *tar* who ploughs the water!
ALL Let the air with joy be laden,
Rend with songs the air above,
For the union of a maiden
With the man who owns her love!
JOS. Never mind the why and wherefore,
Love can level ranks, and therefore
I admit the jurisdiction;
Ably have you played your part;
You have carried firm conviction
To my hesitating heart.
CAPT. and SIR JOSEPH Ring the merry bells on board-ship,
Rend the air with warbling wild,
For the union of {my / his} lordship
With a humble captain's child!
CAPT. For a humble captain's daughter—
JOS. For a gallant captain's daughter—
SIR JOSEPH And a lord who rules the water—
JOS. [*aside*] And a *tar* who ploughs the water!
[*Aloud*] Let the air with joy be laden.
CAPT. and SIR JOSEPH Ring the merry bells on board-ship—
JOS. For the union of a maiden—
CAPT. and SIR JOSEPH For her union with his lordship.
ALL Rend with songs the air above
For the man who owns her love!

[*Exit* JOS.

CAPT. Sir Joseph, I cannot express to you my delight at the happy result of your eloquence. Your argument was unanswerable.

SIR JOSEPH Captain Corcoran, it is one of the happiest characteristics of this glorious country that official utterances are invariably regarded as unanswerable. [*Exit* SIR JOSEPH

CAPT. At last my fond hopes are to be crowned. My only daughter is to be the bride of a Cabinet Minister. The prospect is Elysian. [*During this speech* Dick Deadeye *has entered*]

Dick Captain.

Capt. Deadeye! You here? Don't! [*Recoiling from him*]

Dick Ah, don't shrink from me, Captain. I'm unpleasant to look at, and my name's agin me, but I ain't as bad as I seem.

Capt. What would you with me?

Dick [*mysteriously*] I'm come to give you warning.

Capt. Indeed! do you propose to leave the Navy then?

Dick No, no, you misunderstand me; listen!

Duet

Captain and Dick Deadeye

Dick Kind Captain, I've important information,
Sing hey, the kind commander that you are,
About a certain intimate relation,
Sing hey, the merry maiden and the tar.
Both The merry maiden and the tar.

Capt. Good fellow, in conundrums you are speaking,
Sing hey, the mystic sailor that you are;
The answer to them vainly I am seeking;
Sing hey, the merry maiden and the tar.
Both The merry maiden and the tar.

Dick Kind Captain, your young lady is a-sighing,
Sing hey, the simple captain that you are,
This very night with Rackstraw to be flying;
Sing hey, the merry maiden and the tar.
Both The merry maiden and the tar.

Capt. Good fellow, you have given timely warning,
Sing hey, the thoughtful sailor that you are,
I'll talk to Master Rackstraw in the morning:
Sing hey, the cat-o'-nine-tails and the tar.
[*Producing a "cat"*]

Both The merry cat-o'-nine-tails and the tar!

Capt. Dick Deadeye—I thank you for your warning—I will at once take means to arrest their flight. This boat cloak will afford me ample disguise—So! [*Envelops himself in a mysterious cloak, holding it before his face*]

Dick Ha, ha! They are foiled—foiled—foiled!

Enter Crew on tiptoe, with Ralph *and* Boatswain *meeting* Josephine, *who enters from cabin on tiptoe, with bundle of necessaries, and accompanied by* Little Buttercup.

Ensemble

Carefully on tiptoe stealing,
Breathing gently as we may,
Every step with caution feeling,
We will softly steal away.

[CAPTAIN *stamps*]—*Chord*

ALL [*much alarmed*] Goodness me—
Why, what was that?
DICK Silent be,
It was the cat!
ALL [*reassured*] It was—it was the cat!
CAPT. [*producing cat-o'-nine-tails*] They're right, it was the cat!

ALL Pull ashore, in fashion steady,
Hymen will defray the fare,
For a clergyman is ready
To unite the happy pair!

[*Stamp as before, and Chord*]

ALL Goodness me,
Why, what was that?
DICK Silent be,
Again the cat!
ALL It was again that cat!
CAPT. [*aside*] They're right, it was the cat!
CAPT. [*throwing off cloak*] Hold! [*All start*]
Pretty daughter of mine,
I insist upon knowing
Where you may be going
With these sons of the brine,
For my excellent crew,
Though foes they could thump any,
Are scarcely fit company,
My daughter, for you.
CREW Now, hark at that, do!
Though foes we could thump any,
We are scarcely fit company
For a lady like you!

RALPH Proud officer, that haughty lip uncurl!
Vain man, suppress that supercilious sneer,
For I have dared to love your matchless girl,
A fact well known to all my messmates here!

CAPT. Oh, horror!

RALPH and JOS. {I, / He,} humble, poor, and lowly born,
The meanest in the port division—
The butt of epauletted scorn—
The mark of quarter-deck derision—
{Have / Has} dare to raise {my / his} wormy eyes
Above the dust to which you'd mould {me / him}
In manhood's glorious pride to rise,
{I am / He is} an Englishman—behold {me! / him!}

ALL He is an Englishman!

BOAT. He is an Englishman!
For he himself has said it,
And it's greatly to his credit,
That he is an Englishman!

ALL That he is an Englishman!
BOAT. For he might have been a Roosian,
A French, or Turk, or Proosian,
Or perhaps Itali-an!

ALL Or perhaps Itali-an!
BOAT. But in spite of all temptations
To belong to other nations,
He remains an Englishman!

ALL For in spite of all temptations, etc.

CAPT. [*trying to repress his anger*]
In uttering a reprobation
To any British tar,
I try to speak with moderation,
But you have gone too far.
I'm very sorry to disparage
A humble foremast lad,
But to seek your captain's child in marriage,
Why damme, it's too bad!

[*During this,* COUSIN HEBE *and* FEMALE RELATIVES *have entered.*

ALL [*shocked*] Oh!
CAPT. Yes, damme, it's too bad!
ALL Oh!
CAPT. and DICK DEADEYE Yes, damme, it's too bad.

During this, SIR JOSEPH *has appeared on poop-deck. He is horrified at the bad language.*

HEBE Did you hear him—did you hear him?
Oh, the monster overbearing!
Don't go near him—don't go near him—
He is swearing—he is swearing!
SIR JOSEPH My pain and my distress,
I find it is not easy to express;
My amazement—my surprise—
You may learn from the expression of my eyes!
CAPT. My lord—one word—the facts are not before you
The word was injudicious, I allow—
But hear my explanation, I implore you,
And you will be indignant too, I vow!
SIR JOSEPH I will hear of no defence,
Attempt none if you're sensible.
That word of evil sense
Is wholly indefensible.
Go, ribald, get you hence
To your cabin with celerity.
This is the consequence
Of ill-advised asperity!

[*Exit* CAPTAIN, *disgraced, followed by* JOSEPHINE.

ALL This is the consequence,
Of ill-advised asperity!

SIR JOSEPH For I'll teach you all, ere long,
To refrain from language strong
For I haven't any sympathy for ill-bred taunts!
HEBE No more have his sisters, nor his cousins, nor his aunts.
ALL For he is an Englishman, etc.

SIR JOSEPH Now, tell me, my fine fellow—for you *are* a fine fellow——

RALPH Yes, your honour.

SIR JOSEPH How came your captain so far to forget himself? I am quite sure you had given him no cause for annoyance.

RALPH Please your honour, it was thus-wise. You see I'm only a topman—a mere foremast hand——

SIR JOSEPH Don't be ashamed of that. Your position as a topman is a very exalted one.

RALPH Well, your honour, love burns as brightly in the fo'c'sle as it does on the quarter-deck, and Josephine is the fairest bud that ever blossomed upon the tree of a poor fellow's wildest hopes.

Enter JOSEPHINE; *she rushes to* RALPH'S *arms*

JOS. Darling! [SIR JOSEPH *horrified*]

RALPH She is the figurehead of my ship of life—the bright beacon that guides me into my port of happiness—that the rarest, the purest gem that ever sparkled on a poor but worthy fellow's trusting brow!

ALL Very pretty, very pretty!

SIR JOSEPH Insolent sailor, you shall repent this outrage. Seize him! [*Two Marines seize him and handcuff him*]

JOS. Oh, Sir Joseph, spare him, for I love him tenderly.

SIR JOSEPH Pray, don't. I will teach this presumptuous mariner to discipline his affections. Have you such a thing as a dungeon on board?

ALL We have!

DICK They have!

SIR JOSEPH Then load him with chains and take him there at once!

Octette

RALPH Farewell, my own,
Light of my life, farewell!
For crime unknown
I go to a dungeon cell.

JOS. I will atone.
In the meantime farewell!
And all alone
Rejoice in your dungeon cell!

SIR JOSEPH A bone, a bone
I'll pick with this sailor fell;

Let him be shown
  At once to his dungeon cell.

BOATSWAIN, DICK DEADEYE, and COUSIN HEBE

He'll hear no tone
  Of the maiden he loves so well!
No telephone
  Communicates with his cell!

BUT. [*mysteriously*] But when is known
  The secret I have to tell,
Wide will be thrown
  The door of his dungeon cell.

ALL For crime unknown
  He goes to a dungeon cell!

[RALPH *is led off in custody.*

SIR JOSEPH My pain and my distress
Again it is not easy to express.
My amazement, my surprise,
Again you may discover from my eyes.

ALL How terrible the aspect of his eyes!

BUT. Hold! Ere upon your loss
  You lay much stress,
A long-concealèd crime
  I would confess.

Song—BUTTERCUP

  A many years ago,
When I was young and charming,
  As some of you may know,
I practised baby-farming.

ALL Now this is most alarming!
When she was young and charming,
She practised baby-farming,
  A many years ago.

BUT. Two tender babes I nussed:
  One was of low condition,
The other, upper crust,
  A regular patrician.

ALL [*explaining to each other*]
Now, this is the position:
One was of low condition,

The other a patrician,
A many years ago.

BUT. Oh, bitter is my cup!
However could I do it?
I mixed those children up,
And not a creature knew it!

ALL However could you do it?
Some day, no doubt, you'll rue it,
Although no creature knew it,
So many years ago.

BUT. In time each little waif
Forsook his foster-mother,
The well-born babe was Ralph—
Your captain was the other!!!

ALL They left their foster-mother,
The one was Ralph, our brother,
Our captain was the other,
A many years ago.

SIR JOSEPH Then I am to understand that Captain Corcoran and Ralph were exchanged in childhood's happy hour—that Ralph is really the Captain, and the Captain is Ralph?

BUT. That is the idea I intended to convey, officially!

SIR JOSEPH And very well you have conveyed it.

BUT. Aye! aye! yer 'onour.

SIR JOSEPH Dear me! Let them appear before me, at once!

[RALPH *enters as* CAPTAIN; CAPTAIN *as a common sailor.* JOSEPHINE *rushes to his arms.*

JOS. My father—a common sailor!

CAPT. It is hard, is it not, my dear?

SIR JOSEPH This is a very singular occurrence; I congratulate you both. [*To* RALPH] Desire that remarkably fine seaman to step forward.

RALPH Corcoran. Three paces to the front—march!

CAPT. If what?

RALPH If what? I don't think I understand you.

CAPT. If you please.

SIR JOSEPH The gentleman is quite right. If you *please.*

RALPH Oh! If you *please.* [CAPTAIN *steps forward*]

SIR JOSEPH [*to* CAPTAIN] You are an extremely fine fellow.

CAPT. Yes, your honour.

SIR JOSEPH So it seems that you were Ralph, and Ralph was you.

CAPT. So it seems, your honour.

SIR JOSEPH Well, I need not tell you that after this change in your condition, a marriage with your daughter will be out of the question.

CAPT. Don't say that, your honour—love levels all ranks.

SIR JOSEPH It does to a considerable extent, but it does not level them as much as that. [*Handing* JOSEPHINE *to* RALPH] Here—take her, sir, and mind you treat her kindly.

RALPH and JOS. Oh bliss, oh rapture!

CAPT. and BUT. Oh rapture, oh bliss!

SIR JOSEPH Sad my lot and sorry,
What shall I do? I cannot live alone!
HEBE Fear nothing—while I live I'll not desert you.
I'll soothe and comfort your declining days.
SIR JOSEPH No, don't do that.
HEBE Yes, but indeed I'd rather—
SIR JOSEPH [*resigned*] To-morrow morn our vows shall all be plighted,
Three loving pairs on the same day united!

Quartette

JOSEPHINE, HEBE, RALPH, and DEADEYE

Oh joy, oh rapture unforeseen,
The clouded sky is now serene,
The god of day—the orb of love,
Has hung his ensign high above,
The sky is all ablaze.

With wooing words and loving song,
We'll chase the lagging hours along,
And if {he finds / I find} the maiden coy,
We'll murmur forth decorous joy,
In dreamy roundelay.

CAPT. For he's the Captain of the *Pinafore*.
ALL And a right good captain too!
CAPT. And though before my fall
I was captain of you all,
I'm a member of the crew.
ALL Although before his fall, etc.
CAPT. I shall marry with a wife,
In my humble rank of life! [*turning to* BUT.]
And you, my own, are she—
I must wander to and fro;
But wherever I may go,
I shall never be untrue to thee!
ALL What, never?

CAPT. No, never!
ALL What, *never?*
CAPT. Hardly ever!
ALL Hardly ever be untrue to thee.
Then give three cheers, and one cheer more
For the former Captain of the *Pinafore.*

BUT. For he loves Little Buttercup, dear Little Buttercup,
Though I could never tell why;
But still he loves Buttercup, poor Little Buttercup,
Sweet Little Buttercup, aye!
ALL For he loves, etc.

SIR JOSEPH
I'm the monarch of the sea,
And when I've married thee [*to* HEBE],
I'll be true to the devotion that my love implants,
HEBE Then good-bye to his sisters, and his cousins, and his aunts,
Especially his cousins,
Whom he reckons up by dozens,
His sisters, and his cousins, and his aunts!

ALL For he is an Englishman,
And he himself hath said it,
And it's greatly to his credit
That he is an Englishman!

CURTAIN

THE PIRATES OF PENZANCE

OR

THE SLAVE OF DUTY

DRAMATIS PERSONÆ

MAJOR-GENERAL STANLEY

THE PIRATE KING

SAMUEL [*his Lieutenant*]

FREDERIC [*the Pirate Apprentice*]

SERGEANT OF POLICE

MABEL
EDITH
KATE
ISABEL } [*General Stanley's Daughters*]

RUTH [*a Pirate Maid of all Work*]

Chorus of Pirates, Police, and General Stanley's Daughters

ACT I

A ROCKY SEA-SHORE ON THE COAST OF CORNWALL

ACT II

A RUINED CHAPEL BY MOONLIGHT

First produced at the Opéra Comique on April 3, 1880

THE PIRATES OF PENZANCE

OR

THE SLAVE OF DUTY

ACT I

SCENE.—*A rocky sea-shore on the coast of Cornwall. In the distance is a calm sea, on which a schooner is lying at anchor. As the curtain rises groups of pirates are discovered—some drinking, some playing cards.* SAMUEL, *the Pirate Lieutenant, is going from one group to another, filling the cups from a flask.* FREDERIC *is seated in a despondent attitude at the back of the scene.*

Opening Chorus

Pour, oh, pour the pirate sherry;
  Fill, oh, fill the pirate glass;
And, to make us more than merry,
  Let the pirate bumper pass.

SAM. For to-day our pirate 'prentice
  Rises from indenture freed;
Strong his arm and keen his scent is,
  He's a pirate now indeed!

ALL Here's good luck to Frederic's ventures!
Frederic's out of his indentures.

SAM. Two-and-twenty now he's rising,
  And alone he's fit to fly,
Which we're bent on signalizing
  With unusual revelry.

ALL Here's good luck to Frederic's ventures!
Frederic's out of his indentures.
Pour, oh, pour the pirate sherry, etc.

FREDERIC *rises and comes forward with* PIRATE KING, *who enters*

KING Yes, Frederic, from to-day you rank as a full-blown member of our band.

ALL Hurrah.

FRED. My friends, I thank you all, from my heart, for your kindly wishes. Would that I could repay them as they deserve!

KING What do you mean?

FRED. To-day I am out of my indentures, and to-day I leave you for ever.

KING But this is quite unaccountable; a keener hand at scuttling a Cunarder or cutting out a P. & O. never shipped a handspike.

FRED. Yes, I have done my best for you. And why? It was my duty under my indentures, and I am the slave of duty. As a child I was regularly apprenticed to your band. It was through an error—no matter, the mistake was ours, not yours, and I was in honour bound by it.

SAM. An error? What error?

RUTH *enters*

FRED. I may not tell you; it would reflect upon my well-loved Ruth.

RUTH Nay, dear master, my mind has long been gnawed by the cankering tooth of mystery. Better have it out at once.

Song—RUTH

When Frederic was a little lad he proved so brave and daring,
His father thought he'd 'prentice him to some career seafaring.
I was, alas! his nurserymaid, and so it fell to *my* lot
To take and bind the promising boy apprentice to a *pilot*—
A life not bad for a hardy lad, though surely not a high lot,
Though I'm a nurse, you might do worse than make your boy a pilot.

I was a stupid nurserymaid, on breakers always steering,
And I did not catch the word aright, through being hard of hearing;
Mistaking my instructions, which within my brain did gyrate,
I took and bound this promising boy apprentice to a *pirate*.
A sad mistake it was to make and doom him to a vile lot.
I bound him to a pirate—you—instead of to a pilot.

I soon found out, beyond all doubt, the scope of this disaster,
But I hadn't the face to return to my place, and break it to my master.
A nurserymaid is not afraid of what you people *call* work,
So I made up my mind to go as a kind of piratical maid-of-all-work.
And that is how you find me now, a member of your shy lot,
Which you wouldn't have found, had he been bound apprentice to a pilot.

RUTH Oh, pardon! Frederic, pardon! [*Kneels*]

FRED. Rise, sweet one, I have long pardoned you.

RUTH [*rises*] The two words were so much alike!

FRED. They were. They still are, though years have rolled over their heads. But this afternoon my obligation ceases. Individually, I love you all with affection unspeakable, but, collectively, I look upon you with a disgust that amounts to absolute detestation. Oh! pity me, my beloved friends, for such is my sense of duty that, once out of my indentures, I shall feel myself bound to devote myself heart and soul to your extermination!

ALL Poor lad—poor lad! [*All weep*]

KING Well, Frederic, if you conscientiously feel that it is your duty to destroy us, we cannot blame you for acting on that conviction. Always act in accordance with the dictates of your conscience, my boy, and chance the consequences.

SAM. Besides, we can offer you but little temptation to remain with us. We don't seem to make piracy pay. I'm sure I don't know why, but we don't.

FRED. *I* know why, but, alas! I mustn't tell you; it wouldn't be right.

KING Why not, my boy? It's only half-past eleven, and you are one of us until the clock strikes twelve.

SAM. True, and until then you are bound to protect our interests.

ALL Hear, hear!

FRED. Well, then, it is my duty, as a pirate, to tell you that you are too tender-hearted. For instance, you make a point of never attacking a weaker party than yourselves, and when you attack a stronger party you invariably get thrashed.

KING There is some truth in that.

FRED. Then, again, you make a point of never molesting an orphan!

SAM. Of course: we are orphans ourselves, and know what it is.

FRED. Yes, but it has got about, and what is the consequence? Every one we capture says he's an orphan. The last three ships we took proved to be manned entirely by orphans, and so we had to let them go. One would think that Great Britain's mercantile navy was recruited solely from her orphan asylums—which we know is not the case.

SAM. But, hang it all! you wouldn't have us absolutely merciless?

FRED. There's my difficulty; until twelve o'clock I would, after twelve I wouldn't. Was ever a man placed in so delicate a situation.

RUTH And Ruth, your own Ruth, whom you love so well, and who has won her middle-aged way into your boyish heart, what is to become of *her?*

KING Oh, he will take you with him.

FRED. Well, Ruth, I feel some little difficulty about you. It is true that I admire you very much, but I have been constantly at sea since I was eight years old, and yours is the only woman's face I have seen during that time. I think it is a sweet face.

RUTH It is—oh, it is!

FRED. I say I *think* it is; that is my impression. But as I have never had an opportunity of comparing you with other women, it is just possible I may be mistaken.

KING True.

FRED. What a terrible thing it would be if I were to marry this innocent person, and then find out that she is, on the whole, plain!

KING Oh, Ruth, is very well, very well indeed.

SAM. Yes, there are the remains of a fine woman about Ruth.

FRED. Do you really think so?

SAM. I do.

FRED. Then I will not be so selfish as to take her from you. In justice to her, and in consideration for you, I will leave her behind. [*Hands* RUTH *to* KING]

KING No, Frederic, this must not be. We are rough men who lead a rough life, but we are not so utterly heartless as to deprive thee of thy love. I think I am right in saying that there is not one here who would rob thee of this inestimable treasure for all the world holds dear.

ALL [*loudly*] Not one!

KING No, I thought there wasn't. Keep thy love, Frederic, keep thy love. [*Hands her back to* FREDERIC]

FRED. You're very good, I'm sure. [*Exit* RUTH.

KING Well, it's the top of the tide, and we must be off. Farewell, Frederic. When your process of extermination begins, let our deaths be as swift and painless as you can conveniently make them.

FRED. I will! By the love I have for you, I swear it! Would that you could render this extermination unnecessary by accompanying me back to civilization!

KING No, Frederic, it cannot be. I don't think much of our profession, but, contrasted with respectability, it is comparatively honest. No, Frederic, I shall live and die a Pirate King.

Song—PIRATE KING

Oh better far to live and die
Under the brave black flag I fly,
Than play a sanctimonious part,
With a pirate head and a pirate heart.
Away to the cheating world go you,
Where pirates all are well-to-do;
But I'll be true to the song I sing,
And live and die a Pirate King.
For I am a Pirate King.

ALL You are!
Hurrah for our Pirate King!

KING And it is, it is a glorious thing
To be a Pirate King.

ALL Hurrah!
Hurrah for our Pirate King!

KING When I sally forth to seek my prey
I help myself in a royal way:
I sink a few more ships, it's true,
Than a well-bred monarch ought to do;
But many a king on a first-class throne,
If he wants to call his crown his own,

Must manage somehow to get through
More dirty work than ever *I* do,
Though I am a Pirate King.

ALL You are!
Hurrah for our Pirate King!

KING And it is, it is a glorious thing
To be a Pirate King!

ALL It is!
Hurrah for our Pirate King!

[*Exeunt all except* FREDERIC.

Enter RUTH

RUTH Oh, take me with you! I cannot live if I am left behind.

FRED. Ruth, I will be quite candid with you. You are very dear to me, as you know, but I must be circumspect. You see, you are considerably older than I. A lad of twenty-one usually looks for a wife of seventeen.

RUTH A wife of seventeen! You will find me a wife of a thousand!

FRED. No, but I shall find you a wife of forty-seven, and that is quite enough. Ruth, tell me candidly, and without reserve: compared with other women—how are *you?*

RUTH I will answer you truthfully. master—I have a slight cold, but otherwise I am quite well.

FRED. I am sorry for your cold, but I was referring rather to your personal appearance. Compared with other women, are you beautiful?

RUTH [*bashfully*] I have been told so, dear master.

FRED. Ah, but lately?

RUTH Oh, no, years and years ago.

FRED. What do you think of yourself?

RUTH It is a delicate question to answer, but I think I am a fine woman.

FRED. That is your candid opinion?

RUTH Yes, I should be deceiving you if I told you otherwise.

FRED. Thank you, Ruth, I believe you, for I am sure you would not practise on my inexperience; I wish to do the right thing, and if—I say *if*—you are really a fine woman, your age shall be no obstacle to our union! [*Chorus of Girls heard in the distance*] Hark! Surely I hear voices! Who has ventured to approach our all but inaccessible lair? Can it be Custom House? No, it does not sound like Custom House.

RUTH [*aside*] Confusion! it is the voices of young girls! If he should see them I am lost.

FRED. [*looking off*] By all that's marvellous, a bevy of beautiful maidens!

RUTH [*aside*] Lost! lost! lost!

FRED. How lovely! how surpassingly lovely is the plainest of them! What grace—what delicacy—what refinement! And Ruth—Ruth told me she was beautiful!

Recitative

FRED. Oh, false one, you have deceived me!
RUTH I have deceived you?
FRED. Yes, deceived me!
[*Denouncing her*

Duet—FRED. and RUTH

FRED. You told me you were fair as gold!
RUTH [*wildly*] And, master, am I not so?
FRED. And now I see you're plain and old.
RUTH I am sure I am not a jot so.
FRED. Upon my innocence you play.
RUTH I'm not the one to plot so.
FRED. Your face is lined, your hair is grey.
RUTH It's gradually got so.
FRED. Faithless woman, to deceive me,
I who trusted so!
RUTH Master, master, do not leave me!
Hear me, ere you go!
My love without reflecting,
Oh, do not be rejecting.
Take a maiden tender—her affection raw and green,
At very highest rating,
Has been accumulating
Summers seventeen—summers seventeen.
Don't, beloved master,
Crush me with disaster.
What is such a dower to the dower I have here?
My love unabating
Has been accumulating
Forty-seven year—forty-seven year!

Ensemble

RUTH

Don't, beloved master,
Crush me with disaster.
What is such a dower to the dower
I have here?
My love unabating
Has been accumulating
Forty-seven year—forty-seven year!

FRED

Yes, your former master
Saves you from disaster.
Your love would be uncomfortably
fervid, it is clear,
If, as you are stating,
It's been accumulating
Forty-seven year—forty-seven year!

[*At the end he renounces her, and she goes off in despair.*

Recitative—FRED.

What shall I do? Before these gentle maidens
I dare not show in this alarming costume.

No, no, I must remain in close concealment
Until I can appear in decent clothing!

[*Hides in cave as they enter climbing over the rocks*]

GIRLS Climbing over rocky mountain,
Skipping rivulet and fountain,
Passing where the willows quiver
By the ever-rolling river,
Swollen with the summer rain;
Threading long and leafy mazes
Dotted with unnumbered daisies;
Scaling rough and rugged passes,
Climb the hardy little lasses,
Till the bright sea-shore they gain!

EDITH Let us gaily tread the measure,
Make the most of fleeting leisure;
Hail it as a true ally,
Though it perish by and by.

ALL Hail it as a true ally,
Though it perish by and by.

EDITH Every moment brings a treasure
Of its own especial pleasure,
Though the moments quickly die,
Greet them gaily as they fly.

KATE Far away from toil and care,
Revelling in fresh sea air,
Here we live and reign alone
In a world that's all our own.
Here in this our rocky den,
Far away from mortal men,
We'll be queens, and make decrees—
They may honour them who please.

ALL Let us gaily tread the measure, etc.

KATE What a picturesque spot! I wonder where we are!

EDITH And I wonder where papa is. We have left him ever so far behind.

ISABEL Oh, he will be here presently! Remember poor papa is not as young as we are, and we have come over a rather difficult country.

KATE But how thoroughly delightful it is to be so entirely alone! Why, in all probability we are the first human beings who ever set foot on this enchanting spot.

ISABEL Except the mermaids—it's the very place for mermaids.

KATE Who are only human beings down to the waist!

EDITH And who can't be said strictly to set *foot* anywhere. Tails they may, but feet they *cannot.*

KATE But what shall we do until papa and the servants arrive with the luncheon?

EDITH We are quite alone, and the sea is as smooth as glass. Suppose we take off our shoes and stockings and paddle?

ALL Yes, Yes! The very thing! [*They prepare to carry out the suggestion. They have all taken off one shoe, when* FREDERIC *comes forward from cave*]

FRED. [*recitative*] Stop, ladies, pray!
ALL [*hopping on one foot*] A man!
FRED. I had intended
Not to intrude myself upon your notice
In this effective but alarming costume,
But under these peculiar circumstances
It is my bounden duty to inform you
That your proceedings will not be unwitnessed!
EDITH But who are you, sir? Speak! [*All hopping*]
FRED. I am a pirate!
ALL [*recoiling, hopping*] A pirate! Horror!
FRED. Ladies, do not shun me!
This evening I renounce my wild profession;
And to that end, oh, pure and peerless maidens!
Oh, blushing buds of ever-blooming beauty!
I, sore at heart, implore your kind assistance.
EDITH How pitiful his tale!
KATE How rare his beauty!
ALL How pitiful his tale! How rare his beauty!

Song—FRED.

Oh, is there not one maiden breast
Which does not feel the moral beauty
Of making worldly interest
Subordinate to sense of duty?
Who would not give up willingly
All matrimonial ambition,
To rescue such a one as I
From his unfortunate position?

ALL Alas! there's not one maiden breast
Which seems to feel the moral beauty
Of making worldly interest
Subordinate to sense of duty!

FRED. Oh, is there not one maiden here
  Whose homely face and bad complexion
Have caused all hopes to disappear
  Of ever winning man's affection?
To such a one, if such there be,
  I swear by Heaven's arch above you,
If you will cast your eyes on me–
  However plain you be–I'll love you!

ALL Alas! there's not one maiden here
  Whose homely face and bad complexion
Have caused all hope to disappear
  Of ever winning man's affection!

FRED. [*in despair*] Not one?
ALL No, no–not one!
FRED. Not one?
ALL No, no!

MABEL *enters*

MABEL Yes, one!
ALL 'Tis Mabel!
MABEL Yes, 'tis Mabel!

Recitative–MABEL

Oh, sisters, deaf to pity's name,
  For shame!
It's true that he has gone astray,
  But pray
Is that a reason good and true
  Why you
Should all be deaf to pity's name?

ALL [*aside*] The question is, had he not been
  A thing of beauty,
Would she be swayed by quite as keen
  A sense of duty?

MABEL For shame, for shame, for shame!

Song–MABEL

Poor wandering one!
Though thou has surely strayed,
  Take heart of grace,
  Thy steps retrace,
Poor wandering one!

Poor wandering one!
If such poor love as mine
  Can help thee find
  True peace of mind–
Why, take it, it is thine!
  Take heart, fair days will shine;
  Take any heart–take mine!

ALL — Take heart; no danger lowers;
  Take any heart–but ours!

[*Exeunt* MABEL *and* FREDERIC.

[EDITH *beckons her sisters, who form in a semicircle around her.*]

EDITH

What ought we to do,
  Gentle sisters, say?
Propriety, we know,
  Says we ought to stay;
While sympathy exclaims,
  "Free them from your tether–
Play at other games–
  Leave them here together."

KATE

Her case may, any day,
  Be yours, my dear, or mine.
Let her make her hay
  While the sun doth shine.
Let us compromise,
  (Our hearts are not of leather.)
Let us shut our eyes,
  And talk about the weather.

GIRLS — Yes, yes, let's talk about the weather.

Chattering chorus

How beautifully blue the sky,
The glass is rising very high,
Continue fine I hope it may,
And yet it rained but yesterday.
To-morrow it may pour again
(I hear the country wants some rain),
Yet people say, I know not why,
That we shall have a warm July.

Enter MABEL *and* FREDERIC

[*During* MABEL'S *solo the* GIRLS *continue chatter pianissimo, but listening eagerly all the time.*

Solo—MABEL

Did ever maiden wake
  From dream of homely duty,
To find her daylight break
  With such exceeding beauty?
Did ever maiden close
  Her eyes on waking sadness,
To dream of such exceeding gladness?

FRED. Oh, yes! ah, yes! this is exceeding gladness.
GIRLS How beautifully blue the sky, etc.

Solo—FRED.

[*During this,* GIRLS *continue their chatter pianissimo as before, but listening intently all the time.*

Did ever pirate roll
  His soul in guilty dreaming,
And wake to find that soul
  With peace and virtue beaming?

Ensemble

MABEL	FRED	GIRLS
Did ever maiden wake, etc.	Did ever pirate roll, etc.	How beautifully blue the sky, etc.

Recitative—FRED.

Stay, we must not lose our senses;
  Men who stick at no offences
    Will anon be here.
Piracy their dreadful trade is
  Pray you, get you hence, young ladies,
    While the coast is clear.

[FREDERIC *and* MABEL *retire.*

GIRLS No, we must not lose our senses,
If they stick at no offences
    We should not be here.
Piracy their dreadful trade is—
Nice companions for the young ladies!
    Let us disappear.

[*During this chorus the* PIRATES *have entered stealthily, and formed in a semicircle behind the* GIRLS. *As the* GIRLS *move to go off each* PIRATE *seizes a girl.* KING *seizes* EDITH *and* ISABEL, SAMUEL *seizes* KATE.

ALL Too late!
PIRATES Ha! Ha!
ALL Too late!
PIRATES Ha! Ha!
Ha! ha! ha! ha! Ha! ha! ha! ha!

Ensemble

[*Pirates pass in front of Girls*]

PIRATES

Here's a first-rate opportunity
To get married with impunity,
And indulge in the felicity
Of unbounded domesticity.
You shall quickly be parsonified,
Conjugally matrimonified,
By a doctor of divinity,
Who resides in this vicinity.

[*Girls pass in front of Pirates*]

GIRLS

We have missed our opportunity
Of escaping with impunity;
So farewell to the felicity
Of our maiden domesticity!
We shall quickly be parsonified,
Conjugally matrimonified,
By a doctor of divinity,
Who resides in this vicinity.

MABEL [*coming forward*]

Recitative

Hold, monsters! Ere your pirate caravanserai
Proceed, against our will, to wed us all,
Just bear in mind that we are Wards in Chancery,
And father is a Major-General!

SAM. [*cowed*] We'd better pause, or danger may befall,
Their father is a Major-General.

GIRLS Yes, yes; he is a Major-General!

The MAJOR-GENERAL *has entered unnoticed, on rock*

GEN. Yes, I am a Major-General!
SAM. For he is a Major-General!
ALL He is! Hurrah for the Major-General!
GEN. And it is—it is a glorious thing
To be a Major-General!
ALL It is! Hurrah for the Major-General!

Song—MAJOR-GENERAL

I am the very model of a modern Major-General,
I've information vegetable, animal, and mineral,
I know the kings of England, and I quote the fights
historical,

From Marathon to Waterloo, in order categorical;
I'm very well acquainted too with matters mathematical,
I understand equations, both the simple and quadratical,
About binomial theorem I'm teeming with a lot o' news—
With many cheerful facts about the square of the hypotenuse.

ALL With many cheerful facts, etc.

GEN. I'm very good at integral and differential calculus,
I know the scientific names of beings animalculous;
In short, in matters vegetable, animal, and mineral,
I am the very model of a modern Major-General.

ALL In short, in matters vegetable, animal, and mineral,
He is the very model of a modern Major-General.

GEN. I know our mythic history, King Arthur's and Sir Caradoc's,
I answer hard acrostics, I've a pretty taste for paradox,
I quote in elegiacs all the crimes of Heliogabalus,
In conics I can floor peculiarities parabolous.
I can tell undoubted Raphaels from Gerard Dows and Zoffanies,

I know the croaking chorus from the *Frogs* of
Aristophanes,
Then I can hum a fugue of which I've heard the
music's din afore,
And whistle all the airs from that infernal non-
sense *Pinafore*.

ALL And whistle all the airs, etc.

GEN. Then I can write a washing bill in Babylonic cunei-
form,
And tell you every detail of Caractacus's uniform;
In short, in matters vegetable, animal, and mineral,
I am the very model of a modern Major-General.

ALL In short, in matters vegetable, animal, and mineral,
He is the very model of a modern Major-General.

GEN. In fact, when I know what is meant by "mamelon"
and "ravelin,"
When I can tell at sight a chassepôt rifle from a
javelin,
When such affairs as sorties and surprises I'm more
wary at,
And when I know precisely what is meant by
"commissariat",
When I have learnt what progress has been made
in modern gunnery,
When I know more of tactics than a novice in a
nunnery:
In short, when I've a smattering of elemental
strategy,
You'll say a better Major-Gener*al* has never *sat* a
gee—

ALL You'll say a better, etc.

GEN. For my military knowledge, though I'm plucky
and adventury,
Has only been brought down to the beginning of
the century;
But still in matters vegetable, animal, and mineral,
I am the very model of a modern Major-General.

ALL But still in matters vegetable, animal, and mineral,
He is the very model of a modern Major-General.

GEN. And now that I've introduced myself I should like to have some idea of what's going on.

KATE Oh, papa—we——

SAM. Permit me, I'll explain in two words: we propose to marry your daughters.

GEN. Dear me!

GIRLS Against our wills, papa—against our wills!

GEN. Oh, but you mustn't do that! May I ask—this is a picturesque uniform, but I'm not familiar with it. What are you?

KING We are all single gentlemen.

GEN. Yes, I gathered that—anything else?

KING No, nothing else.

EDITH Papa, don't believe them; they are pirates—the famous Pirates of Penzance!

GEN. The Pirates of Penzance! I have often heard of them.

MABEL All except this gentleman—[*indicating* FREDERIC]—who was a pirate once, but who is out of his indentures to-day, and who means to lead a blameless life evermore.

GEN. But wait a bit. I object to pirates as sons-in-law.

KING We object to Major-Generals as fathers-in-law. But we waive that point. We do not press it. We look over it.

GEN. [*aside*] Hah! an idea! [*Aloud*] And do you mean to say that you would deliberately rob me of these, the sole remaining props of my old age, and leave me to go through the remainder of my life unfriended, unprotected, and alone?

KING Well, yes, that's the idea.

GEN. Tell me, have you ever known what it is to be an orphan?

PIRATES [*disgusted*] Oh, dash it all!

KING Here we are again!

GEN. I ask you, have you ever known what it is to be an orphan?

KING Often!

GEN. Yes, orphan. Have you ever known what it is to be one?

KING I say, often.

ALL [*disgusted*] Often, often, often. [*Turning away*]

GEN. I don't think we quite understand one another. I ask you, have you ever known what it is to be an orphan, and you say "orphan". As I understand you, you are merely repeating the word "orphan" to show that you understand me.

KING I didn't repeat the word often.

GEN. Pardon me, you did indeed.

KING I only repeated it once.

GEN. True, but you repeated it.

KING But not often.

GEN. Stop: I think I see where we are getting confused. When you said "orphan", did you mean "orphan"—a person who has lost his parents, or "often"—frequently?

KING Ah! I beg pardon—I see what you mean—frequently.

GEN. Ah! you said often—frequently.

KING No, only once.
GEN. [*irritated*] Exactly—you said often, frequently, only once.

Recitative—GENERAL

Oh, men of dark and dismal fate,
Forgo your cruel employ,
Have pity on my lonely state,
I am an orphan boy!
KING and SAM. An orphan boy?
GEN. An orphan boy!
PIRATES How sad—an orphan boy.

Solo—GENERAL

These children whom you see
Are all that I can call my own!
PIRATES Poor fellow!
GEN. Take them away from me
And I shall be indeed alone.
PIRATES Poor fellow!
GEN. If pity you can feel,
Leave me my sole remaining joy—
See, at your feet they kneel;
Your hearts you cannot steel
Against the sad, sad tale of the lonely orphan boy!
PIRATES [*sobbing*] Poor fellow!
See at our feet they kneel;
Our hearts we cannot steel
Against the sad, sad tale of the lonely orphan boy!
KING The orphan boy!
SAM. The orphan boy!
ALL The lonely orphan boy! Poor fellow!

Ensemble

GENERAL [*aside*]

I'm telling a terrible story
But it doesn't diminish my glory;
For they would have taken my daughters
Over the billowy waters,
If I hadn't, in elegant diction,
Indulged in an innocent fiction;
Which is not in the same categ*ory*
As a regular terrible story.

GIRLS [*aside*]

He's telling a terrible story,
Which will tend to diminish his glory;
Though they would have taken his daughters
Over the billowy waters.
It's easy, in elegant diction,
To call it an innocent fiction,
But it comes in the same categ*ory*
As a regular terrible story.

PIRATES [*aside*]

If he's telling a terrible story,
He shall die by a death that is gory,
One of the cruellest slaughters
That ever were known in these waters;
And we'll finish his moral affliction
By a very complete malediction,
As a compliment valedict*ory,*
If he's telling a terrible story.

KING Although our dark career
Sometimes involves the crime of stealing,

We rather think that we're
  Not altogether void of feeling.
Although we live by strife,
  We're always sorry to begin it,
For what, we ask, is life
  Without a touch of Poetry in it?

ALL [*kneeling*] Hail, Poetry, thou heaven-born maid!
Thou gildest e'en the pirate's trade:
Hail, flowing fount of sentiment!
All hail, Divine Emollient! [*All rise*]

KING You may go, for you're at liberty, our pirate rules protect you,
And honorary members of our band we do elect you!

SAM. For he is an orphan boy.
CHORUS He is! Hurrah for the orphan boy.
GEN. And it sometimes is a useful thing
  To be an orphan boy.
CHORUS It is! Hurrah for the orphan boy!

Oh, happy day, with joyous glee
They will away and married be;
Should it befall auspiciously,
Our sisters all will bridesmaids be!

RUTH *enters and comes down to* FREDERIC

RUTH Oh, master, hear one word, I do implore you!
Remember Ruth, your Ruth, who kneels before you!
CHORUS Yes, yes, remember Ruth, who kneels before you!
FRED. [PIRATES *threaten* RUTH] Away, you did deceive me!
CHORUS Away, you did deceive him!

RUTH Oh, do not leave me!
CHORUS Oh, do not leave her!

FRED. Away, you grieve me!
CHORUS Away, you grieve him!
FRED. I wish you'd leave me!

[FREDERIC *casts* RUTH *from him*]

CHORUS We wish you'd leave him!

Ensemble

Pray observe the magnanimity
We / They display to lace and dimity!

Never was such opportunity
To get married with impunity,
But {we / they} give up the felicity
Of unbounded domesticity,
Though a doctor of divinity
Resides in this vicinity.

[GIRLS *and* GENERAL *go up rocks, while* PIRATES *indulge in a wild dance of delight on stage. The* GENERAL *produces a British flag, and the* PIRATE KING *produces a black flag with skull and cross-bones. Enter* RUTH, *who makes a final appeal to* FREDERIC, *who casts her from him.*

END OF ACT I

ACT II

SCENE.—*A Ruined Chapel by Moonlight. Ruined Gothic windows at back.* GENERAL STANLEY *discovered seated pensively, surrounded by his daughters.*

Chorus

Oh, dry the glistening tear
  That dews that martial cheek;
Thy loving children hear,
  In them thy comfort seek.
With sympathetic care
  Their arms around thee creep,
For oh, they cannot bear
  To see their father weep!

Enter MABEL

Solo—MABEL

Dear father, why leave your bed
  At this untimely hour,
When happy daylight is dead,
  And darksome dangers lower?
See heaven has lit her lamp,
  The midnight hour is past,
The chilly night air is damp,
  And the dews are falling fast!
Dear father, why leave your bed
When happy daylight is dead?

FREDERIC *enters*

MABEL Oh, Frederic, cannot you, in the calm excellence of your wisdom, reconcile it with your conscience to say something that will relieve my father's sorrow?

FRED. I will try, dear Mabel. But why does he sit, night after night, in this draughty old ruin?

GEN. Why do I sit here? To escape from the pirates' clutches, I described myself as an orphan, and, heaven help me, I am no orphan! I come here to humble myself before the tombs of my ancestors, and to implore their pardon for having brought dishonour on the family escutcheon.

FRED. But you forget, sir, you only bought the property a year ago, and the stucco in your baronial hall is scarcely dry.

GEN. Frederic, in this chapel are ancestors: you cannot deny that. With the estate, I bought the chapel and its contents. I don't know whose ancestors they *were*, but I know whose ancestors they *are*, and I shudder to think that their descendant by purchase (if I may so describe myself) should have brought disgrace upon what, I have no doubt, was an unstained escutcheon.

FRED. Be comforted. Had you not acted as you did, these reckless men would assuredly have called in the nearest clergyman, and have married your large family on the spot.

GEN. I thank you for your proffered solace, but it is unavailing. I assure you, Frederic, that such is the anguish and remorse I feel at the abominable falsehood by which I escaped these easily deluded pirates, that I would go to their simple-minded chief this very night and confess all, did I not fear that the consequences would be most disastrous to myself. At what time does your expedition march against these scoundrels?

FRED. At eleven, and before midnight I hope to have atoned for my involuntary association with the pestilent scourges by sweeping them from the face of the earth—and then, dear Mabel, you will be mine!

GEN. Are your devoted followers at hand?

FRED. They are, they only wait my orders.

Recitative—GENERAL

Then, Frederic, let your escort lion-hearted
Be summoned to receive a General's blessing,
Ere they depart upon their dread adventure.

FRED. Dear sir, they come.

Enter POLICE, *marching in single file. They form in line, facing audience.*

Song—SERGEANT

When the foeman bares his steel,
Tarantara! tarantara!

We uncomfortable feel,
Tarantara!
And we find the wisest thing,
Tarantara! tarantara!
Is to slap our chests and sing
Tarantara!
For when threatened with emeutes,
Tarantara! tarantara!
And your heart is in your boots,
Tarantara!
There is nothing brings it round,
Tarantara! tarantara!
Like the trumpet's martial sound,
Tarantara! tarantara!
Tarantara-ra-ra-ra-ra!

ALL Tarantara-ra-ra-ra-ra!

MABEL Go, ye heroes, go to glory,
Though you die in combat gory,
Ye shall live in song and story.
Go to immortality!
Go to death, and go to slaughter;
Die, and every Cornish daughter
With her tears your grave shall water.
Go, ye heroes, go and die!

ALL Go, ye heroes, go and die!

POLICE Though to us it's evident,
Tarantara! tarantara!
These intentions are well meant,
Tarantara!
Such expressions don't appear,
Tarantara! tarantara!
Calculated men to cheer,
Tarantara!
Who are going to meet their fate
In a highly nervous state,
Tarantara!
Still to us it's evident
These intentions are well meant.
Tarantara!

EDITH Go and do your best endeavour,
And before all links we sever,
We will say farewell for ever.
Go to glory and the grave!

GIRLS For your foes are fierce and ruthless,
False, unmerciful, and truthless.
Young and tender, old and toothless,
All in vain their mercy crave.

SERG. We observe too great a stress,
On the risks that on us press,
And of reference a lack
To our chance of coming back.
Still, perhaps it would be wise
Not to carp or criticise,
For it's very evident
These attentions are well meant.

ALL Yes, to them it's evident
Our attentions are well meant.
Tarantara-ra-ra-ra-ra!

Go, ye heroes, go to glory, etc.

Ensemble

Chorus of all but Police

Go and do your best endeavour,
And before all links we sever
We will say farewell for ever.
Go to glory and the grave!
For your foes are fierce and ruthless,
False, unmerciful, and truthless.
Young and tender, old and toothless,
All in vain their mercy crave.

Chorus of Police

Such expressions don't appear,
Tarantara, tarantara!
Calculated men to cheer,
Tarantara!
Who are going to their fate,
Tarantara, tarantara!
In a highly nervous state—
Tarantara!
We observe too great a stress,
Tarantara, tarantara!
On the risks that on us press,
Tarantara!
And of reference a lack,
Tarantara, tarantara!
To our chance of coming back,
Tarantara!

GEN. Away, away!
POLICE [*without moving*] Yes, yes, we go.
GEN. These pirates slay.
POLICE Tarantara!
GEN. Then do not stay.
POLICE Tarantara!
GEN. Then why this delay?
POLICE All right—we go.
Yes, forward on the foe!
GEN.. Yes, but you *don't* go!
POLICE We go, we go!
Yes, forward on the foe!
GEN. Yes, but you *don't* go!
ALL At last they really go.

[MABEL *tears herself from* FREDERIC *and exits, followed by her sisters, consoling her. The* GENERAL *and others follow.* FREDERIC *remains.*

Recitative—FRED.

Now for the pirates' lair! Oh, joy unbounded!
Oh, sweet relief! Oh, rapture unexampled!
At last I may atone, in some slight measure,
For the repeated acts of theft and pillage
Which, at a sense of duty's stern dictation,
I, circumstance's victim, have been guilty.

[KING *and* RUTH *appear at the window, armed*]

KING Young Frederic! [*Covering him with pistol*]
FRED. Who calls?
KING Your late commander!
RUTH And I, your little Ruth! [*Covering him with pistol*]
FRED. Oh, mad intruders,
How dare ye face me? Know ye not, oh rash ones,
That I have doomed you to extermination?

[KING *and* RUTH *hold a pistol to each ear*]

KING Have mercy on us, hear us, ere you slaughter.
FRED. I do not think I ought to listen to you.
Yet, mercy should alloy our stern resentment,
And so I will be merciful—say on!

Trio—RUTH, KING, and FRED.

RUTH When you had left our pirate fold
We tried to raise our spirits faint,
According to our customs old,
With quips and quibbles quaint.
But all in vain the quips we heard,
We lay and sobbed upon the rocks,
Until to somebody occurred
A startling paradox.
FRED. A paradox?
KING [*laughing*] A paradox!
RUTH A most ingenious paradox!
We've quips and quibbles heard in flocks,
But none to beat this paradox!
Ha! ha! ha! ha! Ho! ho! ho! ho!
KING We knew your taste for curious quips,
For cranks and contradictions queer,

And with the laughter on our lips,
  We wished you there to hear.
We said, "If we could tell it him,
  How Frederic would the joke enjoy!"
And so we've risked both life and limb
  To tell it to our boy.

FRED. [*interested*] That paradox? That paradox?

KING and RUTH [*laughing*] That most ingenious paradox!

We've quips and quibbles heard in flocks,
But none to beat that paradox!
  Ha! ha! ha! ha! Ho! ho! ho! ho!

Chant—KING

For some ridiculous reason, to which, however, I've no desire to be disloyal,
Some person in authority, I don't know who, very likely the Astronomer Royal,
Has decided that, although for such a beastly month as February, twenty-eight days as a rule are plenty.
One year in every four his days shall be reckoned as nine-and-twenty.
Through some singular coincidence—I shouldn't be surprised if it were owing to the agency of an ill-natured fairy—
You are the victim of this clumsy arrangement, having been born in leap-year, on the twenty-ninth of February,
And so, by a simple arithmetical process, you'll easily discover,
That though you've lived twenty-one years, yet, if we go by birthdays, you're only five and a little bit over!

RUTH Ha! ha! ha! ha!
KING Ho! ho! ho! ho!
FRED. Dear me!
Let's see! [*counting on fingers*]
Yes, yes; with yours my figures do agree!

ALL Ha! ha! ha! Ho! ho! ho! ho! [FREDERIC *more amused than any*]

FRED. How quaint the ways of Paradox!
At common sense she gaily mocks!
Though counting in the usual way,
  Years twenty-one I've been alive,
Yet, reckoning by my natal day,
  I am a little boy of five!

He is a little boy of five! Ha! ha!
A paradox, a paradox,

A most ingenious paradox!
Ha! ha! ha! ha! Ho! ho! ho! ho! [Ruth *and* King *throw themselves back on seats, exhausted with laughter*]

Fred. Upon my word, this is most curious—most absurdly whimsical. Five-and-a-quarter! No one would think it to look at me!

Ruth. You are glad now, I'll be bound, that you spared us. You would never have forgiven yourself when you discovered that you had killed *two of your comrades.*

Fred. My comrades?

King [*rises*] I'm afraid you don't appreciate the delicacy of your position. You were apprenticed to us——

Fred. Until I reached my twenty-first year.

King No, until you reached your twenty-first *birthday* [*producing document*], and, going by birthdays, you are as yet only five-and-a-quarter.

Fred. You don't mean to say you are going to hold me to that?

King No, we merely remind you of the fact, and leave the rest to your sense of duty.

Ruth Your sense of duty!

Fred. [*wildly*] Don't put it on that footing! As I was merciful to you just now, be merciful to me! I implore you not to insist on the letter of your bond just as the cup of happiness is at my lips!

Ruth We insist on nothing; we content ourselves with pointing out to you *your duty.*

King Your duty!

Fred [*after a pause*] Well, you have appealed to my sense of duty, and my duty is only too clear. I abhor your infamous calling; I shudder at the thought that I have ever been mixed up with it; but duty is before all—at any price I will do my duty.

King Bravely spoken! Come, you are one of us once more.

Fred. Lead on, I follow. [*Suddenly*] Oh, horror!

King }
Ruth } What is the matter?

Fred. Ought I to tell you? No, no, I cannot do it; and yet, as one of your band——

King Speak out, I charge you by that sense of conscientiousness to which we have never yet appealed in vain.

Fred. General Stanley, the father of my Mabel——

King }
Ruth } Yes, yes!

Fred. He escaped from you on the plea that he was an orphan!

King He did!

Fred. It breaks my heart to betray the honoured father of the girl I adore, but as your apprentice I have no alternative. It is my duty to tell you that General Stanley is no orphan!

KING } What!
RUTH }

FRED. More than that, he never was one!

KING Am I to understand that, to save his contemptible life, he dared to practise on our credulous simplicity? [FREDERIC *nods as he weeps*] Our revenge shall be swift and terrible. We will go and collect our band and attack Tremorden Castle this very night.

FRED. But—stay——

KING Not a word! He is doomed!

Trio

KING and RUTH	FRED
Away, away! my heart's on fire, I burn this base deception to repay, This very night my vengeance dire Shall glut itself in gore. Away, away!	Away, away! ere I expire— I find my duty hard to do to-day! My heart is filled with anguish dire, It strikes me to the core. Away, away!

KING With falsehood foul
He tricked us of our brides.
Let vengeance howl;
The Pirate so decides.
Our nature stern
He softened with his lies,
And, in return,
To-night the traitor dies.

ALL Yes, yes! to-night the traitor dies.

RUTH To-night he dies!
KING Yes, or early to-morrow.
FRED. His girls likewise?
RUTH They will welter in sorrow.
KING The one soft spot
FRED. In their natures they cherish—
RUTH And all who plot
KING To abuse it shall perish!
ALL Yes, all who plot
To abuse it shall perish!
Away, away! etc.

[*Exeunt* KING *and* RUTH.

Enter MABEL

Recitative—MABEL

All is prepared, your gallant crew await you.
My Frederic in tears? It cannot be
That lion-heart quails at the coming conflict?

FRED. No, Mabel, no. A terrible disclosure
Has just been made! Mabel, my dearly-loved one,
I bound myself to serve the pirate captain
Until I reached my one-and-twentieth birthday—

MABEL But you *are* twenty-one?

FRED. I've just discovered
That I was born in leap-year, and that birthday
Will not be reached by me till 1940.

MABEL Oh, horrible! catastrophe appalling!

FRED. And so, farewell!

MABEL No, no! Ah, Frederic, hear me.

Duet—MABEL and FRED

MABEL
Stay, Frederic, stay!
They have no legal claim,
No shadow of a shame
Will fall upon thy name.
Stay, Frederic, stay!

FRED.
Nay, Mabel, nay!
To-night I quit these walls,
The thought my soul appals,
But when stern Duty calls,
I must obey.

MABEL Stay, Frederic, stay!
FRED. Nay, Mabel, nay!
MABEL They have no claim—
FRED. But Duty's name!
The thought my soul appals,
But when stern Duty calls,
I must obey.

Ballad—MABEL

Ah, leave me not to pine
Alone and desolate;
No fate seemed fair as mine,
No happiness so great!
And nature, day by day,
Has sung, in accents clear,
This joyous roundelay,
"He loves thee—he is here.
Fa-la, fa-la, fa-la."

FRED.
Ah, must I leave thee here
In endless night to dream,

Where joy is dark and drear,
And sorrow all supreme!
Where nature, day by day,
Will sing, in altered tone,
This weary roundelay,
"He loves thee—he is gone.
Fa-la, fa-la, fa-la."

FRED. In 1940 I of age shall be,
I'll then return, and claim you—I declare it!
MABEL It seems so long!
FRED. Swear that, till then, you will be true to me.
MABEL Yes, I'll be strong!
By all the Stanleys dead and gone, I swear it!

Ensemble

Oh, here is love, and here is truth,
And here is food for joyous laughter.
{He / She} will be faithful to {his / her} sooth
Till we are wed, and even after.

[FREDERIC *rushes to window and leaps out.*

MABEL [*almost fainting*] No, I am brave! Oh, family descent,
How great thy charm, thy sway how excellent!
Come, one and all, undaunted men in blue,
A crisis, now, affairs are coming to!

Enter Police, marching in single file

SERG. Though in body and in mind,
Tarantara, tarantara!
We are timidly inclined,
Tarantara!
And anything but blind,
Tarantara, tarantara!
To the danger that's behind,
Tarantara!
Yet, when the danger's near,
Tarantara, tarantara!
We manage to appear,
Tarantara!
As insensible to fear
As anybody here.
Tarantara, tarantara-ra-ra-ra-ra!

MABEL Sergeant, approach! Young Frederic was to have led you to death and glory.

ALL That is not a pleasant way of putting it.

MABEL No matter; he will not so lead you, for he has allied himself once more with his old associates.

ALL He has acted shamefully!

MABEL You speak falsely. You know nothing about it. He has acted nobly.

ALL He has acted nobly!

MABEL Dearly as I loved him before, his heroic sacrifice to his sense of duty has endeared him to me tenfold. He has done his duty. I will do mine. Go ye and do yours. [*Exit* MABEL.

ALL Right oh!

SERG. This is perplexing.

ALL We cannot understand it at all.

SERG. Still, as he is actuated by a sense of duty—

ALL That makes a difference, of course. At the same time we repeat, we cannot understand it at all.

SERG. No matter; our course is clear. We must do our best to capture these pirates alone. It is most distressing to us to be the agents whereby our erring fellow-creatures are deprived of that liberty which is so dear to all —but we should have thought of that before we joined the Force.

ALL We should!

SERG. It is too late now!

ALL It is!

Song—SERGEANT

SERG. When a felon's not engaged in his employment—
ALL His employment,
SERG. Or maturing his felonious little plans—
ALL Little plans,
SERG. His capacity for innocent enjoyment—
ALL 'Cent enjoyment
SERG. Is just as great as any honest man's—

ALL — Honest man's.
SERG. — Our feelings we with difficulty smother—
ALL — 'Culty smother
SERG. — When constabulary duty's to be done—
ALL — To be done.
SERG. — Ah, take one consideration with another—
ALL — With another,
SERG. — A policeman's lot is not a happy one.
ALL — When constabulary duty's to be done—
To be done,
The policeman's lot is not a happy one.

SERG. — When the enterprising burglar's not a-burgling—
ALL — Not a-burgling,
SERG. — When the cut-throat isn't occupied in crime—
ALL — 'Pied in crime,
SERG. — He loves to hear the little brook a-gurgling—
ALL — Brook a-gurgling,
SERG. — And listen to the merry village chime—
ALL — Village chime.
SERG. — When the coster's finished jumping on his mother—
ALL — On his mother,
SERG. — He loves to lie a-basking in the sun—
ALL — In the sun.
SERG. — Ah, take one consideration with another—
ALL — With another,
SERG. — The policeman's lot is not a happy one.
ALL — When constabulary duty's to be done—
To be done,
The policeman's lot is not a happy one—
Happy one.

[*Chorus of Pirates without, in the distance*]

A rollicking band of pirates we,
Who, tired of tossing on the sea,
Are trying their hand at a burglaree,
With weapons grim and gory.

SERG. — Hush, hush! I hear them on the manor poaching,
With stealthy step the pirates are approaching.

[*Chorus of Pirates, resumed nearer*]

We are not coming for plate or gold—
A story General Stanley's told—
We seek a penalty fifty-fold,
For General Stanley's story.

POLICE They seek a penalty—
PIRATES [*without*] Fifty-fold,
We seek a penalty—
POLICE Fifty-fold,
ALL We } They } seek a penalty fifty-fold,
For General Stanley's story.
SERG. They come in force, with stealthy stride,
Our obvious course is now—to hide.

[*Police conceal themselves. As they do so, the Pirates are seen appearing at ruined window. They enter cautiously, and come down stage.* SAMUEL *is laden with burglarious tools and pistols, etc.*

Chorus—PIRATES [*very loud*]

With cat-like tread,
Upon our prey we steal,
In silence dread
Our cautious way we feel.
No sound at all,
We never speak a word,
A fly's foot-fall
Would be distinctly heard—
POLICE [*pianissimo*] Tarantara, tarantara!
PIRATES So stealthily the pirate creeps,
While all the household soundly sleeps.
Come, friends, who plough the sea,
Truce to navigation,
Take another station;
Let's vary piracee
With a little burglaree!
POLICE [*pianissimo*] Tarantara, tarantara!
SAM. [*distributing implements to various members of the gang*]
Here's your crowbar and your centrebit,
Your life-preserver—you may want to hit;
Your silent matches, your dark lantern seize,
Take your file and your skeletonic keys.

Enter KING, FREDERIC, and RUTH

ALL [*fortissimo*] With cat-like tread, etc.

Recitative

FRED. Hush, hush, not a word! I see a light inside!
The Major-General comes, so quickly hide!

PIRATES Yes, yes, the Major-General comes!

[*Exeunt* KING, FREDERIC, SAMUEL, *and* RUTH.

POLICE Yes, yes, the Major-General comes!

GEN. [*entering in dressing-gown, carrying a light*]
Yes, yes, the Major-General comes!

Solo—GENERAL

Tormented with the anguish dread
Of falsehood unatoned,
I lay upon my sleepless bed,
And tossed and turned and groaned.
The man who finds his conscience ache
No peace at all enjoys,
And as I lay in bed awake
I thought I heard a noise.

PIRATES } He thought he heard a noise—ha! ha!
POLICE } He thought he heard a noise—ha! ha! [*Very loud*]

GEN. No, all is still
In dale, on hill;
My mind is set at ease.
So still the scene—
It must have been
The sighing of the breeze.

Ballad—GENERAL

Sighing softly to the river
Comes the loving breeze,
Setting nature all a-quiver,
Rustling through the trees—

ALL Through the trees.

GEN. And the brook, in rippling measure,
Laughs for very love,
While the poplars, in their pleasure,
Wave their arms above.

POLICE and PIRATES } Yes, the trees, for very love,
Wave their leafy arms above,
River, river, little river,
May thy loving prosper ever.
Heaven speed thee, poplar tree,
May thy wooing happy be.

GEN. Yet, the breeze is but a rover;
  When he wings away,
Brook and poplar mourn a lover!
  Sighing well-a-day!

ALL Well-a-day!

GEN. Ah! the doing and undoing,
  That the rogue could tell!
When the breeze is out a-wooing,
  Who can woo so well?

POLICE and PIRATES
Shocking tales the rogue could tell
Nobody can woo so well.
  Pretty brook, thy dream is over,
  For thy love is but a rover!
  Sad the lot of poplar trees,
  Courted by the fickle breeze!

[*Enter the* GENERAL's *daughters, all in white peignoirs and night-caps, and carrying lighted candles.*

GIRLS Now what is this, and what is that, and why does father leave his rest
At such a time of night as this, so very incompletely dressed?
Dear father is, and always was, the most methodical of men!
It's his invariable rule to go to bed at half-past ten.
What strange occurrence can it be that calls dear father from his rest
At such a time of night as this, so very incompletely dressed?

Enter KING, SAMUEL, *and* FREDERIC

KING Forward, my men, and seize that General there!
[*They seize the* GENERAL]

GIRLS The pirates! the pirates! Oh, despair!
PIRATES Yes, we're the pirates, so despair!
GEN. Frederic here! Oh, joy! Oh, rapture!
Summon your men and effect their capture!
MABEL Frederic, save us!
FRED. Beautiful Mabel,
I would if I could, but I am not able.
PIRATES He's telling the truth, he is not able.
KING With base deceit
You worked upon our feelings!
Revenge is sweet,
And flavours all our dealings!
With courage rare
And resolution manly,
For death prepare,
Unhappy General Stanley.

MABEL [*wildly*] Is he to die, unshriven—unannealed?
GIRLS Oh, spare him!
MABEL Will no one in his cause a weapon wield?
GIRLS Oh, spare him!
POLICE [*springing up*] Yes, we are here, though hitherto concealed!
GIRLS Oh, rapture!
POLICE So to the Constabulary, pirates, yield!
GIRLS Oh, rapture!

[*A struggle ensues between Pirates and Police. Eventually the Police are overcome, and fall prostrate, the Pirates standing over them with drawn swords.*

Chorus of Police and Pirates

You / We } triumph now, for well we trow
Our mortal career's cut short,
No pirate band will take its stand
At the Central Criminal Court.
SERG. To gain a brief advantage you've contrived.
But your proud triumph will not be long-lived
KING Don't say you are orphans, for we know that game.
SERG. On your allegiance, we've a stronger claim—
We charge you yield, in Queen Victoria's name!
KING [*baffled*] You do!
POLICE We do!
We charge you yield, in Queen Victoria's name!

[*Pirates kneel, Police stand over them triumphantly.*

KING We yield at once, with humbled mien,
Because, with all our faults, we love our Queen
POLICE Yes, yes, with all their faults, they love their Queen.
GIRLS Yes, yes, with all, etc.

[*Police, holding Pirates by the collar, take out handkerchiefs and weep.*

GEN. Away with them, and place them at the bar!

Enter RUTH

RUTH One moment! let me tell you who they are.
They are no members of the common throng;
They are all noblemen who have gone wrong!

GEN. No Englishman unmoved that statement hears,
Because, with all our faults, we love our House of Peers.

Recitative—GENERAL

I pray you, pardon me, ex-Pirate King,
Peers will be peers, and youth will have its fling.
Resume your ranks and legislative duties,
And take my daughters, all of whom are beauties.

Finale

Poor wandering ones!
Though ye have surely strayed,
Take heart of grace.
Your steps retrace,
Poor wandering ones!

Poor wandering ones!
If such poor love as ours
Can help you find
True peace of mind,
Why, take it, it is yours!
Poor wandering ones! etc.

CURTAIN

PATIENCE

OR

BUNTHORNE'S BRIDE

DRAMATIS PERSONÆ

Colonel Calverley Major Murgatroyd Lieut. the Duke of Dunstable	[*Officers of Dragoon Guards*]

Reginald Bunthorne [*a Fleshly Poet*]

Archibald Grosvenor [*an Idyllic Poet*]

Mr. Bunthorne's Solicitor

The Lady Angela The Lady Saphir The Lady Ella The Lady Jane	[*Rapturous Maidens*]

Patience [*a Dairy Maid*]

Chorus of Rapturous Maidens and Officers of Dragoon Guards

ACT I

EXTERIOR OF CASTLE BUNTHORNE

ACT II

A GLADE

First produced at the Opéra Comique on April 23, 1881

PATIENCE

OR

BUNTHORNE'S BRIDE

ACT I

SCENE.—*Exterior of Castle Bunthorne. Entrance to Castle by drawbridge over moat. Young ladies dressed in æsthetic draperies are grouped about the stage. They play on lutes, mandolins, etc., as they sing, and all are in the last stage of despair.* ANGELA, ELLA, *and* SAPHIR *lead them.*

Chorus

Twenty love-sick maidens we,
  Love-sick all against our will.
Twenty years hence we shall be
  Twenty love-sick maidens still.
Twenty love-sick maidens we,
And we die for love of thee.

Solo—ANGELA

Love feeds on hope, they say, or love will die—

ALL — Ah, miserie!

Yet my love lives, although no hope have I!

ALL — Ah, miserie!

Alas, poor heart, go hide thyself away—
To weeping concords tune thy roundelay!
Ah, miserie!

Chorus

All our love is all for one,
  Yet that love he heedeth not.
He is coy and cares for none,
  Sad and sorry is our lot!
    Ah, miserie!

Solo—ELLA

Go, breaking heart,
  Go, dream of love requited;

Go, foolish heart,
  Go, dream of lovers plighted;
Go, madcap heart,
  Go, dream of never waking;
And in thy dream
  Forget that thou art breaking!

CHORUS Ah, miserie!

ELLA Forget that thou art breaking!

CHORUS Twenty love-sick maidens, etc.

ANG. There is a strange magic in this love of ours! Rivals as we all are in the affections of our Reginald, the very hopelessness of our love is a bond that binds us to one another!

SAPH. Jealousy is merged in misery. While he, the very cynosure of our eyes and hearts, remains icy insensible—what have we to strive for?

ELLA The love of maidens is, to him, as interesting as the taxes!

SAPH. Would that it were! He pays his taxes.

ANG. And cherishes the receipts!

Enter LADY JANE

SAPH. Happy receipts!

JANE [*suddenly*] Fools!

ANG. I beg your pardon?

JANE Fools and blind! The man loves—wildly loves!

ANG. But whom? None of us!

JANE No, none of us. His weird fancy has lighted, for the nonce, on Patience, the village milkmaid!

SAPH. On Patience? Oh, it cannot be!

JANE Bah! But yesterday I caught him in her dairy, eating fresh butter with a tablespoon. To-day he is not well!

SAPH. But Patience boasts that she has never loved—that love is, to her, a sealed book! Oh, he cannot be serious!

JANE 'Tis but a fleeting fancy—'twill quickly pass away. [*Aside*] Oh, Reginald, if you but knew what a wealth of golden love is waiting for you, stored up in this rugged old bosom of mine, the milkmaid's triumph would be short indeed!

PATIENCE *appears on an eminence. She looks down with pity on the despondent Ladies.*

Recitative—PATIENCE

Still brooding on their mad infatuation!
  I thank thee, Love, thou comest not to me!

Far happier I, free from thy ministration,
Than dukes or duchesses who love can be!

SAPH. [*looking up*] 'Tis Patience—happy girl! Loved by a Poet!
PA. Your pardon, ladies. I intrude upon you. [*Going*]
ANG. Nay, pretty child, come hither. Is it true
That you have never loved?
PA. Most true indeed.
SOPRANOS Most marvellous!
CONTRALTOS And most deplorable!

Song—PATIENCE

I cannot tell what this love may be
That cometh to all, but not to me.
It cannot be kind as they'd imply,
Or why do these ladies sigh?

It cannot be joy and rapture deep,
Or why do these gentle ladies weep?
It cannot be blissful as 'tis said,
Or why are their eyes so wondrous red?

Though everywhere true love I see
A-coming to all, but not to me
I cannot tell what this love may be!
For I am blithe and I am gay,
While they sit sighing night and day
Think of the gulf 'twixt them and me,
"Fal la la la!"—and "Miserie!"

CHORUS Yes, she is blithe, etc.

PA. If love is a thorn, they show no wit
Who foolishly hug and foster it.
If love is a weed, how simple they
Who gather it, day by day!
If love is a nettle that makes you smart,
Then why do you wear it next your heart?
And if it be none of these, say I,
Ah, why do you sit and sob and sigh?
Though everywhere, etc.

CHORUS For she is blithe, etc.

ANG. Ah, Patience, if you have never loved, you have never known true happiness! [*All sigh*]

PA. But the truly happy always seem to have so much on their minds. The truly happy never seem quite well.

JANE There is a transcendentality of delirium—an acute accentuation of a supremest ecstasy—which the earthy might easily mistake for indigestion. But it is *not* indigestion—it is æsthetic transfiguration! [*To the others*] Enough of babble. Come!

PA. But stay, I have some news for you. The 35th Dragoon Guards have halted in the village, and are even now on their way to this very spot.

ANG. The 35th Dragoon Guards!

SAPH. They are fleshly men, of full habit!

ELLA We care nothing for Dragoon Guards!

PA. But, bless me, you were all engaged to them a year ago!

SAPH. A year ago!

ANG. My poor child, you don't understand these things. A year ago they were very well in our eyes, but since then our tastes have been etherealized, our perceptions exalted. [*To others*] Come, it is time to lift up our voices in morning carol to our Reginald. Let us to his door.

[*The Ladies go off, two and two, into the Castle, singing refrain of "Twenty love-sick maidens we," and accompanying themselves on harps and mandolins.* PATIENCE *watches them in surprise, as she climbs the rock by which she entered.*

March. Enter Officers of Dragoon Guards, led by MAJOR

Chorus of Dragoons

The soldiers of our Queen
  Are linked in friendly tether;
Upon the battle scene
  They fight the foe together.
There every mother's son
  Prepared to fight and fall is;
The enemy of one
  The enemy of all is!

Enter COLONEL

Song—COLONEL

If you want a receipt for that popular mystery,
  Known to the world as a Heavy Dragoon,
Take all the remarkable people in history,
  Rattle them off to a popular tune.
The pluck of Lord Nelson on board of the *Victory*—
  Genius of Bismarck devising a plan—
The humour of Fielding (which sounds contradictory)—
  Coolness of Paget about to trepan—
The science of Jullien, the eminent musico—
  Wit of Macaulay, who wrote of Queen Anne—
The pathos of Paddy, as rendered by Boucicault—
  Style of the Bishop of Sodor and Man—
The dash of a D'Orsay, divested of quackery—
Narrative powers of Dickens and Thackeray—
Victor Emmanuel—peak-haunting Peveril—
Thomas Aquinas, and Doctor Sacheverell—
  Tupper and Tennyson—Daniel Defoe—
  Anthony Trollope and Mr. Guizot!

Take of these elements all that is fusible,
Melt them all down in a pipkin or crucible,
Set them to simmer and take off the scum,
And a Heavy Dragoon is the residuum!

CHORUS Yes! yes! yes! yes!
    A Heavy Dragoon is the residuum!

Col. If you want a receipt for this soldier-like paragon,
Get at the wealth of the Czar (if you can)—
The family pride of a Spaniard from Aragon—
Force of Mephisto pronouncing a ban—
A smack of Lord Waterford, reckless and rollicky—
Swagger of Roderick, heading his clan—
The keen penetration of Paddington Pollaky—
Grace of an Odalisque on a divan—
The genius strategic of Cæsar or Hannibal—
Skill of Sir Garnet in thrashing a cannibal—
Flavour of Hamlet—the Stranger, a touch of him—
Little of Manfred (but not very much of him)—
Beadle of Burlington—Richardson's show—
Mr. Micawber and Madame Tussaud!
Take of these elements all that is fusible,
Melt them all down in a pipkin or crucible,
Set them to simmer and take off the scum,
And a Heavy Dragoon is the residuum!

All Yes! yes! yes! yes!
A Heavy Dragoon is the residuum!

Col. Well, here we are once more on the scene of our former triumphs. But where's the Duke?

Enter Duke, *listlessly, and in low spirits*

Duke Here I am! [*Sighs*]

Col. Come, cheer up, don't give way!

Duke Oh, for that, I'm as cheerful as a poor devil can be expected to be who has the misfortune to be a duke, with a thousand a day!

Maj. Humph! Most men would envy you!

Duke Envy *me?* Tell me, Major, are you fond of toffee?

Maj. Very!

Col. We are all fond of toffee.

All We are!

Duke Yes, and toffee in moderation is a capital thing. But to *live* on toffee—toffee for breakfast, toffee for dinner, toffee for tea—to have it supposed that you care for nothing *but* toffee, and that you would consider yourself insulted if anything but toffee were offered to you—how would you like *that?*

Col. I can quite believe that, under those circumstances, even toffee would become monotonous.

Duke For "toffee" read flattery, adulation, and abject deference, carried to such a pitch that I began, at last, to think that man was born bent at an angle of forty-five degrees! Great Heavens, what is there to adulate in me! Am I particularly intelligent, or remarkably studious, or excruciatingly witty, or unusually accomplished, or exceptionally virtuous?

COL. You're about as commonplace a young man as ever I saw.

ALL You are!

DUKE Exactly! That's it exactly! That describes me to a T! Thank you all very much! Well, I couldn't stand it any longer, so I joined this second-class cavalry regiment. In the Army, thought I, I shall be occasionally snubbed, perhaps even bullied, who knows? The thought was rapture, and here I am.

COL. [*looking off*] Yes, and here are the ladies!

DUKE But who is the gentleman with the long hair?

COL. I don't know.

DUKE He seems popular!

COL. He *does* seem popular!

BUNTHORNE *enters, followed by Ladies, two and two, singing and playing on harps as before. He is composing a poem, and quite absorbed. He sees no one, but walks across the stage, followed by Ladies. They take no notice of Dragoons—to the surprise and indignation of those Officers.*

Chorus of Ladies

In a doleful train
Two and two we walk all day—
For we love in vain!
None so sorrowful as they
Who can only sigh and say,
Woe is me, alackaday!

Chorus of Dragoons

Now is not this ridiculous—and is not this preposterous?
A thorough-paced absurdity—explain it if you can.
Instead of rushing eagerly to cherish us and foster us,
They all prefer this melancholy literary man.
Instead of slyly peering at us,
Casting looks endearing at us,
Blushing at us, flushing at us—flirting with a fan;
They're actually sneering at us, fleering at us, jeering at us!
Pretty sort of treatment for a military man!
Pretty sort of treatment for a military man!

ANG. Mystic poet, hear our prayer,
Twenty love-sick maidens we—
Young and wealthy, dark and fair—
All of county family.
And we die for love of thee—
Twenty love-sick maidens we!

CHORUS OF LADIES

Yes, we die for love of thee—
Twenty love-sick maidens we!

BUN. [*aside—slyly*] Though my book I seem to scan
In a rapt ecstatic way,
Like a literary man
Who despises female clay,
I hear plainly all they say,
Twenty love-sick maidens they!

OFFICERS [*to each other*] He hears plainly, etc.

SAPH. Though so excellently wise,
For a moment mortal be,
Deign to raise thy purple eyes
From thy heart-drawn poesy.
Twenty love-sick maidens see—
Each is kneeling on her knee! [*All kneel*]

CHORUS OF LADIES Twenty love-sick, etc.

BUN. [*aside*] Though, as I remarked before,
Any one convinced would be
That some transcendental lore
Is monopolizing me,
Round the corner I can see
Each is kneeling on her knee!

OFFICERS [*to each other*]

Round the corner, etc.

Ensemble

OFFICERS	LADIES
Now is not this ridiculous, etc.	Mystic poet, hear our prayer, etc.

COL. Angela! what is the meaning of this?

ANG. Oh, sir, leave us; our minds are but ill-tuned to light love-talk.

MAJ. But what in the world has come over you all?

JANE Bunthorne! *He* has come over us. He has come among us, and he has idealized us.

DUKE Has he succeeded in idealizing *you?*

JANE He has!

DUKE Good old Bunthorne!

JANE My eyes are open; I droop despairingly; I am soulfully intense; I am limp and I cling!

[*During this* BUNTHORNE *is seen in all the agonies of composition. The Ladies are watching him intently as he writhes. At last he hits on the word he wants and writes it down. A general sense of relief.*

BUN. Finished! At last! Finished!

[*He staggers, overcome with the mental strain, into arms of* COLONEL.

COL. Are you better now?

BUN. Yes,–oh, it's you–I am better now. The poem is finished, and my soul had gone out into it. That was all. It was nothing worth mentioning, it occurs three times a day. [*Sees* PATIENCE, *who has entered during this scene*] Ah, Patience! Dear Patience! [*Holds her hand; she seems frightened*]

ANG. Will it please you to read it to us, sir?

SAPH. This we supplicate. [*All kneel*]

BUN. Shall I?

ALL THE DRAGOONS No!

BUN. [*annoyed–to* PATIENCE] I will read it if *you* bid me!

PA. [*much frightened*]You can if you like!

BUN. It is a wild, weird, fleshly thing; yet very tender, very yearning, very precious. It is called, "Oh, Hollow! Hollow! Hollow!"

PA. Is it a hunting song?

BUN. A hunting song? No, it is *not* a hunting song. It is the wail of the poet's heart on discovering that everything is commonplace. To understand it, cling passionately to one another and think of faint lilies. [*They do so as he recites*]–

"Oh, Hollow! Hollow! Hollow!"

What time the poet hath hymned
The writhing maid, lithe-limbed,
  Quivering on amaranthine asphodel,
How can he paint her woes,
Knowing, as well he knows,
  That all can be set right with calomel?

When from the poet's plinth
The amorous colocynth
  Yearns for the aloe, faint with rapturous thrills,
How can he hymn their throes
Knowing, as well he knows,
  That they are only uncompounded pills?

Is it, and can it be,
Nature hath this decree,
  Nothing poetic in the world shall dwell?
Or that in all her works
Something poetic lurks,
  Even in colocynth and calomel?
    I cannot tell.

[*Exit* BUNTHORNE.

ANG. How purely fragrant!

SAPH. How earnestly precious!

PA. Well, it seems to me to be nonsense.

SAPH. Nonsense, yes, perhaps—but oh, what precious nonsense!

COL. This is all very well, but you seem to forget that you are engaged to us.

SAPH. It can never be. You are not Empyrean. You are not Della Cruscan. You are not even Early English. Oh, be Early English ere it is too late! [*Officers look at each other in astonishment*]

JANE [*looking at uniform*] Red and yellow! Primary colours! Oh, South Kensington!

DUKE We didn't design our uniforms, but we don't see how they could be improved.

JANE No, you wouldn't. Still, there *is* a cobwebby grey velvet, with a tender bloom like cold gravy, which, made Florentine fourteenth-century, trimmed with Venetian leather and Spanish altar lace, and surmounted with something Japanese—it matters not what—would at least be Early English! Come, maidens.

[*Exeunt Maidens, two and two, singing refrain of "Twenty love-sick maidens we". The Officers watch them off in astonishment.*

DUKE Gentlemen, this is an insult to the British uniform——

COL. A uniform that has been as successful in the courts of Venus as on the field of Mars!

Song—COLONEL

When I first put this uniform on,
I said, as I looked in the glass,
"It's one to a million
That any civilian
My figure and form will surpass.
Gold lace has a charm for the fair,
And I've plenty of that, and to spare,
While a lover's professions,
When uttered in Hessians,
Are eloquent everywhere!"
A fact that I counted upon,
When I first put this uniform on!

Chorus of Dragoons

By a simple coincidence, few
Could ever have counted upon,
The same thing occurred to me, too,
When I first put this uniform on!

COL. I said, when I first put it on,
"It is plain to the veriest dunce
That every beauty
Will feel it her duty
To yield to its glamour at once.
They will see that I'm freely gold-laced
In a uniform handsome and chaste"—
But the peripatetics
Of long-haired æsthetics
Are very much more to their taste—
Which I never counted upon,
When I first put this uniform on!

CHORUS By a simple coincidence, few
Could ever have reckoned upon,
I didn't anticipate that,
When I first put this uniform on!

[*The Dragoons go off angrily.*

Enter BUNTHORNE, *who changes his manner and becomes intensely melodramatic.*

Recitative and Song—BUNTHORNE

Am I alone,
And unobserved? I am!
Then let me own
I'm an æsthetic sham!

This air severe
Is but a mere
Veneer!

This cynic smile
Is but a wile
Of guile!

This costume chaste
Is but good taste
Misplaced!

Let me confess!
A languid love for lilies does *not* blight me!
Lank limbs and haggard cheeks do *not* delight me!
I do *not* care for dirty greens
By any means.
I do *not* long for all one sees
That's Japanese.
I am *not* fond of uttering platitudes
In stained-glass attitudes.
In short, my mediævalism's affectation,
Born of a morbid love of admiration!

Song

If you're anxious for to shine in the high æsthetic line as a man of culture rare,
You must get up all the germs of the transcendental terms, and plant them everywhere.

You must lie upon the daisies and discourse in novel phrases of your complicated state of mind,
The meaning doesn't matter if it's only idle chatter of a transcendental kind.
And every one will say,
As you walk your mystic way,
"If this young man expresses himself in terms too deep for *me*,
Why, what a very singularly deep young man this deep young man must be!"

Be eloquent in praise of the very dull old days which have long since passed away,
And convince 'em, if you can, that the reign of good Queen Anne was Culture's palmiest day.
Of course you will pooh-pooh whatever's fresh and new, and declare it's crude and mean,
For Art stopped short in the cultivated court of the Empress Josephine.
And every one will say,
As you walk your mystic way,
"If that's not good enough for him which is good enough for *me*,
Why, what a very cultivated kind of youth this kind of youth must be!"

Then a sentimental passion of a vegetable fashion must excite your languid spleen,
An attachment *à la* Plato for a bashful young potato, or a not-too-French French bean!
Though the Philistines may jostle, you will rank as an apostle in the high æsthetic band,
If you walk down Piccadilly with a poppy or a lily in your mediæval hand.

And every one will say,
As you walk your flowery way,
"If he's content with a vegetable love which would certainly not suit *me*,
Why, what a most particularly pure young man this pure young man must be!"

At the end of his song PATIENCE *enters. He sees her.*

BUN. Ah! Patience, come hither. I am pleased with thee. The bitter-hearted one, who finds all else hollow, is pleased with thee. For you are not hollow. *Are* you?

PA. No, thanks, I have dined; but–I beg your pardon–I interrupt you.

BUN. Life is made up of interruptions. The tortured soul, yearning for solitude, writhes under them. Oh, but my heart is a-weary! Oh, I am a cursed thing! Don't go.

PA. Really, I'm very sorry——

BUN. Tell me, girl, do you ever yearn?

PA. [*misunderstanding him*] I earn my living.

BUN. [*impatiently*] No, no! Do you know what it is to be heart-hungry? Do you know what it is to yearn for the Indefinable, and yet to be brought face to face, daily, with the Multiplication Table? Do you know what it is to seek oceans and to find puddles?–to long for whirlwinds and yet to have to do the best you can with the bellows? That's my case. Oh, I am a cursed thing! Don't go.

PA. If you please, I don't understand you–you frighten me!

BUN. Don't be frightened–it's only poetry.

PA. Well, if that's poetry, I don't like poetry.

BUN. [*eagerly*] Don't you? [*Aside*] Can I trust her? [*Aloud*] Patience, you don't like poetry–well, between you and me, *I* don't like poetry. It's hollow, unsubstantial–unsatisfactory. What's the use of yearning for Elysian Fields when you know you can't get 'em, and would only let 'em out on building leases if you had 'em?

PA. Sir, I——

BUN. Patience, I have long loved you. Let me tell you a secret. I am not as bilious as I look. If you like, I will cut my hair. There is more innocent fun within me than a casual spectator would imagine. You have never seen me frolicsome. Be a good girl–a very good girl–and one day you shall. If you are fond of touch-and-go jocularity–this is the shop for it.

PA. Sir, I will speak plainly. In the matter of love I am untaught. I have never loved but my great-aunt. But I am quite certain, under any circumstances, I couldn't possibly love *you*.

BUN. Oh, you think not?

PA. I'm quite sure of it. Quite sure. Quite.

BUN. Very good. Life is henceforth a blank. I don't care what becomes of me. I have only to ask that you will not abuse my confidence; though *you* despise me, I am extremely popular with the other young ladies.

PA. I only ask that you will leave me and never renew the subject.

BUN. Certainly. Broken-hearted and desolate, I go. [*Recites*]

"Oh, to be wafted away
 From this black Aceldama of sorrow,
Where the dust of an earthy to-day
 Is the earth of a dusty to-morrow!"

It is a little thing of my own. I call it "Heart Foam." I shall not publish it. Farewell! Patience, Patience, farewell!

[*Exit* BUNTHORNE.

PA. What on earth does it all mean? Why does he love me? Why does he expect me to love him? He's not a relation! It frightens me!

Enter ANGELA

ANG. Why, Patience, what is the matter?

PA. Lady Angela, tell me two things. Firstly, what on earth is this love that upsets everybody; and, secondly, how is it to be distinguished from insanity?

ANG. Poor blind child! Oh, forgive her, Eros! Why, love is of all passions the most essential! It is the embodiment of purity, the abstraction of refinement! It is the one unselfish emotion in this whirlpool of grasping greed!

PA. Oh, dear, oh! [*Beginning to cry*]

ANG. Why are you crying?

PA. To think that I have lived all these years without having experienced this ennobling and unselfish passion! Why, what a wicked girl I must be! For it *is* unselfish, isn't it?

ANG. Absolutely! Love that is tainted with selfishness is no love. Oh, try, try, try to love! It really isn't difficult if you give your whole mind to it.

PA. I'll set about it at once. I won't go to bed until I'm head over ears in love with somebody.

ANG. Noble girl! But is it possible that you have never loved anybody?

PA. Yes, one.

ANG. Ah! Whom?

PA. My great-aunt——

ANG. Great-aunts don't count.

PA. Then there's nobody. At least—no, nobody. Not since I was a baby. But *that* doesn't count, I suppose.

ANG. I don't know. Tell me all about it.

Duet—PATIENCE and ANGELA

Long years ago—fourteen, maybe—
 When but a tiny babe of four,

Another baby played with me,
My elder by a year or more;
A little child of beauty rare,
With marvellous eyes and wondrous hair,
Who, in my child-eyes, seemed to me
All that a little child should be!
Ah, how we loved, that child and I!
How pure our baby joy!
How true our love—and, by the by,
He was a little boy!

ANG. Ah, old, old tale of Cupid's touch!
I thought as much—I thought as much!
He *was* a little boy!

PA. [*shocked*] Pray don't misconstrue what I say—
Remember, pray—remember, pray,
He was a *little* boy!

ANG. No doubt! Yet, spite of all your pains,
The interesting fact remains—
He was a little *boy!*

ENSEMBLE {Ah, yes, in / No doubt! Yet} spite of all {my / your} pains, etc.

[*Exit* ANGELA.

PA. It's perfectly dreadful to think of the appalling state I must be in! I had no idea that love was a duty. No wonder they all look so unhappy! Upon my word, I hardly like to associate with myself. I don't think I'm respectable. I'll go at once and fall in love with—— [*Enter* GROSVENOR] A stranger!

Duet—PATIENCE and GROSVENOR

GROS. Prithee, pretty maiden—prithee, tell me true,
(Hey, but I'm doleful, willow willow waly)
Have you e'er a lover a-dangling after you?
Hey willow waly O!
I would fain discover
If you have a lover?
Hey willow waly O!

PA. Gentle sir, my heart is frolicsome and free—
(Hey, but he's doleful, willow willow waly!)
Nobody I care for comes a-courting me—
Hey willow waly O!
Nobody I care for
Comes a-courting—therefore,
Hey willow waly O!

GROS. Prithee, pretty maiden, will you marry me?
(Hey, but I'm hopeful, willow willow waly!)
I may say, at once, I'm a man of propertee—
Hey willow waly O!
Money, I despise it;
Many people prize it,
Hey willow waly O!

PA. Gentle sir, although to marry I design—
(Hey, but I'm hopeful, willow willow waly!)
As yet I do not know you, and so I must decline.
Hey willow waly O!
To other maidens go you—
As yet I do not know you,
Hey willow waly O!

GROS. Patience! Can it be that you don't recognise me?

PA. Recognise you? No, indeed I don't!

GROS. Have fifteen years so greatly changed me?

PA. Fifteen years? What do you mean?

GROS. Have you forgotten the friend of your youth, your Archibald?—your little playfellow? Oh, Chronos, Chronos, this is too bad of you!

PA. Archibald! Is it possible? Why, let me look! It is! It is! It must be! Oh, how happy I am! I thought we should never meet again! And how you've grown!

GROS. Yes, Patience, I am much taller and much stouter than I was.

PA. And how you've improved!

GROS. Yes, Patience, I am very beautiful! [*Sighs*]

PA. But surely *that* doesn't make you unhappy.

GROS. Yes, Patience. Gifted as I am with a beauty which probably has not its rival on earth, I am, nevertheless, utterly and completely miserable.

PA. Oh—but why?

GROS. My child-love for you has never faded. Conceive, then, the horror of my situation when I tell you that it is my hideous destiny to be madly loved at first sight by every woman I come across!

PA. But why do you make yourself so picturesque? Why not disguise yourself, disfigure yourself, anything to escape this persecution?

GROS. No, Patience, that may not be. These gifts—irksome as they are —were given to me for the enjoyment and delectation of my fellow-creatures. I am a trustee for Beauty, and it is my duty to see that the conditions of my trust are faithfully discharged.

PA. And you, too, are a Poet?

GROS. Yes, I am the Apostle of Simplicity. I am called "Archibald the All-Right"—for I am infallible!

PA. And is it possible that you condescend to love such a girl as I?

GROS. Yes, Patience, is it not strange? I have loved you with a Florentine fourteenth-century frenzy for full fifteen years!

PA. Oh, marvellous! I have hitherto been deaf to the voice of love. I seem now to know what love is! It has been revealed to me—it is Archibald Grosvenor!

GROS. Yes, Patience, it is!

PA. [*as in a trance*] We will never, never part!

GROS. We will live and die together!

PA. I swear it!

GROS. We both swear it!

PA. [*recoiling from him*] But—oh, horror!

GROS. What's the matter?

PA. Why, you are perfection! A source of endless ecstasy to all who know you!

GROS. I know I am. Well?

PA. Then, bless my heart, there can be nothing unselfish in loving *you!*

GROS. Merciful powers! I never thought of that!

PA. To monopolize those features on which all women love to linger! It would be unpardonable!

GROS. Why, so it would! Oh, fatal perfection, again you interpose between me and my happiness!

PA. Oh, if you were but a thought less beautiful than you are!

GROS. Would that I were; but candour compels me to admit that I'm not!

PA. Our duty is clear; we must part, and for ever!

GROS. Oh, misery! And yet I cannot question the propriety of your decision. Farewell, Patience!

PA. Farewell, Archibald! But stay!

GROS. Yes, Patience?

PA. Although I may not love *you*—for you are perfection—there is nothing to prevent your loving *me*. I am plain, homely, unattractive!

GROS. Why, that's true!

PA. The love of such a man as you for such a girl as I must be unselfish!

GROS. Unselfishness itself!

Duet—PATIENCE and GROSVENOR

PA. Though to marry you would very selfish be—
GROS. Hey, but I'm doleful—willow willow waly!
PA. You may, all the same, continue loving me—
GROS. Hey willow waly O!
BOTH All the world ignoring,
You'll / I'll go on adoring—
Hey willow waly O!

[*At the end, exeunt despairingly, in opposite directions.*

Finale—ACT I

Enter BUNTHORNE, *crowned with roses and hung about with garlands, and looking very miserable. He is led by* ANGELA *and* SAPHIR (*each of whom holds an end of the rose-garland by which he is bound*), *and accompanied by procession of Maidens. They are dancing classically, and playing on cymbals, double pipes, and other archaic instruments.*

Chorus

Let the merry cymbals sound,
Gaily pipe Pandæan pleasure,
With a Daphnephoric bound
Tread a gay but classic measure.
Every heart with hope is beating,
For at this exciting meeting
Fickle Fortune will decide
Who shall be our Bunthorne's bride!

Enter Dragoons, led by COLONEL, MAJOR, *and* DUKE. *They are surprised at proceedings.*

Chorus of Dragoons

Now tell us, we pray you,
Why thus they array you—
Oh, poet, how say you—
What is it you've done?

DUKE
Of rite sacrificial,
By sentence judicial,
This seems the initial,
Then why don't you run?

COL.
They cannot have led you
To hang or behead you,
Nor may they *all* wed you,
Unfortunate one!

Chorus of Dragoons

Then tell us, we pray you,
Why thus they array you—
Oh, poet, how say you—
What is it you've done?

Recitative—BUNTHORNE

Heart-broken at my Patience's barbarity,
By the advice of my solicitor
[*introducing his* SOLICITOR],
In aid—in aid of a deserving charity,
I've put myself up to be raffled for!

MAIDENS
By the advice of his solicitor
He's put himself up to be raffled for!

DRAGOONS
Oh, horror! urged by his solicitor,
He's put himself up to be raffled for!

MAIDENS
Oh, heaven's blessing on his solicitor!

DRAGOONS
A hideous curse on his solicitor!

[*The* SOLICITOR, *horrified at the Dragoons' curse, rushes off*.

COL.
Stay, we implore you,
Before our hopes are blighted;
You see before you
The men to whom you're plighted!

Chorus of Dragoons

Stay we implore you,
For we adore you;
To us you're plighted
To be united—
Stay, we implore you!

Solo—DUKE

Your maiden hearts, ah, do not steel
To pity's eloquent appeal,
Such conduct British soldiers feel.
[*Aside to Dragoons*] Sigh, sigh, all sigh! [*They all sigh*]

To foeman's steel we rarely see
A British soldier bend the knee,
Yet, one and all, they kneel to ye—
[*Aside to Dragoons*] Kneel, kneel, all kneel! [*They all kneel*]

Our soldiers very seldom cry,
And yet—I need not tell you why—
A tear-drop dews each martial eye!
[*Aside to Dragoons*] Weep, weep, all weep! [*They all weep*]

Ensemble

Our soldiers very seldom cry,
And yet—I need not tell you why—
A tear-drop dews each manly eye!
Weep, weep, all weep!

BUNTHORNE [*who has been impatient during this appeal*]

Come, walk up, and purchase with avidity,
Overcome your diffidence and natural timidity,
Tickets for the raffle should be purchased with avidity,
Put in half a guinea and a husband you may gain—
Such a judge of blue-and-white and other kinds of pottery—
From early Oriental down to modern terra-cotta-ry—
Put in half a guinea—you may draw him in a lottery—
Such an opportunity may not occur again.

CHORUS Such a judge of blue-and-white, etc.

[MAIDENS *crowd up to purchase tickets; during this* DRAGOONS *dance in single file round stage, to express their indifference.*

DRAGOONS We've been thrown over, we're aware,
But we don't care—but we don't care!
There's fish in the sea, no doubt of it,
As good as ever came out of it,
And some day we shall get our share,
So we don't care—so we don't care!

[*During this the* MAIDENS *have been buying tickets. At last* JANE *presents herself.* BUNTHORNE *looks at her with aversion.*

Recitative

BUN. And are *you* going a ticket for to buy?
JANE [*surprised*] Most certainly I am; why shouldn't I?
BUN. [*aside*] Oh, Fortune, this is hard! [*Aloud*] Blindfold your eyes;
Two minutes will decide who wins the prize! [MAIDENS *blindfold themselves*]

Chorus of MAIDENS

Oh, Fortune, to my aching heart be kind!
Like us, thou art blindfolded, but not blind; [*Each uncovers one eye*]
Just raise your bandage, thus, that you may see,
And give the prize, and give the prize to me! [*They cover their eyes again*]

BUN. Come, Lady Jane, I pray you draw the first!
JANE [*joyfully*] He loves me best!
BUN. [*aside*] I want to know the worst!

[JANE *puts hand in bag to draw ticket.* PATIENCE *enters and prevents her doing so.*

PA. Hold! Stay your hand!
ALL [*uncovering their eyes*] What means this interference?
Of this bold girl I pray you make a clearance!
JANE Away with you, and to your milk-pails go!
BUN. [*suddenly*] She wants a ticket! Take a dozen!
PA. No!

Solo—PATIENCE [*kneeling to* BUNTHORNE]

If there be pardon in your breast
For this poor penitent,
Who, with remorseful thought opprest,
Sincerely doth repent;
If you, with one so lowly, still
Desire to be allied,
Then you may take me, if you will,
For I will be your bride!

ALL Oh, shameless one!
Oh, bold-faced thing!
Away you run,
Go, take you wing,
You shameless one!
You bold-faced thing!

Bun. How strong is love! For many and many a week
She's loved me fondly and has feared to speak
But Nature, for restraint too mighty far,
Has burst the bonds of Art—and here we are!

Pa. No, Mr. Bunthorne, no—you're wrong again;
Permit me—I'll endeavour to explain!

Song—Patience

Pa. True love must single-hearted be—
Bun. Exactly so!
Pa. From every selfish fancy free—
Bun. Exactly so!
Pa. No idle thought of gain or joy
A maiden's fancy should employ—
True love must be without alloy.
All Exactly so!

Pa. Imposture to contempt must lead—
Col. Exactly so!
Pa. Blind vanity's dissension's seed—
Maj. Exactly so!
Pa. It follows, then, a maiden who
Devotes herself to loving you [*indicating* Bunthorne]
Is prompted by no selfish view—
All Exactly so!
Saph. Are you resolved to wed this shameless one?
Ang. Is there no chance for any other?
Bun. [*decisively*] None! [*Embraces* Patience]

[*Exeunt* Patience *and* Bunthorne.

[Angela, Saphir, *and* Ella *take* Colonel, Duke, *and* Major *down, while* Girls *gaze fondly at other* Officers.

Sextette

I hear the soft note of the echoing voice
Of an old, old love, long dead—
It whispers my sorrowing heart "rejoice"—
For the last sad tear is shed—
The pain that is all but a pleasure will change
For the pleasure that's all but pain,
And never, oh never, this heart will range
From that old, old love again!
[Girls *embrace* Officers]

CHORUS Yes, the pain that is all, etc. [*Embrace*]

Enter PATIENCE *and* BUNTHORNE

[*As the* DRAGOONS *and* GIRLS *are embracing, enter* GROSVENOR, *reading. He takes no notice of them, but comes slowly down, still reading. The* GIRLS *are all strangely fascinated by him, and gradually withdraw from* DRAGOONS.

ANG. But who is this, whose god-like grace
Proclaims he comes of noble race?
And who is this, whose manly face
Bears sorrow's interesting trace?

Ensemble—TUTTI

Yes, who is this, etc.

GROS. I am a broken-hearted troubadour,
Whose mind's æsthetic and whose tastes are pure!
ANG. Æsthetic! He is æsthetic!
GROS. Yes, yes—I am æsthetic
And poetic!
ALL THE LADIES Then, we love you!

[*The* GIRLS *leave* DRAGOONS *and group, kneeling, around* GROSVENOR. *Fury of* BUNTHORNE, *who recognizes a rival.*

DRAGOONS They love him! Horror!
BUN. and PA. They love him! Horror!
GROS. They love me! Horror! Horror! Horror!

Ensemble—TUTTI

GIRLS

Oh, list while we a love confess
That words imperfectly express.
Those shell-like ears, ah, do not close
To blighted love's distracting woes!

GROSVENOR

Again my cursed comeliness
Spreads hopeless anguish and distress!
Thine ears, oh Fortune, do not close
To my intolerable woes.

PATIENCE

List, Reginald, while I confess
A love that's all unselfishness;
That it's unselfish, goodness knows,
You won't dispute it, I suppose?

BUNTHORNE

My jealousy I can't express,
Their love they openly confess;
His shell-like ears he does not close
To their recital of their woes.

DRAGOONS Now is not this ridiculous, etc.

END OF ACT I

ACT II

SCENE.—*A glade.* JANE *is discovered leaning on a violon cello, upon which she presently accompanies herself. Chorus of* MAIDENS *are heard singing in the distance.*

JANE The fickle crew have deserted Reginald and sworn allegiance to his rival, and all, forsooth, because he has glanced with passing favour on a puling milkmaid! Fools! of that fancy he will soon weary—and then I, who alone am faithful to him, shall reap my reward. But do not dally too long, Reginald, for my charms are ripe, Reginald, and already they are decaying. Better secure me ere I have gone too far!

Recitative—JANE

Sad is that woman's lot who, year by year,
Sees, one by one, her beauties disappear,
When Time, grown weary of her heart-drawn sighs,
Impatiently begins to "dim her eyes"!
Compelled, at last, in life's uncertain gloamings,
To wreathe her wrinkled brow with well-saved "combings",
Reduced, with rouge, lip-salve, and pearly grey,
To "make up" for lost time as best she may!

Song—JANE

Silvered is the raven hair,
Spreading is the parting straight,
Mottled the complexion fair,
Halting is the youthful gait,
Hollow is the laughter free,
Spectacled the limpid eye—
Little will be left of me
In the coming by and by!

Fading is the taper waist,
Shapeless grows the shapely limb,
And although severely laced,
Spreading is the figure trim!
Stouter than I used to be,
Still more corpulent grow I–
There will be too much of me
In the coming by and by!

[*Exit* JANE.

Enter GROSVENOR, *followed by* MAIDENS, *twc and two, each playing on an archaic instrument, as in Act I. He is reading abstractedly, as* BUNTHORNE *did in Act I, and pays no attention to them.*

Chorus of MAIDENS

Turn, oh, turn in this direction,
Shed, oh, shed a gentle smile,
With a glance of sad perfection
Our poor fainting hearts beguile!
On such eyes as maidens cherish
Let thy fond adorers gaze,
Or incontinently perish
In their all-consuming rays!

[*He sits–they group around him.*

GROS. [*aside*] The old, old tale. How rapturously these maidens love me, and how hopelessly! Oh, Patience, Patience, with the love of thee in my heart, what have I for these poor mad maidens but an unvalued pity? Alas, they will die of hopeless love for me, as I shall die of hopeless love for thee!

ANG. Sir, will it please you read to us?

GROS. [*sighing*] Yes, child, if you will. What shall I read?

ANG. One of your own poems.

GROS. One of my own poems? Better not, my child. *They* will not cure thee of thy love.

ELLA Mr. Bunthorne used to read us a poem of his own every day.

SAPH. And, to do him justice, he read them extremely well.

GROS. Oh, did he so? Well, who am I that I should take upon myself to withhold my gifts from you? What am I but a trustee? Here is a decalet–a pure and simple thing, a very daisy–a babe might understand it. To appreciate it, it is not necessary to think of anything at all.

ANG. Let us think of nothing at all!

GROSVENOR *recites*

Gentle Jane was good as gold,
She always did as she was told;

She never spoke when her mouth was full,
Or caught bluebottles their legs to pull,
Or spilt plum jam on her nice new frock,
Or put white mice in the eight-day clock,
Or vivisected her last new doll,
Or fostered a passion for alcohol.
And when she grew up she was given in marriage
To a first-class earl who keeps his carriage!

GROS. I believe I am right in saying that there is not one word in that decalet which is calculated to bring the blush of shame to the cheek of modesty.

ANG. Not one; it is purity itself.

GROS. Here's another.

Teasing Tom was a very bad boy,
A great big squirt was his favourite toy;
He put live shrimps in his father's boots,
And sewed up the sleeves of his Sunday suits;
He punched his poor little sisters' heads,
And cayenne-peppered their four-post beds,
He plastered their hair with cobbler's wax,
And dropped hot halfpennies down their backs.
The consequence was he was lost totally,
And married a girl in the *corps de bally!*

ANG. Marked you how grandly—how relentlessly—the damning catalogue of crime strode on, till Retribution, like a poiséd hawk, came swooping down upon the Wrong-Doer? Oh, it was terrible!

ELLA Oh, sir, you are indeed a true poet, for you touch our hearts, and they go out to you!

GROS. [*aside*] This is simply cloying. [*Aloud*] Ladies, I am sorry to appear ungallant, but this is Saturday, and you have been following me about ever since Monday. I should like the usual half-holiday. I shall take it as a personal favour if you will kindly allow me to close early to-day.

SAPH. Oh, sir, do not send us from you!

GROS. Poor, poor girls! It is best to speak plainly. I know that I am loved by you, but I never can love you in return, for my heart is fixed elsewhere! Remember the fable of the Magnet and the Churn.

ANG. [*wildly*] But we don't know the fable of the Magnet and the Churn!

GROS. Don't you? Then I will sing it to you.

Song—GROSVENOR

A magnet hung in a hardware shop,
And all around was a loving crop

Of scissors and needles, nails and knives,
Offering love for all their lives;
But for iron the magnet felt no whim,
Though he charmed iron, it charmed not him;
From needles and nails and knives he'd turn,
For he'd set his love on a Silver Churn!

ALL A Silver Churn?

GROS. A Silver Churn!

His most æsthetic,
Very magnetic
Fancy took this turn—
"If I can wheedle
A knife or a needle,
Why not a Silver Churn?"

CHORUS His most æsthetic, etc.

GROS. And Iron and Steel expressed surprise,
The needles opened their well-drilled eyes,
The penknives felt "shut up", no doubt,
The scissors declared themselves "cut out",
The kettles they boiled with rage, 'tis said,
While every nail went off its head,
And hither and thither began to roam,
Till a hammer came up—and drove them home.

ALL It drove them home?
GROS. It drove them home!

While this magnetic,
Peripatetic
Lover he lived to learn,
By no endeavour
Can magnet ever
Attract a Silver Churn!

ALL While this magnetic, etc.

[*They go off in low spirits, gazing back at him from time to time.*

GROS. At last they are gone! What is this mysterious fascination that I seem to exercise over all I come across? A curse on my fatal beauty, for I am sick of conquests!

PATIENCE *appears*

PA. Archibald!

GROS. [*turns and sees her*] Patience!

PA. I have escaped with difficulty from my Reginald. I wanted to see you so much that I might ask you if you still love me as fondly as ever?

GROS. Love you? If the devotion of a lifetime—[*Seizes her hand*]

PA. [*indignantly*] Hold! Unhand me, or I scream! [*He releases her*] If you are a gentleman, pray remember that I am another's! [*Very tenderly*] But you *do* love me, don't you?

GROS. Madly, hopelessly, despairingly!

PA. That's right! I never can be yours; but that's right!

GROS. And you love this Bunthorne?

PA. With a heart-whole ecstasy that withers, and scorches, and burns, and stings! [*Sadly*] It is my duty.

GROS. Admirable girl! But you are not happy with him?

PA. Happy? I am miserable beyond description!

GROS. That's right! I never can be yours; but that's right!

PA. But go now. I see dear Reginald approaching. Farewell, dear Archibald; I cannot tell you how happy it has made me to know that you still love me.

GROS. Ah, if I only dared— [*Advances towards her*]

PA. Sir! this language to one who is promised to another! [*Tenderly*] Oh, Archibald, think of me sometimes, for my heart is breaking! He is so unkind to me, and you would be so loving!

GROS. Loving! [*Advances towards her*]

PA. Advance one step, and as I am a good and pure woman, I scream! [*Tenderly*] Farewell, Archibald! [*Sternly*] Stop there! [*Tenderly*] Think of me sometimes! [*Angrily*] Advance at your peril! Once more, adieu!

[GROSVENOR *sighs, gazes sorrowfully at her, sighs deeply, and exit. She bursts into tears.*

Enter BUNTHORNE, *followed by* JANE. *He is moody and preoccupied*

JANE *sings*

In a doleful train,
  One and one I walk all day;
For I love in vain—
  None so sorrowful as they
    Who can only sigh and say,
    Woe is me, alackaday!

BUN. [*seeing* PATIENCE] Crying, eh? What are you crying about?

PA. I've only been thinking how dearly I love you!

BUN. Love me! Bah!

JANE Love him! Bah!

BUN. [*to* JANE] Don't you interfere.

JANE He always crushes me!

PA. [*going to him*] What is the matter, dear Reginald? If you have any sorrow, tell it to me, that I may share it with you. [*Sighing*] It is my duty!

BUN. [*snappishly*] Whom were you talking with just now?

PA. With dear Archibald.

BUN. [*furiously*] With dear Archibald! Upon my honour, this is too much!

JANE A great deal too much!

BUN. [*angrily to* JANE] Do be quiet!

JANE Crushed again!

PA. I think he is the noblest, purest, and most perfect being I have ever met. But I don't love him. It is true that he is devotedly attached to me, but indeed I don't love *him*. Whenever he grows affectionate, I scream. It is my duty! [*Sighing*]

BUN. I dare say!

JANE So do I! *I* dare say!

PA. Why, how could I love him and love you too? You can't love two people at once!

BUN. Oh, can't you, though!

PA. No, you can't; I only wish you could.

BUN. I don't believe you know what love is!

PA. [*sighing*] Yes, I do. There was a happy time when I didn't, but a bitter experience has taught me.

[*Exeunt* BUNTHORNE *and* JANE.

Ballad—PATIENCE

Love is a plaintive song,
  Sung by a suffering maid,
Telling a tale of wrong,
  Telling of hope betrayed;
Tuned to each changing note,
  Sorry when *he* is sad,
Blind to his every mote,
  Merry when he is glad!
    Love that no wrong can cure,
      Love that is always new,
    Love is the love that's pure,
      That is the love that's true!

Rendering good for ill,
  Smiling at every frown,
Yielding your own self-will,
  Laughing your tear-drops down;
Never a selfish whim,
  Trouble, or pain to stir;
Everything for him,
  Nothing at all for her!
    Love that will aye endure,
      Though the rewards be few,
    That is the love that's pure,
      That is the love that's true!

[*At the end of ballad exit* PATIENCE, *weeping.*

Enter BUNTHORNE *and* JANE

BUN. Everything has gone wrong with me since that smug-faced idiot came here. Before that I was admired—I may say, loved.

JANE Too mild—adored!

BUN. Do let a poet soliloquize! The damozels used to follow me wherever I went; now they all follow him!

JANE Not all! *I* am still faithful to you.

BUN. Yes, and a pretty damozel *you* are!

JANE No, not pretty. Massive. Cheer up! I will never leave you, I swear it!

BUN. Oh, thank you! I know what it is; it's his confounded mildness. They find me too highly spiced, if you please! And no doubt I *am* highly spiced.

JANE Not for my taste!

BUN. [*savagely*] No, but I am for theirs. But I will show the world I can be as mild as he. If they want insipidity, they shall have it. I'll meet this fellow on his own ground and beat him on it.

JANE You shall. And I will help you.

BUN. You will? Jane, there's a good deal of good in you, after all!

Duet—BUNTHORNE and JANE

So go to him and say to him, with compliment ironical—
BUN. Sing "Hey to you—
Good day to you"—
And that's what I shall say!

JANE "Your style is much too sanctified—your cut is too canonical"—
BUN. Sing "Bah to you—
Ha! ha! to you"—
And that's what I shall say!

JANE "I was the beau ideal of the morbid young æsthetical—
To doubt my inspiration was regarded as heretical—
Until you cut me out with your placidity emetical."—
BUN. Sing "Booh to you—
Pooh, pooh to you"—
And that's what I shall say!

BOTH Sing "Hey to you—good day to you"—
Sing "Bah to you—ha! ha! to you"—
Sing "Booh to you—pooh, pooh to you"—
And that's what {you / I} shall say!

BUN. I'll tell him that unless he will consent to be more jocular—
JANE Sing "Booh to you—
Pooh, pooh to you"—
And that's what you should say!

BUN. To cut his curly hair, and stick an eyeglass in his ocular—
JANE Sing "Bah to you—
Ha! ha! to you"—
And that's what you should say!

BUN. To stuff his conversation full of quibble and of quiddity—
To dine on chops and roly-poly pudding with avidity—

He'd better clear away with all convenient rapidity.

JANE Sing "Hey to you—
Good day to you"—
And that's what you should say!

BOTH Sing "Booh to you—pooh, pooh to you"—
Sing "Bah to you—ha! ha! to you"—
Sing "Hey to you—good day to you"—
And that's what {I / you} shall say!

[*Exeunt* JANE *and* BUNTHORNE *together.*

Enter DUKE, COLONEL, *and* MAJOR. *They have abandoned their uniforms, and are dressed and made up in imitation of Æsthetics. They have long hair, and other outward signs of attachment to the brotherhood. As they sing they walk in stiff, constrained, and angular attitudes—a grotesque exaggeration of the attitudes adopted by* BUNTHORNE *and the young Ladies in Act I.*

Trio—DUKE, COLONEL, and MAJOR

It's clear that mediæval art alone retains its zest,
To charm and please its devotees we've done our little best.
We're not quite sure if all we do has the Early English ring;
But, as far as we can judge, it's something like this sort of thing:
You hold yourself like this [*attitude*],
You hold yourself like that [*attitude*],
By hook and crook you try to look both angular and flat [*attitude*].
We venture to expect
That what we recollect,
Though but a part of true High Art, will have its due effect.

If this is not exactly right, we hope you won't upbraid;
You can't get high Æsthetic tastes, like trousers, ready made.
True views on Mediævalism Time alone will bring,
But, as far as we can judge, it's something like this sort of thing:
You hold yourself like this [*attitude*],
You hold yourself like that [*attitude*],
By hook and crook you try to look both angular and flat [*attitude*].
To cultivate the trim
Rigidity of limb,
You ought to get a Marionette, and form your style on him [*attitude*].

COL. [*attitude*] Yes, it's quite clear that our only chance of making a lasting impression on these young ladies is to become as æsthetic as they are.

MAJ. [*attitude*] No doubt. The only question is how far we've succeeded in doing so. I don't know why, but I've an idea that this is not quite right.

DUKE [*attitude*] *I* don't like it. I never did. I don't see what it means. I do it, but I don't like it.

COL. My good friend, the question is not whether we like it, but whether they do. They understand these things—we don't. Now I shouldn't be surprised if this is effective enough—at a distance.

MAJ. I can't help thinking, we're a little stiff at it. It would be extremely awkward if we were to be "struck" so!

COL. I don't think we shall be struck so. Perhaps we're a little awkward at first—but everything must have a beginning. Oh, here they come! 'Tention!

They strike fresh attitudes, as ANGELA *and* SAPHIR *enter*

ANG. [*seeing them*] Oh, Saphir—see—see! The immortal fire has descended on them, and they are of the Inner Brotherhood—perceptively intense and consummately utter. [*The* OFFICERS *have some difficulty in maintaining their constrained attitudes*]

SAPH. [*in admiration*] How Botticellian! How Fra Angelican! Oh, Art, we thank thee for this boon!

COL. [*apologetically*] I'm afraid we're not quite right.

ANG. Not supremely, perhaps, but oh, so, all-but! [*To* SAPHIR] Oh, Saphir, are they not quite too all-but?

SAPHIR They are indeed jolly utter!

MAJ. [*in agony*] I wonder what the Inner Brotherhood usually recommend for cramp?

COL. Ladies, we will not deceive you. We are doing this at some personal inconvenience with a view of expressing the extremity of our devotion to you. We trust that it is not without its effect.

ANG. We will not deny that we are much moved by this proof of your attachment.

SAPH. Yes, your conversion to the principles of Æsthetic Art in its highest development has touched us deeply.

ANG. And if Mr. Grosvenor should remain obdurate—

SAPH. Which we have every reason to believe he will—

MAJ. [*aside, in agony*] I wish they'd make haste.

ANG. We are not prepared to say that our yearning hearts will not go out to you.

COL. [*as giving a word of command*] By sections of threes—Rapture! [*All strike a fresh attitude, expressive of æsthetic rapture*]

SAPH. Oh, it's extremely good—for beginners it's admirable.

MAJ. The only question is, who will take who?

COL. Oh, the Duke chooses first, as a matter of course.

DUKE Oh, I couldn't think of it—you are really too good!

COL. Nothing of the kind. You are a great matrimonial fish, and it's only fair that each of these ladies should have a chance of hooking you. It's perfectly simple. Observe, suppose you choose Angela, I take Saphir, Major takes nobody. Suppose you choose Saphir, Major takes Angela, I take nobody. Suppose you choose neither, I take Angela, Major takes Saphir. Clear as day!

Quintet

DUKE, COLONEL, MAJOR, ANGELA, and SAPHIR

DUKE [*taking* SAPHIR]

If Saphir I choose to marry,
  I shall be fixed up for life;
Then the Colonel need not tarry,
  Angela can be his wife.

[DUKE *dances with* SAPHIR, COLONEL *with* ANGELA, MAJOR *dances alone.*

MAJOR [*dancing alone*]

In that case unprecedented,
  Single I shall live and die—
I shall have to be contented
  With their heartfelt sympathy!

ALL [*dancing as before*]

He will have to be contented
  With our heartfelt sympathy!

DUKE [*taking* ANGELA]

If on Angy I determine,
  At my wedding she'll appear
Decked in diamonds and in ermine,
  Major then can take Saphir!

[DUKE *dances with* ANGELA, MAJOR *with* SAPHIR, COLONEL *dances alone.*]

COLONEL [*dancing*]

In that case unprecedented,
  Single I shall live and die—
I shall have to be contented
  With their heartfelt sympathy!

ALL [*dancing as before*]

He will have to be contented
  With our heartfelt sympathy!

DUKE [*taking both* ANGELA *and* SAPHIR]

After some debate internal,
  If on neither I decide,
Saphir then can take the Colonel,

[*Handing* SAPHIR *to* COLONEL]

  Angy be the Major's bride!

[*Handing* ANGELA *to* MAJOR]

[COLONEL *dances with* SAPHIR, MAJOR *with* ANGELA, DUKE *dances alone*]

DUKE [*dancing*]

In that case unprecedented,
  Single I must live and die–
I shall have to be contented
  With their heartfelt sympathy!

ALL [*dancing as before*]

He will have to be contented
  With our heartfelt sympathy.

[*At the end*, DUKE, COLONEL, *and* MAJOR, *and two girls dance off arm-in-arm.*

Enter GROSVENOR

GROS. It is very pleasant to be alone. It is pleasant to be able to gaze at leisure upon those features which all others may gaze upon at their good will! [*Looking at his reflection in hand-mirror*] Ah, I am a very Narcissus!

Enter BUNTHORNE, *moodily*

BUN. It's no use; I can't live without admiration. Since Grosvenor came here, insipidity has been at a premium. Ah, he is there!

GROS. Ah, Bunthorne! come here–look! Very graceful, isn't it!

BUN. [*taking hand-mirror*] Allow me; I haven't seen it. Yes, it is graceful.

GROS. [*re-taking hand-mirror*] Oh, good gracious! not that–this––

BUN. You don't mean that! Bah! I am in no mood for trifling.

GROS. And what is amiss?

BUN. Ever since you came here, you have entirely monopolized the attentions of the young ladies. I don't like it, sir!

GROS. My dear sir, how can I help it? They are the plague of my life.

My dear Mr. Bunthorne, with your personal disadvantages, you can have no idea of the inconvenience of being madly loved, at first sight, by every woman you meet.

BUN. Sir, until you came here I was adored!

GROS. Exactly—until I came here. That's my grievance. I cut everybody out! I assure you, if you could only suggest some means whereby, consistently with my duty to society, I could escape these inconvenient attentions, you would earn my everlasting gratitude.

BUN. I will do so at once. However popular it may be with the world at large, your personal appearance is highly objectionable to *me*.

GROS. It is? [*Shaking his hand*] Oh, thank you! thank you! How can I express my gratitude?

BUN. By making a complete change at once. Your conversation must henceforth be perfectly matter-of-fact. You must cut your hair, and have a back parting. In appearance and costume you must be absolutely commonplace.

GROS. [*decidedly*] No. Pardon me, that's impossible.

BUN. Take care! When I am thwarted I am very terrible.

GROS. I can't help that. I am a man with a mission. And that mission must be fulfilled.

BUN. I don't think you quite appreciate the consequences of thwarting me.

GROS. I don't care what they are.

BUN. Suppose—I won't go so far as to say that I will do it—but suppose for one moment I were to curse you? [GROSVENOR *quails*] Ah! very well. Take care.

GROS. But surely you would never do that? [*In great alarm*]

BUN. I don't know. It would be an extreme measure, no doubt. Still——

GROS. [*wildly*] But you would not do it—I am sure you would not. [*Throwing himself at* BUNTHORNE's *knees, and clinging to him*] Oh, reflect, reflect! You had a mother once.

BUN. Never!

GROS. Then you had an aunt! [BUNTHORNE *affected*] Ah! I see you had! By the memory of that aunt, I implore you to pause ere you resort to this last fearful expedient. Oh, Mr. Bunthorne, reflect, reflect! [*Weeping*]

BUN. [*aside, after a struggle with himself*] I must not allow myself to be unmanned! [*Aloud*] It is useless. Consent at once, or may a nephew's curse——

GROS. Hold! Are you absolutely resolved?

BUN. Absolutely.

GROS. Will nothing shake you?

BUN. Nothing. I am adamant.

GROS. Very good. [*Rising*] Then I yield.

BUN. Ha! You swear it?

GROS. I do, cheerfully. I have long wished for a reasonable pretext for such a change as you suggest. It has come at last. I do it on compulsion!

BUN. Victory! I triumph!

Duet—BUNTHORNE and GROSVENOR

BUN. When I go out of door,
Of damozels a score
(All sighing and burning,
And clinging and yearning)
Will follow me as before.
I shall, with cultured taste,
Distinguish gems from paste,
And "High diddle diddle"
Will rank as an idyll,
If I pronounce it chaste!

BOTH A most intense young man,
A soulful-eyed young man,
An ultra-poetical, super-æsthetical,
Out-of-the-way young man!

GROS. Conceive me, if you can,
An every-day young man:
A commonplace type,
With a stick and a pipe,
And a half-bred black-and-tan;
Who thinks suburban "hops"
More fun than "Monday Pops",
Who's fond of his dinner,
And doesn't get thinner
On bottled beer and chops.

BOTH A commonplace young man,
A matter-of-fact young man,
A steady and stolid-y, jolly Bank-holiday
Every-day young man!

BUN. A Japanese young man,
A blue-and-white young man,
Francesca da Rimini, miminy, piminy,
Je-ne-sais-quoi young man!

GROS. A Chancery Lane young man,
A Somerset House young man,
A very delectable, highly respectable,
Threepenny-bus young man!

BUN. A pallid and thin young man,
A haggard and lank young man,

A greenery-yallery, Grosvenor Gallery,
Foot-in-the-grave young man!

GROS. A Sewell & Cross young man,
A Howell & James young man,
A pushing young particle—"What's the next article?"—
Waterloo-House young man!

Ensemble

BUN.	GROS.
Conceive me, if you can, A crotchety, cracked young man, An ultra-poetical, super-æsthetical, Out-of-the-way young man!	Conceive me, if you can, A matter-of-fact young man, An alphabetical, arithmetical, Every-day young man!

[*At the end*, GROSVENOR *dances off*. BUNTHORNE *remains.*

BUN. It is all right! I have committed my last act of ill-nature, and henceforth I'm a changed character. [*Dances about stage, humming refrain of last air*]

Enter PATIENCE. *She gazes in astonishment at him*

PA. Reginald! Dancing! And—what in the world is the matter with you?

BUN. Patience, I'm a changed man. Hitherto I've been gloomy, moody, fitful—uncertain in temper and selfish in disposition—

PA. You have, indeed! [*Sighing*]

BUN. All that is changed. I have reformed. I have modelled myself upon Mr. Grosvenor. Henceforth I am mildly cheerful. My conversation will blend amusement with instruction. I shall still be æsthetic; but my æstheticism will be of the most pastoral kind.

PA. Oh, Reginald! Is all this true?

BUN. Quite true. Observe how amiable I am. [*Assuming a fixed smile*]

PA. But, Reginald, how long will this last?

BUN. With occasional intervals for rest and refreshment, as long as I do.

PA. Oh, Reginald, I'm so happy! [*In his arms*] Oh, dear, dear Reginald, I cannot express the joy I feel at this change. It will no longer be a duty to love you, but a pleasure—a rapture—an ecstasy!

BUN. My darling!

PA. But—oh, horror! [*Recoiling from him*]

BUN. What's the matter?

PA. Is it quite certain that you have absolutely reformed—that you are henceforth a perfect being—utterly free from defect of any kind?

BUN. It is quite certain. I have sworn it.

PA. Then I never can be yours!

BUN. Why not?

PA. Love, to be pure, must be absolutely unselfish, and there can be nothing unselfish in loving so perfect a being as you have now become!

BUN. But, stop a bit! I don't want to change—I'll relapse—I'll be as I was—interrupted!

Enter GROSVENOR, *followed by all the young Ladies, who are followed by Chorus of Dragoons. He has had his hair cut, and is dressed in an ordinary suit of dittoes and a pot hat. They all dance cheerfully round the stage in marked contrast to their former languor.*

Chorus—GROSVENOR and GIRLS

GROS.	GIRLS
I'm a Waterloo House young man, A Sewell & Cross young man, A steady and stolid-y, jolly Bank-holiday, Every-day young man!	We're Swears & Wells young girls, We're Madame Louise young girls, We're prettily pattering, cheerily chattering, Every-day young girls!

BUN. Angela—Ella—Saphir—what—what does this mean?

ANG. It means that Archibald the All-Right cannot be all-wrong; and if the All-Right chooses to discard æstheticism, it proves that æstheticism ought to be discarded.

PA. Oh, Archibald! Archibald! I'm shocked—surprised—horrified!

GROS. I can't help it. I'm not a free agent. I do it on compulsion.

PA. This is terrible. Go! I shall never set eyes on you again. But—oh, joy!

GROS. What is the matter?

PA. Is it quite, quite certain that you will always be a commonplace young man?

GROS. Always—I've sworn it.

PA. Why, then, there's nothing to prevent my loving you with all the fervour at my command!

GROS. Why, that's true.

PA. My Archibald!

GROS. My Patience! [*They embrace*]

BUN. Crushed again!

Enter JANE

JANE [*who is still æsthetic*] Cheer up! I am still here. I have never left you, and I never will!

BUN. Thank you, Jane. After all, there is no denying it, you're a fine figure of a woman!

JANE My Reginald!

BUN. My Jane!

Flourish. Enter COLONEL, DUKE, *and* MAJOR

COL. Ladies, the Duke has at length determined to select a bride! [*General excitement*]

DUKE I have a great gift to bestow. Approach such of you as are truly lovely. [*All come forward, bashfully, except* JANE *and* PATIENCE] In personal appearance you have all that is necessary to make a woman happy. In common fairness, I think I ought to choose the only one among you who has the misfortune to be distinctly plain. [*Girls retire disappointed*] Jane!

JANE [*leaving* BUNTHORNE'S *arms*] Duke! [JANE *and* DUKE *embrace.* BUNTHORNE *is utterly disgusted*]

BUN. Crushed again!

Finale

DUKE
After much debate internal,
I on Lady Jane decide,
Saphir now may take the Colonel,
Angy be the Major's bride!

[SAPHIR *pairs off with* COLONEL, ANGELA *with* MAJOR, ELLA *with* SOLICITOR.

BUN.
In that case unprecedented,
Single I must live and die—
I shall have to be contented
With a tulip or li*ly!*

[*Takes a lily from button-hole and gazes affectionately at it*]

ALL
He will have to be contented
With a tulip or li*ly!*

Greatly pleased with one another,
To get married we decide.
Each of us will wed the other,
Nobody be Bunthorne's Bride!

Dance

CURTAIN

IOLANTHE

OR

THE PEER AND THE PERI

DRAMATIS PERSONÆ

THE LORD CHANCELLOR
EARL OF MOUNTARARAT
EARL TOLLOLLER
PRIVATE WILLIS [*of the Grenadier Guards*]
STREPHON [*an Arcadian Shepherd*]
QUEEN OF THE FAIRIES
IOLANTHE [*a Fairy, Strephon's Mother*]
CELIA
LEILA } *Fairies*
FLETA
PHYLLIS [*an Arcadian Shepherdess and Ward in Chancery*]

Chorus of Dukes, Marquises, Earls, Viscounts, Barons, and Fairies

ACT I

AN ARCADIAN LANDSCAPE

ACT II

PALACE YARD, WESTMINSTER

First produced at the Savoy Theatre, November 25, 1882

IOLANTHE

OR

THE PEER AND THE PERI

ACT I

SCENE.—*An Arcadian Landscape. A river runs around the back of the stage. A rustic bridge crosses the river.*

Enter Fairies, led by LEILA, CELIA, *and* FLETA. *They trip around the stage, singing as they dance.*

Chorus

Tripping hither, tripping thither,
Nobody knows why or whither;
We must dance and we must sing
Round about our fairy ring!

Solo—CELIA

We are dainty little fairies,
  Ever singing, ever dancing;
We indulge in our vagaries
  In a fashion most entrancing.
If you ask the special function
  Of our never-ceasing motion,
We reply, without compunction,
  That we haven't any notion!

Chorus

No, we haven't any notion!
  Tripping hither, etc.

Solo—LEILA

If you ask us how we live,
Lovers all essentials give—
We can ride on lovers' sighs,
Warm ourselves in lovers' eyes,
Bathe ourselves in lovers' tears,
Clothe ourselves with lovers' fears,

Arm ourselves with lovers' darts,
Hide ourselves in lovers' hearts.
When you know us, you'll discover
That we almost live on lover!

Chorus

Tripping hither, etc.
[*At the end of Chorus, all sigh wearily*]

CELIA Ah, it's all very well, but since our Queen banished Iolanthe, fairy revels have not been what they were!

LEILA Iolanthe was the life and soul of Fairyland. Why, she wrote all our songs and arranged all our dances! We sing her songs and we trip her measures, but we don't enjoy ourselves!

FLETA To think that five-and-twenty years have elapsed since she was banished! What could she have done to have deserved so terrible a punishment?

LEILA Something awful! She married a mortal!

FLETA Oh! Is it injudicious to marry a mortal?

LEILA Injudicious? It strikes at the root of the whole fairy system! By our laws, the fairy who marries a mortal dies!

CELIA But Iolanthe didn't die!

Enter FAIRY QUEEN

QUEEN No, because your Queen, who loved her with a surpassing love, commuted her sentence to penal servitude for life, on condition that she left her husband and never communicated with him again!

LEILA That sentence of penal servitude she is now working out, on her head, at the bottom of that stream!

QUEEN Yes, but when I banished her, I gave her all the pleasant places of the earth to dwell in. I'm sure I never intended that she should go and live at the bottom of a stream! It makes me perfectly wretched to think of the discomfort she must have undergone!

LEILA Think of the damp! And her chest was always delicate.

QUEEN And the frogs! Ugh! I never shall enjoy any peace of mind until I know why Iolanthe went to live among the frogs!

FLETA Then why not summon her and ask her?

QUEEN Why? Because if I set eyes on her I should forgive her at once!

CELIA Then why not forgive her? Twenty-five years—it's a long time!

LEILA Think how we loved her!

QUEEN Loved her? What was your love to mine? Why, she was invaluable to me! Who taught me to curl myself inside a buttercup? Iolanthe! Who taught me to swing upon a cobweb? Iolanthe! Who taught me to dive into a dewdrop—to nestle in a nutshell—to gambol upon gossamer? Iolanthe!

LEILA She certainly did surprising things!

FLETA Oh, give her back to us, great Queen, for your sake if not for ours! [*All kneel in supplication*]

QUEEN [*irresolute*] Oh, I should be strong, but I am weak! I should be marble, but I am clay! Her punishment has been heavier than I intended. I did not mean that she should live among the frogs—and—well, well, it shall be as you wish—it shall be as you wish!

Invocation—QUEEN

Iolanthe!
From thy dark exile thou art summoned!
Come to our call—
Come, Iolanthe!

CELIA Iolanthe!

LEILA Iolanthe!

ALL Come to our call,
Come, Iolanthe!

[IOLANTHE *rises from the water. She is clad in water-weeds. She approaches the* QUEEN *with head bent and arms crossed.*

IOLANTHE With humbled breast
And every hope laid low,
To thy behest,
Offended Queen, I bow!

QUEEN For a dark sin against our fairy laws
We sent thee into life-long banishment;
But mercy holds her sway within our hearts—
Rise—thou art pardoned!

IOL. Pardoned!

ALL Pardoned!

[*Her weeds fall from her, and she appears clothed as a fairy. The* QUEEN *places a diamond coronet on her head, and embraces her. The others also embrace her.*

Chorus

Welcome to our hearts again,
  Iolanthe! Iolanthe!
We have shared thy bitter pain,
  Iolanthe! Iolanthe!

Every heart, and every hand
In our loving little band
Welcomes thee to Fairyland,
  Iolanthe!

QUEEN And now, tell me, with all the world to choose from, why on earth did you decide to live at the bottom of that stream?

IOL. To be near my son, Strephon.

QUEEN Bless my heart, I didn't know you had a son.

IOL. He was born soon after I left my husband by your royal command—but he does not even know of his father's existence.

FLETA How old is he?

IOL. Twenty-four.

LEILA Twenty-four! No one, to look at you, would think you had a son of twenty-four! But that's one of the advantages of being immortal. We never grow old! Is he pretty?

IOL. He's extremely pretty, but he's inclined to be stout.

ALL [*disappointed*] Oh!

QUEEN I see no objection to stoutness, in moderation.

CELIA And what is he?

IOL. He's an Arcadian shepherd—and he loves Phyllis, a Ward in Chancery.

CELIA A mere shepherd! and he half a fairy!

IOL. He's a fairy down to the waist—but his legs are mortal.

ALL Dear me!

QUEEN I have no reason to suppose that I am more curious than other people, but I confess I should like to see a person who is fairy down to the waist, but whose legs are mortal.

IOL. Nothing easier, for here he comes!

Enter STREPHON, *singing and dancing and playing on a flageolet. He does not see the Fairies, who retire up stage as he enters.*

Song—STREPHON

Good morrow, good mother!
  Good mother, good morrow!
By some means or other,
  Pray banish your sorrow!

With joy beyond telling
My bosom is swelling,
So join in a measure
Expressive of pleasure,
For I'm to be married to-day—to-day—
Yes, I'm to be married to-day!

CHORUS [*aside*] Yes, he's to be married to-day—to-day—
Yes, he's to be married to-day!

IOL. Then the Lord Chancellor has at last given his consent to your marriage with his beautiful ward, Phyllis?

STREPH. Not he, indeed. To all my tearful prayers he answers me, "A shepherd lad is no fit helpmate for a Ward of Chancery." I stood in court, and there I sang him songs of Arcadee, with flageolet accompaniment—in vain. At first he seemed amused, so did the Bar; but quickly wearying of my song and pipe, bade me get out. A servile usher then, in crumpled bands and rusty bombazine, led me, still singing, into Chancery Lane! I'll go no more; I'll marry her to-day, and brave the upshot, be it what it may! [*Sees Fairies*] But who are these?

IOL. Oh, Strephon! rejoice with me, my Queen has pardoned me!

STREPH. Pardoned you, mother? This is good news indeed.

IOL. And these ladies are my beloved sisters.

STREPH. Your sisters! Then they are—my aunts!

QUEEN A pleasant piece of news for your bride on her wedding day!

STREPH. Hush! My bride knows nothing of my fairyhood. I dare not tell her, lest it frighten her. She thinks me mortal, and prefers me so.

LEILA Your fairyhood doesn't seem to have done you much good.

STREPH. Much good! My dear aunt! it's the curse of my existence! What's the use of being half a fairy? My body can creep through a key-hole, but what's the good of that when my legs are left kicking behind? I can make myself invisible down to the waist, but that's of no use when my legs remain exposed to view? My brain is a fairy brain, but from the waist downwards I'm a gibbering idiot. My upper half is immortal, but my lower half grows older every day, and some day or other must die of old age. What's to become of my upper half when I've buried my lower half I really don't know!

FAIRIES Poor fellow!

QUEEN I see your difficulty, but with a fairy brain you should seek an intellectual sphere of action. Let me see. I've a borough or two at my disposal. Would you like to go into Parliament?

IOL. A fairy Member! That would be delightful!

STREPH. I'm afraid I should do no good there—you see, down to the waist, I'm a Tory of the most determined description, but my legs are a couple of confounded Radicals, and, on a division, they'd be sure to take me into the wrong lobby. You see, they're two to one, which is a strong working majority.

QUEEN Don't let that distress you; you shall be returned as a Liberal-Unionist, and your legs shall be our peculiar care.

STREPH. [*bowing*] I see your Majesty does not do things by halves.

QUEEN No, we are fairies down to the feet.

Ensemble

QUEEN Fare thee well, attractive stranger.
FAIRIES Fare thee well, attractive stranger.
QUEEN Shouldst thou be in doubt or danger,
Peril or perplexitee,
Call us, and we'll come to thee!
FAIRIES Call us, and we'll come to thee!
Tripping hither, tripping thither,
Nobody knows why or whither;
We must now be taking wing
To another fairy ring!

[*Fairies and* QUEEN *trip off*, IOLANTHE, *who takes an affectionate farewell of her son, going off last.*

Enter PHYLLIS, *singing and dancing, and accompanying herself on a flageolet.*

Song—PHYLLIS

Good morrow, good lover!
Good lover, good morrow!
I prithee discover,
Steal, purchase, or borrow
Some means of concealing
The care you are feeling,
And join in a measure
Expressive of pleasure,
For we're to be married to-day—to-day!
For we're to be married to-day!

BOTH Yes, we're to be married, etc.

STREPH. [*embracing her*] My Phyllis! And to-day we are to be made happy for ever.

PHYL. Well, we're to be married.

STREPH. It's the same thing.

PHYL. I suppose it is. But oh, Strephon, I tremble at the step I'm taking! I believe it's penal servitude for life to marry a Ward of Court without the Lord Chancellor's consent! I shall be of age in two years. Don't you think you could wait two years?

STREPH. Two years. Have you ever looked in the glass?

PHYL. No, never.

STREPH. Here, look at that [*showing her a pocket mirror*], and tell me if you think it rational to expect me to wait two years?

PHYL. [*looking at herself*] No. You're quite right—it's asking too much. One must be reasonable.

STREPH. Besides, who knows what will happen in two years? Why, you might fall in love with the Lord Chancellor himself by that time!

PHYL. Yes. He's a clean old gentleman.

STREPH. As it is, half the House of Lords are sighing at your feet.

PHYL. The House of Lords are certainly extremely attentive.

STREPH. Attentive? I should think they were! Why did five-and-twenty Liberal Peers come down to shoot over your grass-plot last autumn? It couldn't have been the sparrows. Why did five-and-twenty Conservative Peers come down to fish your pond? Don't tell me it was the gold-fish! No, no—delays are dangerous, and if we are to marry, the sooner the better.

Duet—STREPHON and PHYLLIS

PHYL.
None shall part us from each other,
One in life and death are we:
All in all to one another—
I to thee and thou to me!

BOTH
Thou the tree and I the flower—
Thou the idol; I the throng—
Thou the day and I the hour—
Thou the singer; I the song!

STREPH.
All in all since that fond meeting
When in joy, I woke to find
Mine the heart within thee beating,
Mine the love that heart enshrined!

BOTH
Thou the stream and I the willow—
Thou the sculptor; I the clay—
Thou the ocean; I the billow—
Thou the sunrise; I the day!

[*Exeunt* STREPHON *and* PHYLLIS *together*

March. Enter Procession of Peers

Chorus

Loudly let the trumpet bray!
Tantantara!
Proudly bang the sounding brasses!
Tzing! Boom!
As upon its lordly way
This unique procession passes,
Tantantara! Tzing! Boom!
Bow, bow, ye lower middle classes!
Bow, bow, ye tradesmen, bow, ye masses!
Blow the trumpets, bang the brasses!
Tantantara! Tzing! Boom!
We are peers of highest station,
Paragons of legislation,
Pillars of the British nation!
Tantantara! Tzing! Boom!

Enter the LORD CHANCELLOR, *followed by his train-bearer*

Song—LORD CHANCELLOR

The Law is the true embodiment
Of everything that's excellent.
It has no kind of fault or flaw,
And I, my Lords, embody the Law.
The constitutional guardian I
Of pretty young Wards in Chancery,

All very agreeable girls—and none
Are over the age of twenty-one.
  A pleasant occupation for
  A rather susceptible Chancellor!

ALL — A pleasant, etc.

LORD CH. — But though the compliment implied
Inflates me with legitimate pride,
It nevertheless can't be denied
That it has its inconvenient side.
For I'm not so old, and not so plain,
And I'm quite prepared to marry again,
But there'd be the deuce to pay in the Lords
If I fell in love with one of my Wards!
  Which rather tries my temper, for
  I'm *such* a susceptible Chancellor!

ALL — Which rather, etc.

And every one who'd marry a Ward
Must come to me for my accord,
And in my court I sit all day,

Giving agreeable girls away,
With one for him—and one for he—
And one for you—and one for ye—
And one for thou—and one for thee—
But never, oh, never a one for me!
  Which is exasperating for
  A highly susceptible Chancellor!

ALL — Which is, etc.

Enter LORD TOLLOLLER

LORD TOLL. And now, my Lords, to the business of the day.

LORD CH. By all means. Phyllis, who is a Ward of Court, has so powerfully affected your Lordships, that you have appealed to me in a body to give her to whichever one of you she may think proper to select, and a noble Lord has just gone to her cottage to request her immediate attendance. It would be idle to deny that I, myself, have the misfortune to be singularly attracted by this young person. My regard for her is rapidly undermining my constitution. Three months ago I was a stout man. I need say no more. If I could reconcile it with my duty, I should unhesitatingly award her to myself, for I can conscientiously say that I know no man who is so well fitted to render her exceptionally happy. [*Peers:* Hear, hear!] But such an award would be open to misconstruction, and therefore, at whatever personal inconvenience, I waive my claim.

LORD TOLL. My Lord, I desire, on the part of this House, to express its sincere sympathy with your Lordship's most painful position.

LORD CH. I thank your Lordships. The feelings of a Lord Chancellor who is in love with a Ward of Court are not to be envied. What is his position? Can he give his own consent to his own marriage with his own Ward? Can he marry his own Ward without his own consent? And if he marries his own Ward without his own consent, can he commit himself for contempt of his own Court? And if he commit himself for contempt of his own Court, can he appear by counsel before himself, to move for arrest of his own judgment? Ah, my Lords, it is indeed painful to have to sit upon a woolsack which is stuffed with such thorns as these!

Enter LORD MOUNTARARAT

LORD MOUNT. My Lords, I have much pleasure in announcing that I have succeeded in inducing the young person to present herself at the Bar of this House.

Enter PHYLLIS

Recitative—PHYLLIS

My well-loved Lord and Guardian dear,
You summoned me, and I am here!

Chorus of Peers

Oh, rapture, how beautiful!
How gentle—how dutiful!

Solo—LORD TOLLOLLER

Of all the young ladies I know
This pretty young lady's the fairest;
Her lips have the rosiest show,
Her eyes are the richest and rarest.
Her origin's lowly, it's true,
But of birth and position I've plenty;
I've grammar and spelling for two,
And blood and behaviour for twenty!
Her origin's lowly, it's true,
I've grammar and spelling for two;

CHORUS Of birth and position he's plenty,
With blood and behaviour for twenty!

Solo—LORD MOUNTARARAT

Though the views of the House have diverged
On every conceivable motion,
All questions of Party are merged
In a frenzy of love and devotion;
If you ask us distinctly to say
What Party we claim to belong to,
We reply, without doubt or delay,
The Party I'm singing this song to!

Solo—PHYLLIS

I'm very much pained to refuse,
But I'll stick to my pipes and my tabors;
I can spell all the words that I use,
And my grammar's as good as my neighbours'.
As for birth—I was born like the rest,
My behaviour is rustic but hearty,
And I know where to turn for the best,
When I want a particular Party!

CHORUS Though her station is none of the best,
I suppose she was born like the rest;
And she knows where to look for her hearty,
When she wants a particular Party!

Recitative—PHYLLIS

Nay, tempt me not.
To rank I'll not be bound;
In lowly cot
Alone is virtue found!

CHORUS No, no; indeed high rank will never hurt you,
The Peerage is not destitute of virtue.

Ballad—LORD TOLLOLLER

Spur not the nobly born
With love affected,
Nor treat with virtuous scorn
The well-connected.
High rank involves no shame—
We boast an equal claim
With him of humble name
To be respected!
Blue blood! blue blood!
When virtuous love is sought
Thy power is naught,
Though dating from the Flood,
Blue blood!

CHORUS Blue blood! blue blood! etc.

Spare us the bitter pain
Of stern denials,
Nor with low-born disdain
Augment our trials.

Hearts just as pure and fair
May beat in Belgrave Square
As in the lowly air
Of Seven Dials!
Blue blood! Blue blood!
Of what avail art thou
To serve us now?
Though dating from the Flood,
Blue blood!

CHORUS Blue blood! blue blood! etc.

Recitative—PHYLLIS

My Lords, it may not be.
With grief my heart is riven!
You waste your time on me,
For ah! my heart is given!

ALL Given!
PHYL. Yes, given!
ALL Oh, horror!!!

Recitative—LORD CHANCELLOR

And who has dared to brave our high displeasure,
And thus defy our definite command?

Enter STREPHON

STREPH. 'Tis I—young Strephon! mine this priceless treasure!
Against the world I claim my darling's hand!

[PHYLLIS *rushes to his arms.*

A shepherd I—
ALL A shepherd he!
STREPH. Of Arcady—
ALL Of Arcadee!
STREPH. Betrothed are we!
ALL Betrothed are they—
STREPH. And mean to be—
ALL Espoused to-day!

Ensemble

STREPH.	THE OTHERS
A shepherd I	A shepherd he
Of Arcady,	Of Arcadee,
Betrothed are we,	Betrothed is he,
And mean to be	And means to be
Espoused to-day!	Espoused to-day!

Duet—LORD MOUNTARARAT and LORD TOLLOLLER
[*aside to each other*]

'Neath this blow,
Worse than stab of dagger—
Though we mo-
Mentarily stagger,
In each heart
Proud are we innately—
Let's depart,
Dignified and stately!

ALL
Let's depart,
Dignified and stately!

Chorus of Peers

Though our hearts she's badly bruising,
In another suitor choosing,
Let's pretend it's most amusing.
Ha! ha! ha! Tan-ta-ra!

[*Exeunt all the Peers, marching round stage with much dignity.* LORD CHANCELLOR *separates* PHYLLIS *from* STREPHON *and orders her off. She follows Peers. Manent* LORD CHANCELLOR *and* STREPHON.

LORD CH. Now, sir, what excuse have you to offer for having disobeyed an order of the Court of Chancery?

STREPH. My Lord, I know no Courts of Chancery; I go by Nature's Acts of Parliament. The bees—the breeze—the seas—the rooks—the brooks—the gales—the vales—the fountains and the mountains cry, "You love this maiden—take her, we command you!" 'Tis writ in heaven by the bright barbèd dart that leaps forth into lurid light from each grim thundercloud. The very rain pours forth her sad and sodden sympathy! When chorused Nature bids me take my love, shall I reply, "Nay, but a certain Chancellor forbids it"? Sir, you are England's Lord High

Chancellor, but are you Chancellor of birds and trees, King of the winds and Prince of thunderclouds?

LORD CH. No. It's a nice point. I don't know that I ever met it before. But my difficulty is that at present there's no evidence before the Court that chorused Nature has interested herself in the matter.

STREPH. No evidence! You have my word for it. I tell you that she bade me take my love.

LORD CH. Ah! but, my good sir, you mustn't tell us what she told you—it's not evidence. Now an affidavit from a thunderstorm, or a few words on oath from a heavy shower, would meet with all the attention they deserve.

STREPH. And have you the heart to apply the prosaic rules of evidence to a case which bubbles over with poetical emotion?

LORD CH. Distinctly. I have always kept my duty strictly before my eyes, and it is to that fact that I owe my advancement to my present distinguished position.

Song—LORD CHANCELLOR

When I went to the Bar as a very young man,
(Said I to myself—said I),
I'll work on a new and original plan
(Said I to myself—said I),

I'll never assume that a rogue or a thief
Is a gentleman worthy implicit belief,
Because his attorney has sent me a brief
(Said I to myself—said I!).

Ere I go into court I will read my brief through
(Said I to myself—said I).
And I'll never take work I'm unable to do
(Said I to myself—said I),
My learned profession I'll never disgrace
By taking a fee with a grin on my face,
When I haven't been there to attend to the case
(Said I to myself—said I!).

I'll never throw dust in a juryman's eyes
(Said I to myself—said I),
Or hoodwink a judge who is not over-wise
(Said I to myself—said I),
Or assume that the witnesses summoned in force
In Exchequer, Queen's Bench, Common Pleas, or Divorce,
Have perjured themselves as a matter of course
(Said I to myself—said I!).

In other professions in which men engage
(Said I to myself—said I),
The Army, the Navy, the Church, and the Stage
(Said I to myself—said I),
Professional license, if carried too far,
Your chance of promotion will certainly mar—
And I fancy the rule might apply to the Bar
(Said I to myself—said I!).

[*Exit* LORD CHANCELLOR.

Enter IOLANTHE

STREPH. Oh, Phyllis, Phyllis! To be taken from you just as I was on the point of making you my own! Oh, it's too much—it's too much!

IOL. [*to* STREPHON, *who is in tears*] My son in tears—and on his wedding day!

STREPH. My wedding day! Oh, mother, weep with me, for the Law has interposed between us, and the Lord Chancellor has separated us for ever!

IOL. The Lord Chancellor! [*Aside*] Oh, if he did but know!

STREPH. [*overhearing her*] If he did but know what?

IOL. No matter! The Lord Chancellor has no power over you. Remember you are half a fairy. You can defy him—down to the waist.

STREPH. Yes, but from the waist downwards he can commit me to prison for years! Of what avail is it that my body is free, if my legs are working out seven years' penal servitude?

IOL. True. But take heart—our Queen has promised you her special protection. I'll go to her and lay your peculiar case before her.

STREPH. My beloved mother! how can I repay the debt I owe you?

Finale—QUARTET

As it commences, the Peers appear at the back, advancing unseen and on tiptoe. LORD MOUNTARARAT *and* LORD TOLLOLLER *lead* PHYLLIS *between them, who listens in horror to what she hears.*

STREPH. [*to* IOLANTHE] When darkly looms the day,
And all is dull and grey,
To chase the gloom away,
On thee I'll call!

PHYL. [*speaking aside to* LORD MOUNTARARAT] What was that?

LORD MOUNT. [*aside to* PHYLLIS]
I think I heard him say,
That on a rainy day,
To while the time away,
On her he'd call!

CHORUS We think we heard him say, etc.

[PHYLLIS *is much agitated at her lover's supposed faithlessness.*

IOL. [*to* STREPHON] When tempests wreck thy bark,
And all is drear and dark,
If thou shouldst need an Ark,
I'll give thee one!

PHYL. [*speaking aside to* LORD TOLLOLLER] What was that?

LORD TOLL. [*aside to* PHYLLIS]
I heard the minx remark,
She'd meet him after dark,
Inside St. James's Park,
And give him one!

PHYL. The prospect's very bad,
My heart so sore and sad
Will never more be glad
As summer's sun.

IOL., LORD TOLL., STREPH., LORD MOUNT.
The prospect's not so bad,
{My / Thy} heart so sore and sad
May very soon be glad
As summer's sun;

PHYL., IOL., LORD TOLL., STREPH., LORD MOUNT.
For when the sky is dark
And tempests wreck {my / thy / his} bark,
If {he should / I should / thou shouldst} need an Ark,
{She'll / I'll} give {him / me / thee} one!

PHYL. [*revealing herself*] Ah!

[IOLANTHE *and* STREPHON *much confused.*

PHYL. Oh, shameless one, tremble!
Nay, do not endeavour
Thy fault to dissemble,
We part—and for ever!
I worshipped him blindly,
He worships another—

STREPH. Attend to me kindly,
This lady's my mother!

TOLL. This lady's his *what?*
STREPH. This lady's my mother!
TENORS This lady's his *what?*
BASSES He says she's his mother!

[*They point derisively to* IOLANTHE, *laughing heartily at her. She goes for protection to* STREPHON.

Enter LORD CHANCELLOR. IOLANTHE *veils herself*

LORD CH. What means this mirth unseemly,
That shakes the listening earth?

LORD TOLL. The joke is good extremely,
And justifies our mirth.

LORD MOUNT. This gentleman is seen,
With a maid of seventeen;
A-taking of his *dolce far niente;*
And wonders he'd achieve,
For he asks us to believe
She's his mother—and he's nearly five-and-twenty.

LORD CH. [*sternly*] Recollect yourself, I pray,
And be careful what you say—
As the ancient Romans said, *festina lent.*
For I really do not see
How so young a girl could be
The mother of a man of five-and-twenty.

ALL Ha! ha! ha! ha! ha!

STREPH. My Lord, of evidence I have no dearth—
She is—has been—my mother from my birth!

Ballad

In babyhood
Upon her lap I lay,
With infant food
She moistenèd my clay;
Had she withheld
The succour she supplied,
By hunger quelled,
Your Strephon might have died!

LORD CH. [*much moved*]
Had that refreshment been denied,
Indeed our Strephon might have died!

ALL [*much affected*]
Had that refreshment been denied,
Indeed our Strephon might have died!

LORD MOUNT. But as she's not
His mother, it appears,
Why weep these hot
Unnecessary tears?
And by what laws
Should we so joyously
Rejoice, because
Our Strephon did not die?
Oh, rather let us pipe our eye
Because our Strephon did not die!

ALL That's very true—let's pipe our eye
Because our Strephon did not die!

[*All weep.* IOLANTHE, *who has succeeded in hiding her face from* LORD CHANCELLOR, *escapes unnoticed.*

PHYL. Go, traitorous one—for ever we must part:
To one of you, my Lords, I give my heart!

ALL Oh, rapture!

STREPH. Hear me, Phyllis, ere you leave me.

PHYL. Not a word—you did deceive me.

ALL Not a word—you did deceive her.

[*Exit* STREPHON.

Ballad—PHYLLIS

For riches and rank I do not long—
Their pleasures are false and vain;
I gave up the love of a lordly throng
For the love of a simple swain.
But now that simple swain's untrue,
With sorrowful heart I turn to you—
A heart that's aching,
Quaking, breaking,
As sorrowful hearts are wont to do!

The riches and rank that you befall
Are the only baits you use,
So the richest and rankiest of you all

My sorrowful heart shall choose.
As none are so noble—none so rich
As this couple of lords, I'll find a niche
In my heart that's aching,
Quaking, breaking,
For one of you two—and I don't care which!

Ensemble

PHYL. [*to* LORD MOUNTARARAT *and* LORD TOLLOLLER]
To you I give my heart so rich!
ALL [*puzzled*] To which?
PHYL. I do not care!
To you I yield—it is my doom!
ALL To whom?
PHYL. I'm not aware!
I'm yours for life if you but choose.
ALL She's whose?
PHYL. That's your affair!
I'll be a countess, shall I not?
ALL Of what?
PHYL. I do not care!
ALL Lucky little lady!
Strephon's lot is shady;
Rank, it seems, is vital,
"Countess" is the title,
But of what I'm not aware;

Enter STREPHON

STREPH. Can I inactive see my fortunes fade?
No, no!
Mighty protectress, hasten to my aid!

Enter Fairies, tripping, headed by CELIA, LEILA, *and* FLETA, *and followed by* QUEEN.

CHORUS OF FAIRIES
Tripping hither, tripping thither,
Nobody knows why or whither;
Why you want us we don't know,
But you've summoned us, and so
Enter all the little fairies
To their usual tripping measure!
To oblige you all our care is—
Tell us, pray, what is your pleasure!

STREPH. The lady of my love has caught me talking to another—
PEERS Oh, fie! our Strephon is a rogue!
STREPH. I tell her very plainly that the lady is my mother—
PEERS Taradiddle, taradiddle, tol lol lay!
STREPH. She won't believe my statement, and declares we must be parted,
Because on a career of double-dealing I have started,
Then gives her hand to one of these, and leaves me broken-hearted—
PEERS Taradiddle, taradiddle, tol lol lay!
QUEEN Ah, cruel ones, to separate two lovers from each other!
FAIRIES Oh, fie! our Strephon's not a rogue!
QUEEN You've done him an injustice, for the lady *is* his mother!
FAIRIES Taradiddle, taradiddle, tol lol lay!
LORD CH. That fable perhaps may serve his turn as well as any other.
[*Aside*] I didn't see her face, but if they fondled one another,
And she's but seventeen—I don't believe it was his mother!
Taradiddle, taradiddle.
ALL Tol lol lay!

LORD TOLL. I have often had a use
For a thorough-bred excuse
Of a sudden (which is English for "*repente*"),
But of all I ever heard
This is much the most absurd,
For she's seventeen, and he is five-and-twenty!
ALL Though she is seventeen, and he's four or five-and-twenty!
Oh, fie! our Strephon is a rogue!

LORD MOUNT. Now, listen, pray to me,
For this paradox will be
Carried, nobody at all *contradicente*.
Her age, upon the date
Of his birth, was *minus* eight,
If she's seventeen, and he is five-and-twenty!
ALL To say she is his mother is an utter bit of folly!
Oh, fie! our Strephon is a rogue!
Perhaps his brain is addled, and it's very melancholy!
Taradiddle, taradiddle, tol lol lay!
I wouldn't say a word that could be reckoned as injurious,
But to find a mother younger than her son is very curious,

And that's a kind of mother that is usually spurious.
Taradiddle, taradiddle, tol lol lay!

LORD CH. Go away, madam;
I should say, madam,
You display, madam,
Shocking taste.

It is rude, madam,
To intrude, madam,
With your brood, madam,
Brazen-faced!

You come here, madam,
Interfere, madam,
With a peer, madam.
(I am one.)

You're aware, madam,
What you dare, madam,
So take care, madam,
And begone!

Ensemble

FAIRIES [*to* QUEEN]
Let us stay, madam;
I should say, madam,
They display, madam,
Shocking taste.

It is rude, madam,
To allude, madam,
To your brood, madam,
Brazen-faced!

We don't fear, madam,
Any peer, madam,
Though, my dear madam,
This is one.

They will stare, madam,
When aware, madam,
What they dare, madam—
What they've done!

PEERS
Go away, madam;
I should say, madam,
You display, madam,
Shocking taste.

It is rude, madam,
To intrude, madam,
With your brood, madam,
Brazen-faced!

You come here, madam,
Interfere, madam,
With a peer, madam,
(I am one.)

You're aware, madam,
What you dare, madam,
So take care, madam,
And begone!

QUEEN [*furious*]
Bearded by these puny mortals!
I will launch from fairy portals
All the most terrific thunders
In my armory of wonders!

PHYL. [*aside*]
Should they launch terrific wonders,
All would then repent their blunders.
Surely these must be immortals.

[*Exit* PHYLLIS.

QUEEN
Oh! Chancellor unwary
It's highly necessary
Your tongue to teach
Respectful speech—
Your attitude to vary!

Your badinage so airy,
Your manner arbitrary,
Are out of place
When face to face
With an influential Fairy.

ALL THE PEERS [*aside*]
We never knew
We were talking to
An influential Fairy!

LORD CH.
A plague on this vagary,
I'm in a nice quandary!
Of hasty tone
With dames unknown
I ought to be more chary;
It seems that she's a fairy
From Andersen's library,
And I took her for
The proprietor
Of a Ladies' Seminary!

PEERS
We took her for
The proprietor
Of a Ladies' Seminary!

QUEEN
When next your Houses do assemble,
You may tremble!

CELIA
Our wrath, when gentlemen offend us,
Is tremendous!

LEILA They meet, who underrate our calling,
Doom appalling!

QUEEN Take down our sentence as we speak it,
And *he* shall wreak it!
[*Indicating* STREPHON.

PEERS Oh, spare us!

QUEEN Henceforth, Strephon, cast away
Crooks and pipes and ribbons so gay—
Flocks and herds that bleat and low;
Into Parliament you shall go!

ALL Into Parliament he shall go!
Backed by our supreme authority,
He'll command a large majority!
Into Parliament he shall go!

QUEEN In the Parliamentary hive,
Liberal or Conservative—
Whig or Tory—I don't know—
But into Parliament you shall go!

FAIRIES Into Parliament, etc.

QUEEN [*speaking through music*]

Every bill and every measure
That may gratify his pleasure,
Though your fury it arouses,
Shall be passed by both your Houses!

PEERS Oh!

You shall sit, if he sees reason,
Through the grouse and salmon season;

PEERS No!

He shall end the cherished rights
You enjoy on Friday nights:

PEERS No!

He shall prick that annual blister,
Marriage with deceased wife's sister:

PEERS Mercy!

Titles shall ennoble, then,
All the Common Councilmen:

PEERS — Spare us!
Peers shall teem in Christendom,
And a Duke's exalted station
Be attainable by Com-
Petitive Examination!

PEERS	FAIRIES and PHYLLIS
Oh, horror!	Their horror They can't dissemble Nor hide the fear that makes them tremble!

Ensemble

PEERS	FAIRIES, PHYLLIS and STREPHON
Young Strephon is the kind of lout We do not care a fig about! We cannot say What evils may Result in consequence.	With Strephon for your foe, no doubt, A fearful prospect opens out, And who shall say What evils may Result in consequence?
But lordly vengeance will pursue All kinds of common people who Oppose our views, Or boldly choose To offer us offence.	A hideous vengeance will pursue All noblemen who venture to Oppose his views, Or boldly choose To offer him offence.
He'd better fly at humbler game, Or our forbearance he must claim, If he'd escape In any shape A very painful wrench!	'Twill plunge them into grief and shame; His kind forbearance they must claim, If they'd escape In any shape A very painful wrench.
Your powers we dauntlessly pooh-pooh: A dire revenge will fall on you, If you besiege Our high *prestige*— (The word "*prestige*" is French.)	Although our threats you now pooh-pooh, A dire revenge will fall on you, Should he besiege Your high *prestige*— (The word "*prestige*" is French.)

PEERS — Our lordly style
You shall not quench
With base *canaille!*

FAIRIES — (That word is French.)

PEERS — Distinction ebbs
Before a herd
Of vulgar *plebs!*

FAIRIES — (A Latin word.)

PEERS — 'Twould fill with joy,
And madness stark
The *οἱ πολλοί*!

FAIRIES — (A Greek remark.)

PEERS — One Latin word, one Greek remark,
And one that's French.

FAIRIES Your lordly style
We'll quickly quench
With base *canaille!*
PEERS (That word is French.)
FAIRIES Distinction ebbs
Before a herd
Of vulgar *plebs!*
PEERS (A Latin word.)
FAIRIES 'Twill fill with joy
And madness stark
The *οἱ πολλοί!*
PEERS (A Greek remark.)

FAIRIES One Latin word, one Greek remark,
And one that's French.

PEERS	FAIRIES
You needn't wait:	We will not wait:
Away you fly!	We go sky-high!
Your threatened hate	Our threatened hate
We won't defy!	You won't defy!

[FAIRIES *threaten* PEERS *with their wands.* PEERS *kneel as begging for mercy.* PHYLLIS *implores* STREPHON *to relent. He casts her from him, and she falls fainting into the arms of* LORD MOUNTARARAT *and* LORD TOLLOLLER.

END OF ACT I

ACT II

SCENE.—*Palace Yard, Westminster. Westminster Hall,* L. *Clock Tower up,* R.C. PRIVATE WILLIS *discovered on sentry,* R. *Moonlight.*

Song—PRIVATE WILLIS

When all night long a chap remains
On sentry-go, to chase monotony
He exercises of his brains,
That is, assuming that he's got any.
Though never nurtured in the lap
Of luxury, yet I admonish you,

I am an intellectual chap,
And think of things that would astonish you.
I often think it's comical–Fal, lal, la!
Now Nature always does contrive–Fal, lal, la!
That every boy and every gal
That's born into the world alive
Is either a little Liberal
Or else a little Conservative!
Fal, lal, la!

When in that House M.P.'s divide,
If they've a brain and cerebellum, too,
They've got to leave that brain outside,
And vote just as their leaders tell 'em to.
But then the prospect of a lot
Of dull M.P.'s in close proximity,
All thinking for themselves, is what
No man can face with equanimity.
Then let's rejoice with loud Fal la–Fal lal la!
That Nature always does contrive–Fal lal la!
That every boy and every gal
That's born into the world alive
Is either a little Liberal
Or else a little Conservative!
Fal lal la!

Enter FAIRIES, *with* CELIA, LEILA, *and* FLETA. *They trip round stage*

Chorus of FAIRIES

Strephon's a Member of Parliament!
Carries every Bill he chooses.
To his measures all assent–
Showing that fairies have their uses.
Whigs and Tories
Dim their glories,
Giving an ear to all his stories–
Lords and Commons are both in the blues!
Strephon makes them shake in their shoes!
Shake in their shoes!
Shake in their shoes!
Strephon makes them shake in their shoes!

Enter PEERS *from Westminster Hall.*

Chorus of PEERS

Strephon's a Member of Parliament!
  Running a-muck of all abuses.
His unqualified assent
  Somehow nobody now refuses.
    Whigs and Tories
    Dim their glories,
Giving an ear to all his stories
Carrying every Bill he may wish:
Here's a pretty kettle of fish!
    Kettle of fish!
    Kettle of fish!
Here's a pretty kettle of fish!

Enter LORD MOUNTARARAT *and* LORD TOLLOLLER *from Westminster Hall*

CELIA You seem annoyed.

LORD MOUNT. Annoyed! I should think so! Why, this ridiculous *protégé* of yours is playing the deuce with everything! To-night is the second reading of his Bill to throw the Peerage open to Competitive Examination!

LORD TOLL. And he'll carry it, too!

LORD MOUNT. Carry it? Of course he will! He's a Parliamentary Pickford—he carries everything!

LEILA Yes. If you please, that's our fault!

LORD MOUNT. The deuce it is!

CELIA Yes; we influence the members, and compel them to vote just as he wishes them to.

LEILA It's our system. It shortens the debates.

LORD TOLL. Well, but think what it all means. I don't so much mind for myself, but with a House of Peers with no grandfathers worth mentioning, the country must go to the dogs!

LEILA I suppose it must!

LORD MOUNT. I don't want to say a word against brains—I've a great respect for brains—I often wish I had some myself—but with a House of Peers composed exclusively of people of intellect, what's to become of the House of Commons?

LEILA I never thought of that!

LORD MOUNT. This comes of women interfering in politics. It so happens that if there is an institution in Great Britain which is not susceptible of any improvement at all, it is the House of Peers!

Song—LORD MOUNTARARAT

When Britain really ruled the waves—
  (In good Queen Bess's time)

The House of Peers made no pretence
To intellectual eminence,
  Or scholarship sublime;
Yet Britain won her proudest bays
In good Queen Bess's glorious days!

CHORUS Yes, Britain won, etc.

When Wellington thrashed Bonaparte,
  As every child can tell,
The House of Peers, throughout the war,
Did nothing in particular,
  And did it very well:
Yet Britain set the world ablaze
In good King George's glorious days!

CHORUS Yes, Britain set, etc.

And while the House of Peers withholds
  Its legislative hand,
And noble statesmen do not itch
To interfere with matters which
  They do not understand,
As bright will shine Great Britain's rays
As in King George's glorious days!

CHORUS As bright will shine, etc.

LEILA [*who has been much attracted by the* PEERS *during this song*] Charming persons, are they not?

CELIA Distinctly. For self-contained dignity, combined with airy condescension, give me a British Representative Peer!

LORD TOLL. Then pray stop this *protégé* of yours before it's too late. Think of the mischief you're doing!

LEILA [*crying*] But we *can't* stop him now. [*Aside to Celia*] Aren't they lovely! [*Aloud*] Oh, why did you go and defy us, you great geese!

Duet—LEILA and CELIA

LEILA
In vain to us you plead—
Don't go!
Your prayers we do not heed—
Don't go!
It's true we sigh,
But don't suppose
A tearful eye
Forgiveness shows.
Oh, no!
We're very cross indeed—
Don't go!

FAIRIES
It's true we sigh, etc.

CELIA
Your disrespectful sneers—
Don't go!
Call forth indignant tears—
Don't go!
You break our laws—
You are our foe:

We cry because
We hate you so!
You know!
You very wicked Peers!
Don't go!

FAIRIES

You break our laws–
You are our foe:
We cry because
We hate you so!
You know!
You very wicked peers!
Don't go!

LORDS MOUNT. and TOLL.

Our disrespectful sneers,
Ha, ha!
Call forth indignant tears,
Ha, ha!
If that's the case, my dears–
FAIRIES Don't go!
PEERS We'll go!

[*Exeunt* LORD MOUNTARARAT, LORD TOLLOLLER, *and* PEERS. FAIRIES *gaze wistfully after them.*

Enter FAIRY QUEEN

QUEEN Oh, shame–shame upon you! Is this your fidelity to the laws you are bound to obey? Know ye not that it is death to marry a mortal?

LEILA Yes, but it's not death to *wish* to marry a mortal!

FLETA If it were, you'd have to execute us all!

QUEEN Oh, this is weakness! Subdue it!

CELIA We know it's weakness, but the weakness is so strong!

LEILA We are not all as tough as you are!

QUEEN Tough! Do you suppose that I am insensible to the effect of manly beauty? Look at that man! [*Referring to* SENTRY] A perfect picture! [*To* SENTRY] Who are you, sir?

WILLIS [*coming to "attention"*] Private Willis, B Company, 1st Grenadier Guards.

QUEEN You're a very fine fellow, sir.

WILLIS I am generally admired.

QUEEN I can quite understand it. [*To* FAIRIES] Now here is a man whose physical attributes are simply godlike. That man has a most extraordinary effect upon me. If I yielded to a natural impulse, I should fall down and worship that man. But I mortify this inclination; I wrestle with it, and it lies beneath my feet! That is how I treat my regard for that man!

Song–FAIRY QUEEN

Oh, foolish fay,
Think you, because

His brave array
  My bosom thaws,
I'd disobey
  Our fairy laws?
Because I fly
  In realms above,
In tendency
  To fall in love,
Resemble I
  The amorous dove?

[*Aside*] O, amorous dove!
  Type of Ovidius Naso!
    This heart of mine
    Is soft as thine,
  Although I dare not say so!

CHORUS Oh, amorous dove, etc.

On fire that glows
  With heat intense
I turn the hose
  Of common sense,
And out it goes
  At small expense!
We must maintain
  Our fairy law;
That is the main
  On which to draw—
In that we gain
  A Captain Shaw!

[*Aside*] Oh, Captain Shaw!
Type of true love kept under!
Could thy Brigade
With cold cascade
Quench my great love, I wonder!

CHORUS Oh, Captain Shaw! etc.

[*Exeunt* FAIRIES *and* FAIRY QUEEN, *sorrowfully.*

Enter PHYLLIS

PHYL. [*half crying*] I can't think why I'm not in better spirits. I'm engaged to two noblemen at once. That ought to be enough to make any girl happy. But I'm miserable! Don't suppose it's because I care for Strephon, for I hate him! No girl *could* care for a man who goes about with a mother considerably younger than himself!

Enter LORD MOUNTARARAT and LORD TOLLOLLER

LORD MOUNT. Phyllis! My darling!

LORD TOLL. Phyllis! My own!

PHYL. Don't! How dare you? Oh, but perhaps you're the two noblemen I'm engaged to?

LORD MOUNT. I am one of them.

LORD TOLL. I am the other.

PHYL. Oh, then, my darling! [*To* LORD MOUNTARARAT] My own! [*To* LORD TOLLOLLER] Well, have you settled which it's to be?

LORD TOLL. Not altogether. It's a difficult position. It would be hardly delicate to toss up. On the whole we would rather leave it to you.

PHYL. How can it possibly concern me? You are both Earls, and you are both rich, and you are both plain.

LORD MOUNT. So we are. At least I am.

LORD TOLL. So am I.

LORD MOUNT. No, no!

LORD TOLL. I am indeed. Very plain.

LORD MOUNT. Well, well—perhaps you are.

PHYL. There's really nothing to choose between you. If one of you would forgo his title, and distribute his estates among his Irish tenantry, why, then, I should then see a reason for accepting the other.

LORD MOUNT. Tolloller, are you prepared to make this sacrifice?

LORD TOLL. No!

LORD MOUNT. Not even to oblige a lady?

LORD TOLL. No! not even to oblige a lady.

LORD MOUNT. Then, the only question is, which of us shall give way to the other? Perhaps, on the whole, she would be happier with me. I don't know. I may be wrong.

LORD TOLL. No. I don't know that you are. I really believe she would. But the awkward part of the thing is that if you rob me of the girl of my heart, we must fight, and one of us must die. It's a family tradition that I have sworn to respect. It's a painful position, for I have a very strong regard for you, George.

LORD MOUNT. [*much affected*] My dear Thomas!

LORD TOLL. You are very dear to me, George. We were boys together —at least *I* was. If I were to survive you, my existence would be hopelessly embittered.

LORD MOUNT. Then, my dear Thomas, you must not do it. I say it again and again—if it will have this effect upon you, you must not do it. No, no. If one of us is to destroy the other, let it be me!

LORD TOLL. No, no!

LORD MOUNT. Ah, yes!—by our boyish friendship I implore you!

LORD TOLL. [*much moved*] Well, well, be it so. But, no—no!—I cannot consent to an act which would crush you with unavailing remorse.

LORD MOUNT. But it would not do so. I should be very sad at first—oh, who would not be?—but it would wear off. I like you *very much*—but not, perhaps, as much as you like me.

LORD TOLL. George, you're a noble fellow, but that telltale tear betrays you. No, George; you are very fond of me, and I cannot consent to give you a week's uneasiness on my account.

LORD MOUNT. But, dear Thomas, it would not last a week! Remember, you lead the House of Lords! on your demise I shall take your place! Oh, Thomas, it would not last a day!

PHYL. [*coming down*] Now, I do hope you're not going to fight about me, because it's really not worth while.

LORD TOLL. [*looking at her*] Well, I don't believe it is!
LORD MOUNT. Nor I. The sacred ties of Friendship are paramount.

Quartette—LORD MOUNTARARAT

LORD TOLLOLLER, PHYLLIS, and PRIVATE WILLIS

LORD TOLL. Though p'r'aps I may incur your blame,
The things are few
I would not do
In Friendship's name!

LORD MOUNT. And I may say I think the same;
Not even love
Should rank above
True Friendship's name!

PHYL. Then free me, pray; be mine the blame;
Forget your craze
And go your ways
In Friendship's name!

ALL Oh, many a man, in Friendship's name,
Has yielded fortune, rank, and fame!
But no one yet, in the world so wide,
Has yielded up a promised bride!

WILLIS Accept, O Friendship, all the same,

ALL This sacrifice to thy dear name!

[*Exeunt* LORD MOUNTARARAT *and* LORD TOLLOLLER, *lovingly, in one direction, and* PHYLLIS *in another. Exit* SENTRY.

Enter LORD CHANCELLOR, *very miserable*

Recitative—LORD CHANCELLOR

Love, unrequited, robs me of my rest:
Love, hopeless love, my ardent soul encumbers:
Love, nightmare-like, lies heavy on my chest,
And weaves itself into my midnight slumbers!

Song—LORD CHANCELLOR

When you're lying awake with a dismal headache, and repose is taboo'd by anxiety,

I conceive you may use any language you choose to indulge in, without impropriety;
For your brain is on fire—the bedclothes conspire of usual slumber to plunder you:
First your counterpane goes, and uncovers your toes, and your sheet slips demurely from under you;
Then the blanketing tickles—you feel like mixed pickles—so terribly sharp is the pricking,
And you're hot, and you're cross, and you tumble and toss till there's nothing 'twixt you and the ticking.
Then the bedclothes all creep to the ground in a heap, and you pick 'em all up in a tangle;
Next your pillow resigns and politely declines to remain at its usual angle!
Well, you get some repose in the form of a doze, with hot eye-balls and head ever aching,
But your slumbering teems with such horrible dreams that you'd very much better be waking;
For you dream you are crossing the Channel, and tossing about in a steamer from Harwich—
Which is something between a large bathing machine and a very small second-class carriage—
And you're giving a treat (penny ice and cold meat) to a party of friends and relations—
They're a ravenous horde—and they all came on board at Sloane Square and South Kensington Stations.
And bound on that journey you find your attorney (who started that morning from Devon);
He's a bit undersized, and you don't feel surprised when he tells you he's only eleven.
Well, you're driving like mad with this singular lad (by the by, the ship's now a four-wheeler),
And you're playing round games, and he calls you bad names when you tell him that "ties pay the dealer";
But this you can't stand, so you throw up your hand, and you find you're as cold as an icicle,
In your shirt and your socks (the black silk with gold clocks), crossing Salisbury Plain on a bicycle:
And he and the crew are on bicycles too—which they've somehow or other invested in—
And he's telling the tars all the particu*lars* of a company he's interested in—
It's a scheme of devices, to get at low prices all goods from cough mixtures to cables
(Which tickled the sailors), by treating retailers as though they were all vege*ta*bles—

You get a good spadesman to plant a small tradesman (first take off his
boots with a boot-tree),
And his legs will take root, and his fingers will shoot, and they'll blossom
and bud like a fruit-tree–
From the greengrocer tree you get grapes and green pea, cauliflower,
pineapple, and cranberries,
While the pastrycook plant cherry brandy will grant, apple puffs, and
three-corners, and Banburys–
The shares are a penny, and ever so many are taken by Rothschild and
Baring,
And just as a few are allotted to you, you awake with a shudder despairing–
You're a regular wreck, with a crick in your neck, and no wonder you
snore, for your head's on the floor, and you've needles and pins from
your soles to your shins, and your flesh is a-creep, for your left
leg's asleep, and you've cramp in your toes, and a fly on your nose,
and some fluff in your lung, and a feverish tongue, and a thirst that's
intense, and a general sense that you haven't been sleeping in clover;
But the darkness has passed, and it's daylight at last, and the night has
been long–ditto ditto my song–and thank goodness they're both
of them over!

[LORD CHANCELLOR *falls exhausted on a seat.*

LORDS MOUNTARARAT *and* TOLLOLLER *come forward*

LORD MOUNT. I am much distressed to see your Lordship in this condition.

LORD CH. Ah, my Lords, it is seldom that a Lord Chancellor has reason to envy the position of another, but I am free to confess that I would rather be two Earls engaged to Phyllis than any other half-dozen noblemen upon the face of the globe.

LORD TOLL. [*without enthusiasm*] Yes. It's an enviable position when you're the only one.

LORD MOUNT. Oh yes, no doubt—most enviable. At the same time, seeing you thus, we naturally say to ourselves, "This is very sad. His Lordship is constitutionally as blithe as a bird—he trills upon the bench like a thing of song and gladness. His series of judgments in F sharp minor, given *andante* in six-eight time, are among the most remarkable effects ever produced in a Court of Chancery. He is, perhaps, the only living instance of a judge whose decrees have received the honour of a double *encore*. How can we bring ourselves to do that which will deprive the Court of Chancery of one of its most attractive features?"

LORD CH. I feel the force of your remarks, but I am here in two capacities, and they clash, my Lord, they clash! I deeply grieve to say that in declining to entertain my last application to myself, I presumed to address myself in terms which render it impossible for me ever to apply to myself again. It was a most painful scene, my Lord—most painful!

LORD TOLL. This is what it is to have two capacities! Let us be thankful that we are persons of no capacity whatever.

LORD MOUNT. Come, come. Remember you are a very just and kindly old gentleman, and you need have no hesitation in approaching yourself, so that you do so respectfully and with a proper show of deference.

LORD CH. Do you really think so?

LORD MOUNT. I do.

LORD CH. Well, I will nerve myself to another effort, and, if that fails, I resign myself to my fate!

Trio—LORD CHANCELLOR, LORDS MOUNTARARAT and TOLLOLLER

LORD MOUNT. If you go in
You're sure to win—
Yours will be the charming maidie:
Be your law
The ancient saw,
"Fain heart never won fair lady!"

ALL Faint heart never won fair lady!
Every journey has an end—
When at the worst affairs will mend—

Dark the dawn when day is nigh—
Hustle your horse and don't say die!

LORD TOLL. He who shies
At such a prize
Is not worth a maravedi,
Be so kind
To bear in mind—
Faint heart never won fair lady!

ALL Faint heart never won fair lady!
While the sun shines make your hay—
Where a will is, there's a way—
Beard the lion in his lair—
None but the brave deserve the fair!

LORD CH. I'll take heart
And make a start—
Though I fear the prospect's shady—
Much I'd spend
To gain my end—
Faint heart never won fair lady!

ALL Faint heart never won fair lady!
Nothing venture, nothing win—
Blood is thick, but water's thin—
In for a penny, in for a pound—
It's Love that makes the world go round!

[*Dance, and exeunt arm-in-arm together.*

Enter STREPHON, *in very low spirits*

STREPH. I suppose one ought to enjoy oneself in Parliament, when one leads both Parties, as I do! But I'm miserable, poor, broken-hearted fool that I am! Oh, Phyllis, Phyllis!——

Enter PHYLLIS

PHYL. Yes.

STREPH. [*surprised*] Phyllis! But I suppose I should say "My Lady". I have not yet been informed which title your ladyship has pleased to select?

PHYL. I—I haven't quite decided. You see *I* have no *mother* to advise *me!*

STREPH. No. I have.

PHYL. Yes; a *young* mother.

STREPH. Not very—a couple of centuries or so.

PHYL. Oh! She wears well.

STREPH. She does. She's a fairy.

PHYL. I beg your pardon—a what?

STREPH. Oh, I've no longer any reason to conceal the fact—she's a fairy.

PHYL. A fairy! Well, but—that would account for a good many things! Then—I suppose *you're* a fairy?

STREPH. I'm half a fairy.

PHYL. Which half?

STREPH. The upper half—down to the waistcoat.

PHYL. Dear me! [*Prodding him with her fingers*] There is nothing to show it!

STREPH. Don't do that.

PHYL. But why didn't you tell me this before?

STREPH. I thought you would take a dislike to me. But as it's all off, you may as well know the truth—I'm only half a mortal!

PHYL. [*crying*] But I'd rather have half a mortal I do love, than have a dozen I don't!

STREPH. [*crying*] But I think not—go to your half-dozen.

PHYL. [*crying*] It's only two! and I hate 'em! Please forgive me!

STREPH. I don't think I ought to. Besides, all sorts of difficulties will arise. You know, my grandmother looks quite as young as my mother. So do all my aunts.

PHYL. I quite understand. Whenever I see you kissing a very young lady, I shall know it's an elderly relative.

STREPH. You will? Then, Phyllis, I think we shall be very happy! [*Embracing her*]

PHYL. We won't wait long.

STREPH. No. We might change our minds. We'll get married first.

PHYL. And change our minds afterwards?

STREPH. That's the usual course.

Duet—STREPHON and PHYLLIS

STREPH. If we're weak enough to tarry
Ere we marry,
You and I,
Of the feeling I inspire
You may tire
By and by,
For peers with flowing coffers
Press their offers—
That is why

I am sure we should not tarry
Ere we marry,
You and I!

PHYL. If we're weak enough to tarry
Ere we marry,
You and I,
With a more attractive maiden,
Jewel-laden,
You may fly.
If by chance we should be parted,
Broken-hearted
I should die—
So I think we will not tarry
Ere we marry,
You and I.

PHYL. But does your mother know you're—I mean, is she aware of our engagement?

Enter IOLANTHE

IOL. She is; and thus she welcomes her daughter-in-law! [*Kisses her*]

PHYL. She kisses just like other people! But the Lord Chancellor?

STREPH. I forgot him! Mother, none can resist your fairy eloquence; you will go to him and plead for us?

IOL. [*much agitated*] No, no; impossible!

STREPH. But our happiness—our very lives—depend upon our obtaining his consent!

PHYL. Oh, madam, you cannot refuse to do this!

IOL. You know not what you ask! The Lord Chancellor is—my husband!

STREPH. and PHYL. Your husband!

IOL. My husband and your father! [*Addressing* STREPHON, *who is much moved*]

PHYL. Then our course is plain; on his learning that Strephon is his son, all objection to our marriage will be at once removed!

IOL. No; he must never know! He believes me to have died childless, and, dearly as I love him, I am bound, under penalty of death, not to undeceive him. But see—he comes! Quick—my veil!

[IOLANTHE *veils herself*. STREPHON *and* PHYLLIS *go off on tiptoe.*

Enter LORD CHANCELLOR

LORD CH. Victory! Victory! Success has crowned my efforts, and I may consider myself engaged to Phyllis! At first I wouldn't hear of it—it was out of the question. But I took heart. I pointed out to myself that I was no stranger to myself; that, in point of fact, I had been personally acquainted with myself for some years. This had its effect. I admitted that I had watched my professional advancement with considerable interest, and I handsomely added that I yielded to no one in admiration for my private and professional virtues. This was a great point gained. I then endeavoured to work upon my feelings. Conceive my joy when I distinctly perceived a tear glistening in my own eye! Eventually, after a severe struggle with myself, I reluctantly—most reluctantly—consented.

[IOLANTHE *comes down veiled.*

Recitative—IOLANTHE

My lord, a suppliant at your feet I kneel,
Oh, listen to a mother's fond appeal!
Hear me to-night! I come in urgent need—
'Tis for my son, young Strephon, that I plead!

Ballad—IOLANTHE

He loves! If in the bygone years
  Thine eyes have ever shed
Tears—bitter, unavailing tears,
  For one untimely dead—
If, in the eventide of life,
  Sad thoughts of her arise,
Then let the memory of thy wife
  Plead for my boy—he dies!

He dies! If fondly laid aside
  In some old cabinet,
Memorials of thy long-dead bride
  Lie, dearly treasured yet,
Then let her hallowed bridal dress—
  Her little dainty gloves—
Her withered flowers—her faded tress—
  Plead for my boy—he loves!

[*The* LORD CHANCELLOR *is moved by this appeal. After a pause.*

LORD CH. It may not be—for so the fates decide!
Learn thou that Phyllis is my promised bride.
IOL. [*in horror*] Thy bride! No! no!
LORD CH. It shall be so!
Those who would separate us woe betide!

IOL. My doom thy lips have spoken—
I plead in vain!

CHORUS OF FAIRIES [*without*] Forbear! forbear!

IOL. A vow already broken
I break again!

CHORUS OF FAIRIES [*without*] Forbear! forbear!
IOL. For him—for her—for thee
I yield my life.
Behold—it may not be!
I am thy wife.

CHORUS OF FAIRIES [*without*] Aiaiah! Aiaiah! Willaloo!
LORD CH. [*recognizing her*] Iolanthe! thou livest?
IOL. Aye!
I live! Now let me die!

Enter FAIRY QUEEN *and* FAIRIES. IOLANTHE *kneels to her*

QUEEN Once again thy vows are broken:
Thou thyself thy doom hast spoken!

CHORUS OF FAIRIES Aiaiah! Aiaiah!
Willahalah! Willaloo!
Willahalah! Willaloo!
QUEEN Bow thy head to Destiny:
Death thy doom, and thou shalt die!

CHORUS OF FAIRIES Aiaiah! Aiaiah! etc.

PEERS *and* SENTRY *enter. The* QUEEN *raises her spear*

LEILA Hold! If Iolanthe must die, so must we all; for, as she has sinned, so have we!

QUEEN What?

CELIA We are all fairy duchesses, marchionesses, countesses, viscountesses, and baronesses.

LORD MOUNT. It's our fault. They couldn't help themselves.

QUEEN It seems they *have* helped themselves, and pretty freely, too! [*After a pause*] You have all incurred death; but I can't slaughter the whole company! And yet [*unfolding a scroll*] the law is clear—every fairy must die who marries a mortal!

LORD CH. Allow me, as an old Equity draftsman, to make a suggestion. The subtleties of the legal mind are equal to the emergency. The thing is really quite simple—the insertion of a single word will do it. Let it stand that every fairy shall die who doesn't marry a mortal, and there you are, out of your difficulty at once!

QUEEN We like your humour. Very well! [*Altering the MS. in pencil*] Private Willis!

SENTRY [*coming forward*] Ma'am!

QUEEN To save my life, it is necessary that I marry at once. How should you like to be a fairy guardsman?

SENTRY Well, ma'am, I don't think much of the British soldier who wouldn't ill-convenience himself to save a female in distress.

QUEEN You are a brave fellow. You're a fairy from this moment. [*Wings spring from* SENTRY's *shoulders*] And you, my lords, how say you, will you join our ranks?

[FAIRIES *kneel to* PEERS *and implore them to do so.*

PHYLLIS *and* STREPHON *enter*

LORD MOUNT. [*to* LORD TOLLOLLER] Well, now that the Peers are to be recruited entirely from persons of intelligence, I really don't see what use *we* are, down here, do you, Tolloller?

LORD TOLL. None whatever.

QUEEN Good [*Wings spring from shoulders of* PEERS] Then away we go to Fairyland.

Finale

PHYL.
Soon as we may,
Off and away!
We'll commence our journey airy—
Happy are we—
As you can see,
Every one is now a fairy!

ALL
Every one is now a fairy!

IOL., QUEEN, and PHYL.
Though as a general rule we know
Two strings go to every bow,
Make up your minds that grief 'twill bring,
If you've two beaux to every string.

ALL
Though as a general rule, etc.

LORD CH.
Up in the sky,
Ever so high,

Pleasures come in endless series;
We will arrange
Happy exchange—
House of Peers for House of Peris!

ALL House of Peers for House of Peris!

LORDS CH., MOUNT., and TOLL.
Up in the air, sky-high, sky-high,
Free from Wards in Chancery,
I / He will be surely happier, for
I'm / He's such a susceptible Chancellor.

ALL Up in the air, etc.

CURTAIN

PRINCESS IDA

OR

CASTLE ADAMANT

DRAMATIS PERSONÆ

KING HILDEBRAND
HILARION [*his son*]
CYRIL, FLORIAN [*Hilarion's Friends*]
KING GAMA
ARAC, GURON, SCYNTHIUS [*his Sons*]
PRINCESS IDA [*Gama's Daughter*]
LADY BLANCHE [*Professor of Abstract Science*]
LADY PSYCHE [*Professor of Humanities*]
MELISSA [*Lady Blanche's Daughter*]
SACHARISSA, CHLOE, ADA [*Girl Graduates*]

Soldiers, Courtiers, "Girl Graduates", "Daughters of the Plough", etc.

ACT I

PAVILION IN KING HILDEBRAND'S PALACE

ACT II

GARDENS OF CASTLE ADAMANT

ACT III

COURTYARD OF CASTLE ADAMANT

First produced at the Savoy Theatre, January 5, 1884.

PRINCESS IDA

OR

CASTLE ADAMANT

ACT I

SCENE.—*Pavilion attached to* KING HILDEBRAND'S PALACE. *Soldiers and Courtiers discovered looking out through opera-glasses, telescopes, etc.,* FLORIAN *leading.*

CHORUS Search throughout the panorama
For a sign of royal Gama,
Who to-day should cross the water
With his fascinating daughter—
Ida is her name.

Some misfortune evidently
Has detained them—consequently
Search throughout the panorama
For the daughter of King Gama,
Prince Hilarion's flame!

Solo

FLOR. Will Prince Hilarion's hopes be sadly blighted?
ALL Who can tell?
FLOR. Will Ida break the vows that she has plighted?
ALL Who can tell?
FLOR. Will she back out, and say she did not mean them?
ALL Who can tell?
FLOR. If so, there'll be the deuce to pay between them!

ALL No, no—we'll not despair,
For Gama would not dare
To make a deadly foe
Of Hildebrand, and so,
Search throughout, etc.

Enter KING HILDEBRAND, *with* CYRIL

HILD. See you no sign of Gama?
FLOR. None, my liege!
HILD. It's very odd indeed. If Gama fail
To put in an appearance at our Court

Before the sun has set in yonder west,
And fail to bring the Princess Ida here
To whom our son Hilarion was betrothed
At the extremely early age of one,
There's war between King Gama and ourselves!
[*Aside to* CYRIL] Oh, Cyril, how I dread this interview.
It's twenty years since he and I have met.
He was a twisted monster—all awry—
As though Dame Nature, angry with her work,
Had crumpled it in fitful petulance!

CYR. But, sir, a twisted and ungainly trunk
Often bears goodly fruit. Perhaps he was
A kind, well-spoken gentleman?

HILD. Oh, no!
For, adder-like, his sting lay in his tongue.
(His "sting" is present, though his "stung" is past.)

FLOR. [*looking through glass*] But stay, my liege; o'er yonder mountain's brow
Comes a small body, bearing Gama's arms;
And now I look more closely at it, sir,
I see attached to it King Gama's legs;
From which I gather this corollary
That that small body must be Gama's own!

HILD. Ha! Is the Princess with him?

FLOR. Well, my liege,
Unless her highness is full six feet high,
And wears mustachios too—and smokes cigars—
And rides *en cavalier* in coat of steel—
I do not think she is.

HILD. One never knows.
She's a strange girl, I've heard, and does odd things!
Come, bustle there!
For Gama place the richest robes we own—
For Gama place the coarsest prison dress—
For Gama let our best spare bed be aired—
For Gama let our deepest dungeon yawn—
For Gama lay the costliest banquet out—
For Gama place cold water and dry bread!
For as King Gama brings the Princess here,
Or brings her not, so shall King Gama have
Much more than everything—much less than nothing!

Song and Chorus

HILD. Now hearken to my strict command
On every hand, on every hand—

CHORUS
To your command,
On every hand,
We dutifully bow!

HILD.
If Gama bring the Princess here,
Give him good cheer, give him good cheer.

CHORUS
If she come here
We'll give him a cheer,
And we will show you how.
Hip, hip, hurrah! hip, hip, hurrah!
Hip, hip, hurrah! hurrah! hurrah!
We'll shout and sing
Long live the King,
And his daughter, too, I trow!
Then shout ha! ha! hip, hip, hurrah!
Hip, hip, hip, hip, hurrah!
For the fair Princess and her good papa,
Hurrah! hurrah!

HILD.
But if he fail to keep his troth,
Upon our oath, we'll trounce them both!

CHORUS
He'll trounce them both,
Upon his oath,
As sure as quarter-day!

HILD.
We'll shut him up in a dungeon cell,
And toll his knell on a funeral bell.

CHORUS
From his dungeon cell,
His funeral knell
Shall strike him with dismay!
Hip, hip, hurrah! hip, hip, hurrah!
Hip, hip, hurrah! hurrah! hurrah!
As up we string
The faithless King,
In the old familiar way!
We'll shout ha! ha! hip, hip, hurrah!
Hip, hip, hip, hip, hurrah!
As we make an end of her false papa,
Hurrah! hurrah!

[*Exeunt all.*

Enter HILARION

Recitative—HILARION

To-day we meet, my baby bride and I—
  But ah, my hopes are balanced by my fears!
What transmutations have been conjured by
  The silent alchemy of twenty years!

Ballad—HILARION

Ida was a twelvemonth old,
  Twenty years ago!
I was twice her age, I'm told,
  Twenty years ago!
Husband twice as old as wife
Argues ill for married life
Baleful prophecies were rife,
  Twenty years ago!

Still, I was a tiny prince
  Twenty years ago.
She has gained upon me, since
  Twenty years ago.
Though she's twenty-one, it's true,
I am barely twenty-two—
False and foolish prophets you,
  Twenty years ago!

Enter HILDEBRAND

HIL. Well, father, is there news for me at last?

HILD. King Gama is in sight, but much I fear
With no Princess!

HIL. Alas, my liege, I've heard
That Princess Ida has forsworn the world,
And, with a band of women, shut herself
Within a lonely country house, and there
Devotes herself to stern philosophies!

HILD. Then I should say the loss of such a wife
Is one to which a reasonable man
Would easily be reconciled.

HIL. Oh, no!
Or I am not a reasonable man.
She *is* my wife—has been for twenty years!
[*Holding glass*] I think I see her now.

HILD. Ha! let me look!

HIL. In my mind's eye, I mean—a blushing bride,
All bib and tucker, frill and furbelow!

How exquisite she looked as she was borne,
Recumbent, in her foster-mother's arms!
How the bride wept—nor would be comforted
Until the hireling mother-for-the-nonce
Administered refreshment in the vestry.
And I remember feeling much annoyed
That she should weep at marrying with me.
But then I thought, "These brides are all alike.
You cry at marrying me? How much more cause
You'd have to cry if it were broken off!"
These were my thoughts; I kept them to myself,
For at that age I had not learned to speak.

[*Exeunt.*

Enter Courtiers

Chorus
From the distant panorama
Come the sons of royal Gama.
They are heralds evidently,
And are sacred consequently,
Sons of Gama, hail! oh, hail!

Enter Arac, Guron, *and* Scynthius

Song—Arac

We are warriors three,
Sons of Gama, Rex.
Like most sons are we,
Masculine in sex.

All Three
Yes, yes, yes,
Masculine in sex.

Arac
Politics we bar,
They are not our bent;
On the whole we are
Not intelligent.

All Three
No, no, no,
Not intelligent.

Arac
But with doughty heart,
And with trusty blade
We can play our part—
Fighting is our trade.

ALL THREE Yes, yes, yes,
Fighting is our trade.

ALL THREE Bold, and fierce, and strong, ha! ha!
For a war we burn,
With its right or wrong, ha! ha!
We have no concern.
Order comes to fight, ha! ha!
Order is obeyed,
We are men of might, ha! ha!
Fighting is our trade.
Yes, yes, yes,
Fighting is our trade, ha! ha!

CHORUS They are men of might, ha! ha!
Fighting is their trade.
Order comes to fight, ha! ha!
Order is obeyed, ha! ha!
Fighting is their trade!

Enter KING GAMA

Song—GAMA

If you give me your attention, I will tell you what I am:
I'm a genuine philanthropist—all other kinds are sham.
Each little fault of temper and each social defect
In my erring fellow-creatures I endeavour to correct.
To all their little weaknesses I open people's eyes;
And little plans to snub the self-sufficient I devise;
I love my fellow-creatures—I do all the good I can—
Yet everybody says I'm such a disagreeable man!
And I can't think why!

To compliments inflated I've a withering reply;
And vanity I always do my best to mortify;
A charitable action I can skilfully dissect;
And interested motives I'm delighted to detect;
I know everybody's income and what everybody earns;
And I carefully compare it with the income tax returns;
But to benefit humanity however much I plan,
Yet everybody says I'm such a disagreeable man!
And I can't think why!

I'm sure I'm no ascetic; I'm as pleasant as can be;
You'll always find me ready with a crushing repartee,
I've an irritating chuckle, I've a celebrated sneer,
I've an entertaining snigger, I've a fascinating leer.
To everybody's prejudice I know a thing or two;
I can tell a woman's age in half a minute—and I do.
But although I try to make myself as pleasant as I can,
Yet everybody says I am a disagreeable man!
And I can't think why!

Enter HILDEBRAND, HILARION, CYRIL, *and* FLORIAN

GAMA So this is Castle Hildebrand? Well, well!
Dame Rumour whispered that the place was grand;
She told me that your taste was exquisite,
Superb, unparalleled!
HILD. [*gratified*] Oh, really, King!
GAMA But she's a liar! Why, how old you've grown!
Is this Hilarion? Why, you've changed too—
You were a singularly handsome child!
[*To* FLOR.] Are you a courtier? Come, then, ply your trade,
Tell me some lies. How do you like your King?
Vile rumour says he's all but imbecile.
Now, that's not true?
FLOR. My lord, we love our King.
His wise remarks are valued by his court
As precious stones.
GAMA And for the self-same cause.
Like precious stones, his sensible remarks
Derive their value from their scarcity!
Come now, be honest, tell the truth for once!
Tell it of me. Come, come, I'll harm you not.
This leg is crooked—this foot is ill-designed—
This shoulder wears a hump! Come, out with it!
Look, here's my face! Now, am I not the worst
Of Nature's blunders?

CYR. Nature never errs.
To those who know the workings of your mind,
Your face and figure, sir, suggest a book
Appropriately bound.
GAMA [*enraged*] Why, harkye, sir,
How dare you bandy words with me?
CYR. No need
To bandy aught that appertains to you.
GAMA [*furiously*] Do you permit this, King?
HILD. We are in doubt
Whether to treat you as an honoured guest
Or as a traitor knave who plights his word
And breaks it.
GAMA [*quickly*] If the casting vote's with me,
I give it for the former!
HILD. We shall see.
By the terms of our contract, signed and sealed,
You're bound to bring the Princess here to-day:
Why is she not with you?
GAMA Answer me this:
What think you of a wealthy purse-proud man,
Who, when he calls upon a starving friend,
Pulls out his gold and flourishes his notes,
And flashes diamonds in the pauper's eyes?
What name have you for such an one?
HILD. A snob.
GAMA Just so. The girl has beauty, virtue, wit,
Grace, humour, wisdom, charity, and pluck.
Would it be kindly, think you, to parade
These brilliant qualities before *your* eyes?
Oh no, King Hildebrand, I am no snob!
HILD. [*furiously*] Stop that tongue,
Or you shall lose the monkey head that holds it!
GAMA Bravo! your King deprives me of my head,
That he and I may meet on equal terms!
HILD. Where is she now?
GAMA In Castle Adamant,
One of my many country houses. There
She rules a woman's University,
With full a hundred girls, who learn of her.
CYR. A hundred girls! A hundred ecstasies!
GAMA But no mere girls, my good young gentleman;
With all the college learning that you boast,
The youngest there will prove a match for *you*.
CYR. With all my heart, if she's the prettiest!
[*To* FLOR.] Fancy, a hundred matches—all alight!—

That's if I strike them as I hope to do!
GAMA Despair your hope; their hearts are dead to men.
He who desires to gain their favour must
Be qualified to strike their teeming brains,
And not their hearts. They're safety matches, sir,
And they light only on the knowledge box—
So *you've* no chance!
FLOR. And there are no males whatever in those walls?
GAMA None, gentlemen, excepting letter mails—
And they are driven (as males often are
In other large communities) by women.
Why, bless my heart, she's so particular
She'll scarcely suffer Dr. Watts's hymns—
And all the animals she owns are "hers"!
The ladies rise at cockcrow every morn—
CYR. Ah, then they have male poultry?
GAMA Not at all,
[*Confidentially*] The crowing's done by an accomplished hen!

Duet—GAMA and HILDEBRAND

GAMA
Perhaps if you address the lady
Most politely, most politely—
Flatter and impress the lady,
Most politely, most politely—
Humbly beg and humbly sue—
She may deign to look on you,
But your doing you must do
Most politely, most politely!

ALL
Humbly beg and humbly sue, etc.

HILD.
Go you, and inform the lady,
Most politely, most politely,
If she don't, we'll storm the lady
Most politely, most politely!

[*To* GAMA]
You'll remain as hostage here;
Should Hilarion disappear,
We will hang you, never fear,
Most politely, most politely!

ALL
He'll / I'll / You'll } remain as hostage here, etc.

[GAMA, ARAC, GURON, *and* SCYNTHIUS *are marched off in custody*, HILDEBRAND *following*.

Recitative—HILARION

Come, Cyril, Florian, our course is plain,
To-morrow morn fair Ida we'll engage;
But we will use no force her love to gain,
Nature has armed us for the war we wage!

Trio—HILARION, CYRIL, and FLORIAN

HIL. Expressive glances
Shall be our lances,
And pops of Sillery
Our light artillery.
We'll storm their bowers
With scented showers
Of fairest flowers
That we can buy!

CHORUS Oh, dainty triolet!
Oh, fragrant violet!
Oh, gentle heigho-let
(Or little sigh).
On sweet urbanity,
Though mere inanity,
To touch their vanity
We will rely!

CYR. When day is fading,
With serenading
And such frivolity
We'll prove our quality.
A sweet profusion
Of soft allusion
This bold intrusion
Shall justify.

CHORUS Oh, dainty triolet, etc.

FLOR. We'll charm their senses
With verbal fences,
With ballads amatory
And declamatory.
Little heeding
Their pretty pleading,
Our love exceeding
We'll justify!

CHORUS Oh, dainty triolet, etc.

Re-enter GAMA, ARAC, GURON, *and* SCYNTHIUS *heavily ironed*

Recitative

GAMA Must we, till then, in prison cell be thrust?
HILD. You must!
GAMA This seems unnecessarily severe!
ARAC, GURON, and SCYNTHIUS Hear, hear!

Trio—ARAC, GURON, and SCYNTHIUS

For a month to dwell
In a dungeon cell;
Growing thin and wizen
In a solitary prison,
Is a poor look-out
For a soldier stout,
Who is longing for the rattle
Of a complicated battle—
For the rum-tum-tum
Of the military drum
And the guns that go boom! boom!

ALL The rum-tum-tum
Of the military drum, etc.

HILD. When Hilarion's bride
Has at length complied
With the just conditions
Of our requisitions,
You may go in haste
And indulge your taste
For the fascinating rattle
Of a complicated battle—
For the rum-tum-tum,
Of the military drum,
And the guns that go boom! boom!

ALL For the rum-tum-tum
Of the military drum, etc.

ALL But till that time {we'll / you'll} here remain,

And bail {they / we} will not entertain,
Should she {his / our} mandate disobey,
{Our / Your} lives the penalty will pay!

[GAMA, ARAC, GURON, *and* SCYNTHIUS *are marched off.*

END OF ACT I

ACT II

SCENE.—*Gardens in Castle Adamant. A river runs across the back of the stage, crossed by a rustic bridge. Castle Adamant in the distance.*

Girl graduates discovered seated at the feet of LADY PSYCHE

CHORUS Towards the empyrean heights
Of every kind of lore,
We've taken several easy flights,
And mean to take some more.
In trying to achieve success
No envy racks our heart,
And all the knowledge we possess,
We mutually impart.

Song—MELISSA

Pray, what authors should she read
Who in Classics would succeed?

PSYCHE

If you'd climb the Helicon,
You should read Anacreon,
Ovid's *Metamorphoses*,
Likewise Aristophanes,
And the works of Juvenal:
These are worth attention, all;
But, if you will be advised,
You will get them Bowdlerized!

CHORUS Ah! we will get them Bowdlerized!

Solo—SACHARISSA

Pray you, tell us, if you can,
What's the thing that's known as Man?

PSYCHE

Man will swear and Man will storm—
Man is not at all good form—
Man is of no kind of use—
Man's a donkey—Man's a goose—
Man is coarse and Man is plain—
Man is more or less insane—
Man's a ribald—Man's a rake,
Man is Nature's sole mistake!

CHORUS We'll a memorandum make—
Man is Nature's sole mistake!

And thus to empyrean height
  Of every kind of lore,
In search of wisdom's pure delight,
  Ambitiously we soar.
In trying to achieve success
  No envy racks our heart,
For all we know and all we guess,
  We mutually impart!

Enter LADY BLANCHE. *All stand up demurely*

BLA. Attention, ladies, while I read to you
The Princess Ida's list of punishments.
The first is Sacharissa. She's expelled!
ALL Expelled!
BLA. Expelled, because although she knew
No man of any kind may pass our walls,
She dared to bring a set of chessmen here!
SACH. [*crying*] I meant no harm; they're only men of wood!
BLA. They're men with whom you give each other mate,
And that's enough! The next is Chloe.
CHLOE Ah!
BLA. Chloe will lose three terms, for yesterday,
When looking through her drawing-book, I found
A sketch of a perambulator!
ALL [*horrified*] Oh!
BLA. *Double* perambulator, shameless girl!
That's all at present. Now, attention, pray;

Your Principal the Princess comes to give
Her usual inaugural address
To those young ladies who joined yesterday.

CHORUS Mighty maiden with a mission,
Paragon of common sense,
Running fount of erudition,
Miracle of eloquence,
We are blind, and we would see;
We are bound, and would be free;
We are dumb, and we would talk;
We are lame, and we would walk.

Enter the PRINCESS

Mighty maiden with a mission—
Paragon of common sense;
Running fount of erudition—
Miracle of eloquence!

PRIN. [*recit.*] Minerva, oh, hear me!

Aria

Oh, goddess wise
That lovest light
Endow with sight
Their unillumined eyes.

At this my call,
A fervent few
Have come to woo
The rays that from thee fall.

Let fervent words and fervent thoughts be mine,
That I may lead them to thy sacred shrine!

Women of Adamant, fair Neophytes—
Who thirst for such instruction as we give,
Attend, while I unfold a parable.
The elephant is mightier than Man,
Yet Man subdues him. Why? The elephant
Is elephantine everywhere but here [*tapping her forehead*],
And Man, whose brain is to the elephant's
As Woman's brain to Man's—(that's rule of three),—
Conquers the foolish giant of the woods,

As Woman, in her turn, shall conquer Man.
In Mathematics, Woman leads the way:
The narrow-minded pedant still believes
That two and two make four! Why, we can prove,
We women—household drudges as we are—
That two and two make five—or three—or seven;
Or five-and-twenty, if the case demands!
Diplomacy? The wiliest diplomat
Is absolutely helpless in our hands,
He wheedles monarchs—woman wheedles him!
Logic? Why, tyrant Man himself admits
It's waste of time to argue with a woman!
Then we excel in social qualities:
Though Man professes that he holds our sex
In utter scorn, I venture to believe
He'd rather pass the day with one of you,
Than with five hundred of his fellow-men!
In all things we excel. Believing this,
A hundred maidens here have sworn to place
Their feet upon his neck. If we succeed,
We'll treat him better than he treated us:
But if we fail, why, then let hope fail too!
Let no one care a penny how she looks—
Let red be worn with yellow—blue with green—
Crimson with scarlet—violet with blue!
Let all your things misfit, and you yourselves
At inconvenient moments come undone!
Let hair-pins lose their virtue: let the hook
Disdain the fascination of the eye—
The bashful button modestly evade
The soft embraces of the button-hole!
Let old associations all dissolve,
Let Swan secede from Edgar—Gask from Gask,
Sewell from Cross—Lewis from Allenby!
In other words—let Chaos come again!
[*Coming down*] Who lectures in the Hall of Arts to-day?

BLA. I, madam, on Abstract Philosophy.
There I propose considering, at length,
Three points—The Is, the Might Be, and the Must.
Whether the Is, from being actual fact,
Is more important than the vague Might Be,
Or the Might Be, from taking wider scope,
Is for that reason greater than the Is:
And lastly, how the Is and Might Be stand
Compared with the inevitable Must!

PRIN. The subject's deep—how do you treat it, pray?

BLA. Madam, I take three possibilities,
And strike a balance, then, between the three:
As thus: The Princess Ida Is our head,
The Lady Psyche Might Be,–Lady Blanche,
Neglected Blanche, inevitably Must.
Given these three hypotheses–to find
The actual betting against each of them!

PRIN. Your theme's ambitious: pray you, bear in mind
Who highest soar fall farthest. Fare you well,
You and your pupils! Maidens, follow me.

[*Exeunt* PRINCESS *and maidens singing refrain of chorus*, "*And thus to empyrean heights*", *etc. Manet* LADY BLANCHE.

BLA. I should command here–I was born to rule,
But do I rule? I don't. Why? I don't know.
I shall some day. Not yet. I bide my time.
I once was Some One–and the Was Will Be.
The Present as we speak becomes the Past,
The Past repeats itself, and so is Future!
This sounds involved. It's not. It's right enough.

Song–LADY BLANCHE

Come, mighty Must!
  Inevitable Shall!
In thee I trust.
  Time weaves my coronal!
Go, mocking Is!
  Go, disappointing Was!
That I am this
  Ye are the cursed cause!
Yet humble second shall be first,
    I ween;
And dead and buried be the curst
    Has Been!

Oh, weak Might Be!
  Oh, May, Might, Could, Would, Should!
How powerless ye
  For evil or for good!
In every sense
  Your moods I cheerless call,
Whate'er your tense
  Ye are Imperfect, all!

Ye have deceived the trust I've shown
In ye!
Away! The Mighty Must alone
Shall be!

[*Exit* LADY BLANCHE.

Enter HILARION, CYRIL, *and* FLORIAN, *climbing over wall, and creeping cautiously among the trees and rocks at the back of the stage.*

Trio—HILARION, CYRIL, FLORIAN

Gently, gently,
Evidently
We are safe so far,
After scaling
Fence and paling,
Here, at last, we are!
In this college
Useful knowledge
Everywhere one finds,
And already,
Growing steady,
We've enlarged our minds.

CYR. We've learnt that prickly cactus
Has the power to attract us
When we fall.

ALL When we fall!

HIL. That nothing man unsettles
Like a bed of stinging nettles,
Short or tall.

ALL Short or tall!

FLOR. That bull-dogs feed on throttles—
That we don't like broken bottles
On a wall.

ALL On a wall!

HIL. That spring-guns breathe defiance!
And that burglary's a science
After all!

ALL After all!

Recitative—FLORIAN

A Woman's college! maddest folly going!
What can girls learn within its walls worth knowing?
I'll lay a crown (the Princess shall decide it)
I'll teach them twice as much in half-an-hour outside it.

HILARION

Hush, scoffer; ere you sound your puny thunder,
List to their aims, and bow your head in wonder!

They intend to send a wire
  To the moon—to the moon;
And they'll set the Thames on fire
  Very soon—very soon;
Then they learn to make silk purses
  With their rigs—with their rigs,
From the ears of Lady Circe's
  Piggy-wigs—piggy-wigs.
And weasels at their slumbers
  They trepan—they trepan;
To get sunbeams from cu*cum*bers,
  They've a plan—they've a plan.
They've a firmly rooted notion
They can cross the Polar Ocean,
And they'll find Perpetual Motion,
  If they can—if they can.

ALL
  These are the phenomena
  That every pretty domina

Is hoping we shall see
At her Universitee!

CYR. As for fashion, they forswear it,
So they say—so they say;
And the circle—they will square it
Some fine day—some fine day;
Then the little pigs they're teaching
For to fly—for to fly;
And the niggers they'll be bleaching,
By and by—by and by!
Each newly-joined aspirant
To the clan—to the clan—
Must repudiate the tyrant
Known as Man—known as Man.
They mock at him and flout him,
For they do not care about him,
And they're "going to do without him"
If they can—if they can!

ALL These are the phenomena, etc.

In this college
Useful knowledge
Ev'rywhere one finds,
And already growing steady
We've enlarg'd our minds.

HIL. So that's the Princess Ida's castle! Well,
They must be lovely girls, indeed, if it requires
Such walls as those to keep intruders off!
CYR. To keep men off is only half their charge,
And that the easier half. I much suspect
The object of these walls is not so much
To keep men off as keep the maidens in!
FLOR. But what are these? [*Examining some Collegiate robes*]
HIL. [*looking at them*] Why, Academic robes,
Worn by the lady undergraduates
When they matriculate. Let's try them on. [*They do so*]
Why, see,—we're covered to the very toes.
Three lovely lady undergraduates
Who, weary of the world and all its wooing—
FLOR. And penitent for deeds there's no undoing—
CYR. Looked at askance by well-conducted maids—
ALL Seek sanctuary in these classic shades!

Trio—HILARION, CYRIL, FLORIAN

HIL. I am a maiden, cold and stately,
Heartless I, with a face divine.
What do I want with a heart, innately?
Every heart I meet is mine!

ALL Haughty, humble, coy, or free,
Little care I what maid may be.
So that a maid is fair to see,
Every maid is the maid for me!

[*Dance*]

CYR. I am a maiden frank and simple,
Brimming with joyous roguery;
Merriment lurks in every dimple,
Nobody breaks more hearts than I!

ALL Haughty, humble, coy, or free,
Little care I what maid may be.
So that a maid is fair to see,
Every maid is the maid for me!

[*Dance*]

FLOR. I am a maiden coyly blushing,
Timid am I as a startled hind;
Every suitor sets me flushing:
I am the maid that wins mankind!

ALL Haughty, humble, coy, or free,
Little care I what maid may be.
So that a maid is fair to see,
Every maid is the maid for me!

Enter the PRINCESS *reading. She does not see them*

FLOR. But who comes here? The Princess, as I live! What shall we do?
HIL. [*aside*] Why, we must brave it out!
[*Aloud*] Madam, accept our humblest reverence.

[*They bow, then, suddenly recollecting themselves, curtsey.*
PRIN. [*surprised*] We greet you, ladies. What would you with us?

HIL. [*aside*] What shall I say? [*Aloud*] We are three students, ma'am,
Three well-born maids of liberal estate,
Who wish to join this University.

[HILARION *and* FLORIAN *curtsey again.* CYRIL *bows extravagantly, then, being recalled to himself by* FLORIAN, *curtseys.*

PRIN. If, as you say, you wish to join our ranks,
And will subscribe to all our rules, 'tis well.
FLOR. To all your rules we cheerfully subscribe.
PRIN. You say you're noblewomen. Well, you'll find
No sham degrees for noblewomen here.
You'll find no sizars here, or servitors,
Or other cruel distinctions, meant to draw
A line 'twixt rich and poor: you'll find no tufts
To mark nobility, except such tufts
As indicate nobility of brain.
As for your fellow-students, mark me well:
There are a hundred maids within these walls,
All good, all learned, and all beautiful:
They are prepared to love you: will you swear
To give the fullness of your love to them?
HIL. Upon our words and honours, ma'am, we will!
PRIN. But we go further: will you undertake
That you will never marry any man?
FLOR. Indeed we never will!
PRIN. Consider well,
You must prefer our maids to all mankind!
HIL. To all mankind we much prefer your maids!
CYR. We should be dolts indeed, if we did not,
Seeing how fair——
HIL. [*aside to* CYRIL] Take care—that's rather strong!
PRIN. But have you left no lovers at your home
Who may pursue you here?
HIL. No, madam, none.
We're homely ladies, as no doubt you see,
And we have never fished for lover's love.
We smile at girls who deck themselves with gems,
False hair, and meretricious ornament,
To chain the fleeting fancy of a man,
But do not imitate them. What we have
Of hair, is all our own. Our colour, too,
Unladylike, but not unwomanly,
Is Nature's handiwork, and man has learnt
To reckon Nature an impertinence.
PRIN. Well, beauty counts for naught within these walls;
If all you say is true, you'll pass with us
A happy, happy time!
CYR. If, as you say,
A hundred lovely maidens wait within,

To welcome us with smiles and open arms,
I think there's very little doubt we shall!

Quartette—PRINCESS, HILARION, CYRIL, FLORIAN

PRIN. The world is but a broken toy,
Its pleasure hollow—false its joy,
Unreal its loveliest hue,
Alas!
Its pains alone are true,
Alas!
Its pains alone are true.

HIL. The world is everything you say,
The world we think has had its day.
Its merriment is slow,
Alas!
We've tried it, and we know.
Alas!
We've tried it and we know.

Tutti

PRINCESS	HILARION, CYRIL, FLORIAN
The world is but a broken toy,	The world is but a broken toy,
Its pleasure hollow—false its joy,	We freely give it up with joy,
Unreal its loveliest hue,	Unreal its loveliest hue,
Alas!	Alas!
Its pains alone are true,	Its pains alone are true,
Alas!	Alas!
Its pains alone are true!	Its pains alone are true!

[*Exit* PRINCESS. *The three gentlemen watch her off*. LADY PSYCHE *enters, and regards them with amazement*.

HIL. I'faith, the plunge is taken, gentlemen!
For, willy-nilly, we are maidens now,
And maids against our will we must remain!
[*All laugh heartily*]

PSY. [*aside*] These ladies are unseemly in their mirth.

[*The gentlemen see her, and, in confusion, resume their modest demeanour*.

FLOR. [*aside*] Here's a catastrophe, Hilarion!
This is my sister! She'll remember me,
Though years have passed since she and I have met!

HIL. [*aside to* FLORIAN] Then make a virtue of necessity,
And trust our secret to her gentle care.
FLOR. [*to* PSYCHE, *who has watched* CYRIL *in amazement*] Psyche!
Why, don't you know me? Florian!
PSY. [*amazed*] Why, Florian!
FLOR. My sister [*embraces her*]
PSY. Oh, my dear!
What are you doing here—and who are these?
HIL. I am that Prince Hilarion to whom
Your Princess is betrothed. I come to claim
Her plighted love. Your brother Florian
And Cyril came to see me safely through.
PSY. The Prince Hilarion? Cyril too? How strange!
My earliest playfellows!
HIL. Why, let me look!
Are you that learned little Psyche who
At school alarmed her mates because she called
A buttercup "ranunculus bulbosus"?
CYR. Are you indeed that Lady Psyche, who
At children's parties drove the conjuror wild,
Explaining all his tricks before he did them?
HIL. Are you that learned little Psyche, who
At dinner parties, brought in to dessert,
Would tackle visitors with "You don't know
Who first determined longitude—I do—
Hipparchus 'twas—B.C. one sixty-three!"
Are you indeed that small phenomenon?
PSY. That small phenomenon indeed am I!
But, gentlemen, 'tis death to enter here:
We have all promised to renounce mankind!
FLOR. Renounce mankind? On what ground do you base
This senseless resolution?
PSY. Senseless? No.
We are all taught, and, being taught, believe
That Man, sprung from an Ape, is Ape at heart.
CYR. That's rather strong.
PSY. The truth is always strong!

Song—LADY PSYCHE

A Lady fair, of lineage high,
Was loved by an Ape, in the days gone by.
The Maid was radiant as the sun,
The Ape was a most unsightly one—
So it would not do—
His scheme fell through,

For the Maid, when his love took formal shape,
    Expressed such terror
    At his monstrous error,
That he stammered an apology and made his 'scape,
The picture of a disconcerted Ape.

With a view to rise in the social scale,
He shaved his bristles, and he docked his tail,
He grew mustachios, and he took his tub,
And he paid a guinea to a toilet club—
    But it would not do,
    The scheme fell through—
For the Maid was Beauty's fairest Queen,
    With golden tresses,
    Like a real princess's,
While the Ape, despite his razor keen,
Was the apiest Ape that ever was seen!
He bought white ties, and he bought dress suits,
He crammed his feet into bright tight boots—
And to start in life on a brand-new plan,
He christened himself Darwinian Man!
    But it would not do,
    The scheme fell through—

For the Maiden fair, whom the monkey craved,
    Was a radiant Being,
    With a brain far-seeing—
While a Darwinian Man, though well-behaved,
At best is only a monkey shaved!

ALL   While Darwinian Man, etc.

During this MELISSA *has entered unobserved; she looks on in amazement*

MEL. [*coming down*] Oh, Lady Psyche!
PSY. [*terrified*] What! you heard us then?
    Oh, all is lost!
MEL. Not so! I'll breathe no word!
    [*Advancing in astonishment to* FLORIAN]

How marvellously strange! and are you then
Indeed young men?
FLOR. Well, yes, just now we are—
But hope by dint of study to become,
In course of time, young women.
MEL. [*eagerly*] No, no, no—
Oh, don't do that! Is this indeed a man?
I've often heard of them, but, till to-day,
Never set eyes on one. They told me men
Were hideous, idiotic, and deformed!
They're quite as beautiful as women are!
As beautiful, they're infinitely more so!
Their cheeks have not that pulpy softness which
One gets so weary of in womankind:
Their features are more marked—and—oh, their chins!
How curious! [*Feeling his chin*]
FLOR. I fear it's rather rough.
MEL. [*eagerly*] Oh, don't apologize—I like it so!

Quintette—PSYCHE, MELISSA, HILARION, CYRIL, FLORIAN

PSY.   The woman of the wisest wit
    May sometimes be mistaken, O!
In Ida's views, I must admit,
    My faith is somewhat shaken, O!

CYR.   On every other point than this
    Her learning is untainted, O!

But Man's a theme with which she is
Entirely unacquainted, O!
—acquainted, O!
—acquainted, O!
Entirely unacquainted, O!

ALL Then jump for joy and gaily bound,
The truth is found—the truth is found!
Set bells a-ringing through the air—
Ring here and there and everywhere—
And echo forth the joyous sound,
The truth is found—the truth is found!

[*Dance*]

MEL. My natural instinct teaches me
(And instinct is important, O!)
You're everything you ought to be,
And nothing that you oughtn't, O!

HIL. That fact was seen at once by you
In casual conversation, O!
Which is most creditable to
Your powers of observation, O!
—servation, O!
—servation, O!
Your powers of observation, O!

ALL Then jump for joy, etc.

[*Exeunt* PSYCHE, HILARION, CYRIL, *and* FLORIAN. MELISSA *going*.

Enter LADY BLANCHE

BLA. Melissa!
MEL. [*returning*] Mother!
BLA. Here—a word with you.
Those are the three new students?
MEL. [*confused*] Yes, they are.
They're charming girls.
BLA. Particularly so.
So graceful, and so very womanly!
So skilled in all a girl's accomplishments!
MEL. [*confused*] Yes—very skilled.
BLA. They sing so nicely too!

MEL. They *do* sing nicely!
BLA. Humph! It's very odd.
Two are tenors, one is a baritone!
MEL. [*much agitated*] They've all got colds!
BLA. Colds! Bah! D'ye think I'm blind?
These "girls" are men disguised!
MEL. Oh no–indeed!
You wrong these gentlemen–I mean–why, see,
Here is an *étui* dropped by one of them [*picking up an étui*]
Containing scissors, needles, and——
BLA. [*opening it*] Cigars!
Why, these *are* men! And you knew this, you minx!
MEL. Oh, spare them–they are gentlemen indeed.
The Prince Hilarion (married years ago
To Princess Ida) with two trusted friends!
Consider, mother, he's her husband now,
And has been, twenty years! Consider, too,
You're only second here–you should be first.
Assist the Prince's plan, and when he gains
The Princess Ida, why, you *will* be first.
You will design the fashions–think of that–
And always serve out all the punishments!
The scheme is harmless, mother–wink at it!
BLA. [*aside*] The prospect's tempting! Well, well, well, I'll try–
Though I've not winked at anything for years!
'Tis but one step towards my destiny–
The mighty Must! the inevitable Shall!

Duet–MELISSA and LADY BLANCHE

MEL. Now wouldn't you like to rule the roast,
And guide this University?

BLA. I must agree
'Twould pleasant be.
(Sing hey, a Proper Pride!)

MEL. And wouldn't you like to clear the coast
Of malice and perversity?

BLA. Without a doubt
I'll bundle 'em out,
Sing hey, when I preside!

BOTH Sing, hoity, toity! Sorry for some!
Sing marry, come up and {my / her} day will come!
Sing, Proper Pride
Is the horse to ride,
And Happy-go-lucky, my Lady, O!

BLA. For years I've writhed beneath her sneers,
Although a born Plantaganet!

MEL. You're much too meek,
Or you would speak.
(Sing hey, I'll say no more!)

BLA. Her elder I, by several years,
Although you'd ne'er imagine it.

MEL. Sing, so I've heard
But never a word
Have I e'er believed before!

BOTH Sing, hoity, toity! Sorry for some!
Sing, marry come up and {my / her} day will come!

Sing, she shall learn
That a worm will turn.
Sing Happy-go-lucky, my Lady, O!

[*Exit* LADY BLANCHE.

MEL. Saved for a time, at least!

Enter FLORIAN, *on tiptoe*

FLOR. [*whispering*] Melissa—come!
MEL. Oh, sir! you must away from this at once—
My mother guessed your sex! It was my fault—
I blushed and stammered so that she exclaimed,
"Can these be men?" Then, seeing this, "Why these——"
"*Are men*", she would have added, but "*are men*"
Stuck in her throat! She keeps your secret, sir,
For reasons of her own—but fly from this
And take me with you—that is—no—not that!
FLOR. I'll go, but not without you! [*Bell*] Why, what's that?
MEL. The luncheon bell.
FLOR. I'll wait for luncheon then!

Enter HILARION *with* PRINCESS, CYRIL *with* PSYCHE, LADY BLANCHE *and* LADIES. *Also "Daughters of the Plough" bearing luncheon.*

CHORUS Merrily ring the luncheon bell!
Here in meadow of asphodel,
Feast we body and mind as well,
So merrily ring the luncheon bell!

Solo—BLANCHE

Hunger, I beg to state,
Is highly indelicate,
This is a fact profoundly true,
So learn your appetites to subdue.

ALL Yes, yes,
We'll learn our appetites to subdue!

Solo—CYRIL [*eating*]

Madame, your words so wise,
Nobody should despise,
Cursed with appetite keen I am
And I'll subdue it—
And I'll subdue it—
And I'll subdue it with cold roast lamb!

ALL Yes—yes—
We'll subdue it with cold roast lamb!

CHORUS Merrily ring, etc.

PRIN. You say you know the court of Hildebrand?
There is a Prince there—I forget his name—
HIL. Hilarion?
PRIN. Exactly—is he well?
HIL. If it be well to droop and pine and mope,
To sigh "Oh, Ida! Ida!" all day long,
"Ida! my love! my life! Oh, come to me!"
If it be well, I say, to do all this,
Then Prince Hilarion is very well.
PRIN. He breathes *our* name? Well, it's a common one!
And is the booby comely?
HIL. Pretty well.
I've heard it said that if I dressed myself
In Prince Hilarion's clothes (supposing this

Consisted with my maiden modesty),
I might be taken for Hilarion's self.
But what is this to you or me, who think
Of all mankind with undisguised contempt?

PRIN. Contempt? Why, damsel, when I think of man,
Contempt is not the word.

CYR. [*getting tipsy*] I'm sure of that,
Or if it is, it surely should not be!

HIL. [*aside to* CYRIL] Be quiet, idiot, or they'll find us out.

CYR. The Prince Hilarion's a goodly lad!

PRIN. *You* know him then?

CYR. [*tipsily*] I rather think I do!
We are inseparables!

PRIN. Why, what's this?
You love him then?

CYR. We do indeed—all three!

HIL. Madam, she jests! [*Aside to* CYRIL] Remember where you are!

CYR. Jests? Not at all! Why, bless my heart alive,
You and Hilarion, when at the Court,
Rode the same horse!

PRIN. [*horrified*] Astride?

CYR. Of course! Why not?
Wore the same clothes—and once or twice, I think,
Got tipsy in the same good company!

PRIN. Well, these are nice young ladies, on my word!

CYR. [*tipsy*] Don't you remember that old kissing-song
He'd sing to blushing Mistress Lalage,
The hostess of the Pigeons? Thus it ran:

Song—CYRIL

[*During symphony* HILARION *and* FLORIAN *try to stop* CYRIL. *He shakes them off angrily.*

Would you know the kind of maid
  Sets my heart aflame-a?
Eyes must be downcast and staid,
  Cheeks must flush for shame-a!
    She may neither dance nor sing,
    But, demure in everything,
    Hang her head in modest way,
    With pouting lips that seem to say,
"Oh, kiss me, kiss me, kiss me, kiss me,
  Though I die of shame-a!"
Please you, that's the kind of maid
    Sets my heart aflame-a!

When a maid is bold and gay
  With a tongue goes clang-a,
Flaunting it in brave array,
  Maiden may go hang-a
    Sunflower gay and hollyhock
    Never shall my garden stock;
    Mine the blushing rose of May,
    With pouting lips that seem to say,
  "Oh, kiss me, kiss me, kiss me, kiss me,
    Though I die for shame-a!"
  Please you, that's the kind of maid
    Sets my heart aflame-a!

PRIN. Infamous creature, get you hence away!

[HILARION, *who has been with difficulty restrained by* FLORIAN *during this song, breaks from him and strikes* CYRIL *furiously on the breast.*

HIL. Dog! there is something more to sing about!
CYR. [*sobered*] Hilarion, are you mad?
PRIN. [*horrified*] Hilarion? Help!
Why, these are men! Lost! lost! betrayed, undone!
[*Running on to bridge*]
Girls, get you hence! Man-monsters, if you dare
Approach one step, I— Ah!
[*Loses her balance, and falls into the stream*]

PSY. Oh! save her, sir!
BLA. It's useless, sir,—you'll only catch your death!

[HILARION *springs in*]

SACH. He catches her!
MEL. And now he lets her go!
Again she's in his grasp—

PSY. And now she's not.
He seizes her back hair!
BLA. [*not looking*] And it comes off!
PSY. No, no! She's saved!–she's saved!–she's saved!–she's saved!

Finale

Chorus of LADIES

Oh! joy, our chief is saved,
And by Hilarion's hand;
The torrent fierce he braved,
And brought her safe to land!
For his intrusion we must own
This doughty deed may well atone!

PRIN. Stand forth ye three,
Whoe'er ye be,
And hearken to our stern decree!
HIL., CYR., and FLOR. Have mercy, lady,—disregard your oaths!

PRIN. I know no mercy, men in women's clothes!
The man whose sacrilegious eyes
Invade our strict seclusion, dies.
Arrest these coarse intruding spies!

[*They are arrested by the "Daughters of the Plough"*

FLOR., CYR., and LADIES Have mercy, lady—disregard your oaths!
PRIN. I know not mercy, men in women's clothes!

[CYRIL and FLORIAN *are bound*

Song—HILARION

Whom thou hast chained must wear his chain,
Thou canst not set him free,
He wrestles with his bonds in vain
Who lives by loving thee!
If heart of stone for heart of fire,
Be all thou hast to give,
If dead to me my heart's desire,
Why should I wish to live?

FLOR., CYR., and LADIES Have mercy, O lady!

No word of thine—no stern command
  Can teach my heart to rove,
Then rather perish by thy hand,
  Than live without thy love!
A loveless life apart from thee
  Were hopeless slavery,
If kindly death will set me free,
  Why should I fear to die?

[*He is bound by two of the attendants, and the three gentlemen are marched off.*

Enter MELISSA

MEL. Madam, without the castle walls
  An armed band
Demand admittance to our halls
  For Hildebrand!

ALL Oh, horror!

PRIN. Deny them!
We will defy them!

ALL Too late—too late!
The castle gate
Is battered by them!

[*The gate yields.* SOLDIERS *rush in.* ARAC, GURON, *and* SCYNTHIUS *are with them, but with their hands handcuffed.*

Ensemble

GIRLS	MEN

Rend the air with wailing,
  Shed the shameful tear!
Walls are unavailing,
  Man has entered here!
Shame and desecration
  Are his staunch allies,
Let your lamentation
  Echo to the skies!
	Walls and fences scaling,
	  Promptly we appear;
	Walls are unavailing,
	  We have entered here.
	Female execration
	  Stifle if you're wise,
	Stop your lamentation,
	  Dry your pretty eyes!

Enter HILDEBRAND

Recitative

PRIN. Audacious tyrant, do you dare
To beard a maiden in her lair?

HILD. Since you inquire,
We've no desire
To beard a maiden here, or anywhere!

SOLDIERS No, no—we've no desire
To beard a maiden here, or anywhere!

Solo—HILDEBRAND

Some years ago
No doubt you know
(And if you don't I'll tell you so)
You gave your troth
Upon your oath
To Hilarion my son.
A vow you make
You must not break,
(If you thing you may, it's a great mistake),
For a bride's a bride
Though the knot were tied
At the early age of one!
And I'm a peppery kind of King,
Who's indisposed for parleying
To fit the wit of a bit of a chit,
And that's the long and the short of it!

SOLDIERS For he's a peppery kind of King, etc.

If you decide
To pocket your pride
And let Hilarion claim his bride,
Why, well and good,
It's understood
We'll let bygones go by—
But if you choose
To sulk in the blues
I'll make the whole of you shake in your shoes.
I'll storm your walls,
And level your halls,
In the twinkling of an eye!
For I'm a peppery Potentate,
Who's little inclined his claim to bate,
To fit the wit of a bit of a chit,
And that's the long and the short of it!

SOLDIERS For he's a peppery kind of King, etc.

Trio—Arac, Guron, and Scynthius

We may remark, though nothing can
Dismay us,
That if you thwart this gentleman,
He'll slay us.
We don't fear death, of course—we're taught
To shame it;
But still upon the whole we thought
We'd name it.
[*To each other*] Yes, yes, yes, better perhaps to name it.
Our interests we would not press
With chatter,
Three hulking brothers more or less
Don't matter;
If you'd pooh-pooh this monarch's plan,
Pooh-pooh it,
But when he says he'll hang a man,
He'll do it.
[*To each other*] Yes, yes, yes, devil doubt he'll do it.

Prin. [*recit.*] Be reassured, nor fear his anger blind,
His menaces are idle as the wind.
He dares not kill you—vengeance lurks behind!

Ar., Gur., Scyn. *We* rather think he dares, but never mind!
No, no,—never, never mind!

Hild. I rather think I dare, but never, never mind!
Enough of parley—as a special boon,
We give you till to-morrow afternoon;
Release Hilarion, then, and be his bride,
Or you'll incur the guilt of fratricide!

Ensemble

Princess

To yield at once to such a foe
With shame were rife;
So quick! away with him, although
He saved my life!
That he is fair, and strong, and tall,
Is very evident to all,
Yet I will die before I call
Myself his wife!

The Others

Oh! yield at once, 'twere better so
Than risk a strife!
And let the Prince Hilarion go—
He saved thy life!
Hilarion's fair, and strong, and tall—
A worse misfortune might befall—
It's not so dreadful, after all,
To be his wife!

Solo—PRINCESS

Though I am but a girl,
Defiance thus I hurl,
Our banners all
On outer wall
We fearlessly unfurl.

ALL — Though she is but a girl, etc.

PRINCESS	THE OTHERS
That he is fair, etc.	Hilarion's fair, etc.

[*The* PRINCESS *stands, surrounded by girls kneeling.* HILDEBRAND *and soldiers stand on built rocks at back and sides of stage. Picture.*

CURTAIN

END OF ACT II

ACT III

SCENE.—*Outer Walls and Courtyard of Castle Adamant.* MELISSA, SACHARISSA, *and ladies discovered, armed with battleaxes.*

CHORUS

Death to the invader!
Strike a deadly blow,
As an old Crusader
Struck his Paynim foe!
Let our martial thunder
Fill his soul with wonder,
Tear his ranks asunder,
Lay the tyrant low!

Solo—MELISSA

Thus our courage, all untarnished,
We're instructed to display:
But to tell the truth unvarnished,
We are more inclined to say,
"Please you, do not hurt us."

ALL "Do not hurt us, if it please you!"
MEL. "Please you let us be."
ALL "Let us be—let us be!"
MEL. "Soldiers disconcert us."
ALL "Disconcert us, if it please you!"
MEL. "Frightened maids are we!"
ALL "Maids are we—maids are we!"

MELISSA

But 'twould be an error
To confess our terror,
So, in Ida's name,
Boldly we exclaim:
CHORUS Death to the invader!
Strike a deadly blow,
As an old Crusader
Struck his Paynim foe!

Flourish. Enter PRINCESS, *armed, attended by* BLANCHE *and* PSYCHE

PRIN. I like your spirit, girls! We have to meet
Stern bearded warriors in fight to-day:
Wear naught but what is necessary to
Preserve your dignity before their eyes,
And give your limbs full play.
BLA. One moment, ma'am,
Here is a paradox we should not pass
Without inquiry. We are prone to say,
"This thing is Needful—that, Superfluous"—
Yet they invariably co-exist!
We find the Needful comprehended in
The circle of the grand Superfluous,
Yet the Superfluous cannot be bought
Unless you're amply furnished with the Needful.
These singular considerations are—
PRIN. Superfluous, yet not Needful—so you see
The terms may independently exist.
[*To Ladies*] Women of Adamant, we have to show
That women, educated to the task,
Can meet Man, face to face, on his own ground,
And beat him there. Now let us set to work:
Where is our lady surgeon?
SAC. Madam, here!

PRIN. We shall require your skill to heal the wounds
Of those that fall.

SAC. [*alarmed*] What, heal the wounded?

PRIN. Yes!

SAC. And cut off real live legs and arms?

PRIN. Of course!

SAC. I wouldn't do it for a thousand pounds!

PRIN. Why, how is this? Are you faint-hearted, girl?
You've often cut them off in theory!

SAC. In theory I'll cut them off again
With pleasure, and as often as you like,
But not in practice.

PRIN. Coward! get you hence,
I've craft enough for that, and courage too,
I'll do your work! My fusiliers, advance!
Why, you are armed with axes! Gilded toys!
Where are your rifles, pray?

CHLOE Why, please you, ma'am,
We left them in the armoury, for fear
That in the heat and turmoil of the fight,
They might go off!

PRIN. "They might!" Oh, craven souls!
Go off yourselves! Thank heaven, I have a heart
That quails not at the thought of meeting men;
I will discharge your rifles! Off with you!
Where's my bandmistress?

ADA Please you, ma'am, the band
Do not feel well, and can't come out to-day!

PRIN. Why, this is flat rebellion! I've no time
To talk to them just now. But, happily,
I can play several instruments at once,
And I will drown the shrieks of those that fall
With trumpet music, such as soldiers love!
How stand we with respect to gunpowder?
My Lady Psyche—you who superintend
Our lab'ratory—are you well prepared
To blow these bearded rascals into shreds?

PSY. Why, madam—

PRIN. Well?

PSY. Let us try gentler means.
We can dispense with fulminating grains
While we have eyes with which to flash our rage!
We can dispense with villainous saltpetre
While we have tongues with which to blow them
up!
We can dispense, in short, with all the arts

That brutalize the practical polemist!

PRIN. [*contemptuously*] I never knew a more dispensing chemist!
Away, away—I'll meet these men alone
Since all my women have deserted me!

[*Exeunt all but* PRINCESS, *singing refrain of "Please you, do not hurt us", pianissimo.*

PRIN. So fail my cherished plans—so fails my faith—
And with it hope, and all that comes of hope!

Song—PRINCESS

I built upon a rock,
But ere Destruction's hand
Dealt equal lot
To Court and cot,
My rock had turned to sand!
I leant upon an oak,
But in the hour of need,
Alack-a-day,
My trusted stay
Was but a bruisèd reed!
Ah, faithless rock,
My simple faith to mock!
Ah, trait'rous oak,
Thy worthlessness to cloak.
I drew a sword of steel,
But when to home and hearth
The battle's breath
Bore fire and death,
My sword was but a lath!
I lit a beacon fire,
But on a stormy day
Of frost and rime,
In wintertime,
My fire had died away!
Ah, coward steel,
That fear can unanneal!
False fire indeed,
To fail me in my need!

She sinks on a seat. Enter CHLOE *and all the ladies*

CHLOE Madam, your father and your brothers claim
An audience!

PRIN. What do they do here?

CHLOE They come
To fight for you!

PRIN. Admit them!

BLA. Infamous!
One's brothers, ma'am, are men!

PRIN. So I've heard.
But all my women seem to fail me when
I need them most. In this emergency,
Even one's brothers may be turned to use.

Enter GAMA, *quite pale and unnerved*

GAMA My daughter!

PRIN. Father! thou art free!

GAMA Aye, free!
Free as a tethered ass! I come to thee
With words from Hildebrand. Those duly given
I must return to blank captivity.
I'm free so far.

PRIN. Your message.

GAMA Hildebrand
Is loth to war with women. Pit my sons,
My three brave sons, against these popinjays,
These tufted jack-a-dandy featherheads,
And on the issue let thy hand depend!

PRIN. Insult on insult's head! Are we a stake
For fighting men? What fiend possesses thee,
That thou hast come with offers such as these
From such as he to such an one as I?

GAMA I am possessed
By the pale devil of a shaking heart!
My stubborn will is bent. I dare not face
That devilish monarch's black malignity!
He tortures me with torments worse than death,
I haven't anything to grumble at!
He finds out what particular meats I love,
And gives me them. The very choicest wines,
The costliest robes—the richest rooms are mine:
He suffers none to thwart my simplest plan,
And gives strict orders none should contradict me!
He's made my life a curse! [*Weeps*]

PRIN. My tortured father!

Song—GAMA

Whene'er I poke
Sarcastic joke
Replete with malice spiteful,
This people mild
Politely smiled,
And voted me delightful!

Now when a wight
Sits up all night
Ill-natured jokes devising,
And all his wiles
Are met with smiles
It's hard, there's no disguising!

O, don't the days seem lank and long
When all goes right and nothing goes wrong,
And isn't your life extremely flat
With nothing whatever to grumble at!

When German bands
From music stands
Played Wagner imper*fect*ly—
I bade them go—
They didn't say no,
But off they went directly!

The organ boys
They stopped their noise
With readiness surprising,
And grinning herds
Of hurdy-gurds
Retired apologising!
Oh, don't the days seem lank and long, etc.

I offered gold
In sums untold
To all who'd contradict me—
I said I'd pay
A pound a day
To any one who kicked me—
I bribed with toys
Great vulgar boys
To utter something spiteful,
But, bless you, no!
They *would* be so
Confoundedly politeful!

In short, these aggravating lads,
They tickle my tastes, they feed my fads,
They give me this and they give me that,
And I've nothing whatever to grumble at!

[*He bursts into tears, and falls sobbing on a seat*

PRIN. My poor old father! How he must have suffered!
Well, well, I yield!
GAMA [*hysterically*] She yields! I'm saved, I'm saved! [*Exit*
PRIN. Open the gates—admit these warriors,
Then get you all within the castle walls. [*Exit*

[*The gates are opened, and the girls mount the battlements as soldiers enter. Also* ARAC, GURON, *and* SCYNTHIUS.

Chorus of Soldiers

When anger spreads his wing,
And all seems dark as night for it,
There's nothing but to fight for it,
But ere you pitch your ring,
Select a pretty site for it,
(This spot is suited quite for it),
And then you gaily sing,

"Oh, I love the jolly rattle
Of an ordeal by battle,
There's an end of tittle-tattle
When your enemy is dead.
It's an arrant molly-coddle
Fears a crack upon his noddle
And he's only fit to swaddle
In a downy feather-bed!"—

ALL For a fight's a kind of thing
That I love to look upon,
So let us sing,
Long live the King,
And his son Hilarion!

[*During this,* HILARION, FLORIAN, *and* CYRIL *are brought out by the "Daughters of the Plough". They are still bound and wear the robes. Enter* GAMA.

GAMA Hilarion! Cyril! Florian! dressed as women!
Is this indeed Hilarion?
HIL. Yes, it is!
GAMA Why, you look handsome in your women's clothes!
Stick to 'em! men's attire becomes you not!
[*To* CYRIL *and* FLORIAN] And you, young ladies, will you please to pray
King Hildebrand to set me free again?
Hang on his neck and gaze into his eyes,
He never could resist a pretty face!
HIL. You dog, you'll find, though I wear woman's garb,
My sword is long and sharp!
GAMA Hush, pretty one!
Here's a virago! Here's a termagant!
If length and sharpness go for anything,
You'll want no sword while you can wag your tongue!
CYR. What need to waste your words on such as he?
He's old and crippled.
GAMA Aye, but I've three sons,
Fine fellows, young, and muscular, and brave,
They're well worth talking to! Come, what d'ye say?
ARAC Aye, pretty ones, engage yourselves with us,
If three rude warriors affright you not!
HIL. Old as you are, I'd wring your shrivelled neck
If you were not the Princess Ida's father.
GAMA If I were not the Princess Ida's father,
And so had not her brothers for my sons,

No doubt you'd wring my neck—in safety too!
Come, come, Hilarion, begin, begin!
Give them no quarter—they will give you none.
You've this advantage over warriors
Who kill their country's enemies for pay,—
You know what you are fighting for—look there!

[*Pointing to Ladies on the battlements*]

[*Exit* GAMA. HILARION, FLORIAN, *and* CYRIL *are led off.*

Song—ARAC

This helmet, I suppose,
Was meant to ward off blows,
It's very hot,
And weighs a lot,
As many a guardsman knows,
So off that helmet goes.

ALL Yes, yes, yes,
So off that helmet goes!

[*Giving their helmets to attendants*]

ARAC This tight-fitting cuirass
Is but a useless mass,
It's made of steel,
And weighs a deal,
A man is but an ass
Who fights in a cuirass,
So off goes that cuirass.

ALL Yes, yes, yes,
So off goes that cuirass!

[*Removing cuirasses*]

ARAC These brassets, truth to tell,
May look uncommon well,
But in a fight
They're much too tight,
They're like a lobster shell!

ALL Yes, yes, yes,
They're like a lobster shell.

[*Removing their brassets*]

ARAC These things I treat the same [*indicating leg pieces*]
(I quite forget their name)
They turn one's legs
To cribbage pegs–
Their aid I thus disclaim,
Though I forget their name!

ALL Yes, yes, yes,
Their aid {we / they} thus disclaim!

[*They remove their leg pieces and wear close-fitting shape suits*

Enter HILARION, FLORIAN, *and* CYRIL

[*Desperate fight between the three Princes and the three Knights, during which the Ladies on the battlements and the Soldiers on the stage sing the following chorus.*

This is our duty plain towards
Our Princess all immaculate,
We ought to bless her brothers' swords
And piously ejaculate:
Oh, Hungary!
Oh, Hungary!
Oh, doughty sons of Hungary!
May all success
Attend and bless
Your warlike ironmongery!

Hilarion! Hilarion! Hilarion!

[*By this time,* ARAC, GURON, *and* SCYNTHIUS *are on the ground, wounded*–HILARION, CYRIL, *and* FLORIAN *stand over them.*

PRIN. [*entering through gate and followed by Ladies,* HILDEBRAND, *and* GAMA] Hold! stay your hands–we yield ourselves to you!
Ladies, my brothers all lie bleeding there!
Bind up their wounds–but look the other way.
[*Coming down*] Is this the end? [*bitterly to* LADY BLANCHE] How say you, Lady Blanche–
Can I with dignity my post resign?
And if I do, will you then take my place?

BLA. To answer this, it's meet that we consult
The great Potential Mysteries; I mean
The five Subjunctive Possibilities–

The May, the Might, the Would, the Could, the Should.
Can you resign? The prince May claim you; if
He Might, you Could—and if you Should, I Would!

PRIN. I thought as much! Then, to my fate I yield—
So ends my cherished scheme! Oh, I had hoped
To band all women with my maiden throng,
And make them all abjure tyrannic Man!

HILD. A noble aim!

PRIN. You ridicule it now!
But if I carried out this glorious scheme,
At my exalted name Posterity
Would bow in gratitude!

HILD. But pray reflect—
If you enlist all women in your cause,
And make them all abjure tyrannic Man,
The obvious question then arises, "How
Is this Posterity to be provided?"

PRIN. I never thought of that! My Lady Blanche,
How do you solve the riddle?

BLA. Don't ask me—
Abstract Philosophy won't answer it.
Take him—he is your Shall. Give in to Fate!

PRIN. And you desert me. I alone am staunch!

HIL. Madam, you placed your trust in Woman—well,
Woman has failed you utterly—try Man,
Give him one chance, it's only fair—besides,
Women are far too precious, too divine,
To try unproven theories upon.
Experiments, the proverb says, are made
On humble subjects—try our grosser clay,
And mould it as you will!

CYR. Remember, too,
Dear Madam, if at any time you feel
A-weary of the Prince, you can return
To Castle Adamant, and rule your girls
As heretofore, you know.

PRIN. And shall I find
The Lady Psyche here?

PSY. If Cyril, ma'am,
Does not behave himself, I think you will.

PRIN. And you, Melissa, shall I find *you* here?

MEL. Madam, however Florian turns out,
Unhesitatingly I answer, No!

GAMA Consider this, my love, if your mamma
Had looked on matters from your point of view
(I wish she had), why where would you have been?

BLA. There's an unbounded field of speculation,
On which I could discourse for hours!

PRIN. No doubt!
We will not trouble you. Hilarion,
I have been wrong—I see my error now.
Take me, Hilarion—"We will walk the world
Yoked in all exercise of noble end!
And so through those dark gates across the wild
That no man knows! Indeed, I love thee—Come!"

Finale

PRIN.
With joy abiding,
Together gliding
Through life's variety,
In sweet society,
And thus enthroning
The love I'm owning,
On this atoning
I will rely!

CHORUS
It were profanity
For poor humanity
To treat as vanity
The sway of Love.
In no locality
Or principality
Is our mortality
Its sway above!

HIL.
When day is fading,
With serenading
And such frivolity
Of tender quality—
With scented showers
Of fairest flowers,
The happy hours
Will gaily fly!

CHORUS
It were profanity, etc.

CURTAIN

THE MIKADO

OR

THE TOWN OF TITIPU

DRAMATIS PERSONÆ

THE MIKADO OF JAPAN

NANKI-POO [*his Son, disguised as a wandering minstrel, and in love with* YUM-YUM]

KO-KO [*Lord High Executioner of Titipu*]

POOH-BAH [*Lord High Everything Else*]

PISH-TUSH [*a Noble Lord*]

YUM-YUM
PITTI-SING } *Three Sisters—Wards of* KO-KO
PEEP-BO

KATISHA [*an elderly Lady, in love with* NANKI-POO]

Chorus of School-girls, Nobles, Guards, and Coolies

ACT I

COURTYARD OF KO-KO'S OFFICIAL RESIDENCE

ACT II

KO-KO'S GARDEN

First produced at the Savoy Theatre on March 14, 1885

THE MIKADO

OR

THE TOWN OF TITIPU

ACT I

SCENE.—*Courtyard of* Ko-Ko's *Palace in Titipu. Japanese nobles discovered standing and sitting in attitudes suggested by native drawings.*

Chorus of Nobles

If you want to know who we are,
We are gentlemen of Japan;
On many a vase and jar—
On many a screen and fan,
We figure in lively paint:
Our attitude's queer and quaint—
You're wrong if you think it ain't, oh!

If you think we are worked by strings,
Like a Japanese marionette,
You don't understand these things:
It is simply Court etiquette.
Perhaps you suppose this throng
Can't keep it up all day long?
If that's your idea, you're wrong, oh!

Enter NANKI-POO *in great excitement. He carries a native guitar on his back and a bundle of ballads in his hand.*

Recitative—NANKI-POO

Gentlemen, I pray you tell me
Where a gentle maiden dwelleth,
Named Yum-Yum, the ward of Ko-Ko?
In pity speak—oh, speak, I pray you!
A NOBLE Why, who are you who ask this question?
NANK. Come gather round me, and I'll tell you.

Song and Chorus—NANKI-POO

A wandering minstrel I—
A thing of shreds and patches,
Of ballads, songs and snatches,
And dreamy lullaby!

My catalogue is long,
Through every passion ranging,
And to your humours changing
I tune my supple song!

Are you in sentimental mood?
I'll sigh with you,
Oh, sorrow, sorrow!
On maiden's coldness do you brood?
I'll do so, too—
Oh, sorrow, sorrow!
I'll charm your willing ears
With songs of lovers' fears,
While sympathetic tears
My cheeks bedew—
Oh, sorrow, sorrow!

But if patriotic sentiment is wanted,
I've patriotic ballads cut and dried;
For where'er our country's banner may be planted,
All other local banners are defied!
Our warriors, in serried ranks assembled,
Never quail—or they conceal it if they do—
And I shouldn't be surprised if nations trembled
Before the mighty troops of Titipu!

CHORUS We shouldn't be surprised, etc.

NANK. And if you call for a song of the sea,
We'll heave the capstan round,
With a yeo heave ho, for the wind is free,
Her anchor's a-trip and her helm's a-lee,
Hurrah for the homeward bound!

CHORUS Yeo-ho—heave ho—
Hurrah for the homeward bound!

To lay aloft in a howling breeze
May tickle a landsman's taste,
But the happiest hour a sailor sees
Is when he's down
At an inland town,
With his Nancy on his knees, yeo ho!
And his arm around her waist!

CHORUS

Then man the capstan—off we go,
As the fiddler swings us round,
With a yeo heave ho,
And a rumbelow,
Hurrah for the homeward bound!

A wandering minstrel I, etc.

Enter PISH-TUSH

PISH. And what may be your business with Yum-Yum?

NANK. I'll tell you. A year ago I was a member of the Titipu town band. It was my duty to take the cap round for contributions. While discharging this delicate office, I saw Yum-Yum. We loved each other at once, but she was betrothed to her guardian Ko-Ko, a cheap tailor, and I saw that my suit was hopeless. Overwhelmed with despair, I quitted the town. Judge of my delight when I heard, a month ago, that Ko-Ko had been condemned to death for flirting! I hurried back at once, in the hope of finding Yum-Yum at liberty to listen to my protestations.

PISH. It is true that Ko-Ko was condemned to death for flirting, but he was reprieved at the last moment, and raised to the exalted rank of Lord High Executioner under the following remarkable circumstances:

Song—PISH-TUSH *and Chorus*

Our great Mikado, virtuous man,
When he to rule our land began,
Resolved to try
A plan whereby
Young men might best be steadied.
So he decreed, in words succinct,
That all who flirted, leered or winked
(Unless connubially linked),
Should forthwith be beheaded.

And I expect you'll all agree
That he was right to so decree.
And I am right,
And you are right,
And all is right as right can be!

CHORUS

And you are right,
And we are right, etc.

This stern decree, you'll understand,
Caused great dismay throughout the land!
For young and old
And shy and bold
Were equally affected.
The youth who winked a roving eye,
Or breathed a non-connubial sigh,
Was thereupon condemned to die—
He usually objected.

And you'll allow, as I expect,
That he was right to so object.
And I am right,
And you are right,
And everything is quite correct!

CHORUS And you are right,
And we are right, etc.

And so we straight let out on bail,
A convict from the county jail,
Whose head was next
On some pretext
Condemned to be mown off,
And made *him* Headsman, for we said,
"Who's next to be decapitated
Cannot cut off another's head
Until he's cut his own off."

And we are right, I think you'll say,
To argue in this kind of way;
And I am right,
And you are right,
And all is right—too-looral-lay!

CHORUS And you are right,
And we are right, etc.

[*Exeunt* CHORUS.

Enter POOH-BAH

NANK. Ko-Ko, the cheap tailor, Lord High Executioner of Titipu! Why, that's the highest rank a citizen can attain!

POOH. It is. Our logical Mikado, seeing no moral difference between the dignified judge who condemns a criminal to die, and the industrious mechanic who carries out the sentence, has rolled the two offices into one, and every judge is now his own executioner.

NANK. But how good of you (for I see that you are a nobleman of the highest rank) to condescend to tell all this to me, a mere strolling minstrel!

POOH. Don't mention it. I am, in point of fact, a particularly haughty and exclusive person, of pre-Adamite ancestral descent. You will understand this when I tell you that I can trace my ancestry back to a protoplasmal primordial atomic globule. Consequently, my family pride is something inconceivable. I can't help it. I was born sneering. But I struggle hard to overcome this defect. I mortify my pride continually. When all the great officers of State resigned in a body, because they were too proud to serve under an ex-tailor, did I not unhesitatingly accept all their posts at once?

PISH. And the salaries attached to them? You did.

POOH. It is consequently my degrading duty to serve this upstart as First Lord of the Treasury, Lord Chief Justice, Commander-in-Chief, Lord High Admiral, Master of the Buckhounds, Groom of the Back Stairs, Archbishop of Titipu, and Lord Mayor, both acting and elect, all rolled into one. And at a salary! A Pooh-Bah paid for his services! I a salaried minion! But I do it! It revolts me, but I do it!

NANK. And it does you credit.

POOH. But I don't stop at that. I go and dine with middle-class people on reasonable terms. I dance at cheap suburban parties for a moderate fee. I accept refreshment at any hands, however lowly. I also retail State secrets at a very low figure. For instance, any further information about Yum-Yum would come under the head of a State secret. [NANKI-POO *takes the hint, and gives him money*] [*Aside*] Another insult, and I think, a light one!

Song—POOH-BAH with NANKI-POO and PISH-TUSH

Young man, despair,
    Likewise go to,
Yum-Yum the fair
    You must not woo.
    It will not do:
    I'm sorry for you,
You very imperfect ablutioner!
This very day
    From school Yum-Yum
Will wend her way,
    And homeward come,
    With beat of drum
    And a rum-tum-tum,

To wed the Lord High Executioner!
And the brass will crash,
And the trumpets bray,
And they'll cut a dash
On their wedding day.
She'll toddle away, as all aver,
With the Lord High Executioner!

NANK. and POOH. And the brass will crash, etc.

It's a hopeless case,
As you may see,
And in your place
Away I'd flee;
But don't blame me—
I'm sorry to be
Of your pleasure a diminutioner.
They'll vow their pact
Extremely soon,
In point of fact
This afternoon.
Her honeymoon
With that buffoon
At seven commences, so *you* shun her!

ALL And the brass will crash, etc.

[*Exit* PISH-TUSH.

Recitative—NANKI-POO and POOH-BAH

NANK. And I have journeyed for a month, or nearly,
To learn that Yum-Yum, whom I love so dearly,
This day to Ko-Ko is to be united!

POOH. The fact appears to be as you've recited:
But here he comes, equipped as suits his station;
He'll give you any further information.

[*Exeunt* POOH-BAH *and* NANKI-POO.

Enter Chorus of Nobles

Behold the Lord High Executioner
A personage of noble rank and title—
A dignified and potent officer,
Whose functions are particularly vital!
Defer, defer,
To the Lord High Executioner!

Enter Ko-Ko *attended*

Solo—Ko-Ko

Taken from the county jail
  By a set of curious chances;
Liberated then on bail,
  On my own recognizances;
Wafted by a favouring gale
  As one sometimes is in trances,
To a height that few can scale,
  Save by long and weary dances;
Surely, never had a male
  Under such like circumstances
So adventurous a tale
  Which may rank with most romances.

CHORUS Defer, defer,
  To the Lord High Executioner, etc.

Ko. Gentlemen, I'm much touched by this reception. I can only trust that by strict attention to duty I shall ensure a continuance of those favours which it will ever be my study to deserve. If I should ever be called upon to act professionally, I am happy to think that there will be no difficulty in finding plenty of people whose loss will be a distinct gain to society at large.

Song—Ko-Ko *with Chorus of Men*

As some day it may happen that a victim must be found,
  I've got a little list—I've got a little list
Of society offenders who might well be underground,
  And who never would be missed—who never would be missed!
There's the pestilential nuisances who write for autographs—
All people who have flabby hands and irritating laughs—
All children who are up in dates, and floor you with 'em flat—
All persons who in shaking hands, shake hands with you like *that*—
And all third persons who on spoiling *tête-à-têtes* insist—
  They'd none of 'em be missed—they'd none of 'em be missed!

CHORUS He's got 'em on the list—he's got 'em on the list;
  And they'll none of 'em be missed—they'll none of 'em be missed.

There's the nigger serenader, and the others of his race,
  And the piano-organist—I've got him on the list!

And the people who eat peppermint and puff it in your face,
  They never would be missed—they never would be missed!
Then the idiot who praises, with enthusiastic tone,
All centuries but this, and every country but his own;
And the lady from the provinces, who dresses like a guy,
And who "doesn't think she waltzes, but would rather like to try";
And that singular anomaly, the lady novelist—
  I don't think she'd be missed—I'm *sure* she'd not be missed!

CHORUS He's got her on the list—he's got her on the list;
  And I don't think she'll be missed—I'm *sure* she'll not be missed!

And that *Nisi Prius* nuisance, who just now is rather rife,
  The Judicial humorist—I've got *him* on the list!
All funny fellows, comic men, and clowns of private life—
  They'd none of 'em be missed—they'd none of 'em be missed.
And apologetic statesmen of a compromising kind,
Such as—What d'ye call him—Thing'em-bob, and likewise—Never-mind,
And 'St—'st—'st—and What's-his-name, and also You-know-who—
The task of filling up the blanks I'd rather leave to *you*.
But it really doesn't matter whom you put upon the list,
  For they'd none of 'em be missed—they'd none of 'em be missed!

CHORUS You may put 'em on the list—you may put 'em on the list;
  And they'll none of 'em be missed—they'll none of 'em be missed!

Enter POOH-BAH

KO. Pooh-Bah, it seems that the festivities in connection with my approaching marriage must last a week. I should like to do it handsomely, and I want to consult you as to the amount I ought to spend upon them.

POOH. Certainly. In which of my capacities? As First Lord of the

Treasury, Lord Chamberlain, Attorney-General, Chancellor of the Exchequer, Privy Purse, or Private Secretary?

KO. Suppose we say as Private Secretary.

POOH. Speaking as your Private Secretary, I should say that, as the city will have to pay for it, don't stint yourself, do it well.

KO. Exactly—as the city will have to pay for it. That is your advice.

POOH. As Private Secretary. Of course you will understand that, as Chancellor of the Exchequer, I am bound to see that due economy is observed.

KO. Oh! But you said just now "Don't stint yourself, do it well".

POOH. As Private Secretary.

KO. And now you say that due economy must be observed.

POOH. As Chancellor of the Exchequer.

KO. I see. Come over here, where the Chancellor can't hear us. [*They cross the stage*] Now, as my Solicitor, how do you advise me to deal with this difficulty?

POOH. Oh, as your Solicitor, I should have no hesitation in saying "Chance it——"

KO. Thank you. [*Shaking his hand*] I will.

POOH. If it were not that, as Lord Chief Justice, I am bound to see that the law isn't violated.

KO. I see. Come over here where the Chief Justice can't hear us. [*They cross the stage*] Now, then, as First Lord of the Treasury?

POOH. Of course, as First Lord of the Treasury, I could propose a special vote that would cover all expenses, if it were not that, as Leader of the Opposition, it would be my duty to resist it, tooth and nail. Or, as Paymaster-General, I could so cook the accounts that, as Lord High Auditor, I should never discover the fraud. But then, as Archbishop of Titipu, it would be my duty to denounce my dishonesty and give myself into my own custody as First Commissioner of Police.

KO. That's extremely awkward.

POOH. I don't say that all these distinguished people couldn't be squared; but it is right to tell you that they wouldn't be sufficiently degraded in their own estimation unless they were insulted with a very considerable bribe.

KO. The matter shall have my careful consideration. But my bride and her sisters approach, and any little compliment on your part, such as an abject grovel in a characteristic Japanese attitude, would be esteemed a favour. [*Exeunt together.*

Enter procession of YUM-YUM'S *schoolfellows, heralding* YUM-YUM, PEEP-BO *and* PITTI-SING

Chorus of Girls

Comes a train of little ladies
From scholastic trammels free,

Each a little bit afraid is,
  Wondering what the world can be!

Is it but a world of trouble—
  Sadness set to song?
Is its beauty but a bubble
  Bound to break ere long?

Are its palaces and pleasures
  Fantasies that fade?
And the glory of its treasures
  Shadow of a shade?

Schoolgirls we, eighteen and under,
  From scholastic trammels free,
And we wonder—how we wonder!—
  What on earth the world can be!

Trio

YUM-YUM, PEEP-BO, *and* PITTI-SING, *with Chorus of Girls*

THE THREE Three little maids from school are we,
Pert as a school-girl well can be,
Filled to the brim with girlish glee,
Three little maids from school!

YUM-YUM Everything is a source of fun. [*Chuckle*]

PEEP-BO Nobody's safe, for we care for none! [*Chuckle*]

PITTI-SING Life is a joke that's just begun! [*Chuckle*]

THE THREE — Three little maids from school!
ALL [*dancing*] Three little maids who, all unwary,
Come from a ladies' seminary,
Freed from its genius tutelary—
THE THREE [*suddenly demure*] Three little maids from school!

YUM-YUM — One little maid is a bride, Yum-Yum—
PEEP-BO — Two little maids in attendance come—
PITTI-SING — Three little maids is the total sum.
THE THREE — Three little maids from school!
YUM-YUM — From three little maids take one away.
PEEP-BO — Two little maids remain, and they—
PITTI-SING — Won't have to wait very long, they say—
THE THREE — Three little maids from school!
ALL [*dancing*] Three little maids who, all unwary,
Come from a ladies' seminary,
Freed from its genius tutelary—
THE THREE [*suddenly demure*] Three little maids from school!

Enter KO-KO *and* POOH-BAH

KO. At last, my bride that is to be! [*About to embrace her*]

YUM. You're not going to kiss me before all these people?

KO. Well, that was the idea.

YUM. [*aside to* PEEP-BO] It seems odd, doesn't it?

PEEP. It's rather peculiar.

PITTI. Oh, I expect it's all right. Must have a beginning, you know.

YUM. Well, of course I know nothing about these things; but I've no objection if it's usual.

KO. Oh, it's quite usual, I think. Eh, Lord Chamberlain? [*Appealing to* POOH-BAH]

POOH. I have known it done. [KO-KO *embraces her*]

YUM. Thank goodness that's over! [*Sees* NANKI-POO, *and rushes to him*] Why, that's never you? [*The three girls rush to him and shake his hands, all speaking at once*]

YUM. Oh, I'm so glad! I haven't seen you for ever so long, and I'm right at the top of the school, and I've got three prizes, and I've come home for good, and I'm not going back any more!

PEEP. And have you got an engagement?—Yum-Yum's got one, but she doesn't like it, and she'd ever so much rather it was you! I've come home for good, and I'm not going back any more!

PITTI. Now tell us all the news, because you go about everywhere, and we've been at school, but, thank goodness, that's all over now, and we've come home for good, and we're not going back any more!

[*These three speeches are spoken together in one breath*]

Ko. I beg your pardon. Will you present me?

Yum. Oh, this is the musician who used—
Peep. Oh, this is the gentleman who used—
Pitti. Oh, it is only Nanki-Poo who used—

Ko. One at a time, if you please.

Yum. Oh, if you please, he's the gentleman who used to play so beautifully on the—on the——

Pitti. On the Marine Parade.

Yum. Yes, I think that was the name of the instrument.

Nank. Sir, I have the misfortune to love your ward, Yum-Yum—oh, I know I deserve your anger!

Ko. Anger! not a bit, my boy. Why, I love her myself. Charming little girl, isn't she? Pretty eyes, nice hair. Taking little thing, altogether. Very glad to hear my opinion backed by a competent authority. Thank you very much. Good-bye. [*To* Pish-Tush] Take him away. [Pish-Tush *removes him*]

Pitti. [*who has been examining* Pooh-Bah] I beg your pardon, but what is this? Customer come to try on?

Ko. That is a Tremendous Swell.

Pitti. Oh, it's alive. [*She starts back in alarm*]

Pooh. Go away, little girls. Can't talk to little girls like you. Go away, there's dears.

Ko. Allow me to present you, Pooh-Bah. These are my three wards. The one in the middle is my bride elect.

Pooh. What do you want me to do to them? Mind, I *will not* kiss them.

Ko. No, no, you shan't kiss them; a little bow—a mere nothing—you needn't mean it, you know.

Pooh. It goes against the grain. They are not young ladies, they are young persons.

Ko. Come, come, make an effort, there's a good nobleman.

Pooh [*aside to* Ko-Ko] Well, I shan't mean it. [*With a great effort*] How de do, little girls, how de do? [*Aside*] Oh, my protoplasmal ancestor!

Ko. That's very good. [*Girls indulge in suppressed laughter*]

Pooh. I see nothing to laugh at. It is very painful to me to have to say "How de do, little girls, how de do?" to young persons. I'm not in the habit of saying "How de do, little girls, how de do?" to anybody under the rank of a Stockbroker.

Ko. [*aside to girls*] Don't laugh at him, he can't help it—he's under treatment for it. [*Aside to* Pooh-Bah] Never mind them, they don't understand the delicacy of your position.

Pooh. We know how delicate it is, don't we?

Ko. I should think we did! How a nobleman of your importance can do it at all is a thing I never can, never shall understand.

[Ko-Ko *retires up and goes off.*

Quartet and Chorus of Girls

YUM-YUM, PEEP-BO, PITTI-SING, *and* POOH-BAH

YUM., PEEP. and PITTI. So please you, Sir, we much regret
If we have failed in etiquette
Towards a man of rank so high—
We shall know better by and by.

YUM. But youth, of course, must have its fling,
So pardon us,
So pardon us,

PITTI. And don't, in girlhood's happy spring,
Be hard on us,
Be hard on us,
If we're inclined to dance and sing.
Tra la la, etc. [*Dancing*]

CHORUS OF GIRLS But youth, of course, etc.

POOH. I think you ought to recollect
You cannot show too much respect
Towards the highly titled few;
But nobody does, and why should you?
That youth at us should have its fling,
Is hard on us,
Is hard on us;
To our prerogative we cling—
So pardon us,
So pardon us,
If we decline to dance and sing.
Tra la la, etc. [*Dancing*]

CHORUS OF GIRLS But youth, of course, must have its fling, etc.

[*Exeunt all but* YUM-YUM.

Enter NANKI-POO

NANK. Yum-Yum, at last we are alone! I have sought you night and day for three weeks, in the belief that your guardian was beheaded, and I find that you are about to be married to him this afternoon!

YUM. Alas, yes!

NANK. But you do not love him?

YUM. Alas, no!

NANK. Modified rapture! But why do you not refuse him?

YUM. What good would that do? He's my guardian, and he wouldn't let me marry you!

NANK. But I would wait until you were of age!

YUM. You forget that in Japan girls do not arrive at years of discretion until they are fifty.

NANK. True; from seventeen to forty-nine are considered years of indiscretion.

YUM. Besides–a wandering minstrel, who plays a wind instrument outside tea-houses, is hardly a fitting husband for the ward of a Lord High Executioner.

NANK. But—— [*Aside*] Shall I tell her? Yes! She will not betray me! [*Aloud*] What if it should prove that, after all, I am no musician?

YUM. There! I was certain of it, directly I heard you play!

NANK. What if it should prove that I am no other than the son of his Majesty the Mikado?

YUM. The son of the Mikado! But why is your Highness disguised? And what has your Highness done? And will your Highness promise never to do it again?

NANK. Some years ago I had the misfortune to captivate Katisha, an elderly lady of my father's Court. She misconstrued my customary affability into expressions of affection, and claimed me in marriage, under my father's law. My father, the Lucius Junius Brutus of his race, ordered me to marry her within a week, or perish ignominiously on the scaffold. That night I fled his Court, and, assuming the disguise of a Second Trombone, I joined the band in which you found me when I had the happiness of seeing you! [*Approaching her*]

YUM. [*retreating*] If you please, I think your Highness had better not come too near. The laws against flirting are excessively severe.

NANK. But we are quite alone, and nobody can see us.

YUM. Still, that doesn't make it right. To flirt is capital.

NANK. It *is* capital!

YUM. And we must obey the law.

NANK. Deuce take the law!

YUM. I wish it would, but it won't!

NANK. If it were not for that, how happy we might be!

YUM. Happy indeed!

NANK. If it were not for the law, we should now be sitting side by side, like that. [*Sits by her*]

YUM. Instead of being obliged to sit half a mile off, like that. [*Crosses and sits at other side of stage*]

NANK. We should be gazing into each other's eyes, like that. [*Gazing at her sentimentally*]

YUM. Breathing sighs of unutterable love–like that. [*Sighing and gazing lovingly at him*]

NANK. With our arms round each other's waists, like that. [*Embracing her*]

YUM. Yes, if it wasn't for the law.

NANK. If it wasn't for the law.

YUM. As it is, of course we couldn't do anything of the kind.

NANK. Not for worlds!
YUM. Being engaged to Ko-Ko, you know!
NANK. Being engaged to Ko-Ko!

Duet—YUM-YUM and NANKI-POO

NANK.
Were you not to Ko-Ko plighted,
I would say in tender tone,
"Loved one, let us be united—
Let us be each other's own!"
I would merge all rank and station,
Worldly sneers are nought to us,
And, to mark my admiration,
I would kiss you fondly thus—

[*Kisses her*]

BOTH
{I / He} would kiss {you / me} fondly thus—[*Kiss*]

YUM.
But as I'm engaged to Ko-Ko,
To embrace you thus, *con fuoco*,
Would be distinctly no *giuoco*,
And for yam I should get toko—

BOTH
Toko, toko, toko, toko!

NANK.
So, in spite of all temptation,
Such a theme I'll not discuss,
And on no consideration
Will I kiss you fondly thus—

[*Kissing her*]

Let me make it clear to you,
This is what I'll never do!
This, oh, this, oh, this, oh, this—

[*Kissing her*]

TOGETHER
This, oh, this, etc.

[*Exeunt in opposite directions.*

Enter KO-KO

KO. [*looking after* YUM-YUM] There she goes! To think how entirely my future happiness is wrapped up in that little parcel! Really, it hardly seems worth while! Oh, matrimony!— [*Enter* POOH-BAH *and* PISH-TUSH] Now then, what is it? Can't you see I'm soliloquizing? You have interrupted an apostrophe, sir!

PISH. I am the bearer of a letter from his Majesty the Mikado.

KO. [*taking it from him reverentially*] A letter from the Mikado! What in the world can he have to say to me? [*Reads letter*] Ah, here it is at last! I thought it would come sooner or later! The Mikado is struck by the fact that no executions have taken place in Titipu for a year and decrees that unless somebody is beheaded within one month the post of Lord High Executioner shall be abolished, and the city reduced to the rank of a village!

PISH. But that will involve us all in irretrievable ruin!

KO. Yes. There is no help for it, I shall have to execute somebody at once. The only question is, who shall it be?

POOH. Well, it seems unkind to say so, but as you're already under sentence of death for flirting, everything seems to point to *you.*

KO. To me? What are you talking about? I can't execute myself.

POOH. Why not?

KO. Why not? Because, in the first place, self-decapitation is an extremely difficult, not to say dangerous, thing to attempt, and, in the second, it's suicide, and suicide is a capital offence.

POOH. That is so, no doubt.

PISH. We might reserve that point.

POOH. True, it could be argued six months hence, before the full Court.

KO. Besides, I don't see how a man *can* cut off his own head.

POOH. A man might try.

PISH. Even if you only succeeded in cutting it half off, that would be something.

POOH. It would be taken as an earnest of your desire to comply with the Imperial will.

KO. No. Pardon me, but there I am adamant. As official Headsman, my reputation is at stake, and I can't consent to embark on a professional operation unless I see my way to a successful result.

POOH. This professional conscientiousness is highly creditable to *you,* but it places us in a very awkward position.

KO. My good sir, the awkwardness of your position is grace itself compared with that of a man engaged in the act of cutting off his own head.

PISH. I am afraid that, unless you can obtain a substitute——

KO. A substitute? Oh, certainly—nothing easier. [*To* POOH-BAH] I appoint you Lord High Substitute.

POOH. I should be delighted. Such an appointment would realize my fondest dreams. But no, at any sacrifice, I must set bounds to my insatiable ambition!

Trio

KO-KO

My brain it teems
With endless schemes
Both good and new
For Titipu;
But if I flit,
The benefit

POOH-BAH

I am so proud,
If I allowed
My family pride
To be my guide,
I'd volunteer
To quit this sphere

PISH-TUSH

I heard one day
A gentleman say
That criminals who
Are cut in two
Can hardly feel
The fatal steel,

That I'd diffuse
The town would lose!
Now every man
To aid his clan
Should plot and plan
As best he can,
And so,
Although
I'm ready to go,
Yet recollect
'Twere disrespect
Did I neglect
To thus effect
This aim direct
So I object—
So I object—
So I object—

Instead of you,
In a minute or two.
But family pride
Must be denied,
And set aside,
And mortified.
And so,
Although
I wish to go,
And greatly pine
To brightly shine,
And take the line
Of a hero fine,
With grief condign
I must decline—
I must decline—
I must decline—

And so are slain
Without much pain.
If this is true,
It's jolly for you;
Your courage screw
To bid us adieu,
And go
And show
Both friend and foe
How much you dare.
I'm quite aware
It's your affair,
Yet I declare
I'd take your share,
But I don't much care—
I don't much care—
I don't much care—

ALL To sit in solemn silence in a dull, dark dock,
In a pestilential prison, with a life-long lock,
Awaiting the sensation of a short, sharp shock,
From a cheap and chippy chopper on a big black block!
[*Exeunt* POOH. *and* PISH.

KO. This is simply appalling! I, who allowed myself to be respited at the last moment, simply in order to benefit my native town, am now required to die within a month, and that by a man whom I have loaded with honours! Is this public gratitude? Is this— [*Enter* NANKI-POO, *with a rope in his hands*] Go away, sir! How dare you? Am I never to be permitted to soliloquize?

NANK. Oh, go on—don't mind me.

KO. What are you going to do with that rope?

NANK. I am about to terminate an unendurable existence.

KO. Terminate your existence? Oh, nonsense! What for?

NANK. Because you are going to marry the girl I adore.

KO. Nonsense, sir. I won't permit it. I am a humane man, and if you attempt anything of the kind I shall order your instant arrest. Come, sir, desist at once or I summon my guard.

NANK. That's absurd. If you attempt to raise an alarm, I instantly perform the Happy Despatch with this dagger.

KO. No, no, don't do that. This is horrible! [*Suddenly*] Why, you cold-blooded scoundrel, are you aware that, in taking your life, you are committing a crime which—which—which is— Oh! [*Struck by an idea*] Substitute!

NANK. What's the matter?

KO. Is it *absolutely certain* that you are resolved to die?

NANK. Absolutely!

KO. Will *nothing* shake your resolution?

NANK. Nothing.

KO. Threats, entreaties, prayers—all useless?

NANK. All! My mind is made up.

KO. Then, if you really mean what you say, and if you are absolutely resolved to die, and if nothing whatever will shake your determination —don't spoil yourself by committing suicide, but be beheaded handsomely at the hands of the Public Executioner!

NANK. I don't see how that would benefit me.

KO. You don't? Observe: you'll have a month to live, and you'll live like a fighting-cock at my expense. When the day comes there'll be a grand public ceremonial—you'll be the central figure—no one will attempt to deprive you of that distinction. There'll be a procession—bands—dead march—bells tolling—all the girls in tears—Yum-Yum distracted—then, when it's all over, general rejoicings, and a display of fireworks in the evening. *You* won't see them, but they'll be there all the same.

NANK. Do you think Yum-Yum would really be distracted at my death?

KO. I am convinced of it. Bless you, she's the most tender-hearted little creature alive.

NANK. I should be sorry to cause her pain. Perhaps, after all, if I were to withdraw from Japan, and travel in Europe for a couple of years, I might contrive to forget her.

KO. Oh, I don't think you could forget Yum-Yum so easily; and, after all, what is more miserable than a love-blighted life?

NANK. True.

KO. Life without Yum-Yum—why, it seems absurd!

NANK. And yet there are a good many people in the world who have to endure it.

KO. Poor devils, yes! You are quite right not to be of their number.

NANK. [*suddenly*] I *won't* be of their number!

KO. Noble fellow!

NANK. I'll tell you how we'll manage it. Let me marry Yum-Yum tomorrow, and in a month you may behead me.

KO. No, no. I draw the line at Yum-Yum.

NANK. Very good. If you can draw the line, so can I. [*Preparing rope*]

KO. Stop, stop—listen one moment—be reasonable. How can I consent to your marrying Yum-Yum if I'm going to marry her myself?

NANK. My good friend, she'll be a widow in a month, and you can marry her then.

KO. That's true, of course. I quite see that. But, dear me! my position during the next month will be most unpleasant—most unpleasant.

NANK. Not half so unpleasant as my position at the end of it.

KO. But—dear me!—well—I agree—after all, it's only putting off my wedding for a month. But you won't prejudice her against me, will you? You see, I've educated her to be my wife; she's been taught to regard me as a wise and good man. Now I shouldn't like her views on that point disturbed.

NANK. Trust me, she shall never learn the truth from me.

Finale

Enter CHORUS, POOH-BAH, *and* PISH-TUSH

Chorus

With aspect stern
  And gloomy stride,
We come to learn
  How you decide.

Don't hesitate
  Your choice to name,
A dreadful fate
  You'll suffer all the same.

POOH. To ask you what you mean to do we punctually appear.
KO. Congratulate me, gentlemen, I've found a Volunteer!
ALL The Japanese equivalent for Hear, Hear, Hear!
KO. [*presenting him*] 'Tis Nanki-Poo!
ALL Hail, Nanki-Poo!
KO. I think he'll do
ALL Yes, yes, he'll do!

KO. He yields his life if I'll Yum-Yum surrender.
Now I adore that girl with passion tender,
And could not yield her with a ready will,
  Or her allot
  If I did not
Adore myself with passion tenderer still!

Enter YUM-YUM, PEEP-BO, *and* PITTI-SING

ALL Ah, yes!
He loves himself with passion tenderer still!
KO. [*to* NANKI-POO] Take her—she's yours!

[*Exit* KO-KO.

Ensemble

NANK. The threatened cloud has passed away,
YUM. And brightly shines the dawning day;
NANK. What though the night may come too soon,
YUM. There's yet a month of afternoon!

NANKI-POO, POOH-BAH, YUM-YUM, PITTI-SING, and PEEP-BO

Then let the throng
  Our joy advance,
With laughing song
  And merry dance,

CHORUS With joyous shout and ringing cheer,
Inaugurate our brief career!

PITTI. A day, a week, a month, a year—
YUM. Or far or near, or far or near,
POOH. Life's eventime comes much too soon,
PITTI. You'll live at least a honeymoon!

ALL Then let the throng, etc.

CHORUS With joyous shout, etc.

Solo—POOH-BAH

As in a month you've got to die,
If Ko-Ko tells us true,
'Twere empty compliment to cry
"Long life to Nanki-Poo!"
But as one month you have to live
As fellow-citizen,
This toast with three times three we'll give—
"Long life to you—till then!"

[*Exit* POOH-BAH.

CHORUS May all good fortune prosper you,
May you have health and riches too,
May you succeed in all you do!
Long life to you—till then!

[*Dance*]

Enter KATISHA *melodramatically*

KAT. Your revels cease! Assist me, all of you!
CHORUS Why, who is this whose evil eyes
Rain blight on our festivities?
KAT. I claim my perjured lover, Nanki-Poo!
Oh, fool! to shun delights that never cloy!
CHORUS Go, leave thy deadly work undone!
KAT. Come back, oh, shallow fool! come back to joy!
CHORUS Away, away! ill-favoured one!
NANK. [*aside to* YUM-YUM]Ah!
'Tis Katisha!
The maid of whom I told you.

[*About to go*]

KAT. [*detaining him*] No!
You shall not go,
These arms shall thus enfold you!

Song—KATISHA

KAT. [*addressing* NANKI-POO]
Oh fool, that fleest
My hallowed joys!
Oh blind, that seest
No equipoise!
Oh rash, that judgest
From half, the whole!
Oh base, that grudgest
Love's lightest dole!
Thy heart unbind,
Oh fool, oh blind!
Give me my place,
Oh rash, oh base!

CHORUS If she's thy bride, restore her place,
Oh fool, oh blind, oh rash, oh base!

KAT. [*addressing* YUM-YUM]
Pink cheek, that rulest
Where wisdom serves!
Bright eye, that foolest
Heroic nerves!
Rose lip, that scornest
Lore-laden years!
Smooth tongue, that warnest
Who rightly hears!
Thy doom is nigh,
Pink cheek, bright eye!
Thy knell is rung,
Rose lip, smooth tongue!

CHORUS If true her tale, thy knell is rung,
Pink cheek, bright eye, rose lip, smooth tongue!

PITTI. Away, nor prosecute your quest—
From our intention, well expressed,
You cannot turn us!
The state of your connubial views
Towards the person you accuse
Does not concern us!

For he's going to marry Yum-Yum—
ALL Yum-Yum!
PITTI. Your anger pray bury,
For all will be merry,
I think you had better succumb—
ALL Cumb—cumb!
PITTI. And join our expressions of glee.
On this subject I pray you be dumb—
ALL Dumb—dumb.
PITTI. You'll find there are many
Who'll wed for a penny—
The word for your guidance is "Mum"—
ALL Mum—mum!
PITTI. There's lots of good fish in the sea!

ALL On this subject we pray you be dumb, etc.

Solo—KATISHA

The hour of gladness
Is dead and gone;
In silent sadness
I live alone!
The hope I cherished
All lifeless lies,
And all has perished
Save love, which never dies!
Oh, faithless one, this insult you shall rue!
In vain for mercy on your knees you'll sue.
I'll tear the mask from your disguising!

NANK. [*aside*] Now comes the blow!
KAT. Prepare yourselves for news surprising!
NANK. [*aside*] How foil my foe?
KAT. No minstrel he, despite bravado!
YUM. [*aside, struck by an idea*] Ha! ha! I know!
KAT. He is the son of your——

[NANKI-POO, YUM-YUM, *and* CHORUS, *interrupting, sing Japanese words to drown her voice.*

O ni! bikkuri shakkuri to!
KAT. In vain you interrupt with this tornado!
He is the only son of your——
ALL O ni! bikkuri shakkuri to!
KAT. I'll spoil——

ALL O ni! bikkuri shakkuri to!
KAT. Your gay gambado!
He is the son—
ALL O ni! bikkuri shakkuri to!
KAT. Of your—
ALL O ni! bikkuri shakkuri to!
KAT. The son of your—
ALL O ni! bikkuri shakkuri to! oya! oya!

Ensemble

KATISHA	THE OTHERS
Ye torrents roar!	We'll hear no more,
Ye tempests howl!	Ill-omened owl,
Your wrath outpour	To joy we soar,
With angry growl!	Despite your scowl!
Do ye your worst, my vengeance call	The echoes of our festival
Shall rise triumphant over all!	Shall rise triumphant over all!
Prepare for woe,	Away you go,
Ye haughty lords,	Collect your hordes;
At once I go	Proclaim your woe
Mikado-wards,	In dismal chords;
My wrongs with vengeance shall be crowned!	We do not heed their dismal sound,
My wrongs with vengeance shall be crowned!	For joy reigns everywhere around.

[KATISHA *rushes furiously upstage, clearing the crowd away right and left, finishing on steps at the back of stage.*

END OF ACT I

ACT II

SCENE.—KO-KO'S *Garden.* YUM-YUM *discovered seated at her bridal toilet, surrounded by maidens, who are dressing her hair and painting her face and lips, as she judges of the effect in a mirror.*

Solo—PITTI-SING *and Chorus of Girls*

CHORUS Braid the raven hair—
Weave the supple tress—
Deck the maiden fair,
In her loveliness—
Paint the pretty face—
Dye the coral lip—
Emphasize the grace
Of her ladyship!
Art and nature, thus allied,
Go to make a pretty bride.

Solo—PITTI-SING

Sit with downcast eye—
  Let it brim with dew—
Try if you can cry—
  We will do so, too.
When you're summoned, start
  Like a frightened roe—
Flutter, little heart,
  Colour, come and go!
Modesty at marriage-tide
Well becomes a pretty bride!

Chorus

Braid the raven hair, etc.

[*Exeunt* PITTI-SING, PEEP-BO *and* CHORUS.

YUM. Yes, I am indeed beautiful! Sometimes I sit and wonder, in my artless Japanese way, why it is that I am so much more attractive than anybody else in the whole world. Can this be vanity? No! Nature is lovely and rejoices in her loveliness. I am a child of Nature, and take after my mother.

Song—YUM-YUM

The sun, whose rays
Are all ablaze
  With ever-living glory,
Does not deny
His majesty—
  He scorns to tell a story!
He don't exclaim,

"I blush for shame,
  So kindly be indulgent."
But, fierce and bold,
In fiery gold,
  He glories all effulgent!

  I mean to rule the earth,
    As he the sky—
  We really know our worth,
    The sun and I!

Observe his flame,
That placid dame,
  The moon's Celestial Highness;
There's not a trace
Upon her face
  Of diffidence or shyness:
She borrows light
That, through the night,
  Mankind may all acclaim her!
And, truth to tell,
She lights up well,
  So I, for one, don't blame her!

  Ah, pray make no mistake,
    We are not shy;
  We're very wide awake,
    The moon and I!

Enter PITTI-SING *and* PEEP-BO

YUM. Yes, everything seems to smile upon me. I am to be married to-day to the man I love best, and I believe I am the very happiest girl in Japan!

PEEP. The happiest girl indeed, for she is indeed to be envied who has attained happiness in all but perfection.

YUM. In "all but" perfection?

PEEP. Well, dear, it can't be denied that the fact that your husband is to be beheaded in a month is, in its way, a drawback. It does seem to take the top off it, you know.

PITTI. I don't know about that. It all depends!

PEEP. At all events, *he* will find it a drawback.

PITTI. Not necessarily. Bless you, it all depends!

YUM. [*in tears*] I think it very indelicate of you to refer to such a subject on such a day. If my married happiness *is* to be—to be——

PEEP. Cut short.

YUM. Well, cut short—in a month, can't you let me forget it? [*Weeping*]

Enter NANKI-POO, *followed by* PISH-TUSH

NANK. Yum-Yum in tears—and on her wedding morn!

YUM. [*sobbing*] They've been reminding me that in a month you're to be beheaded! [*Bursts into tears*]

PITTI. Yes, we've been reminding her that you're to be beheaded. [*Bursts into tears*]

PEEP. It's quite true, you know, you *are* to be beheaded! [*Bursts into tears*]

NANK. [*aside*] Humph! Now, some bridegrooms would be depressed by this sort of thing! [*Aloud*] A month? Well, what's a month? Bah! These divisions of time are purely arbitrary. Who says twenty-four hours make a day?

PITTI. There's a popular impression to that effect.

NANK. Then we'll efface it. We'll call each second a minute—each minute an hour—each hour a day—and each day a year. At that rate we've about thirty years of married happiness before us!

PEEP. And, at that rate, this interview has already lasted four hours and three-quarters! [*Exit* PEEP-BO.

YUM. [*still sobbing*] Yes. How time flies when one is thoroughly enjoying oneself.

NANK. That's the way to look at it! Don't let's be downhearted! There's a silver lining to every cloud.

YUM. Certainly. Let's—let's be perfectly happy! [*Almost in tears*]

PISH-TUSH By all means. Let's—let's thoroughly enjoy ourselves.

PITTI. It's—it's absurd to cry. [*Trying to force a laugh*]

YUM. Quite ridiculous! [*Trying to laugh*]

[*All break into a forced and melancholy laugh.*

Madrigal

YUM-YUM, PITTI-SING, NANKI-POO, *and* PISH-TUSH

Brightly dawns our wedding day;
  Joyous hour, we give thee greeting!
  Whither, whither art thou fleeting?
Fickle moment, prithee stay!
  What though mortal joys be hollow?
  Pleasures come, if sorrows follow:
Though the tocsin sound, ere long,
  Ding dong! Ding dong!
Yet until the shadows fall
Over one and over all,
Sing a merry madrigal—
  A madrigal!

Fal-la—fal-la! etc. [*Ending in tears*]
Let us dry the ready tear,
  Though the hours are surely creeping
  Little need for woeful weeping,
Till the sad sundown is near.
  All must sip the cup of sorrow—
  I to-day and thou to-morrow;
This the close of every song—
  Ding dong! Ding dong!
What, though solemn shadows fall,
Sooner, later, over all?
Sing a merry madrigal—
  A madrigal!
Fal-la—fal-la! etc. [*Ending in tears*]

[*Exeunt* PITTI-SING *and* PISH-TUSH.

[NANKI-POO *embraces* YUM-YUM. *Enter* KO-KO. NANKI-POO *releases* YUM-YUM.

KO. Go on—don't mind me.

NANK. I'm afraid we're distressing you.

KO. Never mind, I must get used to it. Only please do it by degrees. Begin by putting your arm round her waist. [NANKI-POO *does so*] There; let me get used to that first.

YUM. Oh, wouldn't you like to retire? It must pain you to see us so affectionate together!

KO. No, I must learn to bear it! Now oblige me by allowing her head to rest on your shoulder.

NANK. Like that? [*He does so.* KO-KO *much affected*]

KO. I am much obliged to you. Now—kiss her! [*He does so.* KO-KO *writhes with anguish*] Thank you—it's simple torture!

YUM. Come, come, bear up. After all, it's only for a month.

KO. No. It's no use deluding oneself with false hopes.

NANK. }
YUM. } What do you mean?

KO. [*to* YUM-YUM] My child—my poor child! [*Aside*] How shall I break it to her? [*Aloud*] My little bride that was to have been?

YUM. [*delighted*] *Was* to have been?

KO. Yes, you never can be mine!

NANK. } [*in ecstasy*] { What!
YUM. } { I'm so glad!

KO. I've just ascertained that, by the Mikado's law, when a married man is beheaded his wife is buried alive.

NANK. }
YUM. } Buried alive!

KO. Buried alive. It's a most unpleasant death.

NANK. But whom did you get that from?

KO. Oh, from Pooh-Bah. He's my Solicitor.

YUM. But he may be mistaken!

KO. So I thought; so I consulted the Attorney-General, the Lord Chief Justice, the Master of the Rolls, the Judge Ordinary and the Lord Chancellor. They're all of the same opinion. Never knew such unanimity on a point of law in my life!

NANK. But stop a bit! This law has never been put in force.

KO. Not yet. You see, flirting is the only crime punishable with decapitation, and married men never flirt.

NANK. Of course, they don't. I quite forgot that! Well, I suppose I may take it that my dream of happiness is at an end!

YUM. Darling—I don't want to appear selfish, and I love you with all my heart—I don't suppose I shall ever love anybody else half as much—but when I agreed to marry you—my own—I had no idea—pet—that I should have to be buried alive in a month!

NANK. Nor I! It's the very first I've heard of it!

YUM. It—it makes a difference, doesn't it?

NANK. It *does* make a difference, of course.

YUM. You see—burial alive—it's such a stuffy death!

NANK. I call it a beast of a death.

YUM. You see my difficulty, don't you?

NANK. Yes, and I see my own. If I insist on your carrying out your promise, I doom you to a hideous death; if I release you, you marry Ko-Ko at once!

Trio—YUM-YUM, NANKI-POO, and KO-KO

YUM. Here's a how-de-do!
If I marry you,
When your time has come to perish,

When the maiden whom you cherish
Must be slaughtered, too!
Here's a how-de-do!

NANK. Here's a pretty mess!
In a month, or less,
I must die without a wedding!
Let the bitter tears I'm shedding
Witness my distress,
Here's a pretty mess!

Ko. Here's a state of things!
To her life she clings!
Matrimonial devotion
Doesn't seem to suit her notion—
Burial it brings!
Here's a state of things!

Ensemble

YUM-YUM and NANKI-POO

With a passion that's intense
I worship and adore,
But the laws of common sense
We oughtn't to ignore.
If what he says is true,
'Tis death to marry you!
Here's a pretty state of things!
Here's a pretty how-de-do!

KO-KO

With a passion that's intense
You worship and adore,
But the laws of common sense
You oughtn't to ignore.
If what I say is true,
'Tis death to marry you!
Here's a pretty state of things!
Here's a pretty how-de-do!

[*Exeunt* YUM-YUM.

Ko. [*going up to* NANKI-POO] My poor boy, I'm really very sorry for you.

NANK. Thanks, old fellow. I'm sure you are.

Ko. You see I'm quite helpless.

NANK. I quite see that.

Ko. I can't conceive anything more distressing than to have one's marriage broken off at the last moment. But you shan't be disappointed of a wedding—you shall come to mine.

NANK. It's awfully kind of you, but that's impossible.

Ko. Why so?

NANK. To-day I die.

Ko. What do you mean?

NANK. I can't live without Yum-Yum. This afternoon I perform the Happy Despatch.

Ko. No, no—pardon me—I can't allow that.

NANK. Why not?

Ko. Why, hang it all, you're under contract to die by the hand of the

Public Executioner in a month's time! If you kill yourself, what's to become of me? Why, I shall have to be executed in your place!

NANK. It would certainly seem so!

Enter POOH-BAH

Ko. Now then, Lord Mayor, what is it?

POOH. The Mikado and his suite are approaching the city, and will be here in ten minutes.

Ko. The Mikado! He's coming to see whether his orders have been carried out! [*To* NANKI-POO] Now look here, you know—this is getting serious—a bargain's a bargain, and you really mustn't frustrate the ends of justice by committing suicide. As a man of honour and a gentleman, you are bound to die ignominiously by the hands of the Public Executioner.

NANK. Very well, then—behead me.

Ko. What, now?

NANK. Certainly; at once.

POOH. Chop it off! Chop it off!

Ko. My good sir, I don't go about prepared to execute gentlemen at a moment's notice. Why, I never even killed a blue-bottle!

POOH. Still, as Lord High Executioner——

Ko. My good sir, as Lord High Executioner, I've got to behead him in a month. I'm not ready yet. I don't know how it's done. I'm going to take lessons. I mean to begin with a guinea pig, and work my way through the animal kingdom till I come to a Second Trombone. Why, you don't suppose that, as a humane man, I'd have accepted the post of Lord High Executioner if I hadn't thought the duties were purely nominal? I *can't* kill you—I can't kill anything! I can't kill anybody! [*Weeps*]

NANK. Come, my poor fellow, we all have unpleasant duties to discharge at times; after all, what is it? If I don't mind, why should you? Remember, sooner or later it must be done.

Ko. [*springing up suddenly*] *Must it?* I'm not so sure about that!

NANK. What do you mean?

Ko. Why should I kill you when making an affidavit that you've been executed will do just as well? Here are plenty of witnesses—the Lord Chief Justice, Lord High Admiral, Commander-in-Chief, Secretary of State for the Home Department, First Lord of the Treasury, and Chief Commissioner of Police.

NANK. But where are they?

Ko. There they are. They'll all swear to it—won't you? [*To* POOH-BAH]

POOH. Am I to understand that all of us high Officers of State are required to perjure ourselves to ensure your safety?

Ko. Why not? You'll be grossly insulted, as usual.

POOH. Will the insult be cash down, or at a date?

Ko. It will be a ready-money transaction.

Pooh. [*Aside*] Well, it will be a useful discipline. [*Aloud*] Very good. Choose your fiction, and I'll endorse it! [*Aside*] Ha! Ha! Family Pride, how do you like *that*, my buck?

Nank. But I tell you that life without Yum-Yum——

Ko. Oh, Yum-Yum, Yum-Yum! Bother Yum-Yum! Here, Commissionaire [*to* Pooh-Bah], go and fetch Yum-Yum. [*Exit* Pooh-Bah] Take Yum-Yum and marry Yum-Yum, only go away and never come back again. [*Enter* Pooh-Bah *with* Yum-Yum] Here she is. Yum-Yum, are you particularly busy?

Yum. Not particularly.

Ko. You've five minutes to spare?

Yum. Yes.

Ko. Then go along with his Grace the Archbishop of Titipu; he'll marry you at once.

Yum. But if I'm to be buried alive?

Ko. Now, don't ask any questions, but do as I tell you, and Nanki-Poo will explain all.

Nank. But one moment——

Ko. Not for worlds. Here comes the Mikado, no doubt to ascertain whether I've obeyed his decree, and if he finds you alive I shall have the greatest difficulty in persuading him that I've beheaded you. [*Exeunt* Nanki-Poo *and* Yum-Yum, *followed by* Pooh-Bah] Close thing that, for here he comes! [*Exit* Ko-Ko.

March—Enter procession, heralding Mikado, *with* Katisha.

Entrance of Mikado *and* Katisha

["*March of the Mikado's troops*"]

Chorus

Miya sama, miya sama,
On n'm-ma no mayé ni
Pira-Pira suru no wa
Nan gia na
Toko tonyaré tonyaré na?

Duet—Mikado and Katisha

Mik.

From every kind of man
  Obedience I expect;
I'm the Emperor of Japan—

Kat.

And I'm his daughter-in-law elect!
  He'll marry his son
  (He's only got one)

To his daughter-in-law elect.

MIK. My morals have been declared
Particularly correct;

KAT. But they're nothing at all, compared
With those of his daughter-in-law elect!
Bow—Bow—
To his daughter-in-law elect!

ALL Bow—Bow—
To his daughter-in-law elect.

MIK. In a fatherly kind of way
I govern each tribe and sect,
All cheerfully own my sway—

KAT. Except his daughter-in-law elect!
As tough as a bone,
With a will of her own,
Is his daughter-in-law elect!

MIK. My nature is love and light—
My freedom from all defect—

KAT. Is insignificant quite,
Compared with his daughter-in-law elect!
Bow—Bow—
To his daughter-in-law elect!

ALL Bow—Bow—
To his daughter-in-law elect!

Song—MIKADO and CHORUS

A more humane Mikado never
Did in Japan exist,
To nobody second,
I'm certainly reckoned
A true philanthropist.
It is my very humane endeavour
To make, to some extent,
Each evil liver
A running river
Of harmless merriment.

My object all sublime
I shall achieve in time—
To let the punishment fit the crime—
The punishment fit the crime;
And make each prisoner pent
Unwillingly represent
A source of innocent merriment!
Of innocent merriment!

All prosy dull society sinners,
Who chatter and bleat and bore,
Are sent to hear sermons
From mystical Germans
Who preach from ten till four.
The amateur tenor, whose vocal villainies
All desire to shirk,
Shall, during off-hours,
Exhibit his powers
To Madame Tussaud's waxwork.

The lady who dyes a chemical yellow
Or stains her grey hair puce,
Or pinches her figger,
Is blacked like a nigger

With permanent walnut juice.
The idiot who, in railway carriages,
Scribbles on window-panes,
We only suffer
To ride on a buffer
In Parliamentary trains.

My object all sublime, etc.

CHORUS His object all sublime, etc.

The advertising quack who wearies
With tales of countless cures,
His teeth, I've enacted,
Shall all be extracted
By terrified amateurs.
The music-hall singer attends a series
Of masses and fugues and "ops"
By Bach, interwoven
With Spohr and Beethoven,
At classical Monday Pops.

The billiard sharp whom any one catches,
His doom's extremely hard—
He's made to dwell—
In a dungeon cell
On a spot that's always barred.
And there he plays extravagant matches
In fitless finger-stalls
On a cloth untrue,
With a twisted cue
And elliptical billiard balls!

My object all sublime, etc.

CHORUS His object all sublime, etc.

Enter POOH-BAH, KO-KO, *and* PITTI-SING. *All kneel.*

[POOH-BAH *hands a paper to* KO-KO]

KO. I am honoured in being permitted to welcome your Majesty. I guess the object of your Majesty's visit—your wishes have been attended to. The execution has taken place.

MIK. Oh, you've had an execution, have you?

Ko. Yes. The Coroner has just handed me his certificate.

Pooh. I am the Coroner. [Ko-Ko *hands certificate to* Mikado]

Mik. And this is the certificate of his death. [*Reads*] "At Titipu, in the presence of the Lord Chancellor, Lord Chief Justice, Attorney-General, Secretary of State for the Home Department, Lord Mayor, and Groom of the Second Floor Front——"

Pooh. They were all present, your Majesty. I counted them myself.

Mik. Very good house. I wish I'd been in time for the performance.

Ko. A tough fellow he was, too—a man of gigantic strength. His struggles were terrific. It was really a remarkable scene.

Mik. Describe it.

Trio and Chorus

Ko-Ko, Pitti-Sing, Pooh-Bah and *Chorus*

Ko. The criminal cried, as he dropped him down,
In a state of wild alarm—
With a frightful, frantic, fearful frown,
I bared my big right arm.
I seized him by his little pig-tail,
And on his knees fell he,
As he squirmed and struggled,
And gurgled and guggled,
I drew my snickersnee!
Oh, never shall I
Forget the cry,
Or the shriek that shriekèd he,
As I gnashed my teeth,
When from its sheath
I drew my snickernee!

Chorus

We know him well,
He cannot tell
Untrue or groundless tales—
He always tries
To utter lies,
And every time he fails.

Pitti. He shivered and shook as he gave the sign
For the stroke he didn't deserve;
When all of a sudden his eye met mine,
And it seemed to brace his nerve;

For he nodded his head and kissed his hand,
And he whistled an air, did he,
As the sabre true
Cut cleanly through
His cervical vertebræ!

When a man's afraid,
A beautiful maid
Is a cheering sight to see;
And it's oh, I'm glad
That moment sad
Was soothed by sight of me!

Chorus

Her terrible tale
You can't assail,
With truth it quite agrees:
Her taste exact
For faultless fact
Amounts to a disease.

Pooh. Now though you'd have said that head was dead
(For its owner dead was he),
It stood on its neck, with a smile well-bred,
And bowed three times to me!
It was none of your impudent off-hand nods,
But as humble as could be;
For it clearly knew
The deference due
To a man of pedigree!
And it's oh, I vow,
This deathly bow
Was a touching sight to see;
Though trunkless, yet
It couldn't forget
The deference due to me!

Chorus

This haughty youth,
He speaks the truth
Whenever he finds it pays:
And in this case
It all took place
Exactly as he says!

[*Exeunt* Chorus

MIK. All this is very interesting, and I should like to have seen it. But we came about a totally different matter. A year ago my son, the heir to the throne of Japan, bolted from our Imperial Court.

KO. Indeed! Had he any reason to be dissatisfied with his position?

KAT. None whatever. On the contrary, I was going to marry him—yet he fled!

POOH. I am surprised that he should have fled from one so lovely!

KAT. That's not true.

POOH. No!

KAT. You hold that I am not beautiful because my face is plain. But you know nothing; you are still unenlightened. Learn, then, that it is not in the face alone that beauty is to be sought. My face is unattractive!

POOH. It is.

KAT. But I have a left shoulder-blade that is a miracle of loveliness. People come miles to see it. My right elbow has a fascination that few can resist.

POOH. Allow me!

KAT. It is on view Tuesdays and Fridays, on presentation of visiting card. As for my circulation, it is the largest in the world.

KO. And yet he fled!

MIK. And is now masquerading in this town, disguised as a Second Trombone.

KO.
POOH. } A Second Trombone!
PITTI.

MIK. Yes; would it be troubling you too much if I asked you to produce him? He goes by the name of——

KAT. Nanki-Poo.

MIK. Nanki-Poo.

KO. It's quite easy. That is, it's rather difficult. In point of fact, he's gone abroad!

MIK. Gone abroad! His address.

KO. Knightsbridge!

KAT. [*who is reading certificate of death*]. Ha!

MIK. What's the matter?

KAT. See here—his name—Nanki-Poo—beheaded this morning. Oh, where shall I find another? Where shall I find another?

[KO-KO, POOH-BAH, *and* PITTI-SING *fall on their knees.*

MIK. [*looking at paper*] Dear, dear, dear! this is very tiresome. [*To* Ko-Ko] My poor fellow, in your anxiety to carry out my wishes you have beheaded the heir to the throne of Japan!

KO. I beg to offer an unqualified apology.

POOH. I desire to associate myself with that expression of regret.

PITTI. We really hadn't the least notion——

MIK. Of course you hadn't. How could you? Come, come, my good fellow, don't distress yourself—it was no fault of yours. If a man of exalted rank chooses to disguise himself as a Second Trombone, he must take the consequences. It really distresses me to see you take on so. I've no doubt he thoroughly deserved all he got. [*They rise.*]

KO. We are infinitely obliged to your Majesty——

PITTI. Much obliged, your Majesty.

POOH. Very much obliged, your Majesty.

MIK. Obliged? not a bit. Don't mention it. How *could* you tell?

POOH. No, of course we couldn't tell who the gentleman really was.

PITTI. It wasn't written on his forehead, you know.

KO. It might have been on his pocket-handkerchief, but Japanese don't use pocket-handkerchiefs! Ha! ha! ha!

MIK. Ha! ha! ha! [*To* KATISHA] I forget the punishment for compassing the death of the Heir Apparent.

KO.
POOH. } Punishment. [*They drop down on their knees again*]
PITTI.

MIK. Yes. Something lingering, with boiling oil in it, I fancy. Something of that sort. I think boiling oil occurs in it, but I'm not sure. I know it's something humorous, but lingering, with either boiling oil or melted lead. Come, come, don't fret—I'm not a bit angry.

KO. [*in abject terror*] If your Majesty will accept our assurance, we had no idea——

MIK. Of course——

PITTI. I knew nothing about it.

POOH. I wasn't there.

MIK. That's the pathetic part of it. Unfortunately, the fool of an Act says "compassing the death of the Heir Apparent." There's not a word about a mistake——

KO., PITTI., and POOH. No!

MIK. Or not knowing——

KO. No!

MIK. Or having no notion——

PITTI. No!

MIK. Or not being there——

POOH. No!

MIK. There should be, of course——

KO., PITTI., and POOH. Yes!

MIK. But there isn't.

KO., PITTI., and POOH. Oh!

MIK. That's the slovenly way in which these Acts are always drawn. However, cheer up, it'll be all right. I'll have it altered next session. Now, let's see about your execution—will after luncheon suit you? Can you wait till then?

KO., PITTI., and POOH. Oh, yes—we can wait till then!

MIK. Then we'll make it after luncheon.

POOH. I don't want any lunch.

MIK. I'm really very sorry for you all, but it's an unjust world, and virtue is triumphant only in theatrical performances.

Glee

PITTI-SING, KATISHA, KO-KO, POOH-BAH, and MIKADO

MIK. See how the Fates their gifts allot,
For A is happy—B is not.
Yet B is worthy, I dare say,
Of more prosperity than A!

KO., POOH., and PITTI. *Is* B more worthy?

KAT. I should say
He's worth a great deal more than A

ENSEMBLE
Yet A is happy!
Oh, so happy!
Laughing, Ha! ha!
Chaffing, Ha! ha!
Nectar quaffing, Ha! ha! ha!
Ever joyous, ever gay,
Happy, undeserving A!

KO., POOH., and PITTI.
If I were Fortune—which I'm not—
B should enjoy A's happy lot,
And A should die in miserie—
That is, assuming I am B.

MIK. and KAT. But *should* A perish?

KO., POOH., and PITTI. That should he
(Of course, assuming I am B).
B should be happy!
Oh, so happy!
Laughing, Ha! ha!
Chaffing, Ha! ha!
Nectar quaffing, Ha! ha! ha!
But condemned to die as he,
Wretched meritorious B!

[*Exeunt* MIKADO *and* KATISHA.

KO. Well, a nice mess you've got us into, with your nodding head and the deference due to a man of pedigree!

POOH. Merely corroborative detail, intended to give artistic verisimilitude to an otherwise bald and unconvincing narrative.

PITTI. Corroborative detail indeed! Corroborative fiddlestick!

KO. And you're just as bad as he is with your cock-and-a-bull stories about catching his eye and his whistling an air. But that's so like you! You must put in your oar!

Pooh. But how about your big right arm?

Pitti. Yes, and your snickersnee!

Ko. Well, well, never mind that now. There's only one thing to be done. Nanki-Poo hasn't started yet—he must come to life again at once. [*Enter* Nanki-Poo *and* Yum-yum *prepared for journey.*] Here he comes. Here, Nanki-Poo, I've good news for you—you're reprieved.

Nank. Oh, but it's too late. I'm a dead man, and I'm off for my honeymoon.

Ko. Nonsense! A terrible thing has just happened. It seems you're the son of the Mikado.

Nank. Yes, but that happened some time ago.

Ko. Is this a time for airy persiflage? Your father is here, and with Katisha!

Nank. My father! And with Katisha!

Ko. Yes, he wants you particularly.

Pooh. So does she.

Yum. Oh, but he's married now.

Ko. But, bless my heart! what has that to do with it?

Nank. Katisha claims me in marriage, but I can't marry her because I'm married already—consequently she will insist on my execution, and if I'm executed, my wife will have to be buried alive.

Yum. You see our difficulty.

Ko. Yes. I don't know what's to be done.

Nank. There's one chance for you. If you could persuade Katisha to marry you, she would have no further claim on me, and in that case I could come to life without any fear of being put to death.

Ko. I marry Katisha!

Yum. I really think it's the only course.

Ko. But, my good girl, have you seen her? She's something appalling!

Pitti. Ah! that's only her face. She has a left elbow which people come miles to see!

Pooh. I am told that her right heel is much admired by connoisseurs.

Ko. My good sir, I decline to pin my heart upon any lady's right heel.

Nank. It comes to this: When Katisha is single, I prefer to be a disembodied spirit. When Katisha is married, existence will be as welcome as the flowers in spring.

Duet—Nanki-Poo and Ko-Ko

[*With* Yum-Yum, Pitti-Sing, *and* Pooh-Bah]

Nank. The flowers that bloom in the spring,
Tra la,
Breathe promise of merry sunshine—

As we merrily dance and we sing,
Tra la,
We welcome the hope that they bring,
Tra la,
Of a summer of roses and wine.
And that's what we mean when we say that a thing
Is welcome as flowers that bloom in the spring.
Tra la la la la la, etc.

ALL Tra la la la, etc.

KO. The flowers that bloom in the spring,
Tra la,
Have nothing to do with the case.
I've got to take under my wing,
Tra la,
A most unattractive old thing,
Tra la,
With a caricature of a face
And that's what I mean when I say, or I sing,
"Oh, bother the flowers that bloom in the spring."
Tra la la la la la, etc.

ALL Tra la, la la, Tra la la la, etc.

[*Dance and exeunt* NANKI-POO, YUM-YUM, POOH-BAH, PITTI-SING, *and* KO-KO.

Enter KATISHA

Recitative and Song—KATISHA

Alone, and yet alive! Oh, sepulchre!
My soul is still my body's prisoner!
Remote the peace that Death alone can give—
My doom, to wait! my punishment, to live!

Song

Hearts do not break!
They sting and ache
For old love's sake,
But do not die,
Though with each breath

They long for death
As witnesseth
The living I!
Oh, living I!
Come, tell me why,
When hope is gone,
Dost thou stay on?
Why linger here,
Where all is drear?
Oh, living I!
Come, tell me why,
When hope is gone,
Dost thou stay on?
May not a cheated maiden die?

Ko. [*entering and approaching her timidly*] Katisha!

Kat. The miscreant who robbed me of my love! But vengeance pursues—they are heating the cauldron!

Ko. Katisha—behold a suppliant at your feet! Katisha—mercy!

Kat. Mercy? Had you mercy on him? See here, you! You have slain my love. He did not love *me*, but he would have loved me in time. I am an acquired taste—only the educated palate can appreciate *me*. I was educating *his* palate when he left me. Well, he is dead, and where shall I find another? It takes years to train a man to love me. Am I to go through the weary round again, and, at the same time, implore mercy for you who robbed me of my prey—I mean my pupil—just as his education was on the point of completion? Oh, where shall I find another?

Ko. [*suddenly, and with great vehemence*] Here!—Here!

Kat. What!!!

Ko. [*with intense passion*] Katisha, for years I have loved you with a white-hot passion that is slowly but surely consuming my very vitals! Ah, shrink not from me! If there is aught of woman's mercy in your heart, turn not away from a love-sick suppliant whose every fibre thrills at your tiniest touch! True it is that, under a poor mask of disgust, I have endeavoured to conceal a passion whose inner fires are broiling the soul within me! But the fire will not be smothered—it defies all attempts at extinction, and, breaking forth, all the more eagerly for its long restraint, it declares itself in words that will not be weighed—that cannot be schooled—that should not be too severely criticised. Katisha, I dare not hope for your love—but I will not live without it! Darling!

Kat. You, whose hands still reek with the blood of my betrothed, dare to address words of passion to the woman you have so foully wronged!

Ko. I do—accept my love, or I perish on the spot!

Kat. Go to! Who knows so well as I that no one ever yet died of a broken heart!

Ko. You know not what you say. Listen!

Song—Ko-Ko

On a tree by a river a little tom-tit
Sang "Willow, titwillow, titwillow!"
And I said to him, "Dicky-bird, why do you sit
Singing 'Willow, titwillow, titwillow'?"
"Is it weakness of intellect, birdie?" I cried,
"Or a rather tough worm in your little inside?"
With a shake of his poor little head, he replied,
"Oh, willow, titwillow, titwillow!"

He slapped at his chest, as he sat on that bough,
Singing "Willow, titwillow, titwillow!"
And a cold perspiration bespangled his brow,
Oh, willow, titwillow, titwillow!
He sobbed and he sighed, and a gurgle he gave,
Then he plunged himself into the billowy wave,
And an echo arose from the suicide's grave—
"Oh, willow, titwillow, titwillow!"

Now I feel just as sure as I'm sure that my name
Isn't Willow, titwillow, titwillow,

That 'twas blighted affection that made him exclaim
"Oh, willow, titwillow, titwillow!"
And if you remain callous and obdurate, I
Shall perish as he did, and you will know why,
Though I probably shall not exclaim as I die,
"Oh, willow, titwillow, titwillow!"

[*During this song* KATISHA *has been greatly affected, and at the end is almost in tears.*

KAT. [*whimpering*] Did he really die of love?

Ko. He really did.

KAT. All on account of a cruel little hen?

Ko. Yes.

KAT. Poor little chap!

Ko. It's an affecting tale, and quite true. I knew the bird intimately.

KAT. Did you? He must have been very fond of her.

Ko. His devotion was something extraordinary.

KAT. [*still whimpering*] Poor little chap! And–and if I refuse you, will you go and do the same?

Ko. At once.

KAT. No, no–you mustn't! Anything but that! [*Falls on his breast*] Oh, I'm a silly little goose!

Ko. [*making a wry face*] You are!

KAT. And you won't hate me because I'm just a little teeny weeny wee bid bloodthirsty, will you?

Ko. Hate you? Oh, Katisha! is there not beauty even in bloodthirstiness?

KAT. My idea exactly.

Duet–KATISHA and KO-KO

KAT. There is beauty in the bellow of the blast,
There is grandeur in the growling of the gale,

There is eloquent outpouring
When the lion is a-roaring,
And the tiger is a-lashing of his tail!

KO. Yes, I like to see a tiger
From the Congo or the Niger,
And especially when lashing of his tail!

KAT. Volcanoes have a splendour that is grim,
And earthquakes only terrify the dolts,
But to him who's scientific
There's nothing that's terrific
In the falling of a flight of thunderbolts!

KO. Yes, in spite of all my meekness,
If I have a little weakness,
It's a passion for a flight of thunderbolts!

BOTH If that is so,
Sing derry down derry!
It's evident, very,
Our tastes are one.
Away we'll go,
And merrily marry,
Nor tardily tarry
Till day is done!

KO. There is beauty in extreme old age–
Do you fancy you are elderly enough?
Information I'm requesting
On a subject interesting:
Is a maiden all the better when she's tough?

KAT. Throughout this wide dominion
It's the general opinion
That she'll last a good deal longer when she's tough.

KO. Are you old enough to marry, do you think?
Won't you wait till you are eighty in the shade?
There's a fascination frantic
In a ruin that's romantic;
Do you think you are sufficiently decayed?

KAT. To the matter that you mention
I have given some attention,
And I think I am sufficiently decayed.

BOTH If that is so,
Sing derry down derry!
It's evident, very,
Our tastes are one!

Away we'll go,
And merrily marry,
Nor tardily tarry
Till day is done!

[*Exeunt together.*

Flourish. Enter the MIKADO, *attended by* PISH-TUSH *and Court.*

MIK. Now then, we've had a capital lunch, and we're quite ready. Have all the painful preparations been made?

PISH. Your Majesty, all is prepared.

MIK. Then produce the unfortunate gentleman and his two well-meaning but misguided accomplices.

Enter KO-KO, KATISHA, POOH-BAH, *and* PITTI-SING. *They throw themselves at the* MIKADO'*s feet.*

KAT. Mercy! Mercy for Ko-Ko! Mercy for Pitti-Sing! Mercy even for Pooh-Bah!

MIK. I beg your pardon, I don't think I quite caught that remark.

POOH. Mercy even for Pooh-Bah.

KAT. Mercy! My husband that was to have been is dead, and I have just married this miserable object.

MIK. Oh! You've not been long about it!

KO. We were married before the Registrar.

POOH. *I* am the Registrar.

MIK. I see. But my difficulty is that, as you have slain the Heir Apparent——

Enter NANKI-POO *and* YUM-YUM. *They kneel.*

NANKI. The Heir Apparent is *not* slain.

MIK. Bless my heart, my son!

YUM. And your daughter-in-law elected!

KAT. [*seizing* KO-KO] Traitor, you have deceived me!

MIK. Yes, you are entitled to a little explanation, but I think he will give it better whole than in pieces.

KO. Your Majesty, it's like this: It is true that I stated that I had killed Nanki-Poo——

MIK. Yes, with most affecting particulars.

POOH. Merely corroborative detail intended to give artistic verisimilitude to a bald and——

KO. *Will* you refrain from putting in your oar? [*To* MIKADO] It's like this: When your Majesty says, "Let a thing be done," it's as good as done—practically, it *is* done—because your Majesty's will is law. Your Majesty says, "Kill a gentleman," and a gentleman is told off to be killed. Consequently, that gentleman is as good as dead—practically, he *is* dead—and if he is dead, why not say so?

MIK. I see. Nothing could possibly be more satisfactory!

Finale

PITTI. For he's gone and married Yum-Yum—
ALL Yum-Yum!
PITTI. Your anger pray bury,
For all will be merry,
I think you had better succumb—
ALL Cumb—cumb!
PITTI. And join our expressions of glee!
KO. On this subject I pray you be dumb—
ALL Dumb—dumb!
KO. Your notions, though many,
Are not worth a penny,
The word for your guidance is "Mum"—
ALL Mum—Mum!
KO. You've a very good bargain in me.
ALL On this subject we pray you be dumb—
Dumb—dumb!
We think you had better succumb—
Cumb—cumb!
You'll find there are many
Who'll wed for a penny,
There are lots of good fish in the sea.
YUM. and NANK. The threatened cloud has passed away,
And brightly shines the dawning day;
What though the night may come too soon,
We've years and years of afternoon!
ALL Then let the throng
Our joy advance,
With laughing song
And merry dance,
With joyous shout and ringing cheer,
Inaugurate our new career!
Then let the throng, etc.

CURTAIN

RUDDIGORE

OR

THE WITCH'S CURSE

DRAMATIS PERSONÆ

MORTALS

SIR RUTHVEN MURGATROYD [*disguised as Robin Oakapple, a Young Farmer*]

RICHARD DAUNTLESS [*his Foster-Brother—a Man-o'-war's-man*]

SIR DESPARD MURGATROYD, OF RUDDIGORE [*a Wicked Baronet*]

OLD ADAM GOODHEART [*Robin's Faithful Servant*]

ROSE MAYBUD [*a Village Maiden*]

MAD MARGARET

DAME HANNAH [*Rose's Aunt*]

ZORAH, RUTH [*Professional Bridesmaids*]

GHOSTS

SIR RUPERT MURGATROYD [*the First Baronet*]

SIR JASPER MURGATROYD [*the Third Baronet*]

SIR LIONEL MURGATROYD [*the Sixth Baronet*]

SIR CONRAD MURGATROYD [*the Twelfth Baronet*]

SIR DESMOND MURGATROYD [*the Sixteenth Baronet*]

SIR GILBERT MURGATROYD [*the Eighteenth Baronet*]

SIR MERVYN MURGATROYD [*the Twentieth Baronet*]

AND

SIR RODERIC MURGATROYD [*the Twenty-first Baronet*]

Chorus of Officers, Ancestors, Professional Bridesmaids, and Villagers

ACT I

THE FISHING VILLAGE OF REDERRING, IN CORNWALL

ACT II

THE PICTURE GALLERY IN RUDDIGORE CASTLE

TIME

EARLY IN THE 19TH CENTURY

First produced at the Savoy Theatre on January 22, 1887

RUDDIGORE

OR

THE WITCH'S CURSE

ACT I

SCENE.—*The fishing village of Rederring (in Cornwall).* ROSE MAYBUD'S *cottage is seen* L.

Enter Chorus of Bridesmaids. They range themselves in front of ROSE'S *cottage.*

Chorus of Bridesmaids

Fair is Rose as the bright May-day;
  Soft is Rose as the warm west-wind;
Sweet is Rose as the new-mown hay—
  Rose is the queen of maiden-kind!
    Rose, all glowing
      With virgin blushes, say—
    Is anybody going
      To marry you to-day?

Solo—ZORAH

Every day, as the days roll on,
Bridesmaids' garb we gaily don,
Sure that a maid so fairly famed
Can't long remain unclaimed.
Hour by hour and day by day,
Several months have passed away,
Though she's the fairest flower that blows,
No one has married Rose!

Chorus

Rose, all glowing
  With virgin blushes, say—
Is anybody going
  To marry you to-day?

Enter DAME HANNAH, *from cottage*

HAN. Nay, gentle maidens, you sing well but vainly, for Rose is still heart-free, and looks but coldly upon her many suitors.

ZOR. It's very disappointing. Every young man in the village is in love with her, but they are appalled by her beauty and modesty, and won't declare themselves; so, until she makes her own choice, there's no chance for anybody else.

RUTH This is, perhaps, the only village in the world that possesses an endowed corps of professional bridesmaids who are bound to be on duty every day from ten to four—and it is at least six months since our services were required. The pious charity by which we exist is practically wasted!

ZOR. We shall be disendowed—that will be the end of it! Dame Hannah—you're a nice old person—*you* could marry if you liked. There's old Adam—Robin's faithful servant—he loves you with all the frenzy of a boy of fourteen.

HAN. Nay—that may never be, for I am pledged!

ALL To whom?

HAN. To an eternal maidenhood! Many years ago I was betrothed to a god-like youth who woo'd me under an assumed name. But on the very day upon which our wedding was to have been celebrated, I discovered that he was no other than Sir Roderic Murgatroyd, one of the bad Baronets of Ruddigore, and the uncle of the man who now bears that title. As a son of that accursed race he was no husband for an honest girl, so, madly as I loved him, I left him then and there. He died but ten years since, but I never saw him again.

ZOR. But why should you not marry a bad Baronet of Ruddigore?

RUTH All baronets are bad; but was he worse than other baronets?

HAN. My child, he was accursed.

ZOR. But who cursed him? Not you, I trust!

HAN. The curse is on all his line and has been, ever since the time of Sir Rupert, the first Baronet. Listen, and you shall hear the legend:

Legend—HANNAH

Sir Rupert Murgatroyd
  His leisure and his riches
He ruthlessly employed
  In persecuting witches.
With fear he'd make them quake—
He'd duck them in his lake—
    He'd break their bones
    With sticks and stones,
And burn them at the stake!

CHORUS
This sport he much enjoyed,
Did Rupert Murgatroyd—

No sense of shame
Or pity came
To Rupert Murgatroyd!

Once, on the village green,
A palsied hag he roasted,
And what took place, I ween,
Shook his composure boasted;
For, as the torture grim
Seized on each withered limb,
The writhing dame
'Mid fire and flame
Yelled forth this curse on him:

"Each lord of Ruddigore,
Despite his best endeavour,
Shall do one crime, or more,
Once, every day, for ever!
This doom he can't defy,
However he may try,
For should he stay
His hand, that day
In torture he shall die!"

The prophecy came true:
Each heir who held the title
Had, every day, to do
Some crime of import vital;
Until, with guilt o'erplied,
"I'll sin no more!" he cried,
And on the day
He said that say,
In agony he died!

CHORUS And thus, with sinning cloyed,
Has died each Murgatroyd,
And so shall fall,
Both one and all,
Each coming Murgatroyd!

[*Exeunt Chorus of Bridesmaids.*

Enter ROSE MAYBUD *from cottage, with small basket on her arm*

HAN. Whither away, dear Rose? On some errand of charity, as is thy wont?

ROSE A few gifts, dear aunt, for deserving villagers. Lo, here is some peppermint rock for old gaffer Gadderby, a set of false teeth for pretty little Ruth Rowbottom, and a pound of snuff for the poor orphan girl on the hill.

HAN. Ah, Rose, pity that so much goodness should not help to make some gallant youth happy for life! Rose, why dost thou harden that little heart of thine? Is there none hereaway whom thou couldst love?

ROSE And if there were such an one, verily it would ill become me to tell him so.

HAN. Nay, dear one, where true love is, there is little need of prim formality.

ROSE Hush, dear aunt, for thy words pain me sorely. Hung in a plated dish-cover to the knocker of the work-house door, with naught that I could call mine own, save a change of baby-linen and a book of etiquette, little wonder if I have always regarded that work as a voice from a parent's tomb. This hallowed volume [*producing a book of etiquette*], composed, if I may believe the title-page, by no less an authority than the wife of a Lord Mayor, has been, through life, my guide and monitor. By its solemn precepts I have learnt to test the moral worth of all who approach me. The man who bites his bread, or eats peas with a knife, I look upon as a lost creature, and he who has not acquired the proper way of entering and leaving a room is the object of my pitying horror. There are those in this village who bite their nails, dear aunt, and nearly all are wont to use their pocket combs in public places. In truth I could pursue this painful theme much further, but behold, I have said enough.

HAN. But is there not one among them who is faultless, in thine eyes? For example—young Robin. He combines the manners of a Marquis with the morals of a Methodist. Couldst thou not love *him?*

ROSE And even if I could, how should I confess it unto him? For lo, he is shy, and sayeth naught!

Ballad—ROSE

If somebody there chanced to be
Who loved me in a manner true,
My heart would point him out to me,
And I would point him out to you.
[*Referring to book*] But here it says of those who point—
Their manners must be out of joint—
You *may* not point—
You *must* not point—
It's manners out of joint, to point!
Had I the love of such as he,
Some quiet spot he'd take me to,
Then he could whisper it to me,
And I could whisper it to you.

[Referring to book] But whispering, I've somewhere met,
Is contrary to etiquette:
Where can it be? [*Searching book*]
Now let me see—[*Finding reference*]
Yes, yes!
It's contrary to etiquette!

[*Showing it to* HANNAH]

If any well-bred youth I knew,
Polite and gentle, neat and trim,
Then I would hint as much to you,
And you could hint as much to him.
[Referring to book] But here it says, in plainest print,
"It's most unladylike to hint"—
You *may* not hint,
You *must* not hint—
It says you mustn't hint, in print!
And if I loved him through and through—
(True love and not a passing whim),
Then I could speak of it to you,
And you could speak of it to him.
[Referring to book] But here I find it doesn't do
To speak until you're spoken to.
Where can it be? [*Searching book*]
Now let me see—[*Finding reference*]
Yes, yes!
"Don't speak until you're spoken to!"

[*Exit* HANNAH.

ROSE Poor aunt! Little did the good soul think, when she breathed the hallowed name of Robin, that he would do even as well as another. But he resembleth all the youths in this village, in that he is unduly bashful in my presence, and lo, it is hard to bring him to the point. But soft, he is here!

[ROSE *is about to go when* ROBIN *enters and calls her.*

ROB. Mistress Rose!
ROSE [*Surprised*] Master Robin!
ROB. I wished to say that—it is fine.
ROSE It is passing fine.
ROB. But we do want rain.
ROSE Aye, sorely! Is that all?
ROB. [*Sighing*] That is all.

Rose Good day, Master Robin!
Rob. Good day, Mistress Rose! [*Both going—both stop*]
Rose } I crave pardon, I——
Rob. } I beg pardon, I——
Rose You were about to say?——
Rob. I would fain consult you——
Rose Truly?
Rob. It is about a friend.
Rose In truth I have a friend myself.
Rob. Indeed? I mean, of course——
Rose And I would fain consult you——
Rob [*Anxiously*] About him?
Rose [*Prudishly*] About *her*.
Rob. [*Relieved*] Let us consult one another.

Duet—Robin and Rose

Rob. I know a youth who loves a little maid—
(Hey, but his face is a sight to see!)
Silent is he, for he's modest and afraid—
(Hey, but he's timid as a youth can be!)

Rose I know a maid who loves a gallant youth,
(Hey, but she sickens as the days go by!)
She cannot tell him all the sad, sad truth—
(Hey, but I think that little maid will die!)

ROB. Poor little man!

ROSE Poor little maid!

ROB. Poor little man!

ROSE Poor little maid!

BOTH Now tell me pray, and tell me true,
What in the world should the {young man / maiden} do?

ROB. He cannot eat and he cannot sleep—
(Hey, but his face is a sight for to see!)
Daily he goes for to wail—for to weep
(Hey, but he's wretched as a youth can be!)

ROSE She's very thin and she's very pale—
(Hey, but she sickens as the days go by!)
Daily she goes for to weep—for to wail—
(Hey, but I think that little maid will die!)

ROB. Poor little maid!

ROSE Poor little man!

ROB. Poor little maid!

ROSE Poor little man!

BOTH Now tell me pray, and tell me true,
What in the world should the {young man / maiden} do?

ROSE If I were the youth I should offer her my name—
(Hey, but her face is a sight for to see!)
ROB. If I were the maid I should fan his honest flame—
(Hey, but he's bashful as a youth can be!)
ROSE If I were the youth I should speak to her to-day—
(Hey, but she sickens as the days go by!)
ROB. If I were the maid I should meet the lad half way—
(For I really do believe that timid youth will die!)

ROSE Poor little man!

ROB. Poor little maid!

ROSE Poor little man!

ROB. Poor little maid!

BOTH I thank you, {miss, / sir,} for your counsel true;
I'll tell that {youth / maid} what {he / she} ought to do!

[*Exit* ROSE.

ROB. Poor child! I sometimes think that if she wasn't quite so particular I might venture—but no, no—even then I should be unworthy of her!

He sits desponding. Enter OLD ADAM

ADAM My kind master is sad! Dear Sir Ruthven Murgatroyd——

ROB. Hush! As you love me, breathe not that hated name. Twenty years ago, in horror at the prospect of inheriting that hideous title, and with it the ban that compels all who succeed to the baronetcy to commit at least one deadly crime per day, for life, I fled my home, and concealed myself in this innocent village under the name of Robin Oakapple. My younger brother, Despard, believing me to be dead, succeeded to the title and its attendant curse. For twenty years I have been dead and buried. Don't dig me up now.

ADAM Dear master, it shall be as you wish, for have I not sworn to obey you for ever in all things? Yet, as we are here alone, and as I belong to that particular description of good old man to whom the truth is a refreshing novelty, let me call you by your own right title once more! [ROBIN *assents*] Sir Ruthven Murgatroyd! Baronet! Of Ruddigore! Whew! It's like eight hours at the seaside!

ROB. My poor old friend! Would there were more like you!

ADAM Would there were indeed! But I bring you good tidings. Your foster-brother, Richard, has returned from sea—his ship the *Tom-Tit* rides yonder at anchor, and he himself is even now in this very village!

ROB. My beloved foster-brother? No, no—it cannot be!

ADAM It is even so—and see, he comes this way!

[*Exeunt together.*

Enter Chorus of Bridesmaids

CHORUS

From the briny sea
Comes young Richard, all victorious!
Valorous is he—
His achievements all are glorious

Let the welkin ring
With the news we bring
Sing it—shout it—
Tell about it—
Safe and sound returneth he,
All victorious from the sea!

Enter RICHARD. *The girls welcome him as he greets old acquaintances*

Ballad—RICHARD

I shipped, d'ye see, in a Revenue sloop,
And, off Cape Finistere,
A merchantman we see,
A Frenchman, going free,
So we made for the bold Mounseer,
D'ye see?
We made for the bold Mounseer.
But she proved to be a Frigate—and she up with her ports,
And fires with a thirty-two!
It come uncommon near,
But we answered with a cheer,
Which paralysed the Parley-voo,
D'ye see?
Which paralysed the Parley-voo!

Then our Captain he up and he says, says he,
"That chap we need not fear,—
We can take her, if we like,
She is sartin for to strike,
For she's only a darned Mounseer,
D'ye see?
She's only a darned Mounseer!
But to fight a French fal-lal—it's like hittin' of a gal!
It's a lubberly thing for to do;
For we, with our faults,
Why we're sturdy British salts,
While she's only a Parley-voo,
D'ye see?
While she's only a Parley-voo!"

So we up with our helm, and we scuds before the breeze
As we gives a compassionating cheer;
Froggee answers with a shout
As he sees us go about,
Which was grateful of the poor Mounseer,
D'ye see?
Which was grateful of the poor Mounseer!

And I'll wager in their joy they kissed each other's cheek
(Which is what them furriners do),
And they blessed their lucky stars
We were hardy British tars
Who had pity on a poor Parley-voo,
D'ye see?
Who had pity on a poor Parley-voo!

[Hornpipe]

[*Exeunt* Chorus.

Enter Robin

Rob. Richard!

Rich. Robin!

Rob. My beloved foster-brother, and very dearest friend, welcome home again after ten long years at sea! It is such deeds as yours that cause our flag to be loved and dreaded throughout the civilized world!

Rich. Why, lord love ye, Rob, that's but a trifle to what we *have* done in the way of sparing life! I believe I may say, without exaggeration, that the marciful little *Tom-Tit* has spared more French frigates than any craft afloat! But 'tain't for a British seaman to brag, so I'll just stow my jawin' tackle and belay. [Robin *sighs*] But 'vast heavin', messmate, what's brought *you* all a-cockbill?

Rob. Alas, Dick, I love Rose Maybud, and love in vain!

Rich. *You* love in vain? Come, that's too good! Why, you're a fine strapping muscular young fellow—tall and strong as a to'-gall'n'-m'st—taut as a forestay—aye, and a barrowknight to boot, if all had their rights!

ROB. Hush, Richard—not a word about my true rank, which none here suspect. Yes, I know well enough that few men are better calculated to win a woman's heart than I. I'm a fine fellow, Dick, and worthy any woman's love—happy the girl who gets me, say I. But I'm timid, Dick; shy—nervous—modest—retiring—diffident—and I cannot tell her, Dick, I cannot tell her! Ah, you've no idea what a poor opinion I have of myself, and how little I deserve it.

RICH. Robin, do you call to mind how, years ago, we swore that, come what might, we would always act upon our hearts' dictates?

ROB. Aye, Dick, and I've always kept that oath. In doubt, difficulty, and danger I've always asked my heart what I should do, and it has never failed me.

RICH. Right! Let your heart be your compass, with a clear conscience for your binnacle light, and you'll sail ten knots on a bowline, clear of shoals, rocks, and quicksands! Well, now, what does my heart say in this here difficult situation? Why, it says, "Dick," it says—(it calls me Dick acos it's known me from a babby)—"Dick," it says, "*you* ain't shy—*you* ain't modest—speak you up for him as is!" Robin, my lad, just you lay me alongside, and when she's becalmed under my lee, I'll spin her a yarn that shall sarve to fish you two together for life!

ROB. Will you do this thing for me? Can you, do you think? Yes [*feeling his pulse*]. There's no false modesty about *you*. Your—what I would call bumptious self-assertiveness (I mean the expression in its complimentary sense) has already made you a bo's'n's mate, and it will make an admiral of you in time, if you work it properly, you dear, incompetent old impostor! My dear fellow, I'd give my right arm for one tenth of your modest assurance!

Song—ROBIN

My boy, you may take it from me,
That of all the afflictions accurst
With which a man's saddled
And hampered and addled,
A diffident nature's the worst.
Though clever as clever can be—
A Crichton of early romance—
You must stir it and stump it,
And blow your own trumpet,
Or, trust me, you haven't a chance!

If you wish in the world to advance,
Your merits you're bound to enhance,
You must stir it and stump it,
And blow your own trumpet,
Or, trust me, you haven't a chance!

Now take, for example, *my* case:
I've a bright intellectual brain—
In all London city
There's no one so witty—
I've thought so again and again.
I've a highly intelligent face—
My features cannot be denied—
But, whatever I try, sir,
I fail in—and why, sir?
I'm modesty personified!

If you wish in the world to advance, etc.

As a poet, I'm tender and quaint—
I've passion and fervour and grace—
From Ovid and Horace
To Swinburne and Morris,
They all of them take a back place.
Then I sing and I play and I paint:
Though none are accomplished as I,
To say so were treason:
You ask me the reason?
I'm diffident, modest, and shy!

If you wish in the world to advance, etc.

[*Exit* ROBIN.

RICH. [*looking after him*] Ah, it's a thousand pities he's such a poor opinion of himself, for a finer fellow don't walk! Well, I'll do my best for him. "Plead for him as though it was for your own father"—that's what my heart's a-remarkin' to me just now. But here she comes! Steady! Steady it is! [*Enter* ROSE—*he is much struck by her*] By the Port Admiral, but she's a tight little craft! Come, come, she's not for you, Dick, and yet—she's fit to marry Lord Nelson! By the Flag of Old England, I can't look at her unmoved.

Rose Sir, you are agitated——

Rich. Aye, aye, my lass, well said! I am agitated, true enough!—took flat aback, my girl; but 'tis naught—'twill pass. [*Aside*] This here heart of mine's a-dictatin' to me like anythink. Question is, Have I a right to disregard its promptings?

Rose Can I do aught to relieve thine anguish, for it seemeth to me that thou art in sore trouble? This apple—[*offering a damaged apple*]

Rich. [*looking at it and returning it*] No, my lass, 'tain't that: I'm—I'm took flat aback—I never see anything like you in all my born days. Parbuckle me, if you ain't the loveliest gal I've ever set eyes on. There—I can't say fairer than that, can I?

Rose No. [*Aside*] The question is, Is it meet that an utter stranger should thus express himself? [*Refers to book*] Yes—"Always speak the truth."

Rich. I'd no thoughts of sayin' this here to you on my own account, for, truth to tell, I was chartered by another; but when I see you my heart it up and it says, says it, "This is the very lass for *you*, Dick"—"speak up to her, Dick," it says—it calls me Dick acos we was at school together—"tell her all, Dick," it says, "never sail under false colours—it's mean!" *That's* what my heart tells me to say, and in my rough, common-sailor fashion, I've said it, and I'm a-waiting for your reply. I'm a-tremblin', miss. Lookye here—[*holding out his hand*] That's narvousness!

Rose [*aside*] Now, how should a maiden deal with such an one? [*Consults book*] "Keep no one in unnecessary suspense." [*Aloud*] Behold I will not keep you in unnecessary suspense. [*Refers to book*] "In accepting an offer of marriage, do so with apparent hesitation." [*Aloud*] I take you, but with a certain show of reluctance. [*Refers to book*] "Avoid any appearance of eagerness." [*Aloud*] Though you will bear in mind that I am far from anxious to do so. [*Refers to book*] "A little show of emotion will not be misplaced!" [*Aloud*] Pardon this tear! [*Wipes her eye*]

Rich. Rose, you've made me the happiest blue-jacket in England! I wouldn't change places with the Admiral of the Fleet, no matter who he's a-huggin' of at this present moment! But, axin' your pardon, miss [*wiping his lips with his hand*], might I be permitted to salute the flag I'm goin' to sail under?

Rose [*referring to book*] "An engaged young lady should not permit too many familiarities." [*Aloud*] Once! [Richard *kisses her.*]

Duet—Richard and Rose

Rich. The battle's roar is over,
O my love!

Embrace thy tender lover,
O my love!
From tempests' welter,
From war's alarms,
O give me shelter
Within those arms!
Thy smile alluring,
All heart-ache curing,
Gives peace enduring,
O my love!

Rose

If heart both true and tender,
O my love!
A life-love can engender,
O my love!
A truce to sighing
And tears of brine,
For joy undying
Shall aye be mine,
And thou and I, love,
Shall live and die, love,
Without a sigh, love–
My own, my love!

Enter Robin, *with Chorus of Bridesmaids*

Chorus

If well his suit has sped,
Oh, may they soon be wed!
Oh, tell us, tell us, pray,
What doth the maiden say?
In singing are we justified,
Hail the Bridegroom–hail the Bride!
Let the nuptial knot be tied:
In fair phrases,
Hymn their praises,
Hail the Bridegroom–hail the Bride?

Rob. Well–what news? Have you spoken to her?
Rich. Aye, my lad, I have–so to speak–spoke her.
Rob. And she refuses?
Rich. Why, no, I can't truly say she do.
Rob. Then she accepts! My darling! [*Embraces her*]

BRIDESMAIDS

Hail the Bridegroom—hail the Bride! etc.

ROSE [*aside, referring to her book*] Now, what should a maiden do when she is embraced by the wrong gentleman?

RICH. Belay, my lad, belay. You don't understand.

ROSE Oh, sir, belay, I beseech you!

RICH. You see, it's like this: she accepts—but it's *me!*

ROB. You! [RICHARD *embraces* ROSE.]

BRIDESMAIDS

Hail the Bridegroom—hail the Bride!
When the nuptial knot is tied——

ROB. [*interrupting angrily*] Hold your tongues, will you! Now then, what does this mean?

RICH. My poor lad, my heart grieves for thee, but it's like this: the moment I see her, and just as I was a-goin' to mention your name, my heart it up and it says, says it—"Dick, you've fell in love with her yourself," it says; "Be honest and sailor-like—don't skulk under false colours—speak up," it says, "take her, you dog, and with her my blessin'!"

BRIDESMAIDS

Hail the Bridegroom—hail the Bride!——

ROB. Will you be quiet! Go away! [CHORUS *make faces at him and exeunt*] Vulgar girls!

RICH. What could I do? I'm bound to obey my heart's dictates.

ROB. Of course—no doubt. It's quite right—I don't mind—that is, not particularly—only it's—it *is* disappointing, you know.

ROSE [*to* ROBIN] Oh, but, sir, I knew not that thou didst seek me in wedlock, or in very truth I should not have hearkened unto this man, for behold, he is but a lowly mariner, and very poor withal, whereas thou art a tiller of the land, and thou hast fat oxen, and many sheep and swine, a considerable dairy farm and much corn and oil!

RICH. That's true, my lass, but it's done now, ain't it, Rob?

ROSE Still it may be that I should not be happy in thy love. I am passing young and little able to judge. Moreover, as to thy character I know naught!

ROB. Nay, Rose, I'll answer for that. Dick has won thy love fairly. Broken-hearted as I am, I'll stand up for Dick through thick and thin!

RICH. [*with emotion*] Thankye, messmate! that's well said. That's spoken honest. Thankye, Rob! [*Grasps his hand*]

ROSE Yet methinks I have heard that sailors are but worldly men, and little prone to lead serious and thoughtful lives!

ROB. And what then? Admit that Dick is *not* a steady character, and that when he's excited he uses language that would make your hair curl. Grant that—he does. It's the truth, and I'm not going to deny it. But look at his *good* qualities. He's as nimble as a pony, and his hornpipe is the talk of the Fleet!

RICH. Thankye, Rob! That's well spoken. Thankye, Rob!

ROSE But it may be that he drinketh strong waters which do bemuse a man, and make him even as the wild beasts of the desert!

ROB. Well, suppose he does, and I don't say he don't, for rum's his bane, and ever has been. He *does* drink—I won't deny it. But what of that? Look at his arms—tattooed to the shoulder! [RICH. *rolls up his sleeves*] No, no—I won't hear a word against Dick!

ROSE But they say that mariners are but rarely true to those whom they profess to love!

ROB. Granted—granted—and I don't say that Dick isn't as bad as any of 'em. [RICH. *chuckles*] You are, you know you are, you dog! a devil of a fellow—a regular out-and-out Lothario! But what then? You can't have everything, and a better hand at turning-in a dead-eye don't walk a deck! And what an accomplishment *that* is in a family man! No, no—not a word against Dick. I'll stick up for him through thick and thin!

RICH. Thankye, Rob, thankye. You're a true friend. I've acted accordin' to my heart's dictates, and such orders as them no man should disobey.

Ensemble—RICHARD, ROBIN, ROSE

In sailing o'er life's ocean wide
Your heart should be your only guide;
With summer sea and favouring wind,
Yourself in port you'll surely find.

Solo—RICHARD

My heart says, "To this maiden strike—
She's captured you.
She's just the sort of girl you like—
You know you do.
If other man her heart should gain,
I shall resign."
That's what it says to me quite plain,
This heart of mine.

Solo—ROBIN

My heart says, "You've a prosperous lot,
With acres wide;

You mean to settle all you've got
Upon your bride."
It don't pretend to shape my acts
By word or sign;
It merely states these simple facts,
This heart of mine!

Solo—ROSE

Ten minutes since my heart said "white"—
It now says "black."
It then said "left"—it now says "right"—
Hearts often tack.

I must obey its latest strain—
You tell me so. [*To* RICHARD.]
But should it change its mind again,
I'll let you know.

[*Turning from* RICHARD *to* ROBIN, *who embraces her.*]

Ensemble

In sailing o'er life's ocean wide
No doubt the heart should be your guide;
But it is awkward when you find
A heart that does not know its mind!

[*Exeunt* ROBIN *with* ROSE L., *and* RICHARD *weeping*, R.

Enter MAD MARGARET. *She is wildly dressed in picturesque tatters, and is an obvious caricature of theatrical madness.*

Scena—MARGARET

Cheerily carols the lark
Over the cot.
Merrily whistles the clerk
Scratching a blot.
But the lark
And the clerk,
I remark,
Comfort me not!

Over the ripening peach
Buzzes the bee.
Splash on the billowy beach
Tumbles the sea.
But the peach
And the beach
They are each
Nothing to me!
And why?
Who am I?
Daft Madge! Crazy Meg!
Mad Margaret! Poor Peg!
He! he! he! he! he! [*chuckling*]

Mad, I?
Yes, very!
But why?
Mystery!
Don't call!
Whisht! whisht!
No crime–
'Tis only
That I'm
Love–lonely!
That's all!

Ballad

To a garden full of posies
Cometh one to gather flowers,
And he wanders through its bowers
Toying with the wanton roses,
Who, uprising from their beds,
Hold on high their shameless heads
With their pretty lips a-pouting,
Never doubting–never doubting
That for Cytherean posies
He would gather aught but roses!

In a nest of weeds and nettles
Lay a violet, half-hidden,
Hoping that his glance unbidden
Yet might fall upon her petals.
Though she lived alone, apart,
Hope lay nestling at her heart,

But, alas, the cruel awaking
Set her little heart a-breaking,
For he gathered for his posies
Only roses—only roses!

[*Bursts into tears*]

Enter ROSE

ROSE A maiden, and in tears? Can I do aught to soften thy sorrow? This apple—[*offering apple*].

MAR. [*examines it and rejects it*] No! [*Mysteriously*] Tell me, are you mad?

ROSE I? No! That is, I think not.

MAR. That's well! Then you don't love Sir Despard Murgatroyd? All mad girls love him. *I* love him. I'm poor Mad Margaret—Crazy Meg—Poor Peg! He! he! he! he! [*chuckling*]

ROSE Thou lovest the bad Baronet of Ruddigore? Oh, horrible—too horrible!

MAR. You pity me? Then be my mother! The squirrel had a mother, but she drank and the squirrel fled! Hush! They sing a brave song in our parts—it runs somewhat thus: [*Sings*]

"The cat and the dog and the little puppee
Sat down in a—down in a—in a——"

I forget what they sat down in, but so the song goes! Listen—I've come to pinch her!

ROSE Mercy, whom?

MAR. You mean "who."

ROSE Nay! it is the accusative after the verb.

MAR. True. [*Whispers melodramatically*] I have come to pinch Rose Maybud!

ROSE [*aside, alarmed*] Rose Maybud!

MAR. Aye: I love him—he loved me once. But that's all gone, Fisht! He gave me an Italian glance—thus [*business*]—and made me his. He will give *her* an Italian glance, and make *her* his. But it shall not be, for I'll stamp on her—stamp on her—stamp on her! Did you ever kill anybody? No? Why not? Listen—I killed a fly this morning! It buzzed, and I wouldn't have it. So it died—pop! So shall she!

ROSE But, behold, *I* am Rose Maybud, and I would fain not die "pop."

MAR. You are Rose Maybud?

ROSE Yes, sweet Rose Maybud!

MAR. Strange! They told me she was beautiful. And *he* loves *you!* No, no! If I thought that, I would treat you as the auctioneer and land-agent treated the lady-bird—I would rend you asunder!

ROSE Nay, be pacified, for behold I am pledged to another, and lo, we are to be wedded this very day!

MAR. Swear me that! Come to a Commissioner and let me have it on affidavit! *I* once made an affidavit—but it died—it died—it died! But, see, they come—Sir Despard and his evil crew! Hide, hide—they are all mad—quite mad!

ROSE What makes you think that?

MAR. Hush! They sing choruses in public. That's mad enough, I think! Go—hide away, or they will seize you! Hush! Quite softly—quite, quite softly!

[*Exeunt together, on tiptoe*

Enter Chorus of Bucks and Blades, heralded by Chorus of Bridesmaids

Chorus of Bridesmaids

Welcome, gentry,
For your entry
Sets our tender hearts a-beating.
Men of station,
Admiration
Prompts this unaffected greeting.
Hearty greeting offer we!

Chorus of Bucks and Blades

When thoroughly tired
Of being admired
By ladies of gentle degree—degree,
With flattery sated,
High-flown and inflated,
Away from the city we flee—we flee!
From charms intramural
To prettiness rural
The sudden transition
Is simply Elysian,
So come, Amaryllis,
Come, Chloe and Phyllis,
Your slaves, for the moment, are we!

ALL From charms intramural, etc.

Chorus of Bridesmaids

The sons of the tillage
Who dwell in this village

Are people of lowly degree—degree.
Though honest and active,
They're most unattractive,
And awkward as awkward can be—can be.
They're clumsy clodhoppers
With axes and choppers,
And shepherds and ploughmen
And drovers and cowmen
And hedgers and reapers
And carters and keepers,
And never a lover for me!

Bridesmaids

So, welcome, gentry, etc.

Bucks and Blades

When thoroughly tired, etc.

Enter SIR DESPARD MURGATROYD

Song and Chorus—SIR DESPARD

SIR D. Oh, why am I moody and sad?
CHORUS Can't guess!
SIR D. And why am I guiltily mad?
CHORUS Confess!
SIR D. Because I am thoroughly bad!
CHORUS Oh yes—
SIR D. You'll see it at once in my face.
Oh, why am I husky and hoarse?
CHORUS Ah, why?
SIR D. It's the workings of conscience, of course.
CHORUS Fie, fie!
SIR D. And huskiness stands for remorse,
CHORUS Oh my!
SIR D. At least it does so in my case!
When in crime one is fully employed—
CHORUS Like you—
SIR D. Your expression gets warped and destroyed:
CHORUS It do.
SIR D. It's a penalty none can avoid;
CHORUS How true!

SIR D. I once was a nice-looking youth;
But like stone from a strong catapult—
CHORUS [*explaining to each other*] A trice—
SIR D. I rushed at my terrible cult—
CHORUS [*explaining to each other*] That's vice—
SIR D. Observe the unpleasant result!
CHORUS Not nice.
SIR D. Indeed I am telling the truth!
Oh, innocent, happy though poor!
CHORUS That's we—
SIR D. If I had been virtuous, I'm sure—
CHORUS Like me—
SIR D. I should be as nice-looking as you're!
CHORUS May be.
SIR D. You are very nice-looking indeed!
Oh, innocents, listen in time—
CHORUS We *doe*,
SIR D. Avoid an existence of crime—
CHORUS Just so—
SIR D. Or you'll be as ugly as I'm—
CHORUS [*loudly*] No! No!
SIR D. And now, if you please, we'll proceed.

[*All the girls express their horror of* SIR DESPARD. *As he approaches them they fly from him, terror-stricken, leaving him alone on the stage.*

SIR D. Poor children, how they loathe me—me whose hands are certainly steeped in infamy, but whose heart is as the heart of a little child. But what *is* a poor baronet to do, when a whole picture gallery of ancestors step down from their frames and threaten him with an excruciating death if he hesitate to commit his daily crime? But ha! ha! I am even with them! [*Mysteriously*] I get my crime over the first thing in the morning, and then, ha! ha! for the rest of the day I do good—I do good—I do good! [*Melodramatically*] Two days since, I stole a child and built an orphan asylum. Yesterday I robbed a bank and endowed a bishopric. To-day I carry off Rose Maybud and atone with a cathedral! This is what it is to be the sport and toy of a Picture Gallery! But I will be bitterly revenged upon them! I will give them all to the Nation, and nobody shall ever look upon their faces again!

Enter RICHARD

RICH. Ax your honour's pardon, but——
SIR D. Ha! observed! And by a mariner! What would you with me, fellow?

Rich. Your honour, I'm a poor man-o'-war's man, becalmed in the doldrums——

Sir D. I don't know them.

Rich. And I make bold to ax your honour's advice. Does your honour know what it is to have a heart?

Sir D. My honour knows what it is to have a complete apparatus for conducting the circulation of the blood through the veins and arteries of the human body.

Rich. Aye, but has your honour a heart that ups and looks you in the face, and gives you quarter-deck orders that it's life and death to disobey?

Sir D. I have not a heart of that description, but I have a Picture Gallery that presumes to take that liberty.

Rich. Well, your honour, it's like this–Your honour had an elder brother——

Sir D. It had.

Rich. Who should have inherited your title and, with it, its cuss.

Sir D. Aye, but he died. Oh, Ruthven!——

Rich. He didn't.

Sir D. He did *not?*

Rich. He didn't. On the contrary, he lives in this here very village, under the name of Robin Oakapple, and he's a-going to marry Rose Maybud this very day.

Sir D. Ruthven alive, and going to marry Rose Maybud! Can this be possible?

Rich. Now the question I was going to ask your honour is–Ought I to tell your honour this?

Sir D. I don't know. It's a delicate point. I think you ought. Mind, I'm not sure, but I think so.

Rich. That's what my heart says. It says, "Dick," it says (it calls me Dick acos it's entitled to take that liberty), "that there young gal would recoil from him if she knowed what he really were. Ought you to stand off and on, and let this young gal take this false step and never fire a shot across her bows to bring her to? No," it says, "you did *not* ought." And I won't ought, accordin'.

Sir D. Then you really feel yourself at liberty to tell me that my elder brother lives–that I may charge him with his cruel deceit, and transfer to his shoulders the hideous thraldom under which I have laboured for so many years! Free–free at last! Free to live a blameless life, and to die beloved and regretted by all who knew me!

Duet–Sir Despard and Richard

Rich. You understand?
Sir D. I think I do;

With vigour unshaken
This step shall be taken.
It's neatly planned.

RICH. I think so too;
I'll readily bet it
You'll never regret it!

BOTH For duty, duty must be done;
The rule applies to every one,
And painful though that duty be,
To shirk the task were fiddle-de-dee!

SIR D. The bridegroom comes—
RICH. Likewise the bride—
The maidens are very
Elated and merry;
They are her chums.
SIR D. To lash their pride
Were almost a pity,
The pretty committee!

BOTH But duty, duty must be done;
The rule applies to every one,
And painful though that duty be,
To shirk the task were fiddle-de-dee!

[*Exeunt* RICHARD *and* SIR DESPARD.

Enter Chorus of Bridesmaids and Bucks

Chorus of Bridesmaids

Hail the bride of seventeen summers:
In fair phrases
Hymn her praises;
Lift your song on high, all comers.
She rejoices
In your voices.
Smiling summer beams upon her,
Shedding every blessing on her:
Maidens greet her—
Kindly treat her—
You may all be brides some day!

Chorus of Bucks

Hail the bridegroom who advances,
Agitated,
Yet elated.
He's in easy circumstances,
Young and lusty,
True and trusty.

Enter ROBIN, *attended by* RICHARD *and* OLD ADAM, *meeting* ROSE, *attended by* ZORAH *and* DAME HANNAH. ROSE *and* ROBIN *embrace.*

Madrigal

ROSE — When the buds are blossoming,
Smiling welcome to the spring,
Lovers choose a wedding day—
Life is love in merry May!

GIRLS — Spring is green—Fal lal la!
Summer's rose—Fal lal la!

ALL — It is sad when summer goes,
Fal la!

MEN — Autumn's gold—Fal lal la!
Winter's grey—Fal lal la!

ALL — Winter still is far away—
Fal la!

Leaves in autumn fade and fall,
Winter is the end of all.
Spring and summer teem with glee:
Spring and summer, then, for me!
Fal la!

HANNAH In the spring-time seed is sown:
In the summer grass is mown:
In the autumn you may reap:
Winter is the time for sleep.

GIRLS Spring is hope—Fal lal la!
Summer's joy—Fal lal la!
ALL Spring and summer never cloy.
Fal la!

MEN Autumn, toil—Fal lal la!
Winter, rest—Fal lal la!
ALL Winter, after all, is best—
Fal la!

ALL Spring and summer pleasure you,
Autumn, aye, and winter too—
Every season has its cheer,
Life is lovely all the year!
Fal la!

[*Gavotte*]

After Gavotte, enter SIR DESPARD

SIR D. Hold, bride and bridegroom, ere you wed each other,
I claim young Robin as my elder brother!
His rightful title I have long enjoyed:
I claim him as Sir Ruthven Murgatroyd!

ALL O wonder!
ROSE [*wildly*] Deny the falsehood, Robin, as you should,
It is a plot!
ROB. I would, if conscientiously I could,
But I cannot!
ALL Ah, base one!

Solo—ROBIN

As pure and blameless peasant,
I cannot, I regret,
Deny a truth unpleasant,
I am that Baronet!

ALL He is that Baronet!

But when completely rated
Bad Baronet am I,
That I am what he's stated
I'll recklessly deny!

ALL He'll recklessly deny!

ROB. When I'm a bad Bart. I will tell taradiddles!
ALL He'll tell taradiddles when he's a bad Bart.
ROB. I'll play a bad part on the falsest of fiddles.
ALL On very false fiddles he'll play a bad part!
ROB. But until that takes place I must be conscientious—
ALL He'll be conscientious until that takes place.
ROB. Then adieu with good grace to my morals sententious!
ALL To morals sententious adieu with good grace!

ZOR. Who is the wretch who hath betrayed thee?
Let him stand forth!
RICH. [*coming forward*] 'Twas I!
ALL Die, traitor!
RICH. Hold! my conscience made me!
Withhold your wrath!

Solo—RICHARD

Within this breast there beats a heart
Whose voice can't be gainsaid.
It bade me thy true rank impart,
And I at once obeyed.
I knew 'twould blight thy budding fate—
I knew 'twould cause thee anguish great—
But did I therefore hesitate?
No! I at once obeyed!
ALL Acclaim him who, when his true heart
Bade him young Robin's rank impart,
Immediately obeyed!

Solo—ROSE [*addressing* ROBIN]

Farewell!
Thou hadst my heart—
'Twas quickly won!

But now we part—
Thy face I shun!
Farewell!

Go bend the knee
At Vice's shrine,
Of life with me
All hope resign.
Farewell!

[*To* SIR DESPARD] Take me—I am thy bride!

Bridesmaids

Hail the Bridegroom—hail the Bride!
When the nuptial knot is tied;
Every day will bring some joy
That can never, never cloy!

Enter MARGARET, *who listens*

SIR D. Excuse me, I'm a virtuous person now—
ROSE That's why I wed you!
SIR D. And I to Margaret must keep my vow!
MAR. Have I misread you?
Oh, joy! with newly kindled rapture warmed,
I kneel before you! [*Kneels*]
SIR D. I once disliked you; now that I've reformed,
How I adore you! [*They embrace*]

Bridesmaids

Hail the Bridegroom—hail the Bride!
When the nuptial knot is tied;
Every day will bring some joy
That can never, never cloy!

ROSE Richard, of him I love bereft,
Through thy design,
Thou art the only one that's left,
So I am thine! [*They embrace*]

Bridesmaids

Hail the Bridegroom—hail the Bride!
Let the nuptial knot be tied!

Duet—Rose and Richard

Oh, happy the lily
When kissed by the bee;
And, sipping tranquilly,
Quite happy is he;
And happy the filly
That neighs in her pride;
But happier than any,
A pound to a penny,
A lover is, when he
Embraces his bride!

Duet—Sir Despard and Margaret

Oh, happy the flowers
That blossom in June,
And happy the bowers
That gain by the boon,
But happier by hours
The man of descent,
Who, folly regretting,
Is bent on forgetting
His bad baronetting,
And means to repent!

Trio—Hannah, Adam, and Zorah

Oh, happy the blossom
That blooms on the lea,
Likewise the opossum
That sits on a tree,
But when you come across 'em,
They cannot compare
With those who are treading
The dance at a wedding,
While people are spreading
The best of good fare!

Solo—Robin

Oh, wretched the debtor
Who's signing a deed!
And wretched the letter
That no one can read!
But very much better
Their lot it must be

Than that of the person
I'm making this verse on,
Whose head there's a curse on—
Alluding to me!

Repeat ensemble with Chorus

[*Dance*]

[*At the end of the dance* ROBIN *falls senseless on the stage. Picture.*

END OF ACT I

ACT II

SCENE.—*Picture Gallery in Ruddigore Castle. The walls are covered with full-length portraits of the Baronets of Ruddigore from the time of* JAMES I.—*the first being that of* SIR RUPERT, *alluded to in the legend; the last that of the last deceased Baronet,* SIR RODERIC.

Enter ROBIN *and* ADAM *melodramatically. They are greatly altered in appearance,* ROBIN *wearing the haggard aspect of a guilty roué;* ADAM, *that of the wicked steward to such a man.*

Duet—ROBIN and ADAM

ROB. I once was as meek as a new-born lamb,
I'm now Sir Murgatroyd—ha! ha!
With greater precision
(Without the elision),
Sir Ruthven Murgatroyd—ha! ha!

ADAM And I, who was once his *valley-de-sham*,
As steward I'm now employed—ha! ha!
The dickens may take him—
I'll never forsake him!
As steward I'm now employed—ha! ha!

BOTH How dreadful when an innocent heart
Becomes, perforce, a bad young Bart.,
And still more hard on old Adam,
His former faithful *valley-de-sham!*

ROB. This is a painful state of things, old Adam!

ADAM Painful, indeed! Ah, my poor master, when I swore that, come what would, I would serve you in all things for ever, I little thought to what a pass it would bring me! The confidential adviser to the greatest villain unhung! Now, sir, to business. What crime do you propose to commit to-day?

ROB. How should I know? As my confidential adviser, it's your duty to suggest something.

ADAM Sir, I loathe the life you are leading, but a good old man's oath is paramount, and I obey. Richard Dauntless is here with pretty Rose Maybud, to ask your consent to their marriage. Poison their beer.

ROB. No—not that—I know I'm a bad Bart., but I'm not as bad a Bart. as all that.

ADAM Well, there you are, you see! It's no use my making suggestions if you don't adopt them.

ROB. [*melodramatically*] How would it be, do you think, were I to lure him here with cunning wile—bind him with good stout rope to yonder post—and then, by making hideous faces at him, curdle the heart-blood in his arteries, and freeze the very marrow in his bones? How say you, Adam, is not the scheme well planned?

ADAM It would be simply rude—nothing more. But soft—they come!

ADAM *and* ROBIN *retire up as* RICHARD *and* ROSE *enter, preceded by Chorus of Bridesmaids*

Duet—RICHARD and ROSE

RICH.
Happily coupled are we,
You see—
I am a jolly Jack Tar,
My star,
And you are the fairest,
The richest and rarest
Of innocent lasses you are,
By far—
Of innocent lasses you are!
Fanned by a favouring gale,
You'll sail
Over life's treacherous sea
With me,
And as for bad weather,
We'll brave it together,
And you shall creep under my lee,
My wee!
And you shall creep under my lee!
For you are such a smart little craft—
Such a neat little, sweet little craft,

Such a bright little, tight little,
Slight little, light little,
Trim little, prim little craft!

CHORUS — For she is such, etc.

ROSE — My hopes will be blighted, I fear,
My dear;
In a month you'll be going to sea,
Quite free,
And all of my wishes
You'll throw to the fishes
As though they were never to be;
Poor me!
As though they were never to be.
And I shall be left all alone
To moan,
And weep at your cruel deceit,
Complete;
While you'll be asserting
Your freedom by flirting
With every woman you meet,
You cheat—
With every woman you meet!

Though I am such a smart little craft—
Such a neat little, sweet little craft,
Such a bright little, tight little,
Slight little, light little,
Trim little, prim little craft!

CHORUS — Though she is such, etc.

Enter ROBIN

ROB. Soho! pretty one—in my power at last, eh? Know ye not that I have those within my call who, at my lightest bidding, would immure ye in an uncomfortable dungeon? [*Calling*] What ho! within there!

RICH. Hold—we are prepared for this [*producing a Union Jack*]. Here is a flag that none dare defy [*all kneel*], and while this glorious rag floats over Rose Maybud's head, the man does not live who would dare to lay unlicensed hand upon her!

ROB. Foiled—and by a Union Jack! But a time will come, and then——

ROSE Nay, let me plead with him. [*To* ROBIN] Sir Ruthven, have pity. In my book of etiquette the case of a maiden about to be wedded to one who unexpectedly turns out to be a baronet with a curse on him is not considered. Time was when you loved me madly. Prove that this was no selfish love by according your consent to my marriage with one who, if he be not you yourself, is the next best thing—your dearest friend!

Ballad—Rose

In bygone days I had thy love—
Thou hadst my heart.
But Fate, all human vows above,
Our lives did part!
By the old love thou hadst for me—
By the fond heart that beat for thee—
By joys that never now can be,
Grant thou my prayer!

All [*kneeling*] Grant thou her prayer!

Rob. [*recit.*] Take her—I yield!

All [*recit.*] Oh, rapture!

Chorus Away to the parson we go—
Say we're solicitous very
That he will turn two into one—
Singing hey, derry down derry!

Rich. For she *is* such a smart little craft—
Rose Such a neat little, sweet little craft—
Rich. Such a bright little—
Rose Tight little—
Rich. Slight little—
Rose Light little—
Both Trim little, slim little craft!

Chorus For she *is* such a smart little craft, etc.

[*Exeunt all but* Robin.

Rob. For a week I have fulfilled my accursed doom! I have duly committed a crime a day! Not a great crime, I trust, but still, in the eyes of one as strictly regulated as I used to be, a crime. But will my ghostly ancestors be satisfied with what I have done, or will they regard it as an unworthy subterfuge? [*Addressing Pictures*] Oh, my forefathers, wallowers in blood, there came at last a day when, sick of crime, you, each and every, vowed to sin no more, and so, in agony, called welcome Death to free you from your cloying guiltiness. Let the sweet psalm of that repentant hour soften your long-dead hearts, and tune your souls to mercy on your poor posterity! [*Kneeling*]

[*The stage darkens for a moment. It becomes light again, and the Pictures are seen to have become animated.*

Chorus of Family Portraits

Painted emblems of a race,
All accurst in days of yore,
Each from his accustomed place
Steps into the world once more.

[*The Pictures step from their frames and march round the stage.*

Baronet of Ruddigore,
Last of our accursèd line,
Down upon the oaken floor—
Down upon those knees of thine.

Coward, poltroon, shaker, squeamer,
Blockhead, sluggard, dullard, dreamer,
Shirker, shuffler, crawler, creeper,
Sniffler, snuffler, wailer, weeper,
Earthworm, maggot, tadpole, weevil!
Set upon thy course of evil,
Lest the King of Spectre-Land
Set on thee his grisly hand!

[*The Spectre of* Sir Roderic *descends from his frame.*

Sir Rod. Beware! beware! beware!
Rob. Gaunt vision, who art thou
That thus, with icy glare
And stern relentless brow,
Appearest, who knows how?

Sir Rod. I am the spectre of the late
Sir Roderic Murgatroyd,
Who comes to warn thee that thy fate
Thou canst not now avoid.

Rob. Alas, poor ghost!
Sir Rod. The pity you
Express for nothing goes:
We spectres are a jollier crew
Than you, perhaps, suppose!
Chorus We spectres are a jollier crew
Than you, perhaps, suppose!

Song—Sir Roderic

When the night wind howls in the chimney cowls, and the bat in the moonlight flies,
And inky clouds, like funeral shrouds, sail over the midnight skies—
When the footpads quail at the night-bird's wail, and black dogs bay at the moon,
Then is the spectre's holiday—then is the ghosts' high-noon!

Chorus Ha! ha!
Then is the ghosts' high-noon!

As the sob of the breeze sweeps over the trees, and the mists lie low on the fen,
From grey tomb-stones are gathered the bones that once were women and men,
And away they go, with a mop and a mow, to the revel that ends too soon,
For cockcrow limits our holiday—the dead of the night's high-noon!

Chorus Ha! ha!
The dead of the night's high-noon!

And then each ghost with his ladye-toast to their churchyard beds takes flight,
With a kiss, perhaps, on her lantern chaps, and a grisly grim "good-night";

Till the welcome knell of the midnight bell rings forth its jolliest tune,
And ushers in our next high holiday—the dead of the night's high-noon!

CHORUS Ha! ha!
The dead of the night's high-noon!

ROB. I recognize you now—you are the picture that hangs at the end of the gallery.

SIR ROD. In a bad light. I am.

ROB. Are you considered a good likeness?

SIR ROD. Pretty well. Flattering.

ROB. Because as a work of art you are poor.

SIR ROD. I am crude in colour, but I have only been painted ten years. In a couple of centuries I shall be an Old Master, and then you will be sorry you spoke lightly of me.

ROB. And may I ask why you have left your frames?

SIR ROD. It is our duty to see that our successors commit their daily crimes in a conscientious and workmanlike fashion. It is our duty to remind you that you are evading the conditions under which you are permitted to exist.

ROB. Really, I don't know what you'd have. I've only been a bad baronet a week, and I've committed a crime punctually every day.

SIR ROD. Let us inquire into this. Monday?

ROB. Monday was a Bank Holiday.

SIR ROD. True. Tuesday?

ROB. On Tuesday I made a false income-tax return.

ALL. Ha! ha!

1ST GHOST That's nothing.

2ND GHOST Nothing at all.

3RD GHOST Everybody does that.

4TH GHOST It's expected of you.

SIR ROD. Wednesday?

ROB. [*melodramatically*] On Wednesday I forged a will.

SIR ROD. Whose will?

ROB. My own.

SIR ROD. My good sir, you can't forge your own will!

ROB. Can't I, though! I like that! I *did!* Besides, if a man can't forge his own will, whose will can he forge?

1ST GHOST There's something in that.

2ND GHOST Yes, it seems reasonable.

3RD GHOST At first sight it does.

4TH GHOST Fallacy somewhere, I fancy!

ROB. A man can do what he likes with his own?

SIR ROD. I suppose he can.

ROB. Well, then, he can forge his own will, stoopid! On Thursday I shot a fox.

1ST GHOST Hear, hear!

SIR ROD. That's better [*addressing Ghosts*]. Pass the fox, I think? [*They assent*] Yes, pass the fox. Friday?

ROB. On Friday I forged a cheque.

SIR ROD. Whose cheque?

ROB. Old Adam's.

SIR ROD. But Old Adam hasn't a banker.

ROB. I didn't say I forged his banker—I said I forged his cheque. On Saturday I disinherited my only son.

SIR ROD. But you haven't got a son.

ROB. No—not yet. I disinherited him in advance, to save time. You see—by this arrangement—he'll be born ready disinherited.

SIR ROD. I see. But I don't think you can do that.

ROB. My good sir, if I can't disinherit my own unborn son, whose unborn son can I disinherit?

SIR ROD. Humph! These arguments sound very well, but I can't help thinking that, if they were reduced to syllogistic form, they wouldn't hold water. Now quite understand us. We are foggy, but we don't permit our fogginess to be presumed upon. Unless you undertake to—well, suppose we say, carry off a lady? [*Addressing Ghosts*] Those who are in favour of his carrying off a lady? [*All hold up their hands except a Bishop*] Those of the contrary opinion? [*Bishop holds up his hands*] Oh, you're never satisfied! Yes, unless you undertake to carry off a lady at once—I don't care what lady—any lady—choose your lady—you perish in inconceivable agonies.

ROB. Carry off a lady? Certainly not, on any account. I've the greatest respect for ladies, and I wouldn't do anything of the kind for worlds! No, no. I'm not that kind of baronet, I assure you! If that's all you've got to say, you'd better go back to your frames.

SIR ROD. Very good—then let the agonies commence.

[*Ghosts make passes.* ROBIN *begins to writhe in agony.*

ROB. Oh! Oh! Don't do that! I can't stand it!

SIR ROD. Painful, isn't it? It gets worse by degrees.

ROB. Oh—Oh! Stop a bit! Stop it, will you? I want to speak.

[SIR RODERIC *makes signs to Ghosts, who resume their attitudes.*

SIR ROD. Better?

ROB. Yes—better now! Whew!

SIR ROD. Well, do you consent?

ROB. But it's such an ungentlemanly thing to do!

SIR ROD. As you please. [*To Ghosts*] Carry on!

ROB. Stop—I can't stand it! I agree! I promise! It shall be done!

SIR ROD. To-day?

ROB. To-day!

SIR ROD. At once?

ROB. At once! I retract! I apologize! I had no idea it was anything like that!

Chorus

He yields! He answers to our call!
We do not ask for more.
A sturdy fellow, after all,
This latest Ruddigore!
All perish in unheard-of woe
Who dare our wills defy;
We want your pardon, ere we go.
For having agonized you so—
So pardon us—
So pardon us—
So pardon us—
Or die!

ROB. I pardon you!
I pardon you!

ALL He pardons us—
Hurrah!

[*The Ghosts return to their frames.*

CHORUS Painted emblems of a race,
All accurst in days of yore,
Each to his accustomed place
Steps unwillingly once more!

[*By this time the Ghosts have changed to pictures again.* ROBIN *is overcome by emotion.*

Enter ADAM

ADAM My poor master, you are not well——

ROB. Gideon Crawle, it won't do—I've seen 'em—all my ancestors—

they're just gone. They say that I must do something desperate at once, or perish in horrible agonies. Go—go to yonder village—carry off a maiden—bring her here at once—any one—I don't care which.

ADAM. But——

ROB. Not a word, but obey! Fly!

[*Exit* ADAM.

Recitative and Song—ROBIN

Away, Remorse!
Compunction, hence!
Go, Moral Force!
Go, Penitence!
To Virtue's plea
A long farewell—
Propriety,
I ring your knell!
Come, guiltiness of deadliest hue!
Come, desperate deeds of derring-do!

Henceforth all the crimes that I find in the *Times*,
I've promised to perpetrate daily;
To-morrow I start, with a petrified heart,
On a regular course of Old Bailey.
There's confidence tricking, bad coin, pocket-picking,
And several other disgraces—
There's postage-stamp prigging, and then, thimble-rigging,
The three-card delusion at races!
Oh! a baronet's rank is exceedingly nice,
But the title's uncommonly dear at the price!

Ye well-to-do squires, who live in the shires,
Where petty distinctions are vital,
Who found Athenæums and local museums,
With views to a baronet's title—
Ye butchers and bakers and candlestick makers
Who sneer at all things that are tradey—
Whose middle-class lives are embarrassed by wives
Who long to parade as "My Lady",
Oh! allow me to offer a word of advice,
The title's uncommonly dear at the price!

Ye supple M.P.'s who go down on your knees,
Your precious identity sinking,

And vote black or white as your leaders indite
    (Which saves you the trouble of thinking),
For your country's good fame, her repute, or her shame,
    You don't care the snuff of a candle—
But you're paid for your game when you're told that your name
    Will be graced by a baronet's handle—
Oh! allow me to give *you* a word of advice—
The title's uncommonly dear at the price!

[*Exit* ROBIN.

Enter DESPARD *and* MARGARET. *They are both dressed in sober black of formal cut, and present a strong contrast to their appearance in Act I.*

Duet

DES. I once was a very abandoned person—
MAR. Making the most of evil chances.
DES. Nobody could conceive a worse 'un—
MAR. Even in all the old romances.
DES. I blush for my wild extravagances,
    But be so kind
    To bear in mind,
MAR. We were the victims of circumstances!

[*Dance*]

That is one of our blameless dances.

MAR. I was once an exceedingly odd young lady—
DES. Suffering much from spleen and vapours.
MAR. Clergymen thought my conduct shady—
DES. She didn't spend much upon linen-drapers.
MAR. It certainly entertained the gapers.
    My ways were strange
    Beyond all range—
DES. Paragraphs got into all the papers.

[*Dance*]

DES. We only cut respectable capers.

DES. I've given up all my wild proceedings.
MAR. My taste for a wandering life is waning.
DES. Now I'm a dab at penny readings.
MAR. They are not remarkably entertaining.
DES. A moderate livelihood we're gaining.

MAR. In fact we rule
A National School.
DES. The duties are dull, but I'm not complaining.
[*Dance*]

This sort of thing takes a deal of training!

DES. We have been married a week.

MAR. One happy, happy week!

DES. Our new life—

MAR. Is delightful indeed!

DES. So calm!

MAR. So unimpassioned! [*Wildly*] Master, all this I owe to you! See, I am no longer wild and untidy. My hair is combed. My face is washed. My boots fit!

DES. Margaret, don't. Pray restrain yourself. Remember, you are now a district visitor.

MAR. A gentle district visitor!

DES. You are orderly, methodical, neat; you have your emotions well under control.

MAR. I have. [*Wildly*] Master, when I think of all you have done for me, I fall at your feet. I embrace your ankles. I hug your knees! [*Doing so*]

DES. Hush. This is not well. This is calculated to provoke remark. Be composed, I beg!

MAR. Ah! you are angry with poor little Mad Margaret!

DES. No, not angry; but a district visitor should learn to eschew melodrama. Visit the poor, by all means, and give them tea and barley-water, but don't do it as if you were administering a bowl of deadly nightshade. It upsets them. Then when you nurse sick people, and find them not as well as could be expected, why go into hysterics?

MAR. Why not?

DES. Because it's too jumpy for a sick-room.

MAR. How strange! Oh, Master! Master!—how shall I express the all-absorbing gratitude that—[*About to throw herself at his feet*]

DES. Now! [*Warningly*]

MAR. Yes, I know, dear—it shan't occur again. [*He is seated—she sits on the ground by him*] Shall I tell you one of poor Mad Margaret's odd thoughts? Well, then, when I am lying awake at night, and the pale moonlight streams through the latticed casement, strange fancies crowd upon my poor mad brain, and I sometimes think that if we could hit upon some word for you to use whenever I am about to relapse—some word that teems with hidden meaning—like "Basingstoke"—it might recall me to my saner self. For, after all, I am only Mad Margaret! Daft Meg! Poor Meg! He! he! he!

DES. Poor child, she wanders! But soft—some one comes—Margaret—

pray recollect yourself—Basingstoke, I beg! Margaret, if you don't Basingstoke at once, I shall be seriously angry.

MAR. [*recovering herself*] Basingstoke it is!

DES. Then make it so.

Enter ROBIN. *He starts on seeing them.*

ROB. Despard! And his young wife! This visit is unexpected.

MAR. Shall I fly at him? Shall I tear him limb from limb? Shall I rend him asunder? Say but the word and——

DES. Basingstoke!

MAR. [*suddenly demure*] Basingstoke it is!

DES. [*aside*] Then make it so. [*Aloud*] My brother—I call you brother still, despite your horrible profligacy—we have come to urge you to abandon the evil courses to which you have committed yourself, and at any cost to become a pure and blameless ratepayer.

ROB. But I've done no wrong yet.

MAR. [*wildly*] No wrong! He has done no wrong! Did you hear that!

DES. Basingstoke!

MAR. [*recovering herself*] Basingstoke it is!

DES. My brother—I still call you brother, you observe—you forget that you have been, in the eye of the law, a Bad Baronet of Ruddigore for ten years—and you are therefore responsible—in the eye of the law—for all the misdeeds committed by the unhappy gentleman who occupied your place.

ROB. I see! Bless my heart, I never thought of that! Was I very bad?

DES. Awful. Wasn't he? [*To* MARGARET]

ROB. And I've been going on like this for how long?

DES. Ten years! Think of all the atrocities you have committed—by attorney as it were—during that period. Remember how you trifled with this poor child's affections—how you raised her hopes on high (don't cry, my love—Basingstoke, you know), only to trample them in the dust when they were at the very zenith of their fullness. Oh fie, sir, fie—she trusted you!

ROB. Did she? What a scoundrel I must have been! There, there—don't cry, my dear [*to* MARGARET, *who is sobbing on* ROBIN'S *breast*], it's all right now. Birmingham, you know—Birmingham——

MAR. [*sobbing*] It's Ba—Ba—Basingstoke!

ROB. Basingstoke! of course it is—Basingstoke.

MAR. Then make it so!

ROB. There, there—it's all right—he's married you now—that is, *I've* married you [*turning to* DESPARD]—I say, which of us has married her?

DES. Oh, *I've* married her.

ROB. [*aside*] Oh, I'm glad of that. [*To* MARGARET] Yes, *he's* married you now [*passing her over to* DESPARD], and anything more disreputable than my conduct seems to have been I've never even heard of. But my mind is made up—I *will* defy my ancestors. I *will* refuse to obey their behests, thus, by courting death, atone in some degree for the infamy of my career!

MAR. I knew it—I knew it—God bless you—[*Hysterically*]

DES. Basingstoke!

MAR. Basingstoke it is! [*Recovers herself*]

Patter-Trio

ROBIN, DESPARD, and MARGARET

ROB. My eyes are fully open to my awful situation—
I shall go at once to Roderic and make him an oration.
I shall tell him I've recovered my forgotten moral senses,
And I don't care twopence-halfpenny for any consequences.
Now I do not want to perish by the sword or by the dagger,
But a martyr may indulge a little pardonable swagger,
And a word or two of compliment my vanity would flatter,
But I've got to die to-morrow, so it really doesn't matter!

DES. So it really doesn't matter—

MAR. So it really doesn't matter—

ALL So it really doesn't matter, matter, matter, matter, matter!

MAR. If I were not a little mad and generally silly
I should give you my advice upon the subject, willy-nilly;
I should show you in a moment how to grapple with the question,
And you'd really be astonished at the force of my suggestion.
On the subject I shall write you a most valuable letter,
Full of excellent suggestions when I feel a little better,
But at present I'm afraid I am as mad as any hatter,
So I'll keep 'em to myself, for my opinion doesn't matter!

DES. Her opinion doesn't matter—

ROB. Her opinion doesn't matter—

ALL Her opinion doesn't matter, matter, matter, matter, matter!

DES. If I had been so lucky as to have a steady brother
Who could talk to me as we are talking now to one another—
Who could give me good advice when he discovered I was erring

(Which is just the very favour which on you I am conferring),
My story would have made a rather interesting idyll,
And I might have lived and died a very decent indiwiddle.
This particularly rapid, unintelligible patter
Isn't generally heard, and if it is it doesn't matter!

ROB. If it is it doesn't matter–

MAR. If it ain't it doesn't matter–

ALL If it is it doesn't matter, matter, matter, matter, matter!

[*Exeunt* DESPARD *and* MARGARET.

Enter ADAM

ADAM [*guiltily*] Master–the deed is done!

ROB. What deed?

ADAM She is here–alone, unprotected––

ROB. Who?

ADAM The maiden. I've carried her off–I had a hard task, for she fought like a tiger-cat!

ROB. Great heaven, I had forgotten her! I had hoped to have died unspotted by crime, but I am foiled again–and by a tiger-cat! Produce her –and leave us!

[ADAM *introduces* DAME HANNAH, *very much excited, and exit.*

ROB. Dame Hannah! This is–this is not what I expected.

HAN. Well, sir, and what would you with me? Oh, you have begun bravely–bravely indeed! Unappalled by the calm dignity of blameless womanhood, your minion has torn me from my spotless home, and dragged me, blindfold and shrieking, through hedges, over stiles, and across a very difficult country, and left me, helpless and trembling, at your mercy! Yet not helpless, coward sir, for approach one step–nay, but the twentieth part of one poor inch–and this poniard [*produces a very small dagger*] shall teach ye what it is to lay unholy hands on old Stephen Trusty's daughter!

ROB. Madam, I am extremely sorry for this. It is not at all what I intended–anything, more correct–more deeply respectful than my intentions towards you, it would be impossible for any one–however particular–to desire.

HAN. Bah, I am not to be tricked by smooth words, hypocrite! But be warned in time, for there are, without, a hundred gallant hearts whose trusty blades would hack him limb from limb who dared to lay unholy hands on old Stephen Trusty's daughter!

ROB. And this is what it is to embark upon a career of unlicensed pleasure!

[HANNAH, *who has taken a formidable dagger from one of the armed figures, throws her small dagger to* ROBIN.

HAN. Harkye, miscreant, you have secured me, and I am your poor prisoner; but if you think I cannot take care of myself you are very much mistaken. Now then, it's one to one, and let the best man win!

[*Making for him*

ROB. [*in an agony of terror*] Don't! don't look at me like that! I can't bear it! Roderic! Uncle! Save me!

RODERIC *enters, from his picture. He comes down the stage.*

ROD. What is the matter? Have you carried her off?

ROB. I have–she is there–look at her–she terrifies me!

ROD. [*looking at* HANNAH] Little Nannikin!

HAN. [*amazed*] Roddy-doddy!

ROD. My own old love! Why, how came *you* here?

HAN. This brute–he carried me off! Bodily! But I'll show him! [*About to rush at* ROBIN]

ROD. Stop! [*To* ROB] What do you mean by carrying off this lady? Are you aware that once upon a time she was engaged to be married to me? I'm very angry–very angry indeed.

ROB. Now I hope this will be a lesson to you in future not to—

ROD. Hold your tongue, sir.

ROB. Yes, uncle.

ROD. Have you given him any encouragement?

HAN. [*to* ROB] Have I given you any encouragement? Frankly now, have I?

ROB. No. Frankly, you have not. Anything more scrupulously correct than your conduct, it would be impossible to desire.

ROD. You go away.

ROB. Yes, uncle. [*Exit* ROBIN.

ROD. This is a strange meeting after so many years!

HAN. Very. I thought you were dead.

ROD. I am. I died ten years ago.

HAN. And are you pretty comfortable?

ROD. Pretty well–that is–yes, pretty well.

HAN. You don't deserve to be, for I loved you all the while, dear; and it made me dreadfully unhappy to hear of all your goings-on, you bad, bad boy!

Ballad—HANNAH

There grew a little flower
'Neath a great oak tree:
When the tempest 'gan to lower
Little heeded she:
No need had she to cower,
For she dreaded not its power—
She was happy in the bower
Of her great oak tree!
Sing hey,
Lackaday!
Let the tears fall free
For the pretty little flower and the great oak tree!

BOTH Sing hey,
Lackaday, etc.

When she found that he was fickle,
Was that great oak tree,
She was in a pretty pickle,
As she well might be—
But his gallantries were mickle,
For Death followed with his sickle,
And her tears began to trickle
For her great oak tree!

BOTH Sing hey,
Lackaday! etc.

Said she, "He loved me never,
Did that great oak tree,
But I'm neither rich nor clever,
And so why should he?
But though fate our fortunes sever,
To be constant I'll endeavour,
Aye, for ever and for ever,
To my great oak tree!"

BOTH Sing hey,
Lackaday! etc.

[*Falls weeping on* RODERIC's *bosom*

Enter Robin, *excitedly, followed by all the characters and Chorus of Bridesmaids.*

Rob. Stop a bit–both of you.

Rod. This intrusion is unmannerly.

Han. I'm surprised at you.

Rob. I can't stop to apologize–an idea has just occurred to me. A Baronet of Ruddigore can only die through refusing to commit his daily crime.

Rod. No doubt.

Rob. Therefore, to refuse to commit a daily crime is tantamount to suicide!

Rod. It would seem so.

Rob. But suicide is, itself, a crime–and so, by your own showing, you ought never to have died at all!

Rod. I see–I understand! Then I'm practically alive!

Rob. Undoubtedly! [Sir Roderic *embraces* Hannah] Rose, when you believed that I was a simple farmer, I believe you loved me?

Rose. Madly, passionately!

Rob. But when I became a bad baronet, you very properly loved Richard instead?

Rose. Passionately, madly!

Rob. But if I should turn out *not* to be a bad baronet after all, how would you love me then?

Rose. Madly, passionately!

Rob. As before?

Rose. Why, of course!

Rob. My darling! [*They embrace*]

Rich. Here, I say, belay!

Rose. Oh sir, belay, if it's absolutely necessary!

Rob. Belay? Certainly not!

Finale

Rob. Having been a wicked baronet a week,
Once again a modest livelihood I seek,
  Agricultural employment
  Is to me a keen enjoyment,
For I'm naturally diffident and meek!

Rose When a man has been a naughty baronet,
And expresses his repentance and regret,
  You should help him, if you're able,
  Like the mousie in the fable,
That's the teaching of my Book of Etiquette.

RICH. If you ask me why I do not pipe my eye,
Like an honest British sailor, I reply,
That with Zorah for my missis,
There'll be bread and cheese and kisses,
Which is just the sort of ration I enjye!

DES. and MAR. Prompted by a keen desire to evoke,
All the blessed calm of matrimony's yoke,
We shall toddle off to-morrow,
From this scene of sin and sorrow,
For to settle in the town of Basingstoke!

ALL For happy the lily
That's kissed by the bee;
And, sipping tranquilly,
Quite happy is he;
And happy the filly
That neighs in her pride;
But happier than any,
A pound to a penny,
A lover is, when he
Embraces his bride!

CURTAIN

THE YEOMEN OF THE GUARD

OR

THE MERRYMAN AND HIS MAID

DRAMATIS PERSONÆ

SIR RICHARD CHOLMONDELEY [*Lieutenant of the Tower*]
COLONEL FAIRFAX [*under sentence of death*]
SERGEANT MERYLL [*of the Yeoman of the Guard*]
LEONARD MERYLL [*his son*]
JACK POINT [*a Strolling Jester*]
WILFRED SHADBOLT [*Head Jailer and Assistant Tormentor*]
THE HEADSMAN
FIRST YEOMAN
SECOND YEOMAN
FIRST CITIZEN
SECOND CITIZEN
ELSIE MAYNARD [*a Strolling Singer*]
PHŒBE MERYLL [*Sergeant Meryll's Daughter*]
DAME CARRUTHERS [*Housekeeper to the Tower*]
KATE [*her Niece*]
Chorus of Yeomen of the Guard, Gentlemen, Citizens, etc.

SCENE—*Tower Green.*

Date, 16th Century.

First produced at the Savoy Theatre on October 3, 1888

THE YEOMEN OF THE GUARD

OR

THE MERRYMAN AND HIS MAID

ACT I

Scene—*Tower Green*

Phœbe *discovered spinning.*

Song—Phœbe

When maiden loves, she sits and sighs,
She wanders to and fro;
Unbidden tear-drops fill her eyes,
And to all questions she replies
With a sad "heigho!"
'Tis but a little word—"heigho!"
So soft, 'tis scarcely heard—"heigho!"
An idle breath—
Yet life and death
May hang upon a maid's "heigho!"

When maiden loves, she mopes apart,
As owl mopes on a tree;
Although she keenly feels the smart,
She cannot tell what ails her heart,
With its sad "Ah me!"
'Tis but a foolish sigh—"Ah me!"
Born but to droop and die—"Ah me!"
Yet all the sense
Of eloquence
Lies hidden in a maid's "Ah me!" [*Weeps*]

Enter Wilfred

Wil. Mistress Meryll!

Phœ. [*looking up*] Eh! Oh! it's you, is it? You may go away, if you like. Because I don't want you, you know.

Wil. Haven't you anything to say to me?

PHŒ. Oh yes! Are the birds all caged? The wild beasts all littered down? All the locks, chains, bolts, and bars in good order? Is the Little Ease sufficiently uncomfortable? The racks, pincers, and thumbscrews all ready for work? Ugh! you brute!

WIL. These allusions to my professional duties are in doubtful taste. I didn't become a head-jailer because I like head-jailing. I didn't become an assistant-tormentor because I like assistant-tormenting. We can't *all* be sorcerers, you know. [PHŒBE, *annoyed*] Ah! you brought that upon yourself.

PHŒ. Colonel Fairfax is *not* a sorcerer. He's a man of science and an alchemist.

WIL. Well, whatever he is, he won't be one long, for he's to be beheaded to-day for dealings with the devil. His master nearly had him last night, when the fire broke out in the Beauchamp Tower.

PHŒ. Oh! how I wish he had escaped in the confusion! But take care; there's still time for a reply to his petition for mercy.

WIL. Ah! I'm content to chance that. This evening at half-past seven—ah!

PHŒ. You're a cruel monster to speak so unfeelingly of the death of a young and handsome soldier.

WIL. Young and handsome! How do *you* know he's young and handsome?

PHŒ. Because I've seen him every day for weeks past taking his exercise on the Beauchamp Tower.

WIL. Curse him!

PHŒ. There, I believe you're jealous of *him*, now. Jealous of a man I've never spoken to! Jealous of a poor soul who's to die in an hour!

WIL. I am! I'm jealous of everybody and everything. I'm jealous of the very words I speak to you—because they reach your ears—and I mustn't go near 'em!

PHŒ. How unjust you are! Jealous of the words you speak to me! Why, you know as well as I do that I don't even like them.

WIL. You used to like 'em.

PHŒ. I used to *pretend* I liked them. It was mere politeness to comparative strangers.

[*Exit* PHŒBE, *with spinning wheel.*

WIL. I don't believe you know what jealousy is! I don't believe you know how it eats into a man's heart—and disorders his digestion—and turns his interior into boiling lead. Oh, you are a heartless jade to trifle with the delicate organization of the human interior!

[*Exit* WILFRED.

Enter Crowd of Men and Women, followed by Yeomen of the Guard.

Chorus [as Yeomen march on]

Tower Warders,
Under orders,
Gallant pikemen, valiant sworders!
Brave in bearing,
Foemen scaring,
In their bygone days of daring!
Ne'er a stranger
There to danger—
Each was o'er the world a ranger;
To the story
Of our glory
Each a bold contributory!

Chorus of Yeomen

In the autumn of our life,
Here at rest in ample clover,
We rejoice in telling over
Our impetuous May and June.
In the evening of our day,
With the sun of life declining,
We recall without repining
All the heat of bygone noon.

Solo—2ND YEOMAN

This the autumn of our life,
This the evening of our day;
Weary we of battle strife,
Weary we of mortal fray.
But our year is not so spent,
And our days are not so faded,
But that we with one consent,
Were our lovèd land invaded,
Still would face a foreign foe,
As in days of long ago.

CHORUS

Still would face a foreign foe,
As in days of long ago.

PEOPLE	YEOMEN
tower warders, under orders, etc.	This the autumn of our life, etc.

[*Exeunt Crowd. Manent Yeomen.*

Enter DAME CARRUTHERS

DAME A good day to you!

2ND YEOMAN Good day, Dame Carruthers. Busy to-day?

DAME Busy, aye! the fire in the Beauchamp last night has given me work enough. A dozen poor prisoners—Richard Colfax, Sir Martin Byfleet, Colonel Fairfax, Warren the preacher-poet, and half-a-score others—all packed into one small cell, not six feet square. Poor Colonel Fairfax, who's to die to-day, is to be removed to No. 14 in the Cold Harbour that he may have his last hour alone with his confessor; and I've to see to that.

2ND YEO. Poor gentleman! He'll die bravely. I fought under him two years since, and he valued his life as it were a feather!

PHŒ. He's the bravest, the handsomest, and the best young gentleman in England! He twice saved my father's life; and it's a cruel thing, a wicked thing, and a barbarous thing that so gallant a hero should lose his head—for it's the handsomest head in England!

DAME For dealings with the devil. Aye! if all were beheaded who dealt with *him*, there'd be busy doings on Tower Green.

PHŒ. You know very well that Colonel Fairfax is a student of alchemy—nothing more, and nothing less; but this wicked Tower, like a cruel giant in a fairy-tale, must be fed with blood, and that blood must be the best and bravest in England, or it's not good enough for the old Blunderbore. Ugh!

DAME Silence, you silly girl; you know not what you say. I was born in the old keep, and I've grown grey in it, and, please God, I shall die and be buried in it; and there's not a stone in its walls that is not as dear to me as my own right hand.

Song with Chorus—DAME CARRUTHERS and YEOMEN

When our gallant Norman foes
  Made our merry land their own,
    And the Saxons from the Conqueror were flying,
At his bidding it arose,
  In its panoply of stone,
    A sentinel unliving and undying.

Insensible, I trow,
  As a sentinel should be,
    Though a queen to save her head should come a-suing,
There's a legend on its brow
  That is eloquent to me,
    And it tells of duty done and duty doing.

    "The screw may twist and the rack may turn,
    And men may bleed and men may burn,

O'er London town and its golden hoard
I keep my silent watch and ward!"

CHORUS The screw may twist, etc.

Within its wall of rock
The flower of the brave
Have perished with a constancy unshaken.
From the dungeon to the block,
From the scaffold to the grave,
Is a journey many gallant hearts have taken.

And the wicked flames may hiss
Round the heroes who have fought
For conscience and for home in all its beauty,
But the grim old fortalice
Takes little heed of aught
That comes not in the measure of its duty.

"The screw may twist and the rack may turn,
And men may bleed and men may burn,
O'er London town and its golden hoard
I keep my silent watch and ward!"

CHORUS The screw may twist, etc.

[*Exeunt all but* PHŒBE. *Enter* SERGEANT MERYLL.

PHŒ. Father! Has no reprieve arrived for the poor gentleman?

MER. No, my lass; but there's one hope yet. Thy brother Leonard, who, as a reward for his valour in saving his standard and cutting his way through fifty foes who would have hanged him, has been appointed a Yeoman of the Guard, will arrive to-day; and as he comes straight from Windsor, where the Court is, it may be—it *may* be—that he will bring the expected reprieve with him.

PHŒ. Oh, that he may!

MER. Amen to that! For the Colonel twice saved my life, and I'd give the rest of my life to save his! And wilt thou not be glad to welcome thy brave brother, with the fame of whose exploits all England is a-ringing?

PHŒ. Aye, truly, if he brings the reprieve.

MER. And not otherwise?

PHŒ. Well, he's a brave fellow indeed, and I love brave men.

MER. *All* brave men?

PHŒ. Most of them, I verily believe! But I hope Leonard will not be too strict with me—they say he is a very dragon of virtue and circumspection! Now, my dear old father is kindness itself, and——

MER. And leaves thee pretty well to thine own ways, eh? Well, I've no fears for thee; thou hast a feather-brain, but thou'rt a good lass.

PHŒ. Yes, that's all very well, but if Leonard is going to tell me that I may not do this and I may not do that, and I must not talk to this one, or walk with that one, but go through the world with my lips pursed up and my eyes cast down, like a poor nun who has renounced mankind—why, as I have *not* renounced mankind, and don't mean to renounce mankind, I won't have it—there!

MER. Nay, he'll not check thee more than is good for thee, Phœbe! He's a brave fellow, and bravest among brave fellows, and yet it seems but yesterday that he robbed the Lieutenant's orchard.

Enter LEONARD MERYLL

LEON. Father!

MER. Leonard! my brave boy! I'm right glad to see thee, and so is Phœbe!

PHŒ. Aye—hast thou brought Colonel Fairfax's reprieve?

LEON. Nay, I have here a despatch for the Lieutenant, but no reprieve for the Colonel!

PHŒ. Poor gentleman! poor gentleman!

LEON. Aye, I would I had brought better news. I'd give my right hand —nay, my body—my life, to save his!

MER. Dost thou speak in earnest, my lad?

LEON. Aye, father—I'm no braggart. Did he not save thy life? and am I not his foster-brother?

MER. Then hearken to me. Thou hast come to join the Yeomen of the Guard!

LEON. Well?

MER. None has seen thee but ourselves?

LEON. And a sentry, who took but scant notice of me.

MER. Now to prove thy words. Give me the despatch and get thee hence at once! Here is money, and I'll send thee more. Lie hidden for a space, and let no one know. I'll convey a suit of Yeoman's uniform to the Colonel's cell—he shall shave off his beard, so that none shall know him, and I'll own him as my son, the brave Leonard Meryll, who saved his flag and cut his way through fifty foes who thirsted for his life. He will be welcomed without question by my brother-Yeomen, I'll warrant that. Now, how to get access to the Colonel's cell? [*To* PHŒBE] The key is with thy sour-faced admirer, Wilfred Shadbolt.

PHŒ. [*demurely*] I think—I say, I *think*—I can get anything I want from Wilfred. I think—mind I say, I *think*—you may leave that to me.

MER. Then get thee hence at once, lad—and bless thee for this sacrifice.

PHŒ. And take my blessing, too, dear, dear Leonard!

LEON. And thine, eh? Humph! Thy love is newborn; wrap it up carefully, lest it take cold and die.

Trio—Phœbe, Leonard, Meryll

Phœ. Alas! I waver to and fro!
Dark danger hangs upon the deed!

All Dark danger hangs upon the deed!

Leon. The scheme is rash and well may fail,
But ours are not the hearts that quail,
The hands that shrink, the cheeks that pale
In hours of need!

All No, ours are not the hearts that quail,
The hands that shrink, the cheeks that pale
In hours of need!

Mer. The air I breathe to him I owe:
My life is his—I count it naught!

Phœ. and Leon. That life is his—so count it naught!

Mer. And shall I reckon risks I run
When services are to be done
To save the life of such an one?
Unworthy thought!

Phœ. and Leon. And shall we reckon risks we run
To save the life of such an one?

All Unworthy thought!
We may succeed—who can foretell?
May heaven help our hope—farewell!

[Leonard *embraces* Meryll *and* Phœbe, *and then exit.* Phœbe *weeping.*

Mer. Nay, lass, be of good cheer, we may save him yet.

Phœ. Oh! see, father—they bring the poor gentleman from the Beauchamp! Oh, father! his hour is not yet come?

Mer. No, no—they lead him to the Cold Harbour Tower to await his end in solitude. But softly—the Lieutenant approaches! He should not see thee weep.

Enter FAIRFAX, *guarded. The* LIEUTENANT *enters, meeting him.*

LIEUT. Halt! Colonel Fairfax, my old friend, we meet but sadly.

FAIR. Sir, I greet you with all good-will; and I thank you for the zealous care with which you have guarded me from the pestilent dangers which threaten human life outside. In this happy little community, Death, when he comes, doth so in punctual and business-like fashion; and, like a courtly gentleman, giveth due notice of his advent, that one may not be taken unawares.

LIEUT. Sir, you bear this bravely, as a brave man should.

FAIR. Why, sir, it is no light boon to die swiftly and surely at a given hour and in a given fashion! Truth to tell, I would gladly have my life; but if that may not be, I have the next best thing to it, which is death. Believe me, sir, my lot is not so much amiss!

PHŒ. [*aside to* MERYLL] Oh, father, father, I cannot bear it!

MER. My poor lass!

FAIR. Nay, pretty one, why weepest thou? Come, be comforted. Such a life as mine is not worth weeping for. [*Sees* MERYLL] Sergeant Meryll, is it not? [*To* LIEUT.] May I greet my old friend? [*Shakes* MERYLL's *hand*] Why, man, what's all this? Thou and I have faced the grim old king a dozen times, and never has his majesty come to me in such goodly fashion. Keep a stout heart, good fellow—we are soldiers, and we know how to die, thou and I. Take my word for it, it is easier to die well than to live well—for, in sooth, I have tried both.

Ballad—FAIRFAX

Is life a boon?
    If so, it must befall,
    That Death, whene'er he call,
Must call too soon.
    Though fourscore years he give,
    Yet one would pray to live
Another moon!
    What kind of plaint have I,
    Who perish in July?
    I might have had to die,
Perchance, in June!

Is life a thorn?
    Then count it not a whit!
    Man is well done with it;
Soon as he's born
    He should all means essay
    To put the plague away;

And I, war-worn,
Poor captured fugitive,
My life most gladly give—
I might have had to live
Another morn!

[*At the end*, PHŒBE *is led off, weeping, by* MERYLL.

FAIR. And now, Sir Richard, I have a boon to beg. I am in this strait for no better reason than because my kinsman, Sir Clarence Poltwhistle, one of the Secretaries of State, has charged me with sorcery, in order that he may succeed to my estate, which devolves to him provided I die unmarried.

LIEUT. As thou wilt most surely do.

FAIR. Nay, as I will most surely *not* do, by your worship's grace! I have a mind to thwart this good cousin of mine.

LIEUT. How?

FAIR. By marrying forthwith, to be sure!

LIEUT. But heaven ha' mercy, whom wouldst thou marry?

FAIR. Nay, I am indifferent on that score. Coming Death hath made of me a true and chivalrous knight, who holds all womankind in such esteem that the oldest, and the meanest, and the worst-favoured of them is good enough for him. So, my good Lieutenant, if thou wouldst serve a poor soldier who has but an hour to live, find me the first that comes—my confessor shall marry us, and her dower shall be my dishonoured name and a hundred crowns to boot. No such poor dower for an hour of matrimony!

LIEUT. A strange request. I doubt that I should be warranted in granting it.

FAIR. There never was a marriage fraught with so little of evil to the contracting parties. In an hour she'll be a widow, and I—a bachelor again for aught I know!

LIEUT. Well, I will see what can be done, for I hold thy kinsman in abhorrence for the scurvy trick he has played thee.

FAIR. A thousand thanks, good sir; we meet again in this spot in an hour or so. I shall be a bridegroom then, and your worship will wish me joy. Till then, farewell. [*To Guard*] I am ready, good fellows.

[*Exit with Guard into Cold Harbour Tower.*

LIEUT. He is a brave fellow, and it is a pity that he should die. Now, how to find him a bride at such short notice? Well, the task should be easy! [*Exit.*

Enter JACK POINT *and* ELSIE MAYNARD, *pursued by a crowd of men and women.* POINT *and* ELSIE *are much terrified;* POINT, *however, assuming an appearance of self-possession.*

Chorus

Here's a man of jollity,
Jibe, joke, jollify!
Give us of your quality,
Come, fool, follify!

If you vapour vapidly,
River runneth rapidly,
Into it we fling
Bird who doesn't sing!

Give us an experiment
In the art of merriment;
Into it we throw
Cock who doesn't crow!

Banish your timidity,
And with all rapidity
Give us quip and quiddity—
Willy-nilly, O!

River none can mollify;—
Into it we throw
Fool who doesn't follify,
Cock who doesn't crow!

POINT [*alarmed*] My masters, I pray you bear with us, and we will satisfy you, for we are merry folk who would make all merry as ourselves. For, look you, there is humour in all things, and the truest philosophy is that which teaches us to find it and to make the most of it.

ELSIE [*struggling with one of the crowd*] Hands off, I say, unmannerly fellow!

POINT [*to 1st Citizen*] Ha! Didst thou hear her say, "Hands off"?

1ST CIT. Aye, I heard her say it, and I felt her do it! What then?

POINT Thou dost not see the humour of that?

1ST CIT. Nay, if I do, hang me!

POINT Thou dost not? Now observe. She said, "Hands off!" Whose hands? Thine. Off whom? Off *her*. Why? Because she is a woman. Now, had she *not* been a woman, thine hands had not been set upon her at all. So the reason for the laying on of hands is the reason for the taking off of hands, and herein is contradiction contradicted! It is the very marriage of *pro* with *con;* and no such lopsided union either, as times go, for *pro* is not more unlike *con* than man is unlike woman—yet men and women marry every day with none to say, "Oh, the pity of it!" but I and fools like me! Now wherewithal shall we please you? We can rhyme you couplet, triolet, quatrain, sonnet, rondolet, ballade, what you will.

Or we can dance you saraband, gondolet, carole, pimpernel, or jumping Joan.

ELSIE Let us give them the singing farce of the Merryman and his Maid—therein is song and dance too.

ALL Aye, the Merryman and his Maid!

Duet—ELSIE and POINT

POINT I have a song to sing, O!

ELSIE Sing me your song, O!

POINT It is sung to the moon
By a love-lorn loon,
Who fled from the mocking throng, O!
It's a song of a merryman, moping mum,
Whose soul was sad, and whose glance was glum,
Who sipped no sup, and who craved no crumb,
As he sighed for the love of a ladye.
Heighdy! heighdy!
Misery me, lackadaydee!
He sipped no sup, and he craved no crumb,
As he sighed for the love of a ladye.

ELSIE I have a song to sing, O!

POINT What is your song, O?

ELSIE
It is sung with the ring
Of the songs maids sing
Who love with a love life-long, O!
It's the song of a merrymaid, peerly proud,
Who loved a lord and who laughed aloud
At the moan of the merryman, moping mum,
Whose soul was sad, and whose glance was glum,
Who sipped no sup, and who craved no crumb,
As he sighed for the love of a ladye.
Heighdy! heighdy!
Misery me, lackadaydee!
He sipped no sup, etc.

POINT
I have a song to sing, O!

ELSIE
Sing me your song, O!

POINT
It is sung to the knell
Of a churchyard bell,
And a doleful dirge, ding dong, O!
It's a song of a popinjay, bravely born,
Who turned up his noble nose with scorn
At the humble merrymaid, peerly proud,
Who loved a lord, and who laughed aloud
At the moan of a merryman, moping mum,
Whose soul was sad, and whose glance was glum,
Who sipped no sup, and who craved no crumb,
As he sighed for the love of a ladye.

BOTH
Heighdy! heighdy!
Misery me, lackadaydee!
He sipped no sup, etc.

ELSIE
I have a song to sing, O!

POINT
Sing me your song, O!

ELSIE
It is sung with a sigh
And a tear in the eye,
For it tells of a righted wrong, O!
It's a song of the merrymaid, once so gay,
Who turned on her heel and tripped away
From the peacock popinjay, bravely born,
Who turned up his noble nose with scorn
At the humble heart that he did not prize:
So she begged on her knees, with downcast eyes,
For the love of the merryman, moping mum,
Whose soul was sad, and whose glance was glum,
Who sipped no sup, and who craved no crumb,
As he sighed for the love of a ladye.

BOTH Heighdy! heighdy!
Misery me, lackadaydee!
His pains were o'er, and he sighed no more,
For he lived in the love of a ladye.

1ST CIT. Well sung and well danced!

2ND CIT. A kiss for that, pretty maid!

ALL Aye, a kiss all round.

ELSIE [*drawing dagger*] Best beware! I am armed!

POINT Back, sirs–back! This is going too far.

2ND CIT. Thou dost not see the humour of it, eh? Yet there is humour in all things–even in this. [*Trying to kiss her*]

ELSIE Help! Help!

Enter LIEUTENANT *with Guard. Crowd falls back.*

LIEUT. What is this pother?

ELSIE Sir, we sang to these folk, and they would have repaid us with gross courtesy, but for your honour's coming.

LIEUT. [*to Mob*] Away with ye! Clear the rabble. [*Guards push Crowd off, and go off with them*] Now, my girl, who are you, and what do you here?

ELSIE May it please you, sir, we are two strolling players, Jack Point and I, Elsie Maynard, at your worship's service. We go from fair to fair, singing, and dancing, and playing brief interludes; and so we make a poor living.

LIEUT. You two, eh? Are ye man and wife?

POINT No, sir; for though I'm a fool, there is a limit to my folly. Her mother, old Bridget Maynard, travels with us (for Elsie is a good girl), but the old woman is a-bed with fever, and we have come here to pick up some silver to buy an electuary for her.

LIEUT. Hark ye, my girl! Your mother is ill?

ELSIE Sorely ill, sir.

LIEUT. And needs good food, and many things that thou canst not buy?

ELSIE Alas! sir, it is too true.

LIEUT. Wouldst thou earn an hundred crowns?

ELSIE An hundred crowns! They might save her life!

LIEUT. Then listen! A worthy but unhappy gentleman is to be beheaded in an hour on this very spot. For sufficient reasons, he desires to marry before he dies, and he hath asked me to find him a wife. Wilt thou be that wife?

ELSIE The wife of a man I have never seen!

POINT Why, sir, look you, I am concerned in this; for though I am not yet wedded to Elsie Maynard, time works wonders, and there's no knowing what may be in store for us. Have we your worship's word for it that this gentleman will die to-day?

LIEUT. Nothing is more certain, I grieve to say.

POINT And that the maiden will be allowed to depart the very instant the ceremony is at an end?

LIEUT. The very instant. I pledge my honour that it shall be so.

POINT An hundred crowns?

LIEUT. An hundred crowns!

POINT For my part, I consent. It is for Elsie to speak.

Trio—ELSIE, POINT, and LIEUTENANT

LIEUT.
How say you, maiden, will you wed
A man about to lose his head?
For half an hour
You'll be a wife,
And then the dower
Is yours for life.
A headless bridegroom why refuse?
If truth the poets tell,
Most bridegrooms, ere they marry, lose
Both head and heart as well!

ELSIE
A strange proposal you reveal,
It almost makes my senses reel.
Alas! I'm very poor indeed,
And such a sum I sorely need.
My mother, sir, is like to die,
This money life may bring.
Bear this in mind, I pray, if I
Consent to do this thing!

POINT
Though as a general rule of life
I don't allow my promised wife,
My lovely bride that is to be,
To marry any one but me,
Yet if the fee is promptly paid,
And he, in well-earned grave,
Within the hour is duly laid,
Objection I will waive!
Yes, objection I will waive!

ALL
Temptation, oh, temptation,
Were we, I pray, intended
To shun, whate'er our station,
Your fascinations splendid;
Or fall, whene'er we view you,
Head over heels into you?
Temptation, oh, temptation, etc.

[*During this, the* LIEUTENANT *has whispered to* WILFRED (*who has entered*). WILFRED *binds* ELSIE'S *eyes with a kerchief, and leads her into the Cold Harbour Tower.*

LIEUT. And so, good fellow, you are a jester?

POINT Aye, sir, and like some of my jests, out of place.

LIEUT. I have a vacancy for such an one. Tell me, what are your qualifications for such a post?

POINT Marry, sir, I have a pretty wit. I can rhyme you extempore; I can convulse you with quip and conundrum; I have the lighter philosophies at my tongue's tip; I can be merry, wise, quaint, grim, and sardonic, one by one, or all at once; I have a pretty turn for anecdote; I know all the jests—ancient and modern—past, present, and to come; I can riddle you from dawn of day to set of sun, and, if that content you not, well on to midnight and the small hours. Oh, sir, a pretty wit, I warrant you—a pretty, pretty wit!

Recitative and Song—POINT

I've jibe and joke
    And quip and crank
For lowly folk
    And men of rank.

I ply my craft
And know no fear,
But aim my shaft
At prince or peer.
At peer or prince—at prince or peer,
I aim my shaft and know no fear!

I've wisdom from the East and from the West,
That's subject to no academic rule;
You may find it in the jeering of a jest,
Or distil it from the folly of a fool.
I can teach you with a quip, if I've a mind;
I can trick you into learning with a laugh;
Oh, winnow all my folly, and you'll find
A grain or two of truth among the chaff!

I can set a braggart quailing with a quip,
The upstart I can wither with a whim;
He may wear a merry laugh upon his lip,
But his laughter has an echo that is grim!
When they're offered to the world in merry guise,
Unpleasant truths are swallowed with a will—
For he who'd make his fellow-creatures wise
Should always gild the philosophic pill!

LIEUT. And how came you to leave your last employ?

POINT Why, sir, it was in this wise. My Lord was the Archbishop of Canterbury, and it was considered that one of my jokes was unsuited to His Grace's family circle. In truth, I ventured to ask a poor riddle, sir—Wherein lay the difference between His Grace and poor Jack Point?

His Grace was pleased to give it up, sir. And thereupon I told him that whereas His Grace was paid £10,000 a year for being good, poor Jack Point was good—for nothing. 'Twas but a harmless jest, but it offended His Grace, who whipped me and set me in the stocks for a scurril rogue, and so we parted. I had as lief not take post again with the dignified clergy.

LIEUT. But I trust you are very careful not to give offence. I have daughters.

POINT Sir, my jests are most carefully selected, and anything objectionable is expunged. If your honour pleases, I will try them first on your honour's chaplain.

LIEUT. Can you give me an example? Say that I had sat me down hurriedly on something sharp?

POINT Sir, I should say that you had sat down on the spur of the moment.

LIEUT. Humph! I don't think much of that. Is that the best you can do?

POINT It has always been much admired, sir, but we will try again.

LIEUT. Well, then, I am at dinner, and the joint of meat is but half cooked.

POINT Why then, sir, I should say that what is *underdone* cannot be helped.

LIEUT. I see. I think that manner of thing would be somewhat irritating.

POINT At first, sir, perhaps; but use is everything, and you would come in time to like it.

LIEUT. We will suppose that I caught you kissing the kitchen wench under my very nose.

POINT Under *her* very nose, good sir—not under yours! *That* is where *I* would kiss her. Do you take me? Oh, sir, a pretty wit—a pretty, pretty wit!

LIEUT. The maiden comes. Follow me, friend, and we will discuss this matter at length in my library.

POINT I am your worship's servant. That is to say, I trust I soon shall be. But, before proceeding to a more serious topic, can you tell me, sir, why a cook's brain-pan is like an overwound clock?

LIEUT. A truce to this fooling—follow me.

POINT Just my luck; my best conundrum wasted!

[*Exeunt.*

Enter ELSIE *from Tower, led by* WILFRED, *who removes the bandage from her eyes, and exit.*

Recitative and Song—ELSIE

'Tis done! I am a bride! Oh, little ring,
That bearest in thy circlet all the gladness

That lovers hope for, and that poets sing,
What bringest thou to me but gold and sadness?
A bridegroom all unknown, save in this wise,
To-day he dies! To-day, alas, he dies!

Though tear and long-drawn sigh
Ill fit a bride,
No sadder wife than I
The whole world wide!
Ah me! Ah me!
Yet maids there be
Who would consent to lose
The very rose of youth,
The flower of life,
To be, in honest truth,
A wedded wife,
No matter whose!

Ah me! what profit we,
O maids that sigh,
Though gold, though gold should live
If wedded love must die?

Ere half an hour has rung,
A widow I!
Ah, heaven, he is too young,
Too brave to die!
Ah me! Ah me!
Yet wives there be
So weary worn, I trow,
That they would scarce complain,
So that they could
In half an hour attain
To widowhood,
No matter how!

O weary wives
Who widowhood would win,
Rejoice that ye have time
To weary in.

[*Exit* ELSIE *as* WILFRED *re-enters.*

WIL. [*looking after* ELSIE] 'Tis an odd freak, for a dying man and his confessor to be closeted alone with a strange singing girl. I would fain have espied them, but they stopped up the keyhole. *My* keyhole!

Enter PHŒBE *with* MERYLL. MERYLL ***remains in the background, unobserved by*** WILFRED.

PHŒ. [*aside*] Wilfred–and alone!

WIL. Now what could he have wanted with her? That's what puzzles me!

PHŒ. [*aside*] Now to get the keys from him. [*Aloud*] Wilfred–has no reprieve arrived?

WIL. None. Thine adored Fairfax is to die.

PHŒ. Nay, thou knowest that I have naught but pity for the poor condemned gentleman.

WIL. I know that he who is about to die is more to thee than I, who am alive and well.

PHŒ. Why, that were out of reason, dear Wilfred. Do they not say that a live ass is better than a dead lion? No, I don't mean that!

WIL. Oh, they say that, do they?

PHŒ. It's unpardonably rude of them, but I believe they put it in that way. Not that it applies to thee, who art clever beyond all telling!

WIL. Oh yes, as an assistant-tormentor.

PHŒ. Nay, as a wit, as a humorist, as a most philosophic commentator on the vanity of human resolution.

[PHŒBE *slyly takes bunch of keys from* WILFRED'S *waistband and hands them to* MERYLL, *who enters the Tower, unnoticed by* WILFRED.

WIL. Truly, I have seen great resolution give way under my persuasive methods [*working a small thumbscrew*]. In the nice regulation of a thumbscrew–in the hundredth part of a single revolution lieth all the difference between stony reticence and a torrent of impulsive unbosoming that the pen can scarcely follow. Ha! ha! I am a mad wag.

PHŒ. [*with a grimace*] Thou art a most light-hearted and delightful companion, Master Wilfred. Thine anecdotes of the torture-chamber are the prettiest hearing.

WIL. I'm a pleasant fellow an I choose. I believe I am the merriest dog that barks. Ah, we might be passing happy together——

PHŒ. Perhaps. I do not know.

WIL. For thou wouldst make a most tender and loving wife.

PHŒ. Aye, to one whom I really loved. For there is a wealth of love within this little heart–saving up for–I wonder whom? Now, of all the world of men, I wonder whom? To think that he whom I am to wed is now alive and somewhere! Perhaps far away, perhaps close at hand! And I know him not! It seemeth that I am wasting time in not knowing him.

WIL. Now say that it is I–nay! suppose it for the nonce. Say that we are wed–suppose it only–say that thou art my very bride, and I thy cheery, joyous, bright, frolicsome husband–and that, the day's work being done, and the prisoners stored away for the night, thou and I are alone together–with a long, long evening before us!

PHŒ. [*with a grimace*] It is a pretty picture—but I scarcely know. It cometh so unexpectedly—and yet—and yet—*were* I thy bride——

WIL. Aye!—wert thou my bride——?

PHŒ. Oh, how I would love thee!

Song—PHŒBE

Were I thy bride,
Then all the world beside
Were not too wide
To hold my wealth of love—
Were I thy bride!

Upon thy breast
My loving head would rest,
As on her nest
The tender turtle dove—
Were I thy bride!

This heart of mine
Would be one heart with thine,
And in that shrine
Our happiness would dwell—
Were I thy bride!

And all day long
Our lives should be a song:
No grief, no wrong
Should make my heart rebel—
Were I thy bride!

The silvery flute,
The melancholy lute,
Were night-owl's hoot
To my low-whispered coo—
Were I thy bride!

The skylark's trill
Were but discordance shrill
To the soft thrill
Of wooing as I'd woo—
Were I thy bride!

MERYLL *re-enters; gives keys to* PHŒBE, *who replaces them at* WILFRED'S *girdle, unnoticed by him. Exit* MERYLL.

The rose's sigh
Were as a carrion's cry
To lullaby
Such as I'd sing to thee,
Were I thy bride!

A feather's press
Were leaden heaviness
To my caress.
But then, of course, you see,
I'm not thy bride!

[*Exit* PHŒBE.

WIL. No, thou'rt not—not yet! But, Lord, how she woo'd; I should be no mean judge of wooing, seeing that I have been more hotly woo'd than most men. I have been woo'd by maid, widow, and wife. I have been woo'd boldly, timidly, tearfully, shyly—by direct assault, by suggestion, by implication, by inference, and by innuendo. But this wooing is not of the common order: it is the wooing of one who must needs woo me, if she die for it!

[*Exit* WILFRED.

Enter MERYLL, *cautiously, from Tower*

MER. [*looking after them*] The deed is, so far, safely accomplished. The slyboots, how she wheedled him! What a helpless ninny is a love-sick man! He is but as a lute in a woman's hands—she plays upon him whatever tune she will. But the Colonel comes. I' faith, he's just in time, for the Yeomen parade here for his execution in two minutes!

Enter FAIRFAX, *without beard and moustache, and dressed in Yeoman's uniform.*

FAIR. My good and kind friend, thou runnest a grave risk for me!

MER. Tut, sir, no risk. I'll warrant none here will recognise you. You make a brave Yeoman, sir! So—this ruff is too high; so—and the sword should hang thus. Here is your halbert, sir; carry it thus. The Yeomen come. Now remember, you are my brave son, Leonard Meryll.

FAIR. If I may not bear mine own name, there is none other I would bear so readily.

MER. Now, sir, put a bold face on it, for they come.

Finale—Act I

Enter Yeomen of the Guard

Chorus

Oh, Sergeant Meryll, is it true—
  The welcome news we read in orders?
Thy son, whose deeds of derring-do
Are echoed all the country through,
  Has come to join the Tower Warders?
If so, we come to meet him,
That we may fitly greet him,
And welcome his arrival here
With shout on shout and cheer on cheer.
    Hurrah! Hurrah! Hurrah!

Recitative—SERGEANT MERYLL

Ye Tower Warders, nursed in war's alarms,
  Suckled on gunpowder, and weaned on glory,
Behold my son, whose all-subduing arms
  Have formed the theme of many a song and story!
    Forgive his aged father's pride; nor jeer
      His aged father's sympathetic tear!

[*Pretending to weep*]

Chorus

Leonard Meryll!
Leonard Meryll!
Dauntless he in time of peril!
Man of power,
Knighthood's flower,

Welcome to the grim old Tower,
To the Tower, welcome thou!

Recitative—FAIRFAX

Forbear, my friends, and spare me this ovation,
I have small claim to such consideration;
The tales that of my prowess are narrated
Have been prodigiously exaggerated!

Chorus

'Tis ever thus!
Wherever valour true is found,
True modesty will there abound.

Couplets

1ST YEOMAN Didst thou not, oh, Leonard Meryll!
Standard lost in last campaign,
Rescue it at deadly peril—
Bear it safely back again?

CHORUS Leonard Meryll, at his peril,
Bore it safely back again!

2ND YEOMAN Didst thou not, when prisoner taken,
And debarred from all escape,
Face, with gallant heart unshaken,
Death in most appalling shape?

CHORUS Leonard Meryll, faced his peril,
Death in most appalling shape!

FAIR. [*aside*] Truly I was to be pitied,
Having but an hour to live,
I reluctantly submitted,
I had no alternative!

[*Aloud*] Oh! the tales that are narrated
Of my deeds of derring-do
Have been much exaggerated,
Very much exaggerated,
Scarce a word of them is true!

CHORUS They are not exaggerated, etc.

Enter PHŒBE. *She rushes to* FAIRFAX. *Enter* WILFRED

Recitative

PHŒ. Leonard!
FAIR. [*puzzled*] I beg your pardon?
PHŒ. Don't you know me?
I'm little Phœbe!
FAIR. [*still puzzled*] Phœbe? Is this Phœbe?
What! little Phœbe? [*Aside*] Who the deuce may *she* be?
It can't be Phœbe, surely?
WIL. Yes, 'tis Phœbe—
Your sister Phœbe! Your own little sister!
ALL Aye, he speaks the truth;
'Tis Phœbe!
FAIR. [*pretending to recognise her*] Sister Phœbe!
PHŒ. Oh, my brother!
FAIR. Why, how you've grown! I did not recognise you!
PHŒ. So many years! Oh, brother!
FAIR. Oh, my sister!
WIL. Aye, hug him, girl! There are three thou mayst hug—
Thy father and thy brother and—myself!
FAIR. Thyself, forsooth? And who art thou thyself?
WIL. Good sir, we are betrothed. [FAIRFAX *turns inquiringly to* PHŒBE]
PHŒ. Or more or less—
But rather less than more!
WIL. To thy fond care
I do commend thy sister. Be to her
An ever-watchful guardian—eagle-eyed!
And when she feels (as sometimes she does feel)
Disposed to indiscriminate caress,
Be thou at hand to take those favours from her!
ALL Be thou at hand to take those favours from her!
PHŒ. Yes, yes.
Be thou at hand to take those favours from me!

Trio—WILFRED, FAIRFAX, and PHŒBE

WIL. To thy fraternal care
Thy sister I commend;
From every lurking snare
Thy lovely charge defend:
And to achieve this end,
Oh! grant, I pray, this boon—
She shall not quit thy sight:

From morn to afternoon—
  From afternoon to night—
From seven o'clock to two—
  From two to eventide—
From dim twilight to 'leven at night
  She shall not quit thy side!

ALL — From morn to afternoon, etc.

PHŒ. — So amiable I've grown,
  So innocent as well,
That if I'm left alone
  The consequences fell
  No mortal can foretell.
So grant, I pray, this boon—
  I shall not quit thy sight:
From morn to afternoon—
  From afternoon to night—
From seven o'clock to two—
  From two to eventide—
From dim twilight to 'leven at night
  I shall not quit thy side.

ALL — From morn to afternoon, etc.

FAIR. — With brotherly readiness,
  For my fair sister's sake,
At once I answer "Yes"—
  That task I undertake—
  My word I never break.
I freely grant that boon,
  And I'll repeat my plight.
From morn to afternoon— [*kiss*]
  From afternoon to night— [*kiss*]
From seven o'clock to two— [*kiss*]
  From two to evening meal— [*kiss*]
From dim twilight to 'leven at night
  That compact I will seal. [*kiss*]

ALL — From morn to afternoon, etc.

[*The bell of St. Peter's begins to toll. The Crowd enters; the block is brought on to the stage, and the Headsman takes his place. The Yeomen of the Guard form up. The* LIEUTENANT *enters and takes his place, and tells off* FAIRFAX *and two others to bring the prisoner to execution.* WILFRED, FAIRFAX, *and two Yeomen exeunt to Tower.*

Chorus [to tolling accompaniment]

The prisoner comes to meet his doom;
The block, the headsman, and the tomb.
The funeral bell begins to toll—
May Heaven have mercy on his soul!

Solo—ELSIE, *with Chorus*

Oh, Mercy, thou whose smile has shone
So many a captive heart upon;
Of all immured within these walls,
To-day the very worthiest falls!

Enter FAIRFAX *and two other Yeomen from Tower in great excitement*

FAIR. My lord! I know not how to tell
The news I bear!
I and my comrades sought the prisoner's cell—
He is not there!

ALL He is not there!
They sought the prisoner's cell—he is not there!

Trio—FAIRFAX *and two Yeomen*

As escort for the prisoner
We sought his cell, in duty bound;
The double gratings open were,
No prisoner at all we found!

We hunted high, we hunted low,
We hunted here, we hunted there—
The man we sought with anxious care
Had vanished into empty air!

[*Exit* LIEUTENANT.

GIRLS Now, by my troth, the news is fair,
The man has vanished into air!

ALL As escort for the prisoner
They sought his cell in duty bound, etc.

Enter WILFRED, *followed by* LIEUTENANT

LIEUT. Astounding news! The prisoner fled!
[*To* WILFRED] Thy life shall forfeit be instead!
[WILFRED *is arrested*]

WIL. My lord, I did not set him free,
I hate the man—my rival he!
[WILFRED *is taken away*]

MER. The prisoner gone—I'm all agape!
Who could have helped him to escape?

PHŒ. Indeed I can't imagine who!
I've no idea at all—have you?

Enter JACK POINT

DAME Of his escape no traces lurk,
Enchantment must have been at work!

ELSIE [*aside to* POINT]
What have I done! Oh, woe is me!
I am his wife, and he is free!

POINT Oh, woe is *you?* Your anguish sink!
Oh, woe is *me*, I rather think!
Oh, woe is *me*, I rather think!
Yes, woe is *me*, I rather think!
Whate'er betide
You are his bride,
And I am left
Alone—bereft!
Yes, woe is *me*, I rather think!
Yes, woe is *me*, I rather think!

Ensemble—LIEUTENANT *and Chorus*

All frenzied with despair I rave,
The grave is cheated of its due.
Who is the misbegotten knave
Who hath contrived this deed to do?
Let search be made throughout the land,
Or {his / my} vindictive anger dread—
A thousand marks to him {he'll / I'll} hand
Who brings him here, alive or dead.

[*At the end,* ELSIE *faints in* FAIRFAX'S *arms; all the Yeomen and populace rush off the stage in different directions, to hunt for the fugitive, leaving only the Headsman on the stage, and* ELSIE *insensible in* FAIRFAX'S *arms.*

END OF ACT I

ACT II

SCENE.—*The same—Moonlight.*

Two days have elapsed.

Women and Yeomen of the Guard discovered.

Chorus

Night has spread her pall once more,
And the prisoner still is free:
Open is his dungeon door,
Useless now his dungeon key!
He has shaken off his yoke—
How, no mortal man can tell!
Shame on loutish jailer-folk—
Shame on sleepy sentinel!

Enter DAME CARRUTHERS *and* KATE

Solo—DAME CARRUTHERS

Warders are ye?
Whom do ye ward?
Bolt, bar, and key,
Shackle and cord,
Fetter and chain,
Dungeon of stone,
All are in vain—
Prisoner's flown!
Spite of ye all, he is free—he is free!
Whom do ye ward? Pretty warders are ye!

CHORUS OF WOMEN Pretty warders are ye, etc.

Chorus

YEOMEN Up and down, and in and out,
Here and there, and round about;
Every chamber, every house,
Every chink that holds a mouse,
Every crevice in the keep,
Where a beetle black could creep,
Every outlet, every drain,
Have we searched, but all in vain.

WOMEN Warders are ye?
Whom do ye ward? etc.

[*Exeunt all.*

Enter JACK POINT, *in low spirits, reading from a huge volume*

POINT [*reads*] "The Merrie Jestes of Hugh Ambrose. No. 7863. The Poor Wit and the Rich Councillor. A certayne poor wit, being an-hungered, did meet a well-fed councillor. 'Marry, fool,' quoth the councillor, 'whither away?' 'In truth,' said the poor wag, 'in that I have eaten naught these two dayes, I do wither away, and that right rapidly!' The councillor laughed hugely, and gave him a sausage." Humph! the councillor was easier to please than my new master the Lieutenant. I would like to take post under that councillor. Ah! 'tis but melancholy mumming when poor heart-broken, jilted Jack Point must needs turn to Hugh Ambrose for original light humour!

Enter WILFRED, *also in low spirits*

WIL. [*sighing*] Ah, Master Point!

POINT [*changing his manner*] Ha! friend jailer! Jailer that wast—jailer that never shalt be more! Jailer that jailed not, or that jailed, if jail he did, so unjailery that 'twas but jerry-jailing, or jailing in joke—though no joke to him who, by unjailerlike jailing, did so jeopardise his jailership. Come, take heart, smile, laugh, wink, twinkle, thou tormentor that tormentest none—thou racker that rackest not—thou pincher out of place—come, take heart, and be merry, as I am!—[*aside, dolefully*]—as I am!

WIL. Aye, it's well for thee to laugh. Thou hast a good post, and hast cause to be merry.

POINT [*bitterly*] Cause? Have we not all cause? Is not the world a big butt of humour, into which all who will may drive a gimlet? See, I am a salaried wit; and is there aught in nature more ridiculous? A poor, dull, heart-broken man, who must needs be merry, or he will be whipped; who must rejoice, lest he starve; who must jest you, jibe you, quip you, crank you, wrack you, riddle you, from hour to hour, from day to day, from year to year, lest he dwindle, perish, starve, pine, and die! Why, when there's naught else to laugh at, I laugh at myself till I ache for it!

WIL. Yet I have often thought that a jester's calling would suit me to a hair.

POINT Thee? Would suit *thee*, thou death's head and cross-bones?

WIL. Aye, I have a pretty wit—a light, airy, joysome wit, spiced with anecdotes of prison cells and the torture chamber. Oh, a very delicate wit! I have tried it on many a prisoner, and there have been some who smiled. Now it is not easy to make a prisoner smile. And it should not be difficult to be a good jester, seeing that thou art one.

POINT Difficult? Nothing easier. Nothing easier. Attend, and I will prove it to thee!

Song—POINT

Oh! a private buffoon is a light-hearted loon,
If you listen to popular rumour;
From the morn to the night he's so joyous and bright,
And he bubbles with wit and good humour!
He's so quaint and so terse, both in prose and in verse;
Yet though people forgive his transgression,
There are one or two rules that all family fools
Must observe, if they love their profession.
There are one or two rules,
Half a dozen, may be,
That all family fools,
Of whatever degree,
Must observe, if they love their profession.

If you wish to succeed as a jester, you'll need
To consider each person's auricular:
What is all right for B would quite scandalise C
(For C is so very particular);
And D may be dull, and E's very thick skull
Is as empty of brains as a ladle;
While F is F sharp, and will cry with a carp
That he's known your best joke from his cradle!
When your humour they flout,
You can't let yourself go;
And it *does* put you out
When a person says, "Oh,
I have known that old joke from my cradle!"

If your master is surly, from getting up early
(And tempers are short in the morning),

An inopportune joke is enough to provoke
  Him to give you, at once, a month's warning.
Then if you refrain, he is at you again,
  For he likes to get value for money;
He'll ask then and there, with an insolent stare,
  "If you know that you're paid to be funny?"
        It adds to the tasks
          Of a merryman's place,
        When your principal asks,
          With a scowl on his face,
    If you know that you're paid to be funny?

Comes a Bishop, maybe, or a solemn D.D.–
  Oh, beware of his anger provoking!
Better not pull his hair–don't stick pins in his chair;
  He don't understand practical joking.
If the jests that you crack have an orthodox smack,
  You may get a bland smile from these sages;
But should they, by chance, be imported from France,
  Half-a-crown is stopped out of your wages!
        It's a general rule,
          Though your zeal it may quench,
        If the family fool
          Tells a joke that's too French,
    Half-a-crown is stopped out of his wages!

Though your head it may rack with a bilious attack,
  And your senses with toothache you're losing,

Don't be mopy and flat—they don't fine you for that,
If you're properly quaint and amusing!
Though your wife ran away with a soldier that day,
And took with her your trifle of money;
Bless your heart, they don't mind—they're exceedingly kind—
They don't blame you—as long as you're funny!
It's a comfort to feel,
If your partner should flit,
Though *you* suffer a deal,
They don't mind it a bit—
They don't blame you—so long as you're funny!

POINT And so thou wouldst be a jester eh?

WIL. Aye!

POINT Now, listen! My sweetheart, Elsie Maynard, was secretly wed to this Fairfax half an hour ere he escaped.

WIL. She did well.

POINT She did nothing of the kind, so hold thy peace and perpend. Now, while he liveth she is dead to me and I to her, and so, my jibes and jokes notwithstanding, I am the saddest and the sorriest dog in England!

WIL. Thou art a very dull dog indeed.

POINT Now, if thou wilt swear that thou didst shoot this Fairfax while he was trying to swim across the river—it needs but the discharge of an arquebus on a dark night—and that he sank and was seen no more, I'll make thee the very Archbishop of jesters, and that in two days' time! Now, what sayest thou?

WIL. I am to lie?

POINT Heartily. But thy lie must be a lie of circumstance, which I will support with the testimony of eyes, ears, and tongue.

WIL. And thou wilt qualify me as a jester?

POINT As a jester among jesters. I will teach thee all my original songs, my self-constructed riddles, my own ingenious paradoxes; nay, more, I will reveal to thee the source whence I get them. Now, what sayest thou?

WIL. Why, if it be but a lie thou wantest of me, I hold it cheap enough, and I say yes, it is a bargain!

Duet—POINT and WILFRED

BOTH Hereupon we're both agreed,
All that we two
Do agree to
We'll secure by solemn deed,
To prevent all
Error mental.

POINT You on Elsie are to call
With a story
Grim and gory;

WIL. How this Fairfax died, and all
I declare to
You're to swear to.

BOTH Tell a tale of cock and bull,
Of convincing detail full
Tale tremendous,
Heaven defend us!
What a tale of cock and bull!

BOTH In return for {your / my} own part
{You are / I am} making
Undertaking
To instruct {me / you} in the art
(Art amazing,
Wonder raising)

POINT Of a jester, jesting free.
Proud position—
High ambition!

WIL. And a lively one I'll be,
Wag-a-wagging,
Never flagging!

BOTH Tell a tale of cock and bull, etc.

[*Exeunt together.*

Enter FAIRFAX

FAIR. Two days gone, and no news of poor Fairfax. The dolts! They seek him everywhere save within a dozen yards of his dungeon. So I am free! Free, but for the cursed haste with which I hurried headlong into the bonds of matrimony with—Heaven knows whom! As far as I remember, she should have been young; but even had not her face been concealed by her kerchief, I doubt whether, in my then plight, I should have taken much note of her. Free? Bah! The Tower bonds were but a thread of silk compared with these conjugal fetters which I, fool that I was, placed upon mine own hands. From the one I broke readily enough—how to break the other!

Ballad—FAIRFAX

Free from his fetters grim—
Free to depart;
Free both in life and limb—
In all but heart!
Bound to an unknown bride
For good and ill;
Ah, is not one so tied
A prisoner still?

Free, yet in fetters held
Till his last hour,
Gyves that no smith can weld,
No rust devour!
Although a monarch's hand
Had set him free,
Of all the captive band
The saddest he!

Enter MERYLL

FAIR. Well, Sergeant Meryll, and how fares thy pretty charge, Elsie Maynard?

MER. Well enough, sir. She is quite strong again, and leaves us to-night.

FAIR. Thanks to Dame Carruthers' kind nursing, eh?

MER. Aye, deuce take the old witch! Ah, 'twas but a sorry trick you played me, sir, to bring the fainting girl to me. It gave the old lady an excuse for taking up her quarters in my house, and for the last two years I've shunned her like the plague. Another day of it and she would have married me! [*Enter* DAME CARRUTHERS *and* KATE] Good Lord, here she is again! I'll e'en go. [*Going*]

DAME Nay, Sergeant Meryll, don't go. I have something of grave import to say to thee.

MER. [*aside*] It's coming.

FAIR. [*laughing*] I'faith, I think I'm not wanted here. [*Going*]

DAME Nay, Master Leonard, I've naught to say to thy father that his son may not hear.

FAIR. [*aside*] True. I'm one of the family; I had forgotten!

DAME 'Tis about this Elsie Maynard. A pretty girl, Master Leonard.

FAIR. Aye, fair as a peach blossom—what then?

DAME She hath a liking for thee, or I mistake not.

FAIR. With all my heart. She's as dainty a little maid as you'll find in a midsummer day's march.

DAME Then be warned in time, and give not thy heart to her. Oh, *I* know what it is to give my heart to one who will have none of it!

MER. [*aside*] Aye, *she* knows all about that. [*Aloud*] And why is my boy to take heed of her? She's a good girl, Dame Carruthers.

DAME Good enough, for aught I know. But she's no girl. She's a married woman.

MER. A married woman! Tush, old lady—she's promised to Jack Point, the Lieutenant's new jester.

DAME Tush in thy teeth, old man! As my niece Kate sat by her bedside to-day, this Elsie slept, and as she slept she moaned and groaned, and turned this way and that way—and, "How shall I marry one I have never seen?" quoth she—then, "An hundred crowns!" quoth she—then, "Is it certain he will die in an hour?" quoth she—then, "I love him not, and yet I am his wife," quoth she! Is it not so, Kate?

KATE Aye, aunt, 'tis even so.

FAIR. Art thou sure of all this?

KATE Aye, sir, for I wrote it all down on my tablets.

DAME Now, mark my words: it was of this Fairfax she spake, and he is her husband, or I'll swallow my kirtle!

MER. [*aside*] Is it true, sir?

FAIR. [*aside to* MERYLL] True? Why, the girl was raving! [*Aloud*] Why should she marry a man who had but an hour to live?

DAME Marry? There be those who would marry but for a minute, rather than die old maids.

MER. [*aside*] Aye, I know one of them!

Quartet—FAIRFAX, SERGEANT MERYLL, DAME CARRUTHERS, and KATE

Strange adventure! Maiden wedded
To a groom she's never seen—
Never, never, never seen!
Groom about to be beheaded,
In an hour on Tower Green!
Tower, Tower, Tower Green!
Groom in dreary dungeon lying,
Groom as good as dead, or dying,
For a pretty maiden sighing—
Pretty maid of seventeen!
Seven—seven—seventeen!

Strange adventure that we're trolling:
Modest maid and gallant groom—
Gallant, gallant, gallant groom!—

While the funeral bell is tolling,
Tolling, tolling, Bim-a-boom!
Bim-a, Bim-a, Bim-a-boom!
Modest maiden will not tarry;
Though but sixteen years she carry,
She must marry, she must marry,
Though the altar be a tomb—
Tower—Tower—Tower tomb!

[*Exeunt* DAME CARRUTHERS, MERYLL, *and* KATE.

FAIR. So my mysterious bride is no other than this winsome Elsie! By my hand, 'tis no such ill plunge in Fortune's lucky bag! I might have fared worse with my eyes open! But she comes. Now to test her principles. 'Tis not every husband who has a chance of wooing his own wife!

Enter ELSIE

FAIR. Mistress Elsie!

ELSIE Master Leonard!

FAIR. So thou leavest us to-night?

ELSIE Yes, Master Leonard. I have been kindly tended, and I almost fear I am loth to go.

FAIR. And this Fairfax. Wast thou glad when he escaped?

ELSIE Why, truly, Master Leonard, it is a sad thing that a young and gallant gentleman should die in the very fullness of his life.

FAIR. Then when thou didst faint in my arms, it was for joy at his safety?

ELSIE It may be so. I was highly wrought, Master Leonard, and I am but a girl, and so, when I am highly wrought, I faint.

FAIR. Now, dost thou know, I am consumed with a parlous jealousy?

ELSIE Thou? And of whom?

FAIR. Why, of this Fairfax, surely!

ELSIE Of Colonel Fairfax?

FAIR. Aye. Shall I be frank with thee? Elsie—I love thee, ardently, passionately! [ELSIE *alarmed and surprised*] Elsie, I have loved thee these two days—which is a long time—and I would fain join my life to thine!

ELSIE Master Leonard! Thou art jesting!

FAIR. Jesting? May I shrivel into raisins if I jest! I love thee with a love that is a fever—with a love that is a frenzy—with a love that eateth up my heart! What sayest thou? Thou wilt not let my heart be eaten up?

ELSIE [*aside*] Oh, mercy! What am I to say?

FAIR. Dost thou love me, or hast thou been insensible these two days?

ELSIE I love all brave men.

FAIR. Nay, there is love in excess. I thank heaven there are many brave men in England; but if thou lovest them all, I withdraw my thanks.

Elsie I love the bravest best. But, sir, I may not listen—I am not free—I—I am a wife!

Fair. Thou a wife? Whose? His name? His hours are numbered—nay, his grave is dug and his epitaph set up! Come, his name?

Elsie Oh, sir! keep my secret—it is the only barrier that Fate could set up between us. My husband is none other than Colonel Fairfax!

Fair. The greatest villain unhung! The most ill-favoured, ill-mannered, ill-natured, ill-omened, ill-tempered dog in Christendom!

Elsie It is very like. He is naught to me—for I never saw him. I was blindfolded, and he was to have died within the hour; and he did not die—and I am wedded to him, and my heart is broken!

Fair. He was to have died, and he did *not* die? The scoundrel! The perjured, traitorous villain! Thou shouldst have insisted on his dying first, to make sure. 'Tis the only way with these Fairfaxes.

Elsie I now wish I had!

Fair [*aside*] Bloodthirsty little maiden! [*Aloud*] A fig for this Fairfax! Be mine—he will never know—he dares not show himself; and if he dare, what art thou to him? Fly with me, Elsie—we will be married to-morrow, and thou shalt be the happiest wife in England!

Elsie Master Leonard! I am amazed! Is it thus that brave soldiers speak to poor girls? Oh! for shame, for shame! I am wed—not the less because I love not my husband. I am a wife, sir, and I have a duty, and—oh, sir!—thy words terrify me—they are not honest—they are wicked words, and unworthy thy great and brave heart! Oh, shame upon thee! shame upon thee!

Fair. Nay, Elsie, I did but jest. I spake but to try thee—— [*Shot heard*]

Enter Meryll *hastily*

Mer. [*recit.*] Hark! What was that, sir?
Fair. Why, an arquebus—
Fired from the wharf, unless I much mistake.
Mer. Strange—and at such an hour! What can it mean?

Enter Chorus

Chorus

Now what can that have been—
A shot so late at night,
Enough to cause a fright!
What can the portent mean?

Are foemen in the land?
Is London to be wrecked?
What are we to expect?

What danger is at hand?
Let us understand
What danger is at hand!

LIEUTENANT *enters, also* POINT *and* WILFRED

Recitative

LIEUT. Who fired that shot? At once the truth declare!
WIL. My lord, 'twas I—to rashly judge forbear!
POINT My lord, 'twas he—to rashly judge forbear!

Duet and Chorus—WILFRED and POINT

WIL. Like a ghost his vigil keeping—
POINT Or a spectre all-appalling—
WIL. I beheld a figure creeping—
POINT I should rather call it crawling—
WIL. He was creeping—
POINT He was crawling—
WIL. He was creeping, creeping—
POINT Crawling!
WIL. He was creeping—
POINT He was crawling—
WIL. He was creeping, creeping—
POINT Crawling!

WIL. Not a moment's hesitation—
I myself upon him flung,
With a hurried exclamation
To his draperies I hung;
Then we closed with one another
In a rough-and-tumble smother;
Colonel Fairfax and no other
Was the man to whom I clung!

ALL Colonel Fairfax and no other
Was the man to whom he clung!

WIL. After mighty tug and tussle—
POINT It resembled more a struggle—
WIL. He, by dint of stronger muscle—
POINT Or by some infernal juggle—
WIL. From my clutches quickly sliding—
POINT I should rather call it slipping—

WIL. With a view, no doubt, of hiding–
POINT Or escaping to the shipping–
WIL. With a gasp, and with a quiver–
POINT I'd describe it as a shiver–
WIL. Down he dived into the river,
And, alas, I cannot swim.

ALL It's enough to make one shiver–
With a gasp and with a quiver,
Down he dived into the river;
It was very brave of him!

WIL. Ingenuity is catching;
With the view my king of pleasing,
Arquebus from sentry snatching–
POINT I should rather call it seizing–
WIL. With an ounce or two of lead
I despatched him through the head!

ALL With an ounce or two of lead
He despatched him through the head!

WIL. I discharged it without winking,
Little time I lost in thinking,
Like a stone I saw him sinking–

POINT I should say a lump of lead.

ALL He discharged it without winking,
Little time he lost in thinking.

WIL. Like a stone I saw him sinking–

POINT I should say a lump of lead.

WIL. Like a stone, my boy, I said–

POINT Like a heavy lump of lead.

WIL. Anyhow, the man is dead,
Whether stone or lump of lead!

ALL Anyhow, the man is dead,
Whether stone or lump of lead!

Arquebus from sentry seizing,
With the view his king of pleasing,
Wilfred shot him through the head,
And he's very, very dead.
And it matters very little whether stone or lump of lead;
It is very, very certain that he's very, very dead!

Recitative—LIEUTENANT

The river must be dragged—no time be lost;
The body must be found, at any cost.
To this attend without undue delay;
So set to work with what despatch ye may! [*Exit.*

ALL Yes, yes,
We'll set to work with what despatch we may!

[*Four men raise* WILFRED, *and carry him off on their shoulders.*

Chorus

Hail the valiant fellow who
Did this deed of derring-do!
Honours wait on such an one;
By my head, 'twas bravely done!
Now, by my head, 'twas bravely done!

[*Exeunt all but* ELSIE, POINT, FAIRFAX, *and* PHŒBE.

POINT [*to* ELSIE, *who is weeping*] Nay, sweetheart, be comforted. This Fairfax was but a pestilent fellow, and, as he had to die, he might as well die thus as any other way. 'Twas a good death.

ELSIE Still, he was my husband, and had he not been, he was nevertheless a living man, and now he is dead; and so, by your leave, my tears may flow unchidden, Master Point.

FAIR. And thou didst see all this?

POINT Aye, with both eyes at once—this and that. The testimony of one eye is naught—he may lie. But when it is corroborated by the other, it is good evidence that none may gainsay. Here are both present in court, ready to swear to him!

PHŒ. But art thou sure it was Colonel Fairfax? Saw you his face?

POINT Aye, and a plaguey ill-favoured face too. A very hang-dog face —a felon face—a face to fright the headsman himself, and make him strike awry. Oh, a plaguey, bad face, take my word for it. [PHŒBE *and* FAIRFAX *laugh*] How they laugh! 'Tis ever thus with simple folk—an accepted wit has but to say "Pass the mustard," and they roar their ribs out!

FAIR. [*aside*] If ever I come to life again, thou shalt pay for this, Master Point!

POINT Now, Elsie, thou art free to choose again, so behold me: I am young and well-favoured. I have a pretty wit. I can jest you, jibe you, quip you, crank you, wrack you, riddle you——

FAIR. Tush, man, thou knowest not how to woo. 'Tis not to be done with time-worn jests and thread-bare sophistries; with quips, conundrums, rhymes, and paradoxes. 'Tis an art in itself, and must be studied gravely and conscientiously.

Trio—ELSIE, PHŒBE, and FAIRFAX

FAIR.
A man who would woo a fair maid
Should 'prentice himself to the trade,
And study all day,
In methodical way,
How to flatter, cajole, and persuade;

He should 'prentice himself at fourteen,
And practise from morning to e'en;
And when he's of age,
If he will, I'll engage,
He may capture the heart of a queen!

ALL
It is purely a matter of skill,
Which all may attain if they will:
But every Jack,
He must study the knack
If he wants to make sure of his Jill!

ELSIE
If he's made the best use of his time,
His twig he'll so carefully lime
    That every bird
    Will come down at his word,
Whatever its plumage or clime.

He must learn that the thrill of a touch
May mean little, or nothing, or much:
    It's an instrument rare,
    To be handled with care,
And ought to be treated as such.

ALL
It is purely a matter of skill, etc.

PHŒ.
Then a glance may be timid or free,
It will vary in mighty degree,
    From an impudent stare
    To a look of despair
That no maid without pity can see!
And a glance of despair is no guide–
It may have its ridiculous side;
    It may draw you a tear
    Or a box on the ear;
You can never be sure till you've tried!

ALL
It is purely a matter of skill, etc.

FAIR. [*aside to* POINT] Now, listen to me–'tis done thus–[*aloud*]–Mistress Elsie, there is one here who, as thou knowest, loves thee right well!

POINT [*aside*] That he does–right well!

FAIR. He is but a man of poor estate, but he hath a loving, honest heart. He will be a true and trusty husband to thee, and if thou wilt be his wife, thou shalt lie curled up in his heart, like a little squirrel in its nest!

POINT [*aside*] 'Tis a pretty figure. A maggot in a nut lies closer, but a squirrel will do.

FAIR. He knoweth that thou wast a wife–an unloved and unloving wife, and his poor heart was near to breaking. But now that thine unloving husband is dead, and thou art free, he would fain pray that thou wouldst hearken unto him, and give him hope that thou wouldst one day be his!

PHŒ. [*alarmed*] He presses her hands–and he whispers in her ear! Ods bodikins, what does it mean?

FAIR. Now, sweetheart, tell me–wilt thou be this poor good fellow's wife?

ELSIE If the good, brave man–*is* he a brave man?

FAIR. So men say.

POINT [*aside*] That's not true, but let it pass.

ELSIE If the brave man will be content with a poor, penniless, untaught maid——

POINT [*aside*] Widow—but let *that* pass.

ELSIE I will be his true and loving wife, and that with my heart of hearts!

FAIR. My own dear love! [*Embracing her*]

PHŒ. [*in great agitation*] Why, what's all this? Brother—brother—it is not seemly!

POINT. [*also alarmed, aside*] Oh, I can't let *that* pass! [*Aloud*] Hold, enough, Master Leonard! An advocate should have his fee, but methinks thou art over-paying thyself!

FAIR. Nay, that is for Elsie to say. I promised thee I would show thee how to woo, and herein lies the proof of the virtue of my teaching. Go thou, and apply it elsewhere! [PHŒBE *bursts into tears*]

Quartet—ELSIE, PHŒBE, FAIRFAX, and POINT

ELSIE and FAIR.

When a wooer
  Goes a-wooing,
Naught is truer
  Than his joy.
Maiden hushing
  All his suing—
Boldly blushing—
  Bravely coy!

ALL

Oh, the happy days of doing!
Oh, the sighing and the suing!
When a wooer goes a-wooing,
  Oh, the sweets that never cloy!

PHŒ. [*weeping*]

When a brother
  Leaves his sister
For another,
  Sister weeps.
Tears that trickle,
  Tears that blister—
'Tis but mickle
  Sister reaps!

ALL

Oh, the doing and undoing,
Oh, the sighing and the suing,
When a brother goes a-wooing,
  And a sobbing sister weeps!

POINT

When a jester
Is outwitted,
Feelings fester,
Heart is lead!
Food for fishes
Only fitted,
Jester wishes
He was dead!

ALL

Oh, the doing and undoing,
Oh, the sighing and the suing,
When a jester goes a-wooing,
And he wishes he was dead!

[*Exeunt all but* PHŒBE, *who remains weeping.*

PHŒ. And I helped that man to escape, and I've kept his secret, and pretended that I was his dearly loving sister, and done everything I could think of to make folk believe I *was* his loving sister, and this is his gratitude! Before I pretend to be sister to anybody again, I'll turn nun, and be sister to everybody—one as much as another!

Enter WILFRED

WIL. In tears, eh? What a plague art thou grizzling for now?

PHŒ. Why am I grizzling? Thou hast often wept for jealousy—well, 'tis for jealousy I weep now. Aye, yellow, bilious, jaundiced jealousy. So make the most of that, Master Wilfred.

WIL. But I have never given thee cause for jealousy. The Lieutenant's cook-maid and I are but the merest gossips!

PHŒ. Jealous of thee! Bah! I'm jealous of no craven cock-on-a-hill, who crows about what he'd do an he dared! I am jealous of another and a better man than thou—set that down, Master Wilfred. And he is to marry Elsie Maynard, the little pale fool—set that down, Master Wilfred—and my heart is wellnigh broken! There, thou hast it all! Make the most of it!

WIL. The man thou lovest is to marry Elsie Maynard? Why, that is no other than thy brother, Leonard Meryll!

PHŒ. [*aside*] Oh, mercy! what have I said?

WIL. Why, what manner of brother is this, thou lying little jade? Speak! Who is this man whom thou hast called brother, and fondled, and coddled, and kissed!—with my connivance, too! Oh Lord! with my connivance! Ha! should it be this Fairfax! [PHŒBE *starts*] It is! It is this accursed Fairfax! It's Fairfax! Fairfax, who——

PHŒ. Whom thou hast just shot through the head, and who lies at the bottom of the river!

WIL. A—I—I may have been mistaken. We are but fallible mortals, the best of us. But I'll make sure—I'll make sure. [*Going*]

PHŒ. Stay—one word. I think it cannot be Fairfax—mind, I say I *think*—because thou hast just slain Fairfax. But whether he be Fairfax or no Fairfax, he is to marry Elsie—and—and—as thou hast shot him through the head, and he is dead, be content with that, and I will be thy wife!

WIL. Is that sure?

PHŒ. Aye, sure enough, for there's no help for it! Thou art a very brute —but even brutes must marry, I suppose.

WIL. My beloved! [*Embraces her*]

PHŒ [*aside*] Ugh!

Enter LEONARD, *hastily*

LEON. Phœbe, rejoice, for I bring glad tidings. Colonel Fairfax's reprieve was signed two days since, but it was foully and maliciously kept back by Secretary Poltwhistle, who designed that it should arrive after the Colonel's death. It hath just come to hand, and it is now in the Lieutenant's possession!

PHŒ. Then the Colonel is free? Oh, kiss me, kiss me, my dear! Kiss me, again, and again!

WIL. [*dancing with fury*] Ods bobs, death o' my life! Art thou mad? Am *I* mad? Are we *all* mad?

PHŒ. Oh, my dear—my dear, I'm wellnigh crazed with joy! [*Kissing* LEONARD]

WIL. Come away from him, thou hussy—thou jade—thou kissing, clinging cockatrice! And as for thee, sir, devil take thee, I'll rip thee like a herring for this! I'll skin thee for it! I'll cleave thee to the chine! I'll—oh! Phœbe! Phœbe! Who is this man?

PHŒ. Peace, fool. He is my brother!

WIL. Another brother! Are there any more of them? Produce them all at once, and let me know the worst!

PHŒ. This is the real Leonard, dolt; the other was but his substitute. The *real* Leonard, I say—my father's own son.

WIL. How do I know this? Has he "brother" writ large on his brow? I mistrust thy brothers! Thou art but a false jade! [*Exit* LEONARD.

PHŒ. Now, Wilfred, be just. Truly I did deceive thee before—but it was to save a precious life—and to save it, not for me, but for another. They are to be wed this very day. Is not this enough for thee? Come—I am thy Phœbe—thy very own—and we will be wed in a year—or two—or three, at the most. Is not that enough for thee?

Enter MERYLL, *excitedly, followed by* DAME CARRUTHERS, *who listens, unobserved.*

MER. Phœbe, hast thou heard the brave news?

PHŒ. [*still in* WILFRED'S *arms*] Aye, father.

MER. I'm nigh mad with joy! [*Seeing* WILFRED] Why, what's all this?

PHŒ. Oh, father, he discovered our secret through my folly, and the price of his silence is——

WIL. Phœbe's heart.

PHŒ. Oh dear, no—Phœbe's hand.

WIL. It's the same thing!

PHŒ. *Is* it? [*Exeunt* WILFRED *and* PHŒBE.

MER. [*looking after them*] 'Tis pity, but the Colonel had to be saved at any cost, and as thy folly revealed our secret, thy folly must e'en suffer for it! [DAME CARRUTHERS *comes down*] Dame Carruthers!

DAME. So this is a plot to shield this arch-fiend, and I have detected it. A word from me, and three heads besides his would roll from their shoulders!

MER. Nay, Colonel Fairfax is reprieved. [*Aside*] Yet, if my complicity in his escape were known! Plague on the old meddler! There's nothing for it—[*aloud*]—Hush, pretty one! Such bloodthirsty words ill become those cherry lips! [*Aside*] Ugh!

DAME [*bashfully*] Sergeant Meryll!

MER. Why, look ye, chuck—for many a month I've—I've thought to myself—"There's snug love saving up in that middle-aged bosom for some one, and why not for thee—that's me—so take heart and tell her—that's thee—that thou—that's me—lovest her—thee—and—and—well, I'm a miserable old man, and I've done it—and that's me!" But not a word about Fairfax! The price of thy silence is——

DAME Meryll's heart?

MER. No, Meryll's *hand.*

DAME. It's the same thing!

MER. *Is* it?

Duet—DAME CARRUTHERS and SERGEANT MERYLL

DAME

Rapture, rapture
When love's votary,
Flushed with capture,
Seeks the notary,
Joy and jollity
Then is polity;
Reigns frivolity!
Rapture, rapture!

MER.

Doleful, doleful!
When humanity
With its soul full
Of satanity,
Courting privity,
Down declivity
Seeks captivity!
Doleful, doleful!

DAME Joyful, joyful!
When virginity
Seeks, all coyful,
Man's affinity;
Fate all flowery,
Bright and bowery,
Is her dowery!
Joyful, joyful!

MER. Ghastly, ghastly!
When man, sorrowful,
Firstly, lastly,
Of to-morrow full,
After tarrying,
Yields to harrying–
Goes a-marrying.
Ghastly, ghastly!

BOTH Rapture, etc.

[*Exeunt* DAME *and* MERYLL.

FINALE

Enter Yeomen and Women

Chorus of Women

[ELEGIACS]

Comes the pretty young bride, a-blushing, timidly shrinking–
Set all thy fears aside–cheerily, pretty young bride! 2 1-2 ms
Brave is the youth to whom thy lot thou art willingly linking!
Flower of valour is he–loving as loving can be!
Brightly thy summer is shining,
Fair as the dawn of the day;
Take him, be true to him–
Tender his due to him–
Honour him, love and obey!

Enter DAME, PHŒBE, *and* ELSIE *as Bride*

Trio–PHŒBE, ELSIE, and DAME CARRUTHERS

'Tis said that joy in full perfection
Comes only once to womankind–
That, other times, on close inspection,
Some lurking bitter we shall find.

If this be so, and men say truly,
My day of joy has broken duly.
With happiness {my / her} soul is cloyed—
This is {my / her} joy-day unalloyed!

ALL — Yes, yes, with happiness her soul is cloyed!
This is her joy-day unalloyed!

Flourish. Enter LIEUTENANT

LIEUT. — Hold, pretty one! I bring to thee
News—good or ill, it is for thee to say.
Thy husband lives—and he is free,
And comes to claim his bride this very day!

ELSIE — No! no! recall those words—it cannot be!

Ensemble

KATE AND CHORUS

Oh, day of terror! Day of tears!
Who is the man who, in his pride,
Claims thee as his bride?

DAME CARRUTHERS and PHŒBE

Oh, day of terror! Day of tears!
The man to whom thou art allied
Appears to claim thee as his bride.

LIEUT., MERYLL, and WILFRED

Come, dry these unbecoming tears,
Most joyful tidings greet thine ears,
The man to whom thou art allied
Appears to claim thee as his bride.

ELSIE

Oh, Leonard, come thou to my side,
And claim me as thy loving bride!
Oh, day of terror! Day of tears!

Flourish. Enter COLONEL FAIRFAX, *handsomely dressed, and attended by other Gentlemen*

FAIR. [*sternly*] All thought of Leonard Meryll set aside.
Thou art mine own! I claim thee as my bride.

ALL — Thou art his own! Alas! he claims thee as his bride.

ELSIE — A suppliant at thy feet I fall;
Thine heart will yield to pity's call!

FAIR. — Mine is a heart of massive rock,
Unmoved by sentimental shock!

ALL — Thy husband he!

ELSIE [*aside*] Leonard, my loved one—come to me.
They bear me hence away!
But though they take me far from thee,
My heart is thine for aye!
My bruised heart,
My broken heart,
Is thine, my own, for aye!

[*To* FAIRFAX] Sir, I obey!
I am thy bride;
But ere the fatal hour
I said the say
That placed me in thy power
Would I had died!
Sir, I obey!
I am thy bride!

[*Looks up and recognises* FAIRFAX] Leonard!

FAIR. My own!

ELSIE Ah! [*Embrace*]

ELSIE and FAIR. With happiness my soul is cloyed,
This is our joy-day unalloyed!

ALL Yes, yes!
With happiness their souls are cloyed,
This is their joy-day unalloyed!

Enter JACK POINT

POINT Oh, thoughtless crew!
Ye know not what ye do!
Attend to me, and shed a tear or two—
For I have a song to sing, O!

ALL Sing me your song, O!

POINT It is sung to the moon
By a love-lorn loon,
Who fled from the mocking throng, O!
It's the song of a merryman, moping mum,
Whose soul was sad, and whose glance was glum,
Who sipped no sup, and who craved no crumb,
As he sighed for the love of a ladye!

ALL
Heighdy! heighdy!
Misery me, lackadaydee!
He sipped no sup, and he craved no crumb,
As he sighed for the love of a ladye!

ELSIE
I have a song to sing, O!

ALL
What is your song, O?

ELSIE
It is sung with the ring
Of the songs maids sing
Who love with a love life-long, O!
It's the song of a merrymaid, nestling near,
Who loved her lord—but who dropped a tear
At the moan of the merryman, moping mum,
Whose soul was sad, and whose glance was glum,
Who sipped no sup, and who craved no crumb,
As he sighed for the love of a ladye!

ALL
Heighdy! heighdy!
Misery me, lackadaydee!
He sipped no sup, and he craved no crumb,
As he sighed for the love of a ladye!

[FAIRFAX *embraces* ELSIE *as* POINT *falls insensible at their feet.*

CURTAIN

THE GONDOLIERS

OR

THE KING OF BARATARIA

DRAMATIS PERSONAE

THE DUKE OF PLAZA-TORO [*a Grandee of Spain*]
LUIZ [*his Attendant*]
DON ALHAMBRA DEL BOLERO [*the Grand Inquisitor*]
MARCO PALMIERI
GIUSEPPE PALMIERI
ANTONIO
FRANCESCO
GIORGIO
ANNIBALE
} [*Venetian Gondoliers*]
THE DUCHESS OF PLAZA-TORO
CASILDA [*her Daughter*]
GIANETTA
TESSA
FIAMETTA
VITTORIA
GIULIA
} [*Contadine*]
INEZ [*the King's Foster-Mother*]
Chorus of Gondoliers and Contadine, Men-at-Arms, Heralds and Pages

ACT I

THE PIAZZETTA, VENICE

ACT II

PAVILION IN THE PALACE OF BARATARIA

[*An interval of three months is supposed to elapse between Acts I and II*]

Date, 1750

First produced at the Savoy Theatre on December 7, 1889

THE GONDOLIERS

OR

THE KING OF BARATARIA

ACT I

SCENE.—*The Piazzetta, Venice. The Ducal Palace on the right.*

FIAMETTA, GIULIA, VITTORIA, *and other Contadine discovered, each tying a bouquet of roses.*

Chorus of Contadine

List and learn, ye dainty roses,
Roses white and roses red,
Why we bind you into posies
Ere your morning bloom has fled.
By a law of maiden's making,
Accents of a heart that's aching,
Even though that heart be breaking,
Should by maiden be unsaid:
Though they love with love exceeding,
They must seem to be unheeding—
Go ye then and do their pleading,
Roses white and roses red!

FIAMETTA

Two there are for whom in duty,
Every maid in Venice sighs—
Two so peerless in their beauty
That they shame the summer skies.
We have hearts for them, in plenty,
They have hearts, but all too few,
We, alas, are four-and-twenty!
They, alas, are only two!
We, alas!

CHORUS Alas!

FIA. Are four-and-twenty,
They, alas!

CHORUS Alas!

FIA. Are only two.

CHORUS They, alas, are only two, alas!
Now ye know, ye dainty roses,
Why we bind you into posies,
Ere your morning bloom has fled,
Roses white and roses red!

[*During this chorus* ANTONIO, FRANCESCO, GIORGIO, *and other Gondoliers have entered unobserved by the Girls—at first two, then two more, then four, then half a dozen, then the remainder of the Chorus.*

Soli

FRANC. Good morrow, pretty maids; for whom prepare ye
These floral tributes extraordinary?

FIA. For Marco and Giuseppe Palmieri,
The pink and flower of all the Gondolieri.

GIU. They're coming here, as we have heard but lately,
To choose two brides from us who sit sedately.

ANT. Do all you maidens love them?

ALL Passionately!

ANT. These gondoliers are to be envied greatly!

GIOR. But what of us, who one and all adore you?
Have pity on our passion, we implore you!

FIA. These gentlemen must make their choice before you;

VIT. In the meantime we tacitly ignore you.

GIU. When they have chosen two that leaves you plenty—
Two dozen we, and ye are four-and-twenty.

FIA. and VIT. Till then, enjoy your *dolce far niente*.

ANT. With pleasure, nobody *contradicente!*

Song—Antonio and Chorus

For the merriest fellows are we, tra la,
That ply on the emerald sea, tra la;
With loving and laughing,
And quipping and quaffing,
We're happy as happy can be, tra la—
As happy as happy can be!

With sorrow we've nothing to do, tra la,
And care is a thing to pooh-pooh, tra la;
And Jealousy yellow,
Unfortunate fellow,
We drown in the shimmering blue, tra la—
We drown in the shimmering blue!

Fia. [*looking off*] See, see, at last they come to make their choice—
Let us acclaim them with united voice.

[Marco *and* Giuseppe *appear in gondola at back.*

Chorus [*Girls*] Hail, hail! gallant gondolieri, ben venuti!
Accept our love, our homage, and our duty.

[Marco *and* Giuseppe *jump ashore—the Girls salute them.*

Duet—Marco *and* Giuseppe, *with Chorus of Girls*

Mar. and Giu. Buon' giorno, signorine!

Girls Gondolieri carissimi!
Siamo contadine!

Mar. and Giu. [*bowing*] Servitori umilissimi!
Per chi questi fiori—
Questi fiori bellissimi?

Girls Per voi, bei signori
O eccellentissimi!

[*The Girls present their bouquets to* Marco *and* Giuseppe, *who are overwhelmed with them, and carry them with difficulty.*

Mar. and Giu. [*their arms full of flowers*] O ciel'!

Girls Buon' giorno, cavalieri!

MAR. and GIU. [*deprecatingly*]	Siamo gondolieri.
[*To* FIA. *and* VIT.]	Signorina, io t' amo!
GIRLS [*deprecatingly*]	Contadine siamo.
MAR. and GIU.	Signorine!
GIRLS [*deprecatingly*]	Contadine!
[*Curtseying to* MAR. *and* GIU.]	Cavalieri.
MAR. and GIU. [*deprecatingly*]	Gondolieri!
	Poveri gondolieri!

CHORUS Buon' giorno, signorine, etc.

Duet—MARCO and GIUSEPPE

We're called *gondolieri*,
But that's a vagary,
It's quite honorary
The trade that we ply.
For gallantry noted
Since we were short-coated,
To beauty devoted,
Giuseppe / Are Marco } and I;

When morning is breaking,
Our couches forsaking,
To greet their awaking
With carols we come,
At summer day's nooning,
When weary lagooning,
Our mandolins tuning,
We lazily thrum.

When vespers are ringing,
To hope ever clinging,
With songs of our singing
A vigil we keep,
When daylight is fading,
Enwrapt in night's shading,
With soft serenading
We sing them to sleep.

We're called *gondolieri*, etc.

Recitative—MARCO and GIUSEPPE

MAR. And now to choose our brides!

GIU. As all are young and fair,
And amiable besides,

BOTH We really do not care
A preference to declare.

MAR. A bias to disclose
Would be indelicate—

GIU. And therefore we propose
To let impartial Fate
Select for us a mate!

ALL Viva!

GIRLS A bias to disclose
Would be indelicate—

MEN But how do they propose
To let impartial Fate
Select for them a mate?

GIU. These handkerchiefs upon our eyes be good enough to bind,

MAR. And take good care that both of us are absolutely blind;

BOTH Then turn us round—and we, with all convenient despatch,
Will undertake to marry any two of you we catch!

ALL Viva!

They undertake to marry any two of {us they catch! / them they catch!}

[*The girls prepare to bind their eyes as directed.*

FIA. [*to* MARCO] Are you peeping?
Can you see me?

MAR. Dark I'm keeping,
Dark and dreamy!

[MARCO *slyly lifts bandage*]

VIT. [*to* GIUSEPPE] If you're blinded
Truly, say so.

GIU. All right-minded
Players play so! [*slyly lifts bandage*]

FIA. [*detecting* MARCO] Conduct shady!
They are cheating!
Surely they de-
Serve a beating! [*replaces bandage*]

VIT. [*detecting* GIUSEPPE] This too much is;
Maidens mocking–
Conduct such is
Truly shocking! [*replaces bandage*]

ALL You can spy, sir!
Shut your eye, sir!
You may use it by and by, sir!
You can see, sir!
Don't tell me, sir!
That will do–now let it be, sir!

CHORUS OF GIRLS My papa he keeps three horses,
Black, and white, and dapple grey, sir;
Turn three times, then take your courses,
Catch whichever girl you may, sir!

CHORUS OF MEN My papa, etc.

[MARCO *and* GIUSEPPE *turn round, as directed, and try to catch the girls. Business of blind-man's buff. Eventually* MARCO *catches* GIANETTA, *and* GIUSEPPE *catches* TESSA. *The two girls try to escape, but in vain. The two men pass their hands over the girls' faces to discover their identity.*

GIU. I've at length achieved a capture!
[*Guessing*] This is Tessa! [*removes bandage*] Rapture, rapture!
MAR. [*guessing*] To me Gianetta fate has granted!
[*removes bandage*]
Just the very girl I wanted!
GIU. [*politely to* MAR.] If you'd rather change——
TESS. My goodness!
This indeed is simple rudeness.

MAR. [*politely to* GIU.] I've no preference whatever–

GIA. Listen to him! Well, I never!
[*Each man kisses each girl*]

GIA. Thank you, gallant *gondolieri!*
In a set and formal measure
It is scarcely necessary
To express our pleasure.
Each of us to prove a treasure,
Conjugal and monetary,
Gladly will devote our leisure,
Gay and gallant *gondolieri.*
Tra, la, la, la, la, la, etc.

TESS. Gay and gallant *gondolieri,*
Take us both and hold us tightly,
You have luck extraordinary;
We might both have been unsightly!
If we judge your conduct rightly,
'Twas a choice involuntary;
Still we thank you most politely,
Gay and gallant *gondolieri!*
Tra, la, la, la, la, la, etc.

CHORUS OF GIRLS Thank you, gallant *gondolieri;*
In a set and formal measure,
It is scarcely necessary
To express our pleasure.
Each of us to prove a treasure
Gladly will devote our leisure,
Gay and gallant *gondolieri!*
Tra, la, la, la, la, la, etc.

ALL Fate in this has put his finger—
Let us bow to Fate's decree,
Then no longer let us linger,
To the altar hurry we!

[*They all dance off two and two*—GIANETTA *with* MARCO, TESSA *with* GIUSEPPE.

Flourish. A gondola arrives at the Piazzetta steps, from which enter the DUKE OF PLAZA-TORO, *the* DUCHESS, *their daughter* CASILDA, *and their attendant* LUIZ, *who carries a drum. All are dressed in pompous but old and faded clothes.*

Entrance of DUKE, DUCHESS, CASILDA, *and* LUIZ

DUKE From the sunny Spanish shore,
The Duke of Plaza-Tor!–

DUCH. And His Grace's Duchess true–

CAS. And His Grace's daughter, too–

LUIZ. And His Grace's private drum
To Venetia's shores have come:

ALL If ever, ever, ever
They get back to Spain,
They will never, never, never
Cross the sea again–

DUKE Neither that Grandee from the Spanish shore,
The noble Duke of Plaza Tor'–

DUCH. Nor His Grace's Duchess, staunch and true–

CAS. You may add, His Grace's daughter, too–

LUIZ. Nor His Grace's own particular drum
To Venetia's shores will come:

ALL If ever, ever, ever
They get back to Spain,
They will never, never, never
Cross the sea again!

DUKE At last we have arrived at our destination. This is the Ducal Palace, and it is here that the Grand Inquisitor resides. As a Castilian hidalgo of ninety-five quarterings, I regret that I am unable to pay my state visit on a horse. As a Castilian hidalgo of that description, I should have preferred to ride through the streets of Venice; but owing, I presume, to an unusually wet season, the streets are in such a condition that equestrian exercise is impracticable. No matter. Where is our suite?

LUIZ [*coming forward*] Your Grace, I am here.

DUCH. Why do you not do yourself the honour to kneel when you address His Grace?

DUKE My love, it is so small a matter! [*To* LUIZ] Still, you may as well do it. [LUIZ *kneels.*]

CAS. The young man seems to entertain but an imperfect appreciation of the respect due from a menial to a Castilian hidalgo.

DUKE My child, you are hard upon our suite.

CAS. Papa, I've no patience with the presumption of persons in his plebeian position. If he does not appreciate that position, let him be whipped until he does.

DUKE Let us hope the omission was not intended as a slight. I should be much hurt if I thought it was. So would he. [*To* LUIZ] Where are the halberdiers who were to have had the honour of meeting us here, that our visit to the Grand Inquisitor might be made in becoming state?

LUIZ Your Grace, the halberdiers are mercenary people who stipulated for a trifle on account.

DUKE How tiresome! Well, let us hope the Grand Inquisitor is a blind gentleman. And the band who were to have had the honour of escorting us? I see no band!

LUIZ Your Grace, the band are sordid persons who required to be paid in advance.

DUCH. That's so like a band!

DUKE [*annoyed*] Insuperable difficulties meet me at every turn!

DUCH. But surely they know His Grace?

LUIZ Exactly–they know His Grace.

DUKE Well let us hope that the Grand Inquisitor is a deaf gentleman. A cornet-à-piston would be something. You do not happen to possess the accomplishment of tootling like a cornet-à-piston?

LUIZ Alas, no, Your Grace! But I can imitate a farmyard.

DUKE [*doubtfully*] I don't see how that would help us. I don't see how we could bring it in.

CAS. It would not help us in the least. We are not a parcel of graziers come to market, dolt!

DUKE My love, our suite's feelings! [*To* LUIZ] Be so good as to ring the bell and inform the Grand Inquisitor that his Grace the Duke of Plaza-Toro, Count Matadoro, Baron Picadoro——

DUCH. And suite–

DUKE And suite–have arrived at Venice, and seek——

CAS. Desire–

DUCH. Demand!

DUKE And demand an audience.

LUIZ Your Grace has but to command. [*Rising*]

DUKE [*much moved*] I felt sure of it–I felt sure of it! [*Exit* LUIZ *into Ducal Palace*] And now my love–[*aside to* DUCHESS] Shall we tell her? I think so– [*aloud to* CASILDA] And now, my love, prepare for a magnificent surprise. It is my agreeable duty to reveal to you a secret which should make you the happiest young lady in Venice!

CAS. A secret?

DUCH. A secret which, for state reasons, it has been necessary to preserve for twenty years.

DUKE When you were a prattling babe of six months old you were married by proxy to no less a personage than the infant son and heir of His Majesty the immeasurably wealthy King of Barataria!

CAS. Married to the infant son of the King of Barataria? Was I consulted? [DUKE *shakes his head*] Then it was a most unpardonable liberty!

DUKE Consider his extreme youth and forgive him. Shortly after the ceremony that misguided monarch abandoned the creed of his forefathers, and became a Wesleyan Methodist of the most bigoted and persecuting type. The Grand Inquisitor, determined that the innovation should not be perpetuated in Barataria, caused your smiling and unconscious husband to be stolen and conveyed to Venice. A fortnight since the Methodist Monarch and all his Wesleyan Court were killed in an insurrection, and we are here to ascertain the whereabouts of your husband, and to hail you, our daughter, as Her Majesty, the reigning Queen of Barataria! [*Kneels*]

During this speech Luiz *re-enters*

Duch. Your Majesty! [*Kneels*]

Duke It is at such moments as these that one feels how necessary it is to travel with a full band.

Cas. I, the Queen of Barataria! But I've nothing to wear! We are practically penniless!

Duke That point has not escaped me. Although I am unhappily in straitened circumstances at present, my social influence is something enormous; and a Company, to be called the Duke of Plaza-Toro, Limited, is in course of formation to work me. An influential directorate has been secured, and I shall myself join the Board after allotment.

Cas. Am I to understand that the Queen of Barataria may be called upon at any time to witness her honoured sire in process of liquidation?

Duch. The speculation is not exempt from that drawback. If your father should stop, it will, of course, be necessary to wind him up.

Cas. But it's so undignified—it's so degrading! A Grandee of Spain turned into a public company? Such a thing was never heard of!

Duke My child, the Duke of Plaza-Toro does not follow fashions—he leads them. He always leads everybody. When he was in the army he led his regiment. He occasionally led them into action. He invariably led them out of it.

Song—Duke of Plaza-Toro

In enterprise of martial kind,
When there was any fighting,
He led his regiment from behind—
He found it less exciting.
But when away his regiment ran,
His place was at the fore, O—
That celebrated,
Cultivated,
Underrated
Nobleman,
The Duke of Plaza-Toro!

ALL

In the first and foremost flight, ha, ha!
You always found that knight, ha, ha!
That celebrated,
Cultivated,
Underrated
Nobleman,
The Duke of Plaza-Toro!

When, to evade Destruction's hand,
To hide they all proceeded,
No soldier in that gallant band
Hid half as well as he did.
He lay concealed throughout the war,
And so preserved his gore, O!
That unaffected,
Undetected,
Well-connected
Warrior,
The Duke of Plaza-Toro!

ALL

In every doughty deed, ha, ha!
He always took the lead, ha, ha!
That unaffected,
Undetected,
Well-connected
Warrior,
The Duke of Plaza-Toro!

When told that they would all be shot
Unless they left the service,
That hero hesitated not,
So marvellous his nerve is.
He sent his resignation in,
The first of all his corps, O!
That very knowing,
Overflowing,
Easy-going
Paladin,
The Duke of Plaza-Toro!

ALL
To men of grosser clay, ha, ha!
He always showed the way, ha, ha!
That very knowing,
Overflowing,
Easy-going
Paladin,
The Duke of Plaza-Toro!

[*Exeunt* DUKE *and* DUCHESS *into Grand Ducal Palace. As soon as they have disappeared,* LUIZ *and* CASILDA *rush to each other's arms.*

Recitative and Duet—CASILDA and LUIZ

O rapture, when alone together
Two loving hearts and those that bear them
May join in temporary tether,
Though Fate apart should rudely tear them.

CAS.
Necessity, Invention's mother,
Compelled me to a course of feigning—
But, left alone with one another,
I will atone for my disdaining!

Ah, well-beloved,
Mine angry frown
Is but a gown
That serves to dress
My gentleness!

LUIZ

Ah, well-beloved,
Thy cold disdain,
It gives no pain—
'Tis mercy, played
In masquerade!

BOTH

Ah, well-beloved, etc.

CAS. O Luiz, Luiz—what have you said? What have I done? What have I allowed you to do?

LUIZ Nothing, I trust, that you will ever have reason to repent. [*Offering to embrace her*]

CAS. [*withdrawing from him*] Nay, Luiz, it may not be. I have embraced you for the last time.

LUIZ [*amazed*] Casilda!

CAS. I have just learnt, to my surprise and indignation, that I was wed in babyhood to the infant son of the King of Barataria!

LUIZ The son of the King of Barataria? The child who was stolen in infancy by the Inquisition?

CAS. The same. But of course, you know his story.

LUIZ Know his story? Why, I have often told you that my mother was the nurse to whose charge he was entrusted!

CAS. True. I had forgotten. Well, he has been discovered, and my father has brought me here to claim his hand.

LUIZ But you will not recognize this marriage? It took place when you were too young to understand its import.

CAS. Nay, Luiz, respect my principles and cease to torture me with vain entreaties. Henceforth my life is another's.

LUIZ But stay—the present and the future—*they* are another's; but the past—that at least is ours, and none can take it from us. As we may revel in naught else, let us revel in that!

CAS. I don't think I grasp your meaning.

LUIZ Yet it is logical enough. You say you cease to love me?

CAS. [*demurely*] I say I *may* not love you.

LUIZ Ah, but you do not say you *did* not love me?

CAS. I loved you with a frenzy that words are powerless to express—and that but ten brief minutes since!

LUIZ Exactly. My own—that is, until ten minutes since, my own—my lately loved, my recently adored—tell me that until, say a quarter of an hour ago, I was all in all to thee! [*Embracing her*]

CAS. I see your idea. It's ingenious, but don't do that. [*Releasing herself*]

LUIZ There can be no harm in revelling in the past.

CAS. None whatever, but an embrace cannot be taken to act retrospectively.

LUIZ Perhaps not!

CAS. We may recollect an embrace—I recollect many—but we must not repeat them.

LUIZ Then let us recollect a few! [*A moment's pause, as they recollect, then both heave a deep sigh*]

LUIZ Ah, Casilda, you were to me as the sun is to the earth!

CAS. A quarter of an hour ago?

LUIZ About that.

CAS. And to think that, but for this miserable discovery, you would have been my own for life!

LUIZ Through life to death—a quarter of an hour ago!

CAS. How greedily my thirsty ears would have drunk the golden melody of those sweet words a quarter—well, it's now about twenty minutes since. [*Looking at her watch*]

LUIZ About that. In such a matter one cannot be too precise.

CAS. And now our love, so full of life, is but a silent, solemn memory!

LUIZ Must it be so Casilda?

CAS. Luiz, it must be so!

Duet—CASILDA and LUIZ

LUIZ There was a time—
A time for ever gone—ah, woe is me!
It was no crime
To love but thee alone—ah, woe is me!
One heart, one life, one soul,
One aim, one goal—
Each in the other's thrall,
Each all in all, ah, woe is me!

BOTH Oh, bury, bury—let the grave close o'er
The days that were—that never will be more!
Oh, bury, bury love that all condemn,
And let the whirlwind mourn its requiem!

CAS. Dead as the last year's leaves—
As gathered flowers—ah, woe is me!
Dead as the garnered sheaves,
That love of ours—ah, woe is me!
Born but to fade and die
When hope was high,

Dead and as far away
As yesterday!—ah, woe is me!

BOTH Oh, bury, bury—let the grave close o'er, etc.

Re-enter from the Ducal Palace the DUKE *and* DUCHESS, *followed by* DON ALHAMBRA DEL BOLERO, *the Grand Inquisitor.*

DUKE My child, allow me to present to you His Distinction Don Alhambra del Bolero, the Grand Inquisitor of Spain. It was His Distinction who so thoughtfully abstracted your infant husband and brought him to Venice.

DON AL. So this is the little lady who is so unexpectedly called upon to assume the functions of Royalty! And a very nice little lady, too!

DUKE Jimp, isn't she?

DON AL. Distinctly jimp. Allow me! [*Offers his hand. She turns away scornfully.*] Naughty temper!

DUKE You must make some allowance. Her Majesty's head is a little turned by her access of dignity.

DON AL. I could have wished that Her Majesty's access of dignity had turned it in this direction.

DUCH. Unfortunately, if I am not mistaken, there appears to be some little doubt as to His Majesty's whereabouts.

CAS. [*aside*] A doubt as to his whereabouts? Then we may yet be saved!

DON AL. A doubt? Oh dear, no—no doubt at all! He is here, in Venice, plying the modest but picturesque calling of a gondolier. I can give you his address—I see him every day! In the entire annals of our history there is absolutely no circumstance so entirely free from all manner of doubt of any kind whatever! Listen, and I'll tell you all about it.

Song—DON ALHAMBRA
[*with* DUKE, DUCHESS, CASILDA, *and* LUIZ]

I stole the Prince, and brought him here,
And left him gaily prattling
With a highly respectable gondolier,
Who promised the Royal babe to rear,
And teach him the trade of a timeoneer
With his own beloved bratling.

Both of the babes were strong and stout,
And considering all things, clever.
Of that there is no manner of doubt—
No probable, possible shadow of doubt—
No possible doubt whatever.

But owing, I'm much disposed to fear,
To his terrible taste for tippling,
That highly respectable gondolier
Could never declare with a mind sincere
Which of the two was his offspring dear,
And which the Royal stripling!

Which was which he could never make out
Despite his best endeavour.
Of *that* there is no manner of doubt—
No probable, possible shadow of doubt—
No possible doubt whatever.

Time sped, and when at the end of a year
I sought that infant cherished,
That highly respectable gondolier
Was lying a corpse on his humble bier—
I dropped a Grand Inquisitor's tear—
That gondolier had perished.

A taste for drink combined with gout,
Had doubled him up for ever.
Of *that* there is no manner of doubt—
No probable, possible shadow of doubt—
No possible doubt whatever.

The children followed his old career—
(This statement can't be parried)
Of a highly respectable gondolier:
Well, one of the two (who will soon be here)—

But *which* of the two is not quite clear—
Is the Royal Prince you married!

Search in and out and round about,
And you'll discover never
A tale so free from every doubt—
All probable, possible shadow of doubt—
All possible doubt whatever!

CAS. Then do you mean to say that I am married to one of two gondoliers, but it is impossible to say which?

DON AL. Without any doubt of any kind whatever. But be reassured: the nurse to whom your husband was entrusted is the mother of the musical young man who is such a past-master of that delicately modulated instrument [*indicating the drum*]. She can, no doubt, establish the King's identity beyond all question.

LUIZ Heavens, how did he know that?

DON AL. My young friend, a Grand Inquisitor is always up to date. [*To* CAS.] His mother is at present the wife of a highly respectable and old-established brigand, who carries on an extensive practice in the mountains around Cordova. Accompanied by two of my emissaries, he will set off at once for his mother's address. She will return with them, and if she finds any difficulty in making up her mind, the persuasive influence of the torture chamber will jog her memory.

Recitative—CASILDA and DON ALHAMBRA

CAS. But, bless my heart, consider my position!
I am the wife of one, that's very clear;
But who can tell, except by intuition,
Which is the Prince, and which the Gondolier?

DON AL. Submit to Fate without unseemly wrangle:
Such complications frequently occur—
Life is one closely complicated tangle:
Death is the only true unraveller!

Quintet—DUKE, DUCHESS, CASILDA, LUIZ, and GRAND INQUISITOR

ALL Try we life-long, we can never
Straighten out life's tangled skein,
Why should we, in vain endeavor,
Guess and guess and guess again?

LUIZ Life's a pudding full of plums,

DUCH. Care's a canker that benumbs.

ALL
Life's a pudding full of plums,
Care's a canker that benumbs.
Wherefore waste our elocution
On impossible solution?
Life's a pleasant institution,
Let us take it as it comes!

Set aside the dull enigma,
We shall guess it all too soon;
Failure brings no kind of stigma—
Dance we to another tune!

LUIZ
String the lyre and fill the cup,

DUCH.
Lest on sorrow we should sup.

ALL
String the lyre and fill the cup,
Lest on sorrow we should sup.
Hop and skip to Fancy's fiddle,
Hands across and down the middle—
Life's perhaps the only riddle
That we shrink from giving up!

[*Exeunt all into Ducal Palace except* LUIZ, *who goes off in gondola.*

Enter Gondoliers and Contadine, followed by MARCO, GIANETTA, GIUSEPPE, *and* TESSA.

Chorus

Bridegroom and bride!
Knot that's insoluble,
Voices all voluble
Hail it with pride.

Bridegroom and bride!
We in sincerity
Wish you prosperity,
Bridegroom and bride!

Song—Tessa

Tess. When a merry maiden marries,
Sorrow goes and pleasure tarries;
Every sound becomes a song,
All is right, and nothing's wrong!
From to-day and ever after
Let our tears be tears of laughter.
Every sigh that finds a vent
Be a sigh of sweet content!
When you marry, merry maiden,
Then the air with love is laden;
Every flower is a rose,
Every goose becomes a swan,
Every kind of trouble goes
Where the last year's snows have gone!

Chorus Sunlight takes the place of shade
When you marry, merry maid!

Tess. When a merry maiden marries,
Sorrow goes and pleasure tarries;
Every sound becomes a song,
All is right, and nothing's wrong.

Gnawing Care and aching Sorrow,
Get ye gone until to-morrow;
Jealousies in grim array,
Ye are things of yesterday!
When you marry, merry maiden,
Then the air with joy is laden;
All the corners of the earth
Ring with music sweetly played,
Worry is melodious mirth,
Grief is joy in masquerade;

CHORUS Sullen night is laughing day–
All the year is merry May!

At the end of the song, DON ALHAMBRA *enters at back. The Gondoliers and Contadine shrink from him, and gradually go off, much alarmed.*

GIU. And now our lives are going to begin in real earnest! What's a bachelor? A mere nothing–he's a chrysalis. He can't be said to live–he exists.

MAR. What a delightful institution marriage is! Why have we wasted all this time? Why didn't we marry ten years ago?

TESS. Because you couldn't find anybody nice enough.

GIA. Because you were waiting for *us.*

MAR. I suppose that *was* the reason. We were waiting for you without knowing it. [DON ALHAMBRA *comes forward.*] Hallo!

DON AL. Good morning.

GIU. If this gentleman is an undertaker it's a bad omen.

DON AL. Ceremony of some sort going on?

GIU. [*aside*] He *is* an undertaker! [*Aloud*] No–a little unimportant family gathering. Nothing in *your* line.

DON AL. Somebody's birthday I suppose?

GIA. Yes, mine!

TESS. And mine!

MAR. And mine!

GIU. And mine!

DON AL. Curious coincidence! And how old may you all be?

TESS. It's a rude question–but about ten minutes.

DON AL. Remarkably fine children! But surely you are jesting?

TESS. In other words, we were married about ten minutes since.

DON AL. Married! You don't mean to say you are married?

MAR. Oh yes, we are married.

DON AL. What, both of you?

ALL All four of us.

DON AL. [*aside*] Bless my heart, how extremely awkward!

GIA. You don't mind, I suppose?

TESS. You were not thinking of either of us for yourself, I presume? Oh, Giuseppe, look at him—he was. He's heart-broken!

DON AL. No, no, I wasn't! I wasn't!

GIU. Now, my man [*slapping him on the back*], we don't want anything in your line to-day, and if your curiosity's satisfied—you can go!

DON AL. You mustn't call me your man. It's a liberty. I don't think you know who I am.

GIU. Not we, indeed! We are jolly gondoliers, the sons of Baptisto Palmieri, who led the last revolution. Republicans, heart and soul, we hold all men to be equal. As we abhor oppression, we abhor kings: as we detest vain-glory, we detest rank: as we despise effeminacy, we despise wealth. We are Venetian gondoliers—your equals in everything except our calling, and in that at once your masters and your servants.

DON AL. Bless my heart, how unfortunate! One of you may be Baptisto's son, for anything I know to the contrary; but the other is no less a personage than the only son of the late King of Barataria.

ALL What!

DON AL. And I trust—I *trust* it was that one who slapped me on the shoulder and called me his man!

GIU. One of us a king!
MAR. Not brothers!
TESS. The King of Barataria!
GIA. Well, who'd have thought it!
} *Together*

MAR. But which is it?

DON AL. What does it matter? As you are both Republicans, and hold kings in detestation, of course you'll abdicate at once. Good morning! [*Going.*]

GIA. and TESS. Oh, don't do that! [MARCO *and* GIUSEPPE *stop him.*]

GIU. Well, as to that, of course there are kings and kings. When I say that I detest kings, I mean I detest *bad* kings.

DON AL. I see. It's a delicate distinction.

GIU. Quite so. Now I can conceive a kind of king—an ideal king—the creature of my fancy, you know—who would be absolutely unobjectionable. A king, for instance, who would abolish taxes and make everything cheap, except gondolas——

MAR. And give a great many free entertainments to the gondoliers——

GIU. And let off fireworks on the Grand Canal, and engage all the gondolas for the occasion——

MAR. And scramble money on the Rialto among the gondoliers.

GIU. Such a king would be a blessing to his people, and if I were a king, that is the sort of king I would be.

MAR. And so would I!

DON AL. Come, I'm glad to find your objections are not insuperable.

MAR. and GIU. Oh, they're not insuperable.

GIA and TESS. No, they're not insuperable.

GIU. Besides, we are open to conviction.

GIA. Yes; they are open to conviction.

TESS. Oh! they've often been convicted.

GIU. Our views may have been hastily formed on insufficient grounds. They may be crude, ill-digested, erroneous. I've a very poor opinion of the politician who is not open to conviction.

TESS. [*to* GIA] Oh, he's a fine fellow!

GIA. Yes, that's the sort of politician for *my* money!

DON AL. Then we'll consider it settled. Now, as the country is in a state of insurrection, it is absolutely necessary that you should assume the reins of Government at once; and, until it is ascertained which of you is to be king, I have arranged that you will reign jointly, so that no question can arise hereafter as to the validity of any of your acts.

MAR. As one individual.

DON AL. As one individual.

GIU. [*linking himself with* MARCO] Like this?

DON AL. Something like that.

MAR. And we may take our friends with us, and give them places about the Court?

DON AL. Undoubtedly. That's always done!

MAR. I'm convinced!

GIU. So am I!

TESS. Then the sooner we're off the better.

GIA. We'll just run home and pack up a few things [*going*]—

DON AL. Stop, stop—that won't do at all—ladies are not admitted.

ALL. What!

DON AL. Not admitted. Not at present. Afterwards, perhaps. We'll see.

GIU. Why, you don't mean to say you are going to separate us from our wives!

DON AL. [*aside*] This is very awkward! [*Aloud*] Only for a time—a few months. After all, what is a few months?

TESS. But we've only been married half an hour! [*Weeps*]

FINALE—ACT I

Song—GIANETTA

Kind sir, you cannot have the heart
Our lives to part
From those to whom an hour ago
We were united!
Before our flowing hopes you stem,
Ah, look at them,
And pause before you deal this blow,
All uninvited!
You men can never understand
That heart and hand

Cannot be separated when
We go a-yearning;
You see, you've only women's eyes
To idolize
And only women's hearts, poor men,
To set *you* burning!
Ah me, you men will never understand
That woman's heart is one with woman's hand!

Some kind of charm you seem to find
In womankind—
Some source of unexplained delight
(Unless you're jesting),
But what attracts you, I confess,
I cannot guess,
To me a woman's face is quite
Uninteresting!
If from my sister I were torn
It could be borne—
I should, no doubt, be horrified,
But I could bear it;—
But Marco's quite another thing—
He is my King,
He has my heart and none beside
Shall ever share it!
Ah me, you men will never understand
That woman's heart is one with woman's hand!

Recitative—DON ALHAMBRA

Do not give way to this uncalled-for grief,
Your separation will be very brief.
To ascertain which is the King
And which the other,
To Barataria's Court I'll bring
His foster-mother;
Her former nurseling to declare
She'll be delighted
That settled, let each happy pair
Be reunited.

MAR., GIU., GIA., Viva! His argument is strong!
TESS. Viva! We'll not be parted long!
Viva! It will be settled soon!
Viva! Then comes our honeymoon!
[*Exit* DON ALHAMBRA.

Quartet—Marco, Giuseppe, Gianetta, Tessa

Gia. Then one of us will be a Queen,
And sit on a golden throne,
With a crown instead,
Of a hat on her head,
And diamonds all her own!
With a beautiful robe of gold and green,
I've always understood;
I wonder whether
She'd wear a feather?
I rather think she should!

All Oh, 'tis a glorious thing, I ween,
To be a regular Royal Queen!
No half-and-half affair, I mean,
But a right-down regular Royal Queen!

Mar. She'll drive about in a carriage and pair,
With the King on her left-hand side,
And a milk-white horse,
As a matter of course,
Whenever she wants to ride!
With beautiful silver shoes to wear
Upon her dainty feet;
With endless stocks
Of beautiful frocks
And as much as she wants to eat!

All Oh, 'tis a glorious thing, I ween, etc.

Tess. Whenever she condescends to walk,
Be sure she'll shine at that,
With her haughty stare
And her nose in the air,
Like a well-born aristocrat!
At elegant high society talk
She'll bear away the bell,
With her "How de do?"
And her "How are you?"
And "I trust I see you well!"

All Oh, 'tis a glorious thing, I ween, etc.

Giu. And noble lords will scrape and bow,
And double themselves in two,

And open their eyes
In blank surprise
At whatever she likes to do.
And everybody will roundly vow
She's fair as flowers in May,
And say, "How clever!"
At whatsoever
She condescends to say!

ALL Oh, 'tis a glorious thing, I ween,
To be a regular Royal Queen!
No half-and-half affair, I mean,
But a right-down regular Royal Queen!

Enter Chorus of Gondoliers and Contadine

Chorus

Now, pray, what is the cause of this remarkable hilarity?
This sudden ebullition of unmitigated jollity?
Has anybody blessed you with a sample of his charity?
Or have you been adopted by a gentleman of quality?

MAR. and GIU. Replying, we sing
As one individual,
As I find I'm a king,
To my kingdom I bid you all.
I'm aware you object
To pavilions and palaces,
But you'll find I respect
Your Republican fallacies.

CHORUS As they know we object
To pavilions and palaces,
How can they respect
Our Republican fallacies?

MARCO and GIUSEPPE

MAR. For every one who feels inclined,
Some post we undertake to find
Congenial with his frame of mind—
And all shall equal be.

GIU. The Chancellor in his peruke—
The Earl, the Marquis, and the Dook,
The Groom, the Butler, and the Cook—
They all shall equal be.

MAR. The Aristocrat who banks with Coutts—
The Aristocrat who hunts and shoots—
The Aristocrat who cleans our boots—
They all shall equal be!

GIU. The Noble Lord who rules the State—
The Noble Lord who cleans the plate—

MAR. The Noble Lord who scrubs the grate—
They all shall equal be!

GIU. The Lord High Bishop orthodox—
The Lord High Coachman on the box—

MAR. The Lord High Vagabond in the stocks—
They all shall equal be!

BOTH For every one, etc.

Sing high, sing low,
Wherever they go,
They all shall equal be!

CHORUS Sing high, sing low,
Wherever they go,
They all shall equal be!

The Earl, the Marquis, and the Dook,
The Groom, the Butler, and the Cook,
The Aristocrat who banks with Coutts,
The Aristocrat who cleans the boots,
The Noble Lord who rules the State,
The Noble Lord who scrubs the grate,
The Lord High Bishop orthodox,
The Lord High Vagabond in the stocks—

For every one, etc.

Sing high, sing low,
Wherever they go,
They all shall equal be!

Then hail! O King,
  Whichever you may be,
To you we sing,
  But do not bend the knee.
Then hail! O King.

MARCO and GIUSEPPE [*together*]

Come, let's away–our island crown awaits me–
  Conflicting feelings rend my soul apart!
The thought of Royal dignity elates me,
  But leaving thee behind me breaks my heart!

[*Addressing* GIANETTA *and* TESSA]

GIANETTA and TESSA [*together*]

Farewell, my love; on board you must be getting;
  But while upon the sea you gaily roam,
Remember that a heart for thee is fretting–
  The tender little heart you've left at home!

GIA. Now, Marco dear,
My wishes hear:
  While you're away
It's understood
You will be good,
  And not too gay.
To every trace
Of maiden grace
  You will be blind,

And will not glance
By any chance
On womankind!

If you are wise,
You'll shut your eyes
Till we arrive,
And not address
A lady less
Than forty-five.
You'll please to frown
On every gown
That you may see;
And, O my pet,
You won't forget
You've married me!

And O my darling, O my pet,
Whatever else you may forget
In yonder isle beyond the sea,
Do not forget you've married me!

TESS. You'll lay your head
Upon your bed
At set of sun.
You will not sing
Of anything
To any one.
You'll sit and mope
All day, I hopc,
And shed a tear
Upon the life
Your little wife
Is passing here.

And if so be
You think of me,
Please tell the moon!
I'll read it all
In rays that fall
On the lagoon:
You'll be so kind
As tell the wind
How you may be,
And send me words
By little birds
To comfort me!

And O my darling, O my pet,
Whatever else you may forget,
In yonder isle beyond the sea,
Do not forget you've married me!

QUARTET Oh, my darling, O my pet, etc.

Chorus [*during which a "Xebeque" is hauled alongside the quay*]

Then away we go to an island fair
That lies in a Southern sea:
We know not where, and we don't much care,
Wherever that isle may be.

THE MEN [*hauling on boat*]

One, two, three,
Haul!
One, two, three,
Haul!
One, two, three,
Haul!
With a will!

ALL When the breezes are a-blowing
The ship will be going,
When they don't we shall all stand still!
Then away we go to an island fair,
We know not where, and we don't much care,
Wherever that isle may be.

Solo—MARCO

Away we go
To a balmy isle,
Where the roses blow
All the winter while.

ALL [*hoisting sail*]

Then away we go to an island fair
That lies in a Southern sea:
Then away we go to an island fair,
Then away, then away, then away!

[*The men embark on the "Xebeque."* MARCO *and* GIUSEPPE *embracing* GIANETTA *and* TESSA. *The girls wave a farewell to the men as the curtain falls.*

END OF ACT I

ACT II

SCENE.—*Pavilion in the Court of Barataria.* MARCO *and* GIUSEPPE, *magnificently dressed, are seated on two thrones, occupied in cleaning the crown and the sceptre. The Gondoliers are discovered, dressed, some as courtiers, officers of rank, etc., and others as private soldiers and servants of various degrees. All are enjoying themselves without reference to social distinctions—some playing cards, others throwing dice, some reading, others playing cup and ball, "morra", etc.*

Chorus of men with MARCO *and* GIUSEPPE

Of happiness the very pith
In Barataria you may see:
A monarchy that's tempered with
Republican Equality.
This form of government we find
The beau-ideal of its kind—
A despotism strict combined
With absolute equality!

MARCO and GIUSEPPE

Two kings, of undue pride bereft,
Who act in perfect unity,
Whom you can order right and left
With absolute impunity.
Who put their subjects at their ease
By doing all they can to please!
And thus, to earn their bread-and-cheese,
Seize every opportunity.

CHORUS Of happiness, the very pith, etc.

MAR. Gentlemen, we are much obliged to you for your expressions of satisfaction and good feeling—I say, we are much obliged to you for your expressions of satisfaction and good feeling.

ALL We heard you.

MAR. We are delighted, at any time, to fall in with sentiments so charmingly expressed.

ALL That's all right.

GIU. At the same time there is just one little grievance that we should like to ventilate.

ALL [*angrily*] What?

GIU. Don't be alarmed—it's not serious. It is arranged that, until it is decided which of us two is the actual King, we are to act as one person.

GIOR. Exactly.

GIU. Now, although we act as *one* person, we are, in point of fact, *two* persons.

ANNI. Ah, I don't think we can go into that. It is a legal fiction, and legal fictions are solemn things. Situated as we are, we can't recognize two independent responsibilities.

GIU. No; but you can recognize two independent appetites. It's all very well to say we act as one person, but when you supply us with only one ration between us, I should describe it as a legal fiction carried a little too far.

ANNI. It's rather a nice point. I don't like to express an opinion offhand. Suppose we reserve it for argument before the full Court?

MAR. Yes, but what are we to do in the meantime?

MAR. and GIU. We want our tea.

ANNI. I think we may make an interim order for double rations on their Majesties entering into the usual undertaking to indemnify in the event of an adverse decision?

GIOR. That, I think, will meet the case. But you must work hard—stick to it—nothing like work.

GIU. Oh, certainly. We quite understand that a man who holds the magnificent position of King should do something to justify it. We are called "Your Majesty", we are allowed to buy ourselves magnificent clothes, our subjects frequently nod to us in the streets, the sentries always return our salutes, and we enjoy the inestimable privilege of heading the subscription lists to all the principal charities. In return for these advantages the least we can do is to make ourselves useful about the Palace.

Song—GIUSEPPE *with Chorus*

Rising early in the morning,
We proceed to light the fire,
Then our Majesty adorning
In its workaday attire,
We embark without delay
On the duties of the day.

First, we polish off some batches
Of political despatches,
    And foreign politicians circumvent:
Then, if business isn't heavy,
We may hold a Royal *levée*,
    Or ratify some Acts of Parliament.
Then we probably review the household troops—
With the usual "shalloo humps!" and "Shalloo hoops!"
Or receive with ceremonial and state
An interesting Eastern potentate.
    After that we generally
    Go and dress our private *valet*—
(It's a rather nervous duty—he's a touchy little man)—
    Write some letters literary
    For our private secretary—
He is shaky in his spelling, so we help him if we can.
    Then, in view of cravings inner,
    We go down and order dinner;
Then we polish the Regalia and the Coronation Plate—
    Spend an hour in titivating
    All our Gentlemen-in-Waiting;
Or we run on little errands for the Ministers of State.

    Oh, philosophers may sing
    Of the troubles of a King;
Yet the duties are delightful, and the privileges great;
    But the privilege and pleasure
    That we treasure beyond measure
Is to run on little errands for the Ministers of State.

CHORUS Oh, philosophers may sing, etc.

After luncheon (making merry
On a bun and glass of sherry),
    If we've nothing in particular to do,
We may make a Proclamation,
Or receive a deputation—
    Then we possibly create a Peer or two.
Then we help a fellow-creature on his path
With the Garter or the Thistle or the Bath
Or we dress and toddle off in semi-state
To a festival, a function, or a *fête*.
    Then we go and stand as sentry
    At the Palace (private entry),
Marching hither, marching thither, up and down and to and fro,
    While the warrior on duty
    Goes in search of beer and beauty
(And it generally happens that he hasn't far to go).
    He relieves us, if he's able,
    Just in time to lay the table,
Then we dine and serve the coffee, and at half-past twelve or one,
    With a pleasure that's emphatic,
    We retire to our attic
With the gratifying feeling that our duty has been done!
    Oh, philosophers may sing
    Of the troubles of a King,
But of pleasures there are many and of worries there are none;
    And the culminating pleasure
    That we treasure beyond measure
Is the gratifying feeling that our duty has been done!

CHORUS Oh, philosophers may sing, etc.

[*Exeunt all but* MARCO *and* GIUSEPPE

GIU. Yes, it really is a very pleasant existence. They're all so singularly kind and considerate. You don't find them wanting to do this, or wanting to do that, or saying "It's my turn now." No, they let us have all the fun to ourselves, and never seem to grudge it.

MAR. It makes one feel quite selfish. It almost seems like taking advantage of their good nature.

GIU. How nice they were about the double rations.

MAR. Most considerate. Ah! there's only one thing wanting to make us thoroughly comfortable.

GIU. And that is?

MAR. The dear little wives we left behind us three months ago.

GIU. Yes, it *is* dull without female society. We can do without everything else, but we can't do without that.

MAR. And if we have that in perfection, we have everything. There is only one recipe for perfect happiness.

Song—MARCO

Take a pair of sparkling eyes
Hidden, ever and anon,
In a merciful eclipse—
Do not heed their mild surprise—
Having passed the Rubicon,
Take a pair of rosy lips;
Take a figure trimly planned—
Such as admiration whets
(Be particular in this);
Take a tender little hand,
Fringed with dainty fingerettes,
Press it—in parenthesis;—
Ah! Take all these, you lucky man—
Take and keep them, if you can!

Take a pretty little cot—
Quite a miniature affair—
Hung about with trellised vine,
Furnish it upon the spot
With the treasures rich and rare
I've endeavoured to define.
Live to love and love to live—
You will ripen at your ease,
Growing on the sunny side—
Fate has nothing more to give.
You're a dainty man to please
If you are not satisfied.
Ah! Take my counsel, happy man;
Act upon it, if you can!

Enter Chorus of Contadine, running in, led by FIAMETTA *and* VITTORIA. *They are met by all the Ex-Gondoliers, who welcome them heartily.*

Scene—Chorus of Girls, Quartet, Duet and Chorus

Here we are, at the risk of our lives,
From ever so far, and we've brought your wives—
And to that end we've crossed the main,
And don't intend to return again!

FIA. Though obedience is strong,
Curiosity's stronger—
We waited for long,
Till we couldn't wait longer.

VIT. It's imprudent, we know,
But without your society
Existence was slow,
And we wanted variety—

ALL So here we are, at the risk of our lives,
From ever so far, and we've brought your wives—
And to that end we've crossed the main,
And don't intend to return again!

Enter GIANETTA *and* TESSA. *They rush to the arms of* MARCO *and* GIUSEPPE.

GIU. Tessa!
TESS. Giuseppe!
GIA. Marco!
MAR. Gianetta!
Embrace

TESSA and GIANETTA

TESS. After sailing to this island—
GIA. Tossing in a manner frightful,
TESS. We are all once more on dry land—
GIA. And we find the change delightful,
TESS. As at home we've been remaining—
We've not seen you both for ages,
GIA. Tell me, are you fond of reigning?—
How's the food, and what's the wages?
TESS. Does your new employment please ye?—
GIA. How does the Royalizing strike you?
TESS. Is it difficult or easy?—
GIA. Do you think your subjects like you?
TESS. I am anxious to elicit,
Is it plain and easy steering?

GIA. Take it altogether, is it—
Better fun than gondoliering?
BOTH We shall both go on requesting
Till you tell us, never doubt it;
Everything is interesting,
Tell us, tell us all about it!

CHORUS They will both go on requesting, etc.

TESS. Is the populace exacting?
GIA. Do they keep you at a distance?
TESS. All unaided are you acting,
GIA. Or do they provide assistance?
TESS. When you're busy, have you got to
Get up early in the morning?
GIA. If you do what you ought not to,
Do they give the usual warning?
TESS. With a horse do they equip you?
GIA. Lots of trumpeting and drumming?
TESS. Do the Royal tradesmen tip you?
GIA. Ain't the livery becoming!
TESS. Does your human being inner
Feed on everything that nice is?
GIA. Do they give you wine for dinner;
Peaches, sugar-plums, and ices?
BOTH We shall both go on requesting
Till you tell us, never doubt it;
Everything is interesting,
Tell us, tell us all about it!

CHORUS They will both go on requesting, etc.

MAR. This is indeed a most delightful surprise!

TESS. Yes, we thought you'd like it. You see, it was like this. After you left we felt very dull and mopey, and the days crawled by, and you never wrote; so at last I said to Gianetta, "I can't stand this any longer; those two poor monarchs haven't got any one to mend their stockings or sew on their buttons or patch their clothes—at least, I hope they haven't—let us all pack up a change and go and see how they're getting on." And she said, "Done," and they all said, "Done"; and we asked old Giacopo to lend us his boat, and *he* said, "Done"; and we've crossed the sea, and, thank goodness, *that's* done; and here we are, and—and—*I've* done!

GIA. And now—which of you is King?

TESS. And which of us is Queen?

GIU. That we shan't know until Nurse turns up. But never mind that—

the question is, how shall we celebrate the commencement of our honeymoon? Gentlemen, will you allow us to offer you a magnificent banquet?

ALL We will!

GIU. Thanks very much; and, ladies, what do you say to a dance?

TESS. A banquet *and* a dance! O, it's too much happiness!

Chorus and Dance

Dance a cachucha, fandango, bolero,
Xeres we'll drink–Manzanilla, Montero–
Wine, when it runs in abundance, enhances
The reckless delight of that wildest of dances!
To the pretty pitter-pitter-patter,
And the clitter-clitter-clitter-clatter–
Clitter–clitter–clatter,
Pitter–pitter–patter,
Patter, patter, patter, patter, we'll dance.
Old Xeres we'll drink–Manzanilla, Montero;
For wine, when it runs in abundance, enhances
The reckless delight of that wildest of dances!

[*Cachucha*]

The dance is interrupted by the unexpected appearance of DON ALHAMBRA, *who looks on with astonishment.* MARCO *and* GIUSEPPE *appear embarrassed. The others run off, except Drummer Boy, who is driven off by* DON ALHAMBRA.

DON AL. Good evening. Fancy ball?

GIU. No, not exactly. A little friendly dance. That's all. Sorry you're late.

DON AL. But I saw a groom dancing, and a footman!

MAR. Yes. That's the Lord High Footman.

DON AL. And, dear me, a common little drummer boy!

GIU. Oh no! That's the Lord High Drummer Boy.

DON AL. But surely, surely the servants'-hall is the place for these gentry?

GIU. Oh dear no! *We* have appropriated the servants'-hall. It's the Royal Apartment, and accessible only by tickets obtainable at the Lord Chamberlain's office.

MAR. We really must have some place that we can call our own.

DON AL. [*puzzled*] I'm afraid I'm not quite equal to the intellectual pressure of the conversation.

GIU. You see, the Monarchy has been re-modelled on Republican principles.

DON AL. What!

GIU. All departments rank equally, and everybody is at the head of his department.

DON AL. I see.

MAR. I'm afraid you're annoyed.

DON AL. No. I won't say that. It's not quite what I expected.

GIU. I'm awfully sorry.

MAR. So am I.

GIU. By the by, can I offer you anything after your voyage? A plate of macaroni and a rusk?

DON AL. [*preoccupied*] No, no–nothing–nothing.

GIU. Obliged to be careful?

DON AL. Yes–gout. You see, in every Court there are distinctions that must be observed.

GIU. [*puzzled*] There are, are there?

DON AL. Why, of course. For instance, you wouldn't have a Lord High Chancellor play leapfrog with his own cook.

MAR. Why not?

DON AL. Why not! Because a Lord High Chancellor is a personage of great dignity, who should never, under any circumstances, place himself in a position of being told to tuck in his tuppenny, except by noblemen of his own rank. A Lord High Archbishop, for instance, might tell a Lord High Chancellor to tuck in his tuppenny, but certainly not a cook, gentlemen, certainly not a cook.

GIU. Not even a Lord High Cook?

DON AL. My good friend, that is a rank that is not recognized at the Lord Chamberlain's office. No, no, it won't do. I'll give you an instance in which the experiment was tried.

Song–DON ALHAMBRA, *with* MARCO *and* GIUSEPPE

DON AL. There lived a King, as I've been told,
In the wonder-working days of old,
When hearts were twice as good as gold,
And twenty times as mellow.
Good-temper triumphed in his face,
And in his heart he found a place
For all the erring human race
And every wretched fellow.
When he had Rhenish wine to drink
It made him very sad to think
That some, at junket or at jink,
Must be content with toddy.

MAR. and GIU. With toddy, must be content with toddy.

DON AL. He wished all men as rich as he
(And he was rich as rich could be),
So to the top of every tree
Promoted everybody.

MAR. and GIU. Now, that's the kind of King for me—
He wished all men as rich as he,
So to the top of every tree
Promoted everybody.

DON AL. Lord Chancellors were cheap as sprats,
And Bishops in their shovel hats
Were plentiful as tabby cats—
In point of fact, too many.
Ambassadors cropped up like hay,
Prime Ministers and such as they
Grew like asparagus in May,
And Dukes were three a penny.
On every side Field-Marshals gleamed,
Small beer were Lords-Lieutenant deemed,
With Admirals the ocean teemed
All round his wide dominions.

MAR. and GIU. With Admirals all round his wide dominions.

DON AL. And Party Leaders you might meet
In twos and threes in every street
Maintaining, with no little heat,
Their various opinions.

MAR. and GIU. Now that's a sight you couldn't beat—
Two Party Leaders in each street
Maintaining, with no little heat,
Their various opinions.

DON AL. That King, although no one denies
His heart was of abnormal size,
Yet he'd have acted otherwise
If he had been acuter.
The end is easily foretold,
When every blessed thing you hold
Is made of silver, or of gold,
You long for simple pewter.
When you have nothing else to wear
But cloth of gold and satins rare,
For cloth of gold you cease to care—
Up goes the price of shoddy.

MAR. and GIU. Of shoddy, up goes the price of shoddy.

DON AL. In short, whoever you may be,
To this conclusion you'll agree,
When every one is somebodee,
Then no one's anybody!

MAR. and GIU. Now that's as plain as plain can be,
To this conclusion we agree—

ALL When every one is somebodee,
Then no one's anybody!

GIANETTA *and* TESSA *enter unobserved. The two girls, impelled by curiosity, remain listening at the back of the stage.*

DON AL. And now I have some important news to communicate. His Grace the Duke of Plaza-Toro, Her Grace the Duchess, and their beautiful daughter Casilda—I say their beautiful daughter Casilda——

GIU. We heard you.

DON AL. Have arrived at Barataria, and may be here at any moment.

MAR. The Duke and Duchess are nothing to us.

DON AL. But the daughter—the beautiful daughter! Aha! Oh, you're a lucky dog, one of you!

GIU. I think you're a very incomprehensible old gentleman.

DON AL. Not a bit—I'll explain. Many years ago when you (whichever you are) were a baby, you (whichever you are) were married to a little girl who has grown up to be the most beautiful young lady in Spain. That beautiful young lady will be here to claim you (whichever you are) in half an hour, and I congratulate that one (whichever it is) with all my heart.

MAR. Married when a baby!

GIU. But we were married three months ago!

DON AL. One of you—only one. The other (whichever it is) is an unintentional bigamist.

GIA. and TESS. [*coming forward*] Well, upon my word!

DON AL. Eh? Who are these young people?

TESS. Who are we? Why their wives, of course. We've just arrived.

DON AL. Their wives! Oh dear, this is very unfortunate! Oh dear, this complicates matters! Dear, dear, what will Her Majesty say?

GIA. And do you mean to say that one of these Monarchs was already married?

TESS. And that neither of us will be a Queen?

DON AL. That is the idea I intended to convey. [TESSA *and* GIANNETTA *begin to cry.*]

GIU. [*to* TESSA] Tessa, my dear, dear child——

TESS. Get away! perhaps it's you!

MAR. [*to* GIA.] My poor, poor little woman!

GIA. Don't! Who knows whose husband you are?

TESS. And pray, why didn't you tell us all about it before they left Venice?

DON AL. Because, if I had, no earthly temptation would have induced these gentlemen to leave two such extremely fascinating and utterly irresistible little ladies!

TESS. There's something in that.

DON AL. I may mention that you will not be kept long in suspense, as the old lady who nursed the Royal child is at present in the torture chamber, waiting for me to interview her.

GIU. Poor old girl. Hadn't you better go and put her out of her suspense?

DON AL. Oh no—there's no hurry—she's all right. She has all the illustrated papers. However, I'll go and interrogate her, and, in the meantime, may I suggest the absolute propriety of your regarding yourselves as single young ladies. Good evening!

[*Exit* DON ALHAMBRA.

GIA. Well, here's a pleasant state of things!

MAR. Delightful. One of us is married to two young ladies, and nobody knows which; and the other is married to one young lady whom nobody can identify!

GIA. And one of us is married to one of you, and the other is married to nobody.

TESS. But which of you is married to which of us, and what's to become of the other? [*About to cry*]

GIU. It's quite simple. Observe. Two husbands have managed to acquire three wives. Three wives—two husbands. [*Reckoning up*] That's two-thirds of a husband to each wife.

TESS. O Mount Vesuvius, here we are in arithmetic! My good sir, one can't marry a vulgar fraction!

GIU. You've no right to call me a vulgar fraction.

MAR. We are getting rather mixed. The situation entangled. Let's try and comb it out.

Quartet—MARCO, GIUSEPPE, GIANETTA, TESSA

In a contemplative fashion,
    And a tranquil frame of mind,
Free from every kind of passion,
    Some solution let us find.
Let us grasp the situation,
    Solve the complicated plot—
Quiet, calm deliberation
    Disentangles every knot.

TESS. I, no doubt, Giuseppe wedded—
That's, of course, a slice of luck.
He is rather dunder-headed,
Still distinctly, he's a duck.

THE OTHERS. In a contemplative fashion, etc.

GIA. I, a victim, too, of Cupid,
Marco married—that is clear.
He's particularly stupid,
Still distinctly, he's a dear.

THE OTHERS. Let us grasp the situation, etc.

MAR. To Gianetta I was mated;
I can prove it in a trice:
Though her charms are overrated,
Still I own she's rather nice.

THE OTHERS. In a contemplative fashion, etc.

GIU. I to Tessa, willy-nilly,
All at once a victim fell.
She is what is called a silly,
Still she answers pretty well.

THE OTHERS. Let us grasp the situation, etc.

MAR. Now when we were pretty babies
Some one married us, that's clear—

GIA. And if I can catch her
I'll pinch her and scratch her,
And send her away with a flea in her ear.

GIU. He whom that young lady married,
To receive her can't refuse.

TESS. If I overtake her
I'll warrant I'll make her
To shake in her aristocratical shoes!

GIA. [*to* TESS.] If she married your Giuseppe
You and he will have to part—

TESS. [*to* GIA.] If I have to do it
I'll warrant she'll rue it—
I'll teach her to marry the man of my heart!

TESS. [*to* GIA.] If she married Messer Marco
You're a spinster, that is plain—

GIA. [*to* TESS.] No matter—no matter
If I can get at her
I doubt if her mother will know her again!

ALL Quiet, calm deliberation
Disentangles every knot!

[*Exeunt, pondering.*

March. Enter procession of Retainers, heralding approach of Duke, Duchess, *and* Casilda. *All three are now dressed with the utmost magnificence.*

Chorus of men, with Duke *and* Duchess

With ducal pomp and ducal pride
(Announce these comers,
O ye kettle-drummers!)
Comes Barataria's high-born bride.
(Ye sounding cymbals clang!)
She comes to claim the Royal hand—
(Proclaim their Graces,
O ye double basses!)
Of the King who rules this goodly land.
(Ye brazen brasses bang!)

Duke and Duch. This polite attention touches
Heart of Duke and heart of Duchess.
Who resign their pet
With profound regret.
She of beauty was a model
When a tiny tiddle-toddle,
And at twenty-one
She's excelled by none!

Chorus With ducal pomp and ducal pride, etc.

Duke [*to his attendants*] Be good enough to inform His Majesty that His Grace the Duke of Plaza-Toro, Limited, has arrived, and begs—

Cas. Desires—

Duch. Demands—

Duke And demands an audience. [*Exeunt attendants*] And now, my child, prepare to receive the husband to whom you were united under such interesting and romantic circumstances.

Cas. But which is it? There are two of them!

Duke It is true that at present His Majesty is a double gentleman; but as soon as the circumstances of his marriage are ascertained, he will, *ipso facto*, boil down to a single gentleman—thus presenting a unique example of an individual who becomes a single man and a married man by the same operation.

Duch. [*severely*] I have known instances in which the characteristics of both conditions existed concurrently in the same individual.

Duke Ah, he couldn't have been a Plaza-Toro.

Duch. Oh! couldn't he, though!

CAS. Well, whatever happens, I shall, of course, be a dutiful wife, but I can never love my husband.

DUKE I don't know. It's extraordinary what unprepossessing people one can love if one gives one's mind to it.

DUCH. I loved your father.

DUKE My love—that remark is a little hard, I think? Rather cruel, perhaps? Somewhat uncalled-for, I venture to believe?

DUCH. It was very difficult, my dear; but I said to myself, "That man is a Duke, and I *will* love him." Several of my relations bet me I couldn't, but I did—desperately!

Song—DUCHESS

On the day when I was wedded
  To your admirable sire,
I acknowledge that I dreaded
  An explosion of his ire.
I was overcome with panic—
For his temper was volcanic,
  And I didn't dare revolt,
  For I feared a thunderbolt!
I was always very wary,
  For his fury was ecstatic—
His refined vocabulary
  Most unpleasantly emphatic.
    To the thunder
      Of this Tartar
    I knocked under
      Like a martyr;
    When intently
      He was fuming,
    I was gently
      Unassuming—
    When reviling
      Me completely,
    I was smiling
      Very sweetly:
Giving him the very best, and getting back the very worst—
That is how I tried to tame your great progenitor—at first!
But I found that a reliance
  On my threatening appearance,
And a resolute defiance
  Of marital interference,
And a gentle intimation
Of my firm determination
  To see what I could do
  To be wife and husband too

Was the only thing required
For to make his temper supple,
And you couldn't have desired
A more reciprocating couple.
Ever willing
To be wooing,
We were billing—
We were cooing;
When I merely
From him parted,
We were nearly
Broken-hearted—
When in sequel
Reunited,
We were equal-
Ly delighted.
So with double-shotted guns and colors nailed unto the mast,
I tamed your insignificant progenitor—at last!

CAS. My only hope is that when my husband sees what a shady family he has married into he will repudiate the contract altogether.

DUKE Shady? A nobleman shady, who is blazing in the lustre of unaccustomed pocket-money? A nobleman shady, who can look back upon ninety-five quarterings? It is not every nobleman who is ninety-five quarters in arrear—I mean, who can look back upon ninety-five of them! And this, just as I have been floated at a premium! Oh fie!

DUCH. Your Majesty is surely unaware that directly Your Majesty's father came before the public he was applied for over and over again.

DUKE My dear, Her Majesty's father was in the habit of being applied for over and over again—and very urgently applied for, too—long before he was registered under the Limited Liability Act.

Recitative—DUKE

To help unhappy commoners, and add to their enjoyment,
Affords a man of noble rank congenial employment;
Of our attempts we offer you examples illustrative:
The work is light, and, I may add, it's most remunerative.

Duet—DUKE and DUCHESS

DUKE Small titles and orders
For Mayors and Recorders
I get—and they're highly delighted—

DUCH. They're highly delighted!

DUKE — M.P.'s baronetted,
Sham Colonels gazetted,
And second-rate Aldermen knighted—

DUCH. — Yes, Aldermen knighted.

DUKE — Foundation-stone laying
I find very paying:
It adds a large sum to my makings—

DUCH. — Large sums to his makings.

DUKE — At charity dinners
The best of speech-spinners,
I get ten per cent on the takings—

DUCH. — One-tenth of the takings.

DUCH. — I present my lady
Whose conduct is shady
Or smacking of doubtful propriety—

DUKE — Doubtful propriety.

DUCH. — When Virtue would quash her,
I take and whitewash her,
And launch her in first-rate society—

DUKE — First-rate society!

DUCH. I recommend acres
Of clumsy dressmakers–
Their fit and their finishing touches–

DUKE Their finishing touches.

DUCH. A sum in addition
They pay for permission
To say that they make for the Duchess–

DUKE They make for the Duchess!

DUKE Those pressing prevailers,
The ready-made tailors,
Quote me as their great double-barrel–

DUCH. Their great double-barrel.

DUKE I allow them to do so,
Though Robinson Crusoe
Would jib at their wearing apparel–

DUCH. Such wearing apparel!

DUKE I sit, by selection,
Upon the direction
Of several Companies bubble–

DUCH. All Companies bubble!

DUKE As soon as they're floated,
I'm freely bank-noted–
I'm pretty well paid for my trouble–

DUCH. He's paid for his trouble!

DUCH. At middle-class party
I play at *écarté*–
And I'm by no means a beginner–

DUKE [*significantly*] She's not a beginner.

DUCH. To one of my station
The remuneration–
Five guineas a night and my dinner–

DUKE And wine with her dinner.

DUCH. I write letters blatant
On medicines patent—
And use any other you mustn't—

DUKE Believe me, you mustn't—

DUCH. And vow my complexion
Derives its perfection
From somebody's soap—which it doesn't—

DUKE [*significantly*] It certainly doesn't!

DUKE We're ready as witness
To any one's fitness
To fill any place or preferment—

DUCH. A place or preferment.

DUCH. We're often in waiting
At junket or *fêting*,
And sometimes attend an interment—

DUKE We enjoy an interment.

BOTH In short, if you'd kindle
The spark of a swindle,
Lure simpletons into your clutches—
Yes; into your clutches.
Or hoodwink a debtor,
You cannot do better

DUCH. Than trot out a Duke or a Duchess—

DUKE A Duke or a Duchess!

Enter MARCO *and* GIUSEPPE

DUKE Ah! Their Majesties. Your Majesty! [*Bows with great ceremony*]

MAR. The Duke of Plaza-Toro, I believe?

DUKE The same. [MARCO *and* GIUSEPPE *offer to shake hands with him. The* DUKE *bows ceremoniously. They endeavour to imitate him*] Allow me to present——

GIU. The young lady one of us married?

[MARCO *and* GIUSEPPE *offer to shake hands with her.* CASILDA *curtsies formally. They endeavour to imitate her.*]

CAS. Gentlemen, I am the most obedient servant of one of you. [*Aside*] Oh, Luiz!

DUKE I am now about to address myself to the gentleman whom my daughter married; the other may allow his attention to wander if he likes, for what I am about to say does not concern him. Sir, you will find in this young lady a combination of excellences which you would search for in vain in any young lady who had not the good fortune to be my daughter. There is some little doubt as to which of you is the gentleman I am addressing, and which is the gentleman who is allowing his attention to wander; but when that doubt is solved, I shall say (still addressing the attentive gentleman), "Take her, and may she make you happier than her mother has made me."

DUCH. Sir!

DUKE If possible. And now there is a little matter to which I think I am entitled to take exception. I come here in state with Her Grace the Duchess and Her Majesty my daughter, and what do I find? Do I find, for instance, a guard of honour to receive me? No!

MAR. and GIU. No.

DUKE The town illuminated? No!

MAR. and GIU. No.

DUKE Refreshment provided? No!

MAR. and GIU. No.

DUKE A Royal salute fired? No!

MAR. and GIU. No.

DUKE Triumphal arches erected? No!

MAR. and GIU. No.

DUKE The bells set ringing?

MAR. and GIU. No.

DUKE Yes–one–the Visitors', and I rang it myself. It is not enough! It is not enough!

GIU. Upon my honour, I'm very sorry; but you see, I was brought up in a gondola, and my ideas of politeness are confined to taking off my cap to my passengers when they tip me.

DUCH. That's all very well in its way, but it is not enough.

GIU. I'll take off anything else in reason.

DUKE But a Royal Salute to my daughter—it costs so little.

CAS. Papa, I don't want a salute.

GIU. My dear sir, as soon as we know which of us is entitled to take that liberty she shall have as many salutes as she likes.

MAR. As for guards of honour and triumphal arches, you don't know our people—they wouldn't stand it.

GIU. They are very off-hand with us—very off-hand indeed.

DUKE Oh, but you mustn't allow that—you must keep them in proper discipline, you must impress your Court with your importance. You want deportment—carriage——

GIU. We've got a carriage.

DUKE Manner—dignity. There must be a good deal of this sort of thing—[*business*]—and a little of this sort of thing—[*business*]—and possibly just a *Soupçon* of this sort of thing!—[*business*]—and so on. Oh, it's very useful, and most effective. Just attend to me. You are a King—I am a subject. Very good——

[*Gavotte*]

DUKE, DUCHESS, CASILDA, MARCO, GIUSEPPE

DUKE
I am a courtier grave and serious
  Who is about to kiss your hand:
Try to combine a pose imperious
  With a demeanour nobly bland.

MAR. and GIU.
Let us combine a pose imperious
  With a demeanour nobly bland.

[MARCO *and* GIUSEPPE *endeavour to carry out his instructions*]

DUKE
That's, if anything, *too* unbending—
  Too aggressively stiff and grand;

[*They suddenly modify their attitudes*]

Now to the other extreme you're tending—
Don't be so deucedly condescending!

DUCH. and CAS.
Now to the other extreme you're tending—
Don't be so dreadfully condescending!

MAR. and GIU.
Oh, hard to please some noblemen seem!
  At first, if anything, *too* unbending;
Off we go to the other extreme—
  Too confoundedly condescending!

DUKE — Now a gavotte perform sedately—
Offer your hand with conscious pride;
Take an attitude not too stately,
Still sufficiently dignified.

MAR. and GIU. — Now for an attitude not too stately,
Still sufficiently dignified.

[*They endeavour to carry out his instructions.*]

DUKE [*beating time*]

Oncely, twicely—oncely, twicely—
Bow impressively ere you glide.

[*They do so.*]

Capital both—you've caught it nicely!
That is the style of thing precisely!

DUCH. and CAS. — Capital both—they've caught it nicely!
That is the style of thing precisely!

MAR. and GIU. — Oh, sweet to earn a nobleman's praise!
Capital both—we've caught it nicely!
Supposing he's right in what he says,
This is the style of thing precisely!

[*Gavotte. At the end exeunt* DUKE *and* DUCHESS, *leaving* CASILDA *with* MARCO *and* GIUSEPPE.

GIU. [*to* MARCO] The old birds have gone away and left the young chickens together. That's called tact.

MAR. It's very awkward. We really ought to tell her how we are situated. It's not fair to the girl.

GIU. Then why don't you do it?

MAR. I'd rather not—you.

GIU. I don't know how to begin. [*To* CASILDA] A—Madam—I—we, that is, several of us——

CAS. Gentlemen, I am bound to listen to you; but it is right to tell you that, not knowing I was married in infancy, I am over head and ears in love with somebody else.

GIU. Our case exactly! *We* are over head and ears in love with somebody else! [*Enter* GIANETTA *and* TESSA.] In point of fact, with our wives!

CAS. Your wives! Then you are married?

TESS. It's not our fault.

GIA. We knew nothing about it.

BOTH. We are sisters in misfortune.

CAS. My good girls, I don't blame you. Only before we go any further we must really arrive at some satisfactory arrangement, or we shall get hopelessly complicated.

Quintet and Finale

MARCO, GIUSEPPE, CASILDA, GIANETTA, TESSA

ALL Here is a case unprecedented!
Here are a King and Queen ill-starred!
Ever since marriage was first invented
Never was known a case so hard!

MAR. and GIU. I may be said to have been bisected,
By a profound catastrophe!

CAS., GIA., TESS. Through a calamity unexpected
I am divisible into three!

ALL O moralists all,
How can you call
Marriage a state of unitee,
When excellent husbands are bisected,
And wives divisible into three?
O moralists all,
How can you call
Marriage a state of union true?

CAS., GIA., TESS. One-third of myself is married to half of ye or you,

MAR. and GIU. When half of myself has married one-third of ye or you?

Enter DON ALHAMBRA, *followed by* DUKE, DUCHESS, *and all the Chorus*

Finale

Recitative—DON ALHAMBRA

Now let the loyal lieges gather round—
The prince's foster-mother has been found!
She will declare, to silver clarion's sound,
The rightful King—let him forthwith be crowned!

CHORUS She will declare, etc.

[DON ALHAMBRA *brings forward* INEZ, *the Prince's foster-mother.*

TESS. Speak, woman, speak—
DUKE We're all attention!
GIA. The news we seek—
DUCH. This moment mention.
CAS. To us they bring—
DON AL. His foster-mother.
MAR. Is he the King?
GIU. Or this my brother?

ALL Speak, woman, speak, etc.

Recitative—INEZ

The Royal Prince was by the King entrusted
To my fond care, ere I grew old and crusted;
When traitors came to steal his son reputed,
My own small boy I deftly substituted!
The villains fell into the trap completely—
I hid the Prince away—still sleeping sweetly:
I called him "son" with pardonable slyness—
His name, Luiz! Behold his Royal Highness!

[*Sensation.* LUIZ *ascends the throne, crowned and robed as King.*

CAS. [*rushing to his arms*] Luiz!
LUIZ. Casilda! [*Embrace*]

ALL Is this indeed the King?
Oh, wondrous revelation!
Oh, unexpected thing!
Unlooked-for situation!

MAR., GIA., GIU., TESS. This statement we receive
With sentiments conflicting;
Our hearts rejoice and grieve,
Each other contradicting;
To those whom we adore
We can be reunited—
On one point rather sore,
But, on the whole, delighted!

LUIZ When others claimed thy dainty hand,
I waited—waited—waited,

DUKE As prudence (so I understand)
Dictated–tated–tated.

CAS. By virtue of our early vow
Recorded–corded–corded.

DUCH. Your pure and patient love is now
Rewarded–warded–warded.

ALL Then hail, O King of a Golden Land,
And the high-born bride who claims his hand!
The past is dead, and you gain your own,
A royal crown and a golden throne!

[*All kneel:* LUIZ *crowns* CASILDA.

ALL Once more *gondolieri*,
Both skilful and wary,
Free from this quandary
Contented are we.
From Royalty flying,
Our gondolas plying,
And merrily crying
Our "*premé*," "*stalì!*"

So good-bye, cachucha, fandango, bolero—
We'll dance a farewell to that measure—
Old Xeres, adieu—Manzanilla—Montero—
We leave you with feelings of pleasure!

CURTAIN